Raabiah Ahmed

CHILDREN'S CLASSICS

What Katy Did at School

SUSAN COOLIDGE

What Katy Did at School

PARRAGON

What Katy Did At School
A Parragon Classic

First published in 1873

This is a Siena book
Siena is an imprint of Parragon

This edition published in 1998 by
Parragon
13 Whiteladies Road
Clifton
Bristol BS8 1PB

Printed and bound in the UK

CHAPTER 1

CONIC SECTION

It was just after that happy visit mentioned at the end of "What Katy Did," that Elsie and John made their famous excursion to Conic Section—an excursion which neither of them ever forgot, and about which the family teased them for a long time afterward.

The summer had been cool; but, as often happens after cool summers, the autumn proved unusually hot. It seemed as if the months had been playing a game, and had "changed places" all round; and as if September were determined to show that he knew how to make himself just as disagreeable as August, if only he chose to do so.

All the last half of Cousin Helen's stay the weather was excessively sultry. She felt it very much, though the children did all they could to make her comfortable, with shaded rooms, and iced water, and fans. Every evening the boys would wheel her sofa out on the porch, in hopes of coolness; but it was of no use: the evenings were as warm as the days, and the yellow dust hanging in the air made the sunshine look thick and hot. A few bright leaves appeared on the trees, but they were wrinkled, and of an ugly colour. Clover said she thought they had been boiled red like lobsters. Altogether, the month was a trying one, and the coming of October made little or no difference; still the dust continued, and the heat; and the wind, when it blew, had no refreshment in it, but seemed to have passed over some great furnace, which had burned out of it all life and flavour.

5

In spite of this, however, it was wonderful to see how Katy gained and improved. Every day added to her powers. First she came down to dinner, then to breakfast. She sat on the porch in the afternoons; she poured the tea. It was like a miracle to the others, in the beginning, to watch her going about the house; but they got used to it surprisingly soon—one does to pleasant things. One person, however, never got used to it, never took it as a matter of course; and that was Katy herself. She could not run downstairs, or out into the garden; she could not open the kitchen door to give an order, without a sense of gladness and exultation which was beyond words. The wider and more active life stimulated her in every way. Her cheeks grew round and pink, her eyes bright. Cousin Helen and papa watched this change with indescribable pleasure; and Mrs. Worrett, who dropped in to lunch one day, fairly screamed with surprise at the sight of it.

To think of it! she cried, "why, the last time I was here you looked as if you had taken root in that chair of yours for the rest of your days, and here you are stepping around as lively as I be! Well, well! wonders will never cease. It does my eyes good to see you, Katherine. I wish your poor aunt were here to-day; that I do. How pleased she'd be!

It is doubtful whether Aunt Izzie would have been so pleased, for the lived-in look of the best parlour would have horrified her extremely; but Katy did not recollect that just then. She was touched at the genuine kindness of Mrs. Worrett's voice, and took very willingly her offered kiss. Clover brought lemonade and grapes, and they all devoted themselves to making the poor lady comfortable. Just before she went away, she said:—

6

How is it that I can't never get any of you to come out to Conic Section? I'm sure I've asked you often enough. There's Elsie, now, and John; they're just the age to enjoy being in the country. Why won't you send 'em out for a week? Johnnie can feed chickens, and chase 'em too, if she likes," she added, as Johnnie dashed then into view, pursuing one of Phil's bantams round the house. "Tell her so, won't you, Katherine? There is lots of chickens on the farm. She can chase 'em from morning to night, if she's a mind to."

Katy thanked her, but she didn't think the children would care to go. She gave Johnnie the message, and then the whole matter passed out of her mind. She was surprised, a few days later, by having it brought up again by Elsie. The family were in low spirits that morning because of Cousin Helen's having just gone away; and Elsie was lying on the sofa, fanning herself with a great palm-leaf fan.

"Oh, dear!" she sighed. "Do you suppose it's ever going to be cool again in this world? It does seem as if I couldn't bear it any longer.

Aren't you well, darling? inquired Katy, anxiously.

"Oh, yes! well enough," replied Elsie. "It's only this horrid heat, and never going away to where it's cooler. I keep thinking about the country, and wishing I was there feeling the wind blow. I wonder if papa wouldn't let John and me go to Conic Section and see Mrs. Worrett. Do you think he would if you asked him?

But," said Katy, amazed, "Conic Section isn't exactly country, you know. It is just out of the city—only six miles from here. And Mrs. Worrett's house is close to the road, papa said. Do you think you'd like it, dear? It can't be very much cooler than this."

"Oh, yes! it can," rejoined Elsie, in a tone which was a little fretful. "It's quite near woods; Mrs. Worrett told me so. Besides, it's always cooler on a farm. There's more room for the wind, and—oh everything's pleasanter! You can't think how tired I am of this hot house. Last night I hardly slept at all; and, when I did, I dreamed that I was a loaf of brown bread, and Debby was putting me into the oven to bake. It was a horrid dream. I was so glad to wake up. Won't you ask papa if we may go, Katy?

"Why, of course I will, if you wish it so much. Only"— Katy stopped, and did not finish her sentence. A vision of fat Mrs Worrett had risen before her, and she could not help doubting if Elsie would find the farm as pleasant as she expected. But sometimes the truest kindness is in giving people their own unwise way, and Elsie's 'eyes looked so wistful that Katy had no heart to argue or refuse.

Dr. Carr looked doubtful when the plan was proposed to him.

"It's too hot, he said. "I don't believe the girls will like it."

"Oh, yes; we will, papa; indeed we will," pleaded Elsie and John, who had lingered near the door to learn the fate of their request.

Dr. Carr smiled at the imploring faces, but he looked a little quizzical. "Very well, he said, "you may go. Mr. Worrett is coming into town to-morrow on some bank business. I'll send word by him; and in the afternoon, when it is cooler, Alexander can drive you out. "

"Goody! Goody!" cried John, jumping up and down, while Elsie put her arms round papa's neck and gave him a hug.

"And Thursday I'll send for you," he continued.

"But, papa," expostulated Elsie, "that's only two days. Mrs. Worrett said a week. "

"Yes, she said a week," chimed in John; "and she's got ever so many chickens, and I'm to feed 'em, and chase 'em about as much as I like. Only it's too hot to run much," she added reflectively.

"You won't really send for us on Thursday, will you, papa? urged Elsie, anxiously. "I'd like to stay ever and ever so long; but Mrs. Worrett said a week. "

"I shall send on Thursday," repeated Dr. Carr in a decided tone. Then, seeing that Elsie's lip was trembling, and her eyes were full of tears, he continued: "Don't look so woeful, Pussy. Alexander shall drive out for you; but if you want to stay longer, you may send him back with a note to say what day you would like to have him come again. Will that do?"

"Oh, yes! said Elsie, wiping her eyes; "that will do beautifully, papa. Only, it seems such a pity that Alexander should have to go twice when it's so hot; for we're sure to want to stay a week."

Papa only laughed as he kissed her. All being settled, the children began to get ready. It was quite an excitement packing the bags, and deciding what to take and what not to take. Elsie grew bright and gay with the bustle. Just to think of being in the country— the cool, green country—made her perfectly happy, she declared. The truth was, she was a little feverish, and not quite well, and didn't know exactly how she felt or what she wanted.

The drive out was pleasant, except that Alexander upset John's gravity, and hurt Elsie's dignity very much, by inquiring, a they left the gate, Do the little misses know where it is that they want to go? Part of the way the road ran through woods. They were rather boggy woods; but the dense shade kept off the sun, and there was a spicy smell of evergreens and sweet fern. Elsie felt that the good time had fairly begun, and her spirits rose with every turn of the wheels.

By and by they left the woods, and came out again into the sunshine. The road was dusty, and so were the fields, and the ragged sheaves of cornstalks which dotted them here and there looked dusty too. Piles of dusty-red apples lay on the grass, under the orchard trees. Some cows going down a lane toward their milking shed mooed in a dispirited and thirsty way, which made the children feel thirsty also.

"I want a drink of water very badly," said John. "Do you suppose it's much farther? How long will it be before we get to Mrs. Worrett's, Alexander?"

"'Most there, miss," replied Alexander laconically.

Elsie put her head out of the carriage, and looked eagerly round. Where was the delightful farm? She saw a big, pumpkin-coloured house by the roadside, a little farther on; but surely that couldn't be it! Yes; Alexander drew up at the gate, and jumped down to lift them out. It really was! The surprise quite took away her breath.

She looked about. There were the woods, to be sure, but half a mile away across the fields. Near the house there were no trees at all; only some lilac bushes at one side; there was no green grass either. A gravel path took up the whole of the narrow front yard; and, what with the blazing colour of the paint, and the wide-awake look of the blindless windows, the house had somehow the air of standing on tiptoe and staring hard at something—the dust in the road, perhaps, for there seemed nothing else to stare at.

Elsie's heart sank indescribably, as she and John got very slowly out of the vehicle, and Alexander, putting his arm over the fence, rapped loudly at the front door. It was some minutes before the rap was answered. Then a heavy step was heard creaking through the hall, and somebody began fumbling at an obstinate bolt, which would not move. Next, a voice which they recognised as Mrs. Worrett's, called, "Isaphiny! Isaphiny! come and see if you can open this door."

"How funny!" whispered Johnnie, beginning to giggle.

"Isaphiny" seemed to be upstairs, for presently they heard her running down, after which a fresh rattle began at the obstinate bolt. But still the door did not open, and at length Mrs. Worrett put her lips to the keyhole, and asked—

"Who is it?"

The voice sounded so hollow and ghostly, that Elsie jumped, as she answered: "It's I, Mrs. Worrett—Elsie Carr. And Johnnie's here, too. "

"Ts, ts, ts!" sounded from within, and then came a whispering, after which Mrs. Worrett put her mouth again to the keyhole, and called out:—

"Go round to the back, children. I can't make this door open anyway. It's all swelled up with the damp."'

"Damp!" whispered Johnnie, "why, it hasn't rained since the third week in August; Papa said so yesterday."

"That's nothing, Miss Johnnie," put in Alexander, overhearing her. "Folks here away don't open their front doors much—only for weddings, and funerals, and such like. Very likely this has stood shut these five years. I know the last time I drove Miss Carr out before she died, it was just so; and she had to go round to the back as you're a-doing now."

John's eyes grew wide with wonder, but there was no time to say anything, for they had turned the corner of the house, and there was Mrs. Worrett waiting at the kitchen door to receive them. She looked fatter than ever, Elsie thought; but she kissed them both, and said she was real glad to see a Carr in her house at last.

"It was too bad," she went on, "to keep you waiting so. But the fact is I got asleep, and when you knocked I waked up all in a daze, and for a minute it didn't come to me who it must be. Take the bags right upstairs, Isaphiny, and put them in the keeping-room chamber. How's your pa, 1:Elsie—and Katy? Not laid up again, I hope.

"Oh, no; she seems to get better all the time.

"That's right, responded Mrs. Worrett, heartily." I didn't know, but what, with hot weather, and company in the house, and all— there's a chicken, Johnnie," she exclaimed, suddenly interrupting herself, as a long-legged hen ran past the door. Want to chase it right away? You can if you like. Or would you rather go upstairs first?"

"upstairs, please," replied John, while Elsie went to the door, and watched Alexander driving away down the dusty road. She felt as if their last friend had deserted them. Then she and Johnnie followed Isaphiny upstairs. Mrs. Worrett never amounted" in hot weather, she told them.

The spare chamber was just under the roof. It was very hot, and smelled as if the windows had never been opened since the house was built. As soon as they were alone, Elsie ran across the room and threw up the sash; but the moment she let go down it fell again, with a crash that shook the floor and made the pitcher dance and rattle in the washbowl. The children were dreadfully frightened, especially when they heard Mrs. Worrett at the foot of the stairs calling to ask what was the matter.

12

"It's only the window," explained Elsie, going into the hall. "I'm so sorry, but it won't stay open. Something's the matter with it."

"Did you stick the nail in?" inquired Mrs. Worrett.

"The nail? No, ma'am.

"Why, how on earth did you expect it to stay up, then? You young folks never see what's before your eyes. Look on the windowsill, and you'll find it. It's put there a-purpose.

Elsie returned, much discomfited. She looked, and, sure enough, there was a big nail, and there was a hole in the side of the window frame in which to stick it. This time she got the window open without accident; but a long blue paper shade caused her much embarrassment. It hung down, and kept the air from coming in. She saw no way of fastening it.

"Roll it up and put in a pin," suggested John.

I'm afraid of tearing the paper. Dear, what a horrid thing it is! replied Elsie, in a disgusted tone.

However, she stuck in a couple of pins and fastened the shade out of the way. After that they looked about the room. It was plainly furnished, but very nice and neat. The bureau was covered with a white towel, on which stood a pincushion, with "Remember Ruth" stuck upon it in pins. John admired this very much, and felt that she could never make up her mind to spoil the pattern by taking out a pin, however great her need of one might be.

What a high bed!" she exclaimed. Elsie, you'll have to climb on a chair to get into it; and so shall I.

Elsie felt it. "Feathers!" she cried, in a tone of horror. O John! why did we come? What shall we do?

"I guess we shan't mind it much, replied John, who was perfectly well, and considered these little variations on home habits rather as fun than otherwise. But Elsie gave a groan. Two nights on a feather bed! How should she bear it!

Tea was ready in the kitchen when they went downstairs. A little fire had been lighted to boil the water. It was almost out, but the room felt stiflingly warm, and the butter was so nearly melted that Mrs. Worrett had to help it with a teaspoon. Buzzing flies hovered above the table, and gathered thick on the plate of cake. The bread was excellent, and so were the cottage cheeses and the stewed quince; but Elsie could eat nothing. She was in a fever of heat. Mrs. Worrett was distressed at this want of appetite, and so was Mr. Worrett, to whom the children had just been introduced. He was a kindly-looking old man, with a bald head, who came to supper in his shirt sleeves, and was as thin as his wife was fat.

"I'm afraid the little girl don't like her supper, Lucinda," he said. "You must see about getting her something different to-morrow.

"Oh! it isn't that. Everything is very nice, only I'm not hungry," pleaded Elsie, feeling as if she should like to cry. She did cry a little after tea, as they sat in the dusk; Mr. Worrett smoking his pipe and slapping mosquitoes outside the door, and Mrs. Worrett sleeping rather noisily in a big rocking-chair. But not even Johnnie found out that she was crying, for Elsie felt that she was the naughtiest child in the world to behave so badly when everybody was so kind to her. She repeated this to herself many times, but it didn't do much good. As often as the thought of home and Katy and papa came, a wild longing to get back to them would rush over her, and her eyes would fill again with sudden tears.

The night was very uncomfortable. Not a breath of

wind was stirring, or none found its way to the stifling bed where the little sisters lay. John slept pretty well, in spite of heat and mosquitoes, but Elsie hardly closed her eyes. Once she got up and went to the window, but the blue-paper shade had become unfastened, and rattled down upon her head with a sudden bump, which startled her very much. She could find no pins in the dark, so she left it hanging; whereupon it rustled and flapped through the rest of the night, and did its share toward keeping her awake. About three o'clock she fell into a doze; and it seemed only a minute after that before she waked up to find bright sunshine in the room, and half-a-dozen roosters crowing and calling under the windows. Her head ached violently. She longed to stay in bed, but feared Mrs. Worrett would think it impolite: so she dressed and went down with Johnnie; but she looked so pale, and ate so little breakfast, that Mrs. Worrett was quite troubled, and said she had better not try to go out, but just lie on the lounge in the best room, and amuse herself with a book.

The lounge in the best room was covered with slippery, purple chintz. It was a high lounge, and very narrow. There was nothing at the end to hold the pillow in its place; so the pillow constantly tumbled off and jerked Elsie's head suddenly backward, which was not at all comfortable. Worse, Elsie having dropped into a doze, she herself tumbled to the floor, rolling from the glassy, smooth chintz as if it had been a slope of ice. This adventure made her so nervous that she dared not go to sleep again, though Johnnie fetched two chairs, and placed them beside the sofa to hold her on. So she followed Mrs. Worrett's advice, and "amused herself with a book." There were not many books in the best room. The one Elsie chose was a fat black volume called

"Complete Works of Mrs. Hannah More". Part of it was prose, and part was poetry. Elsie began with a chapter called "Hints on the Formation of the Character of a Youthful Princess". But there were a great many long words in it; so she turned to a story named "Cælebs in Search of a Wife". It was about a young gentleman who wanted to get married, but who didn't feel sure that there were any young ladies nice enough for him; so he went about making visits, first to one and then to another; and, when he had stayed a few days at a house, he would always say, "No, she won't do," and then he would go away. At last he found a young lady who seemed the very person, who visited the poor, and got up early in the morning, and always wore white, and never forgot to wind up her watch or do her duty; and Elsie almost thought that now the difficult young gentleman must be satisfied, and say, "This is the very thing." When, lo! her attention wandered a little, and the next thing she knew she was rolling off the lounge for the second time, in company with Mrs. Hannah More. They landed in the chairs, and Johnnie ran and picked them both up. Altogether, lying on the best parlour sofa was not very restful; and as the day went on, and the sun beating on the blindless windows made the room hotter, Elsie grew continually more and more feverish and home-sick and disconsolate.

Meanwhile Johnnie was kept in occupation by Mrs. Worrett, who had got the idea firmly fixed in her mind that the chief joy in a child's life was to chase chickens. Whenever a hen fluttered past the kitchen door, which was about once in three minutes, she would cry, "Here, Johnnie, here's another chicken for you to chase"; and poor Johnnie would feel obliged to dash out into the sun. Being a very polite little girl, she did not like to say to Mrs. Worrett that running in the heat was disagreeable; so by dinner-time she was thoroughly tired out, and would have been cross if she had known how; but she didn't—Johnnie was never cross. After dinner it was even worse; for the sun was hotter, and the chickens, who didn't mind sun, seemed to be walking all the time. "Hurry, Johnnie, here's another!" came so constantly, that at last Elsie grew desperate, got up, and went to the kitchen with a languid appeal, "Please, Mrs. Worrett, won't you let Johnnie stay by me, because my head aches so hard?" After that, Johnnie had rest; for Mrs. Worrett was the kindest of women, and had no idea that she was not amusing her little guest in the most delightful manner.

A little before six, Elsie's head felt better; and she and Johnnie put on their hats, and went for a walk in the garden. There was not much to see: beds of vegetables, a few currant bushes, that was all. Elsie was leaning against a paling, and trying to make out why the Worrett house had that queer tiptoe expression, when a sudden loud grunt startled her, and something touched the top of her head. She turned, and there was an enormous pig standing on his hind legs on the other side of the paling. He was taller than Elsie as he stood thus, and it was his cold nose which had touched her head. Somehow, appearing in this unexpected way, he seemed to the children like some dreadful wild beast. They screamed with fright, and fled to the house, from which Elsie never ventured to stir again during their visit. John chased chickens at intervals, but it was a doubtful pleasure; and all the time she kept a wary eye on the distant pig.

That evening, while Mrs. Worrett slept and Mr. Worrett smoked outside the door, Elsie felt so very miserable that she broke down altogether. She put her head in Johnnie's lap, as they sat together in the darkest corner of the room, and sobbed and cried, making as little noise as she possibly could. Johnnie comforted her with soft pats and strokings; but did not dare to say a word, for fear Mrs. Worrett should wake up and find them out.

When the morning came, Elsie's one thought was, would Alexander come for them in the afternoon? All day she watched the clock and the road with feverish anxiety. Oh, if papa had changed his mind, had decided to let them stay for a week at Conic Section, what should she do? It was just possible to worry through and keep alive till afternoon, she thought; but if they were forced to spend another night in that feather-bed, with those mosquitoes, hearing the blue shade rattle and quiver hour after hour, she should die, she was sure she should die!

But Elsie was not called upon to die, or even to discover how easy it is to survive a little discomfort. About five, her anxious watch was rewarded by the appearance of a cloud of dust, out of which presently emerged old Whitey's ears and the top of the well-known carriage. They stopped at the gate. There was Alexander, brisk and smiling, ve_ glad to see his "little misses again," and to find them so glad to go home. Mrs. Worrett, however, did not discover that they were glad—no, indeed! Elsie and John were much too polite for that. They thanked the old lady, and said good-bye so prettily that, after they were gone, she told Mr. Worrett that it hadn't been a bit of trouble having them there, and she hoped they would come again, they enjoyed everything so much; only it was a pity that Elsie looked so peaked. And at that very moment Elsie was sitting on the floor of the vehicle with her head in John's lap, crying and sobbing for joy that the visit was over, and that she was on the way home. "If only I live to get there," she said, "I'll never, no, never, go into the country again!n which was silly enough; but we must forgive her.

Ah, how charming home did look, with the family grouped in the shady porch, Katy in her white wrapper, Clover with rose-buds in her belt, and everybody ready to welcome and pet the little absentees! There was much hugging and kissing, and much to tell of what had happened in the two days: how a letter had come from Cousin Helen; how Daisy White had four kittens as white as herself; how Dorry had finished his water-wheel—a wheel which turned in the bath-tub, and was "really ingenious," papa said; and Phil had "swapped" one of his bantam chicks for one of Eugene Slack's Brahmapootras. It was not till they were all seated round the tea table that anybody demanded an account of the visit. Elsie felt this a relief, and was just thinking how delicious everything was, from the sliced peaches to the clinking ice in the milk-pitcher, when papa put the dreaded question—

"Well, Elsie, so you decided to come, after all. How was it? Why didn't you stay your week out? You look pale, it seems to me. Have you been enjoying yourself too much? Tell us all about it."

Elsie looked at papa, and papa looked at Elsie. Dr. Carr's eyes twinkled just a little, but otherwise he was perfectly grave. Elsie began to speak, then to laugh, then to cry, and the explanation, when it came, was given in a mingled burst of all three.

"O papa, it was horrid! That is, Mrs. Worrett was just as kind as could be, but so fat; and oh, such a pig! I

19

never imagined such a pig. And the calico on that horrid sofa was so slippery that I rolled off five times, and once I hurt myself very badly. And we had a feather-bed; and I was so home-sick that I cried all the evening."

That must have been gratifying to Mrs. Worrett," put in Dr. Carr.

"Oh! she didn't know it, papa. She was asleep, and snoring so that nobody could hear. And the flies!—such flies, Katy!—and the mosquitoes, and our window wouldn't open till I put in a nail. I am so glad to get home! I never want to go into the country again, never, never! Oh, if Alexander hadn't come!—why, Clover, what are you laughing for? And Dorry, I think it's very unkind," and Elsie ran to Katy, hid her face, and began to cry.

Never mind, darling, they didn't mean to be unkind. Papa, her hands are quite hot; you must give her something.n Katy's voice shook a little; but she would not hurt Elsie's feelings by showing that she was amused. Papa gave Elsie "something" before she went to bed—a very mild dose, I fancy; for doctor's little girls, as a general rule, do take no medicine, and next day she was much better. As the adventures of the Conic Section visit leaked out bid by bit, the family laughed till it seemed as if they would never stop. Phil was for ever enacting the pig, standing on his triumphant hind legs, and patting Elsie's head with his nose; and many and many a time, "It will end like your visit to Mrs. Worrett" proved a useful check when Elsie was in a self-willed mood and bent on some scheme which for the moment struck her as delightful. For one of the good things about our child-ish mistakes is, that each one teaches us something; and so, blundering on, we grow wiser, till, when the time comes, we are ready to take our places among the wonderful grown-up people who never make mistakes.

CHAPTER 2

A NEW YEAR AND A NEW PLAN

When summer lingers on into October, it often seems as if winter, anxious to catch a glimpse of her, hurries a little; and so people are cheated out of their autumn It was so that year. Almost as soon as it ceased to be hot, it began to be cold. The leaves, instead of drifting away in soft, dying colours, like sunset clouds, turned yellow all at once; and were whirled off the trees in a single gusty night, leaving everything bare and desolate. Thanksgiving came; and before the smell of the turkey was fairly out of the house, it was time to hang up stockings and dress the Christmas-tree. They had a tree that year in honour of Katy's being downstairs. Cecy, who had gone away to boarding-school, came home; and it was all delightful, except that the days flew too fast. Clover said it seemed to her very queer that there was so much less time than usual in the world. She couldn't imagine what had become of it; there used to be plenty. And she was certain that Dorry must have been tinkering all the clocks— they struck so often.

It was just after New Year that Dr. Carr walked in one day with a letter in his hand, and remarked, "Mr. and Mrs. Page are coming to stay with us.

"Mr. and Mrs. Page," repeated Katy: "did I ever see them?"

"Once, when you were four years old, and Elsie a baby. Of course you don't remember it."

"But who are they, papa?"

"Mrs. Page was your dear mother's second cousin; and at one time she lived in your grandfather's family, and was like a sister to mamma and Uncle Charles. It is a good many years since I have seen her. Mr. Page is a railroad engineer. He is coming this way on business, and they will stop for a few days with us. Your Cousin Olivia writes that she is anxious to see all you children. Have everything as nice as you can, Katy."

"Of course, I will. What day are they coming?"

"Thursday—no, Friday," replied Dr. Carr, consulting the letter, Friday evening, at half-past six. Order something substantial for tea that night, Katy. They'll be hungry after travelling."

Katy worked with a will for the next two days. Twenty times, at least, she went into the blue-room to make sure that nothing was forgotten; repeating, as if it had been a lesson in geography, "Bath towels, face towels, matches, soap, candles, cologne, extra blanket, ink." A nice little fire was lighted in the bedroom on Friday afternoon, and a big, beautiful one in the parlour, which looked very pleasant with the lamp lit and Clover's geraniums and china roses in the window. The tea-table was set with the best linen and the pink and white china. Debby's muffins were very light. The crab-apple jelly came out of its mould clear and whole, and the cold chicken looked appetising, with its green wreath of parsley. There was stewed potato, too, and, of course, oysters. Everybody in Burnet had oysters for tea when company was expected. They were counted a special treat; because they were rather dear, and could not always be procured. Burnet was a thousand miles from the sea, so the oysters were of the tin-can variety. The cans gave the oysters a curious taste —tinny, or was it more like solder? At all events, Burnet people liked it, and always insisted that it was a striking improvement on the flavour which oysters have on their native shores. Everything was as nice as could be when Katy stood in the dining-room to take a last look at her arrangements; and she hoped papa would be pleased, and that mamma's cousin would think her a good housekeeper.

"I don't want to have on my other jacket," observed Phil, putting his head in at the door. "Need I? This is nice."

"Let me see," said Katy, gently turning him round. Well, it does pretty well; but I think I'd rather you should put on the other, if you don't mind much. We want everything as nice as possible, you know; because this is papa's company, and he hardly ever has any."

"Just one little sticky place isn't much," said Phil, rather gloomily, wetting his finger and rubbing at a shiny place on his sleeve. "Do you really think I'd better? Well, then, I will."

"That's a dear" – kissing him. "Be quick, Philly, for it's almost time they were here. And please tell Dorry to make haste. It's ever so long since he went upstairs."

"Dorry's an awful dandy," remarked Phil, confidentially. "He looks in the glass, and makes faces if he can't get his parting straight. I wouldn't care so much about my clothes for a good deal. It's like a girl. Jim Slack says a boy who shines his hair up like that never'll get to be President, not if he lives a thousand years."

"Well," said Katy, laughing; "it's something to be clean, even if you cannot be President."

She was not at all alarmed by Dorry's recent reaction in favour of personal adornment. He came down pretty soon, very spick and span in his best suit, and asked her to fasten the blue ribbon under his collar, which she did most obligingly; though he was very particular as to the

23

size of the bows and length of the ends, and made her tie and re-tie more than once. She had just arranged it to suit him when a carriage stopped.

"There they are," she cried. "Run and open the door, Dorry."

Dorry did so; and Katy, following, found papa ushering in a tall gentleman, and a lady who was not tall, but whose Roman nose and long neck, and general air of style and fashion, made her look so. Katy bent quite over to be kissed; but for all that she felt small, and young, and unformed, as the eyes of mamma's cousin looked her over and over, and through and through, and Mrs. Page said—

Why, Philip, is it possible that this tall girl is one of yours? Dear me how the time flies! I was thinking of the little creatures I saw when I was her last. And this other great creature can't be Elsie? That mite of a baby! Impossible! I cannot realize it. I really cannot realize it in the least."

"Won't you come to the fire, Mrs. Page?" said Katy, rather timidly.

"Don't call me Mrs. Page, my dear. Call me Cousin Olivia."

Then the newcomer rustled into the parlour, where Johnnie and Phil were waiting to be introduced; and again she remarked that she "couldn't realize it." I don't know why Mrs. Page's not realizing it should have made Katy uncomfortable, but it did.

Supper went off well. The guests ate and praised; and Dr. Carr looked pleased, and said: "We think Katy an excellent housekeeper for her age." At which Katy blushed and was delighted, till she caught Mrs. Page's eyes fixed upon her with a look of scrutiny and amusement, whereupon she felt awkward and ill at ease.

It was so all the evening. Mamma's cousin was entertaining and bright, and told lively stories; but the children felt that she was watching them, and passing judgment on their ways. Children are very quick to suspect when older people hold within themselves these little private courts of inquiry, and they always resent it.

Next morning Mrs. Page sat by while Katy washed the breakfast things, fed the birds, and did various odd jobs about the room and house.

My dear," she said at last, "what a solemn girl you are! I should think from your face that you were at least five-and-thirty. Don't you ever laugh or frolic, like other girls of your age? Why, my Lilly, who is four months older than you, is a perfect child still; impulsive as a baby, bubbling over with fun from morning till night."

"I've been shut up a good deal," said Katy, trying to defend herself; "but I didn't know I was solemn."

"My dear, that's the very thing I complain of; you don't know it! You are altogether ahead of your age. It's very bad for you, in my opinion. All this housekeeping and care, for young girls like you and Clover, is wrong and unnatural. I don't like it; indeed I don't."

Oh! housekeeping doesn't hurt me a bit," protested Katy, trying to smile. "We have lovely times; indeed we do, Cousin Olivia"

Cousin Olivia only pursed up her mouth, and repeated, It's wrong, my dear. It's unnatural It's not the thing for you. Depend upon it, it's not the thing."

This was unpleasant; but what was worse, had Katy known it, Mrs. Page attacked Dr. Carr upon the subject. He was quite troubled to learn that she considered Katy grave and careworn, and unlike what girls of her age should be. Katy caught him looking at her with a puzzled expression.

What is it, dear papa? Do you want anything?"

No, child, nothing. What are you doing there? Mending the parlour curtain, eh? Can't old Mary attend to that, and give you a chance to frisk about with the other girls?"

"Papa! As if I wanted to frisk! I declare you're as bad as Cousin Olivia. She's always telling me that I ought to bubble over with mirth. I don't wish to bubble. I don't know how."

"I'm afraid you don't," said Dr. Carr, with an odd sigh, which set Katy to wondering. What should papa sigh for? Had she done anything wrong? She began to rack her brains and memory as to whether it could be this or that; or, if not, what could it be? Such needless self-examination does no good Katy looked "more solemn" than ever after it.

Altogether, Mrs. Page was not a favourite in the family. She had every intention of being kind to her cousin's children, so dreadfully in want of a mother, poor things!" but she could not hide the fact that their ways puzzled and did not please her, and the children detected this, as children always will. She and Mr. Page were very polite. They praised the housekeeping, and the excellent order of everything, and said that there never were better children in the world than John, and Dorry, and Phil. But, through all, Katy perceived the hidden disapproval; and she couldn't help feeling glad when the visit ended, and they went away.

With their departure, matters went back to their old train, and Katy forgot her disagreeable feelings. Papa seemed a little grave and preoccupied; but doctors often are when they have bad cases to think of, and nobody noticed it particularly, or remarked that several letters came from Mrs. Page, and nothing was heard of their contents, except that "Cousin Olivia sent her love." So it was a shock, when one day papa called Katy into the study to tell her of a new plan. She knew at once that it was something important when she heard his voice; it sounded so grave. Beside, he said, "My daughter" —a phrase he never used except upon the most impressive occasions.

"My daughter," he began, "I want to talk to you about something which I have been thinking of. How would you and Clover like going away to school together?"

"To school? To Mrs. Knight's?"

"No, not to Mrs. Knight's. To a boarding-school at the East, where Lilly Page has been for two years. Didn't you hear Cousin Olivia speak of it when she was here?"

"I believe I did. But, papa, you won't really?"

Yes, I think so," said Dr. Carr, gently. "Listen, Katy, and don't feel so badly, my dear child. I've thought the plan over carefully; and it seems to me a good one, though I hate to part from you. It is pretty much as your cousin says; these home cares, which I can't take from you while you are at home, are making you old before your time. Heaven knows, I don't want to turn you into a silly, giggling miss; but I should like you to enjoy your youth while you have it, and not grow middle-aged before you are twenty."

"What is the name of the school?" asked Katy. Her voice sounded a good deal like a sob.

The girls call it 'The Nunnery.' It is at Hillsover, on the Connecticut River, pretty far north. And the winters are pretty cold, I fancy; but the air is sure to be good and bracing. That is one thing which has inclined me to the plan. The climate is just what you need."

"Hillsover? Isn't there a college there, too?"

"Yes; Arrowmouth College. I believe there is always a college where there is a boarding-school; though why, I can't for the life of me imagine. That's neither here nor there, however, I'm not afraid of your getting into silly scrapes, as girls sometimes do."

"College scrapes? Why, how could I? We don't have anything to do with the college, do we?" said Katy, opening her candid eyes with such a wondering stare, that Dr. Carr laughed, as he patted her cheek, and replied, "No, my dear, not a thing."

"The term opens the third week in April," he went on. You must begin to get ready at once. Mrs. Hall has just fitted out Cecy; so she can tell you what you will need. You'd better consult her tomorrow."

"But, papa," cried Katy, beginning to realise it, "what are you going to do? Elsie's a darling, but she's so very little. I don't see how you can possibly manage. I'm sure you'll miss U5, and so will the children. "

"I rather think we shall," said Dr. Carr, with a smile, which ended in a sigh; "but we shall do very well, Katy; never fear. Miss Finch will see to us. "

"Miss Finch? Do you mean Mrs. Knight's sister-in-law?"

"Yes. Her mother died in the summer; so she has no particular home now, and is glad to come for a year and keep house for us. Mrs. Knight says she is a good manager; and I dare say she'll fill your place suffi-ciently well, as far as that goes. We can't expect her to be you, you know: that would be unreasonable." And Dr. Carr put his arm round Katy, and kissed her so fondly that she was quite overcome, and clung to him, crying—

"O papa! don't make us go. I'll frisk, and be as young as I can and not grow middle-aged or anything disagreeable, if only you'll let us stay. Never mind what Cousin Olivia says; she doesn't know. Cousin Helen wouldn't say so, I'm sure."

"On the contrary, Helen thinks well of the plan; only she wishes the school were nearer," said Dr. Carr. "No, Katy, don't coax. My mind is made up. It will do you and Clover both good; and once you are settled at Hillsover, you'll be very happy, I hope."

When papa spoke in this decided tone, it was never any use to urge him. Katy knew this, and ceased her pleadings. She went to find Clover and tell her the news, and the two girls had a hearty cry together. A sort of "clearing-up shower" it turned out to be; for when once they had wiped their eyes, everything looked brighter, and they began to see a pleasant side to the plan.

"The travelling part of it will be very nice," pronounced Clover. "We never went so far away from home before."

Elsie, who was still looking very woeful, burst into tears afresh at this remark.

"Oh, don't, darling!" said Katy. "Think how pleasant it will be to send letters, and to get them from us. I shall write to you every Saturday. Run for the big atlas—there's a dear, and let us see where we are going."

Elsie brought the atlas; and the three heads bent eagerly over it, as Clover traced the route of the journey with her forefinger. How exciting it looked! There was the railroad, twisting and curving over half a dozen States. The black dots which followed it were towns and villages, all of which they should see. By and by the road made a bend, and swept northward by the side of the Connecticut River and toward the hills. They had heard how beautiful the Connecticut valley is.

"Only think! we shall be close to it," remarked Clover;

"and we shall see the hills. I suppose they are very high, a great deal higher than the hill at Bolton."

"I hope so," laughed Dr. Carr, who came into the room just then. The hill at Bolton was one of his favourite jokes. When mamma first came to Burnet, she had paid a visit to some friends at Bolton; and one day, when they were all out walking, they asked her if she felt strong enough to go to the top of the hill. Mamma was used o hills, so she said yes, and walked on, very glad to find that there was a hill in that flat country, but wondering a little why they did not see it. At last she asked where it was, and, behold, they had just reached the top! The slope had been so gradual that she had never found out that they were going uphill at all. Dr. Carr had told this story to the children, but had never been able to make them see the joke very clearly. In fact, when Clover went to Bolton, she was quite struck with the hill: it was so much higher than the sand-bank which bordered the lake at Burnet.

There was a great deal to do to make the girls ready for school by the third week in April. Mrs. Hall was very kind, and her advice was sensible; though, except for Dr. Carr, the girls would hardly have had furs and flannels enough for so cold a place as Hillsover. Everything for winter, as well as for summer, had to be thought of; for it had been arranged that the girls should not come home for the autumn vacation, but should spend it with Mrs. Page. This was the hardest thing about the plan. Katy begged very hard for Christmas; but when she learned that it would take three days to come and three to go, and that the holidays lasted less than a week, she saw it was of no use, and gave up the idea, while Elsie tried to comfort herself by planning a Christmas-box. The preparations kept them so busy that there was no time for anything else. Mrs. Hall was always wanting them to go with her to shops, or Miss Petingill demanding that they should try on linings; and so the days flew by. At last all was ready. The nice half-dozens of pretty underclothes came home from the sewing-machine woman's, and were done up by Brigitte, who dropped many a tear into the starch at the thought of the young ladies going away. Mrs. Hall, who was a good packer, put the things into the new trunks. Everybody gave the girls presents, as if they had been brides starting on a wedding journey.

Papa's was a watch for each. They were not new, but the girls thought them beautiful. Katy's had belonged to her mother. It was large and old-fashioned, with a finely-wrought case. Clover's, which had been her grandmother's, was larger still. It had a quaint ornament on the back—a sort of true-love knot, done in gold of different tints. The girls were excessively pleased with these watches. They wore them with guard-chains of black watered ribbon, and every other minute they looked to see what the time was.

Elsie had been in papa's confidence, so her presents were watch-cases, embroidered on perforated paper. Johnnie gave Katy a box of pencils, and Clover a penknife with a pearl handle. Dorry and Phil clubbed to buy a box of notepaper and envelopes, which the girls were requested to divide between them. Miss Petingill contributed a bottle of ginger balsam, and a box of opodeldoc salve, to be used in case of possible chilblains. Old Mary's offering was a couple of needle-books, full of bright, sharp needles.

I wouldn't give you scissors," she said; "but you can't cut love— or, for the matter of that, anything else—with a needle."

31

Miss Finch, the new housekeeper, arrived a few days before they started: so Katy had time to take her over the house and explain all the different things she wanted done and not done to secure papa's comfort and the children's. Miss Finch was meek and gentle. She seemed glad of a comfortable home. And Katy felt that she would be kind to the boys, and not fret Debby, and drive her into marrying Alexander and going away—an event which Aunt Izzie had been used to predict. Now that all was settled, she and Clover found themselves looking forward to the change with pleasure. There was something new and interesting about it which excited their imaginations.

The last evening was a melancholy one. Elsie had been too much absorbed in the preparations to realise her loss; but when it came to locking the trunks, her courage gave way altogether. She was in such a state of affliction that everybody else became afflicted too; and there is no knowing what would have happened, had not a parcel arrived by express and distracted their attention. The parcel was from Cousin Helen, whose things, like herself, had a knack of coming at the moment when most wanted. It contained two pretty silk umbrellas—one brown, and one dark green, with Katy's initials on one handle, and Clover's on the other. Opening these treasures, and exclaiming over them, helped the family through the evening wonderfully; and next morning there was such a bustle of getting off that nobody had time to cry.

After the last kisses had been given, and Philly, who had climbed on the horse-block, was clamouring for "one more—just one more," Dr. Carr, looking at the sober faces, was struck by a bright idea; and calling Alexander, told him to hurry old Whitey into the carriage, and drive the children down to Willett's Point, that they might wave their handkerchiefs to the boat as she went by. This suggestion worked like a charm on the spirits of the party. Phil began to caper, and Elsie and John ran in to get their hats. Half an hour later, when the boat rounded the point, there stood the little crew, radiant with smiles, fluttering their handkerchiefs and kissing their hands as cheerfully as possible. It was a pleasant last look to the two who stood beside papa on the deck; and, as they waved back their greetings to the little ones, and then looked forward across the blue water to the unknown places they were going to see, Katy and Clover felt that the new life opened well, and promised to be very interesting indeed.

CHAPTER 3

ON THE WAY

The journey from Burnet to Hillsover was a very long one. It took the greater part of three days, and as Dr. Carr was in a hurry to get back to his patients, they travelled without stopping; spending the first night on the boat, and the second on a railroad train. Papa found this tiresome; but the girls, to whom everything was new, thought it delightful. They enjoyed their state-room, with its narrow shelves of beds, as much as if it had been a baby-house, and they two children playing in it. To tuck themselves away for the night in a car-section seemed the greatest fun in the world. When older people fretted, they laughed. Everything was interesting, from the telegraph-poles by the wayside, to the faces of their fellow-passengers. It amused them to watch strange people, and make up stories about them—where they were going, and what relation they could be to each other. The strange people, in their turn, cast curious glances toward the bright, happy-faced sisters; but Katy and Clover did not mind that, or, in fact, notice it. They were too much absorbed to think of themselves, or the impression they were making on others.

It was early on the third morning that the train, puffing and shrieking, ran into the Springfield depot. Other trains stood waiting; and there was such a chorus of snorts and whistles, and such clouds of smoke, that Katy was half frightened. Papa, who was half asleep, jumped up, and told the girls to collect their bags and books; for they were to breakfast here, and to meet Lilly Page, who was going on to Hillsover with them.

"Do you suppose she is here already? asked Katy, tucking the railway-guide into the shawl-strap, and closing her bag with a snap.

Yes; we shall meet her at the Massasoit. She and her father were to pass the night there. "

The Massasoit was close at hand, and in less than five minutes the girls and papa were seated at a table in its pleasant dining-room. They were ordering their breakfast, when Mr. Page came in, accompanied by his daughter—a pretty girl, with light hair, delicate, rather sharp features, and her mother's stylish ease of manner. Her travelling-dress was simple, but had the finish which a French dressmaker knows how to give to a simple thing; and all its appointments —boots, hat, gloves, collar, neck ribbon—were so perfect, each in its way, that Clover, glancing down at her own grey alpaca, and then at Katy's, felt suddenly countrified and shabby.

"Well, Lilly, here they are; here are your cousins," said Mr. Page, giving the girls a cordial greeting. Lilly only said, "How do you do?" Clover saw her glancing at the grey alpacas, and was conscious of a sudden flush. But perhaps Lilly looked at something beside the alpaca; for after a minute her manner changed, and became more friendly.

Did you order waffles?" she asked.

Waffles? no, I think not," replied Katy.

"Oh! why not? Don't you know how celebrated they are for waffles at this hotel? I thought everybody knew that. Then she tinkled her fork against her glass, and when the waiter came, said, "Waffles, please," with an air which impressed Clover extremely. Lilly seemed to her like a young lady in a story, so elegant and self-possessed. She wondered if all the girls at Hillsover were going to be like her.

The waffles came, crisp and hot, with delicious maple syrup to eat on them; and the party made a satisfactory breakfast. Lilly, in spite of all her elegance, displayed a wonderful appetite. "You see," she explained to Clover, a I don't expect to have another decent thing to eat till next September—not a thing, so I'm making the most of this." Accordingly she disposed of nine waffles in quick succession, before she found time to utter anything further, except, "Butter, please," or, "May I trouble you for the molasses?" As she swallowed the last morsel, Dr. Carr, looking at his watch, said that it was time to start for the train; and they set off. Mr. Page went with them. As they crossed the street, Katy was surprised to see that Lilly, who had seemed quite happy only a minute before, had begun to cry. After they reached the car, her tears increased to sobs; she grew almost hysterical.

"Oh! don't make me go, papa," she implored, clinging to her father's arm. "I shall be so homesick! It will kill me, I know it will. Please let me stay. Please let me go home with you."

"Now, my darling, protested Mr. Page, "this is foolish: you know it is. "

"I can't help it," blubbered Lilly. "I ca—n't help it. Oh! don't, don't make me go. Don't, papa, dear. I ca—n't bear it."

Katy and Clover felt embarrassed during this scene. They had always been used to considering tears as things to be rather ashamed of—to be kept back, if possible; or, if not, shed in private corners, in dark closets, or behind the bed in the nursery. To see the stylish Lilly crying like a baby, in the midst of a railway carriage, with strangers looking on, quite shocked them. It did not last long, however. The whistle sounded, the conductor shouted, "All right!" and Mr. Page, giving Lilly a last kiss, disengaged her clinging arms, put her into the seat beside Clover, and hurried out of the car. Lilly sobbed loudly for a few seconds; then she dried her eyes, lifted her head, adjusted her veil and the wrists of her three-buttoned gloves, and remarked—

"I always go on in this way. Ma says I am a real cry-baby; and I suppose I am. I don't see how people can be calm and composed when they're leaving home, do you? You'll be just as bad to-morrow, when you come to say good-bye to your papa."

"Oh! I hope not," said Katy. "Because papa would feel so badly."

Lilly stared. "I shall think you real cold-hearted if you don't," she said, in an offended tone.

Katy took no notice of the tone; and before long Lilly recovered from her pettishness, and began to talk about the school. Katy and lover asked eager questions. They were eager to hear all that Lilly could tell.

"You'll adore Mrs. Florence," she said. "All the girls do. She's the most fascinating woman! She does just what she likes with everybody. Why, even the students think her perfectly splendid; and yet she's just as strict as she can be."

"Strict with the students?" asked Clover, looking puzzled.

"No; strict with us girls. She never lets any one call, unless it's a brother or a first cousin; and then you must have a letter from your parents, asking permission. I wanted ma to write and say that George Hickman might call on me. He isn't a first cousin exactly, but his father married pa's sister-in-law's sister. So it's just as good. But ma was real mean about it. She says I'm too young to have gentlemen coming to see me! I can't think why. Ever so many girls who are younger than I have 'em. Which row are you going to sleep in?" she went on.

"I don't know. Nobody told us that there were any rows.'

"Oh, yes! Shaker Row, and Quaker Row, and Attic Row. Attic Row is the nicest, because it's highest up, and furthest away from Mrs. Florence. My room is in Attic Row. Annie Silsbie and I engaged it last term. You'll be in Quaker Row, I guess. Most of the new girls are."

"Is that a nice row?" asked Clover, greatly interested.

"Pretty nice. It isn't so good as Attic, but it's very much better than Shaker; because there you're close to Mrs. Florence, and can't have a bit of fun without her hearing you. I'd try to get the end room, if I were you. Mary Andrews and I had it once. There is a splendid view of Berry Searles's windows."

"Berry Searles?"

Yes; President Searles, you know; his youngest son. He's an elegant fellow. All the girls are cracked about him—perfectly cracked! The President's house is next door to the Nunnery, you know; and Berry rooms at the very end of the back building, just opposite Quaker Row. It used to be such fun! He'd sit at his window, and we'd sit at ours, in silent study hour, you know; and he'd pretend to read, and all the time keep looking over the top of his book at us, and trying to make us laugh. Once Mary did laugh right out; and Miss Jane heard her, and came in. But Berry is just as quick as a flash, and he ducked down under the window-sill; so she didn't see him. It was such fun!"

"Who's Miss Jane?" asked Katy.

"The horridest old thing. She's Mrs. Florence's niece, and engaged to a missionary. Mrs. Florence keeps her on purpose to spy on us girls, and report when we break the rules. Oh, those rules! Just wait till you come to read 'em over. They're nailed up on all the doors— thirty-two of them—and you can't help breaking 'em if you try ever so much."

"What are they? what sort of rules?" cried Katy and Clover in a breath

"Oh! about being punctual to prayers, and turning your mattress, and smoothing over the under sheet before you leave your room, and never speaking a word in the hall, or in private-study hour, and hanging your towel on your own nail in the wash-room, and all that."

"Wash-room? what do you mean?" said Katy, aghast.

"At the head of Quaker Row, you know. All the girls wash there, except on Saturdays, when they go to the bath-house. You have your own bowl and soap-dish, and a hook for your towel. Why, what's the matter? How big your eyes are!"

"I never heard anything so horrid!" cried Katy, when she had recovered her breath. "Do you really mean that the girls don't have wash-stands in their own rooms?"

"You'll get used to it. All the girls do," responded Lilly.

"I don't want to get used to it," said Katy, resolving to appeal to papa; but papa had gone into the smoking-car, and she had to wait. Meantime Lilly went on talking.

"If you have. that end room in Quaker Row, you'll see all the fun that goes on at commencement time. Mrs. Searles always has a big party, and you can look right in, and watch the people and the supper-table, just as if you were there. Last summer Berry and Alpheus

Seccomb got a lot of cakes and mottoes from the table and came out into the yard, and threw them up one by one to Rose Red and her room-mate. They didn't have the end room, though; but the one next to it."

"What a funny name!—Rose Red," said Clover.

"Oh! her real name is Rosamond Redding; but the girls call her Rose Red. She's the greatest witch in the school; not exactly pretty, you know, but sort of killing and fascinating. She's always getting into the most awful scrapes. Mrs. Florence would have expelled her long ago if she hadn't been such a favourite; and Mr. Redding's daughter, beside. He's a member of Congress, you know, and all that; and Mrs. Florence is quite proud of having Rose in her school.

"Berry Scarles is so funny!" she continued. His mother is a horrid old thing, and always interfering with him. Sometimes when he has a party of fellows in his room, and they're playing cards, we can see her coming with her candle through the house; and when she gets to his door, she tries it, and then she knocks, and calls out, 'Abernethy, my son!' And the fellows whip the cards into their pockets, and stick the bottles under the table and get out their books and dictionaries in a minute; and when Berry unlocks the door, there they sit, studying away; and Mrs. Searles looks so disappointed! I thought I should die one night, me and Mary Andrews laughed so.

I verily believe that if Dr. Carr had been present at this conversation, he would have stopped at the next station, and taken the girls back to Burnet. But he did not return from the smoking-car till the anecdotes about Berry were finished, and Lilly had begun again on Mrs. Florence.

"She's a sort of queen, you know. Everybody minds her. She's tall, and always dresses beautifully. Her eyes are lovely; but, when she gets angry, they're perfectly awful. Rose Red says she'd rather face a mad bull any day than Mrs. Florence in a fury; and Rose ought to know, for she's had more reprimands than any girl in the school."

"How many girls are there?" inquired Dr. Carr.

"There were forty-eight last term. I don't know how many there'll be this, for they say Mrs. Florence is going to give up. It's she who makes the school so popular."

All this time the train was moving northward. With every mile the country grew prettier. Spring had not fairly opened; but the grass was green, and the buds on the trees gave a tender mist-like colour to the woods. The road followed the river, which here and there turned upon itself in long links and windings. Ranges of blue hills closed the distance. Now and then a nearer mountain rose, single and alone, from the plain. The air was cool, and full of a brilliant zest, which the Western girls had never before tasted. Katy felt as if she were drinking champagne. She and Clover flew from window to window, exclaiming with such delight that Lilly was surprised.

I can't see what there is to make such a fuss about," she remarked. "That's only Deerfield. It's quite a small place."

But how pretty it looks, nestled in among the hills! Hills are lovely, Clover, aren't they?

These hills are nothing. You should see the White Mountains," said the experienced Lilly. "Ma and me spent three weeks at the Profile House last vacation. It was perfectly elegant."

In the course of the afternoon Katy drew papa away to a distant seat, and confided her distress about the wash-stands.

"Don't you think it is horrid, papa? Aunt Izzie always said it isn't lady-like not $o take a sponge-bath every morning; but how can we, with forty-eight girls in the room? I don't see what we are going to do."

"I fancy we can arrange it; don't be distressed, my dear," replied Dr. Carr. And Katy was satisfied; for when papa undertook to arrange things, they were very apt to be done.

It was almost evening when they reached their final stopping-place.

"Now, two miles in the stage, and then we're at the horrid old Nunnery," said Lilly. "Ugh! look at that snow. It never melts here till long after it's all gone at home. How I do hate this station! I'm going to be frightfully home-sick: I know I am."

But just then she caught sight of the stagecoach, which stood waiting, and her mood changed; for the stage was full of girls who had come by the other train.

"Hurrah! there's Mary Edwards and Mary Silver," she exclaimed; "and, I declare, Rose Red! Oh, you precious darling! how do you do?" Scrambling up the steps, she plunged at a girl with waving hair, and a rosy, mischievous face; and began kissing her with effusion.

Rose Red did not seem equally enchanted. "Well, Lilly, how are you? she said, and then went on talking to a girl who sat by her side, and whose hand she held; while Lilly rushed up and down the line, embracing and being embraced. She did not introduce Katy and Clover; and, as papa was outside, on the driver's box, they felt a little lonely and strange. All the rest were chattering merrily, and were evidently well acquainted: they were the only ones left out.

Clover watched Rose Red, to whose face she had taken a fancy. It made her think of a pink carnation, or of a twinkling wild rose, with saucy whiskers of brown calyx. Whatever she said or did seemed full of a flavour especially her own. Her eyes, which were blue, and not very large, sparkled with fun and mischief. Her cheeks were round and soft, like a baby's: when she laughed, two dimples broke their pink, and made you want to laugh too. A cunning white throat supported this pretty head, as a stem supports a flower; and, altogether, she was like a flower, except that flowers don't talk, and she talked all the time. What she said seemed very droll, for the girls about her were in fits of laughter; but Clover only caught a word now and then, the stage made such a noise.

Suddenly Rose Red leaned forward, and touched Clover's hand.

"What's your name?" she said. You've got eyes like my sister's. Are you coming to the Nunnery?"

"Yes," replied Clover, smiling back. "My name is Clover—Clover Carr."

"What a dear little name! It sounds just as you look! "

"So does your name—Rose Red," said Clover, shyly.

"It's a ridiculous name," protested Rose Red, trying to pout.

Just then the stage stopped.

"Why? Who's going to the hotel?" cried the school-girls in a chorus.

" I am," said Dr. Carr, putting his head in at the door, with a smile which captivated every girl there. "Come, Katy; come, Clover. I've decided that you shan't begin school till to-morrow."

"Oh, my! Don't I wish he was my pa!" cried Rose Red. Then the stage moved on.

"Who are they? What's their name?" asked the girls. "They look nice."

"They're sort of cousins of mine, and they come from the West," replied Lilly, not unwilling to own the relationship, now that she perceived that Dr. Carr had made a favourable impression.

"Why on earth didn't you introduce them, then? I declare that was just like you, Lilly Page," put in Rose Red, indignantly. "They looked so lonesome that I wanted to pat and stroke both of 'em. That little one has the sweetest eyes!"

Meantime Katy and Clover entered the hotel, very glad of the reprieve, and of one more quiet evening alone with papa. They needed to get their ideas straightened out and put to rights after the confusions of the day and Lilly's extraordinary talk. It was very evident that the Nunnery was to be quite different from their expectations; but another thing was equally evident—it would not be dull! Rose Red by herself, and without any one to help her, would be enough to prevent that!

CHAPTER 4

THE NUNNERY

The night seemed short; for the girls, tired by their journey, slept like dormice. About seven o'clock Katy was roused by the click of a blind; and, opening her eyes, saw Clover standing in the window, and peeping out through the half-opened shutters. When she heard Katy move, she cried out—

"Oh, do come! It's so interesting! I can see the colleges and the church, and, I guess, the Nunnery; only I am not quite sure, because the houses are all so much alike."

Katy jumped up and hurried to the window. The hotel stood on one side of a green common, planted with trees. The common had a lead-coloured fence, and gravel-paths, which ran across it from corner to corner. Opposite the hotel was a long row of red buildings, broken by one or two brown ones, with cupolas. These were evidently the colleges, and a large grey building with a spire was as evidently the church; but which one of the many white, green-blinded houses which filled the other sides of the common, was the Nunnery, the girls could not tell. Clover thought it was one with a garden at the side; but Katy thought not, because Lilly had said nothing of a garden. They discussed the point so long, that the breakfast-bell took them by surprise; and they were forced to rush through their dressing as fast as possible, so as not to keep papa waiting.

When breakfast was over, Dr. Carr told them to put on their hats, and get ready to walk with him to the school. Clover took one arm, and Katy the other; and the

45

three passed between some lead-coloured posts, and took one of the diagonal paths which led across the common.

"That's the house," said Dr. Carr, pointing.

"It isn't the one you picked out, Clover," said Katy.

No," replied Cover, a little disappointed. The house papa indicated was by no means so pleasant as the one she had chosen.

It was a tall, narrow building, with dormer windows in the roof, and a square porch supported by white-washed pillars. A pile of trunks stood in the porch. From above came sounds of voices. Girls' heads were popped out of upper windows at the swinging of the gate; and, as the door opened, more heads appeared looking over the balusters from the hall above.

The parlour into which they were taken was full of heavy, old-fashioned furniture, stiffly arranged. The sofa and chairs were covered with black haircloth, and stood closely against the wall. Some books lay upon the table, arranged two by two; each upper book being exactly at a right angle with each lower book. A bunch of dried grasses stood in the fire-place. There were no pictures, except one portrait in oils, of a forbidding old gentleman in a wig and glasses, sitting with his middle finger majestically inserted in a half-open Bible. Altogether, it was not a cheerful room, nor one calculated to raise the spirits of new-comers; and Katy, whose long seclusion had made her sensitive on the subject of rooms, shrank instinctively nearer papa as they went in.

Two ladies rose to receive them. One, a tall, dignified person, was Mrs. Florence. The other she introduced as, "My assistant principal, Mrs. Nipson." Mrs. Nipson was not tall. She had a round face, pinched lips, and half-shut grey eyes.

This lady is fully associated with me in the management of the school," explained Mrs. Florence. When I go, she will assume the entire control."

"Is that likely to be soon?" inquired Dr. Carr, surprised, and not well pleased that the teacher of whom he had heard, and with whom he had proposed to leave his children, was planning to yield her place to a stranger.

"The time is not yet determined," replied Mrs. Florence. Then she changed the subject—gracefully, but so decidedly, that Dr. Carr had no chance for further question. She spoke of classes, and discussed what Katy and Clover were to study. Finally, she proposed to take them upstairs to see their room. Papa might come too, she said.

"I dare say that Lilly Page, who tells me that she is a cousin of yours, has described the arrangements of the house, she remarked to Katy. "The room I have assigned to you is in the back building. 'Quaker Row,' the girls call it."

She smiled as she spoke; and Katy, meeting her eyes for the first time, felt that there was something in what Lilly had said Mrs. Florence *was* a sort of queen.

They went upstairs. Some girls, who were peeping over the baluster, hurried away at their approach Mrs. Florence shook her head at the

"The first day is always one of license, she said, leading the way along an uncarpeted entry to a door at the end, from which, by a couple of steps, they went down into a square room—round three sides of which ran a shelf, on which stood rows of wash-bowls and pitchers. Above were hooks for towels. Katy perceived that this was the much-dreaded wash-room.

"Our lavatory," remarked Mrs. Florence, blandly. Opening from the wash-room was a very long hall, lighted at each end by a window. The doors on either side were numbered "one", "two", "three", and so on. Some of them were half open; as they went by, Katy and Clover caught glimpses of girls and trunks, and beds strewed with things. At No. 6 Mrs. Florence paused.

"Here is the room which I propose to give you," she said.

Katy and Clover looked eagerly about. It was a small room, but the sun shone in cheerfully at the window. There was a maple bedstead and table, a couple of chairs, and a row of hooks; that was all, except that in the wall was set a case of black-handled drawers, with cupboard-doors above them.

"These take the place of a bureau, and hold your clothes," explained Mrs. Florence, pulling out one of the drawers. "I hope, when once you are settled, you will find yourselves comfortable. The rooms are small; but young people do not require so much space as older ones. Though, indeed, your elder daughter, Dr. Carr, looks more advanced and grown up than I was prepared to find her. What did you say was her age?"

"She is past sixteen; but she has been so long confined to her room by the illness of which I wrote, that you may probably find her behindhand in some respects, which reminds me" (this was very adroit of Papa!) "I am anxious that she should keep up the system to which she has been accustomed at home—among other things, sponge-baths of cold water every morning; and, as I see that the bedrooms are not furnished with washstands, I will ask your permission to provide one for the use of my little girls. Perhaps you will kindly tell me where I had better look for it?

Mrs. Florence was not pleased, but she could not object, so she mentioned a shop. Katy's heart gave a bound of relief. She thought No. 6 with a washstand might be very comfortable. Its bareness and simplicity had the charm of novelty. Then there was something very interesting to her in the idea of a whole house full of girls.

They did not stay long after seeing the room, but went off on a shopping excursion. Shops were few and far between at Hillsover, but they found a neat little maple washstand and rocking-chair, and Papa also bought a comfortable low chair, with a slatted back and a cushion. This was for Katy.

"Never study till your back aches," he told her; "when you are tired, lie flat on the bed for half an hour, and tell Mrs. Florence that it was by my direction."

"Or Mrs. Nipson," said Katy, laughing rather ruefully. She had taken no fancy to Mrs. Nipson, and did not enjoy the idea of a divided authority.

A hurried lunch at the hotel followed, and then it was time for Dr. Carr to go away. They all walked to the school together, and said good-bye on the steps. The girls would not cry, but they clung very tightly to Papa, and put as much feeling into their last kisses as would have furnished forth half-a-dozen fits of tears. Lilly might have thought them cold-hearted, but Papa did not; he knew better.

"That's my brave girls!" he said. Then he kissed them once more and hurried away. Perhaps he did not wish them to see that his eyes too were a little misty.

As the door closed behind them, Katy and Clover realized that they were alone among strangers. The sensation was not pleasant, and they felt forlorn as they went upstairs, and down Quaker Row, toward No. 6.

"Aha! so you're going to be next door," said a gay voice, as they passed No. 5, and Rose Red popped her head into the hall. Well, I'm glad," she went on, shaking hands cordially. "I was in hopes you would, and yet I didn't know; and there are some awful stiffies among the new girls. How do you both do?"

"Oh, are we next door to you?" cried Clover, brightening.

"Yes. It's rather good of me not to hate you, for I wanted the end room myself, and Mrs. Florence wouldn't give it to me. Come in, and let me introduce you to my room-mate. It's against the rules, but that's no matter; nobody pretends to keep rules the first day."

They went in. No. 5 was precisely like No. 6 in shape, size, and furniture; but Rose had unpacked her trunk, and decorated her room with odds and ends of all sorts. The table was covered with books and boxes; coloured lithographs were pinned on the walls; a huge blue rosette ornamented the head-board of the bed; the blinds were tied together with pink ribbon; over the top of the window was a festoon of hemlock boughs, fresh and spicy. The effect was fantastic, but cheery, and Katy and Clover exclaimed with one voice, How pretty! "

The room-mate was a pale, shy girl, with a half-scared look in her eyes, and small hands which twisted uneasily together when she moved and spoke. Her name was Mary Silver. She and Rose were so utterly unlike, that Katy thought it odd that they should have chosen to be together. Afterwards she understood it better. Rose liked to protect, and Mary to be protected; Rose to talk, and Mary to listen. Mary evidently considered Rose the most entertaining creature in the world; she giggled violently at all her jokes, and then stopped short and covered her mouth with her fingers, in a frightened way, as if giggling were wrong.

Only think, Mary," began Rose, after introducing Katy and Clover, these young ladies have got the end room. What do you suppose was the reason that Mrs. Florence did not give it to us? It's very peculiar."

Mary laughed her uneasy laugh. She looked as if she could tell the reason, but did not dare.

"Never mind," continued Rose. "Trials are good for one, they say. It's something to have nice people in that room, if we can't be there ourselves. You are nice, aren't you?" turning to Clover.

"Very," replied Clover, laughing.

I thought so. I can almost always tell without asking; still, it is something to have it on the best authority. We'll be good neighbours, won't we? Look here," and she pulled one of the black-handled drawers completely out and laid it on the bed. "Do you see? your drawers are exactly behind ours. Any time in silent study hour, if I have something I want to say, I'll ;just rap and pop a note into your drawer, and you can do the same to me. Isn't it fun?

Clover said, "Yes"; but Katy, though she laughed, shook her head.

Don't entice us into mischief," she said. l

"Oh, gracious!" exclaimed Rose. "Now, are you going to be good, —you two? If you are, just break the news at once, and have it over. I can bear it." She fanned herself in such a comical way that no one could help laughing. Mary Silver joined, but stopped pretty soon in her sudden manner.

"There's Mary, now," went on Rose; "she's named Silver, but she's as good as gold. She's a paragon. It's quite a trial to me, rooming with a paragon. But if any more are coming into the entry just give me fair notice, and I pack and move up among the sinners in Attic

Row. Somehow, you don't look like paragons either—you especially," nodding to Clover. "Your eyes are like violets; but so are Sylvia's—that's my sister—and she's the greatest witch in Massachusetts. Eyes are dreadfully deceitful things. As for you"—to Katy —"you're so tall that I can't take you all in at once; but the piece I see doesn't look dreadful a bit.

Rose was sitting in the window as she made these remarks, and, leaning forward suddenly, she gave a pretty, blushing nod to some one below. Katy glanced down, and saw a handsome young man replacing the cap he had lifted from his head.

"That's Berry Searles," said Rose. "He's the President's son, you know. He always comes through the side yard to get to his room. That's it—the one with the red curtain. It's exactly opposite your window. Don't you see?"

"So it is!" exclaimed Katy, remembering what Lilly had said. "Oh! was that the reason——" she stopped, afraid of being rude.

"The reason we wanted the room? inquired Rose, coolly. "Well, I don't know. It hadn't occurred to me to look at it in that ,light. Mary," with sudden severity, "is it possible that you had Berry Searles in your mind when you were so pertinacious about that room?"

"Rose! How can you? You know I never thought of such a thing," protested poor Mary. "I hope not; otherwise I should feel it my duty to consult with Mrs. Florence on the subject, went on Rose, with an air of dignified admonition. "I consider myself responsible for you and your morals, Mary. Let us change this painful subject." She looked gravely at the three girls for a moment; then her lips began to twitch, the irresistible dimples appeared in her cheeks, and, throwing herself back in her chair, she burst into a fit of laughter.

"O Mary, you little goose! Some day or other you'll be the death of me! Dear, dear! how I am behaving! It's perfectly horrid of me. And I didn't mean it. I'm going to be real good this term; I promised mother. Please forget it, and don't take a dislike to me, and never come again," she added, coaxingly, as Katy and Clover rose to go.

"Indeed, we won't," replied Katy. As for sensible Clover, she was already desperately in love with Rose, on that very first day.

"After a couple of hours of hard work, No. 6 was in order, and looked like a different place. Fringed towels were laid over the washstand and the table. Dr. Carr's photograph and some pretty chromos ornamented the walls; the rocking-chair and the study chair stood by the window; the trunks were hidden by chintz covers, made for the purpose by old Mary. On the window-sill stood Cousin Helen's vase which Katy had brought carefully packed among her clothes. "Now," she said, tying the blinds together with a knot of ribbon in imitation of Rose Red's, "when we get a bunch of wild flowers for my vase, we shall be all right."

A tap at the door. Rose entered.

Are you done?" she asked; "may I come in and see?"

Oh, this is pretty!n she exclaimed, looking about. "How you can tell in one minute what sort of a girl one is, just by looking at her room! I should know you had been neat and dainty and housekeeperly all your days. And you would see in a minute that I am a Madge Wildfire, and that Ellen Gray is a saint, and Sally Satterlee a scatterbrain, and Lilly Page an affected little hum—oh, I forgot! she is your cousin, isn't she? How dreadfully rude of me!" dimpling at Clover, who couldn't help dimpling back again.

"Oh, my!" she went on, a wash-stand, I declare! Where did you get it?

"Papa bought it," explained Katy; he asked Mrs. Florence's permission. "

"How nice of him! I shall just write to my father to ask for permission too. Which she did; and the result was that it set the fashion of wash-stands, and so many papas wrote to "ask permission, that Mrs. Florence found it necessary to give up the lavatory system, and provide wash-stands for the whole house. Katy's request had been the opening wedge. I do not think this fact made her more popular with the principals.

"By the way, where is Lilly?" asked Katy. "I haven't seen her today.

"Do you want to know? I can tell you. She's sitting on the edge of one chair, with her feet on the stave of another chair, and her head on the shoulder of her room-mate (who is dying to get away and arrange her drawers); and she's crying _ _ r

'"How do you know? Have you been up to see her?"

"Oh! I haven't seen her. It isn't necessary. I saw her last term, and the term before. She always spends the first day at school in that way. I'll take you up, if you'd like to examine for yourselves.

Katy and Clover, much amused, followed as she led the way upstairs. Sure enough, Lilly was sitting exactly as Rose predicted. Her face was swollen with crying. When she saw the girls, her sobs redoubled.

"Oh! isn't it dreadful?" she demanded. "I shall die, I know I shall. Oh! why did pa make me come?"

"Now, Lilly, don't be an idiot, said the unsympathising Rose. Then she sat down and proceeded to make a series of the most grotesque faces, winking her eyes and twinkling her finger round the head of "Niobe," as she called Lilly, till the other girls were in fits of laughter, and Niobe, though she shrugged her shoulders pettishly and said, "Don't be so ridiculous, Rose Red," was forced to give way. First she smiled, then a laugh was heard; afterwards she announced that she felt better.

"That's right, Niobe," said Rose. "Wash your face now, and get ready for tea, for the bell is just going to ring. As for you, Annie, you might as well put your drawers in order," with a wicked wink. Annie hurried away with a laugh, which she tried in vain to hide.

"You heartless creature!" cried the exasperated Lilly. I believe you're made of marble; you haven't one bit of feeling. Nor you either, Katy. You haven't cried a drop."

"Given this problem, said the provoking Rose; "when the nose without is as red as a lobster, what must be the temperature of the heart within, and vice versa?"

The tea-bell rang just in time to avert a fresh flood of tears from Lilly. She brushed her hair in angry haste, and they all hurried down by a side staircase which, as Rose explained, the school-girls were expected to use. The dining-room was not large; only part of the girls could be seated at a time; so they took turns at dining at the first table, half one week and half the next.

Mrs. Nipson sat at the tea-tray, with Mrs. Florence beside her. At the other end of the long board sat a severe-looking person, whom Lilly announced in a whisper as "that horrid Miss Jane. The meal was very simple—tea, bread and butter, and dried beef: it was eaten in silence; the girls were not allowed to speak, except to ask for what they wanted. Rose Red, indeed, who sat next to Mrs. Florence, talked to her, and even ventured once or twice on daring little jokes, which caused Clover to regard her with admiring astonishment. No one else said anything, except, Butter, please,

"Pass the bread". As they filed upstairs after this cheerless meal, they were met by rows of hungry girls, who were waiting to go down, and who whispered, "How long you have been! What's for tea?"

The evening passed in making up classes and arranging for recitation-rooms and study-hours. Katy was glad when bed-time came. The day, with all its new impressions and strange faces, seemed to her like a confused dream. She and Clover undressed very quietly. Among the printed rules, which hung on the bedroom door, they read: "All communication between room-mates, after the retiring bell has rung, is strictly prohibited." Just then it did not seem difficult to keep this rule. It was only after the candle was blown out, that Clover ventured to whisper—very low indeed, for who knew but Miss Jane was listening outside the door?—"Do you think you're going to like it?" and Katy, in the same cautious whisper, responded, "I'm not quite sure." And so ended the first day at the Nunnery.

CHAPTER 5

ROSES AND THORNS

"Oh! What is it? What has happened?" cried Clover, starting up in bed, the next morning, as a clanging sound roused her suddenly from sleep. It was only the rising-bell, ringing at the end of Quaker Row.

Katy held her watch up to the dim light. She could just see the hands. Yes, they pointed to six. It was actually morning! She and Clover jumped up, and began to dress as fast as possible.

"We've only got half an hour," said Clover, unhooking the rules, and carrying them to the window—"half an hour; and this says we must turn the mattress, smooth the under-sheet over the bolster, and spend five minutes in silent devotion. We'll have to be quick to do all that, besides dressing ourselves!"

It is never easy to be quick, when one is in a hurry. Everything sets itself against you. Fingers turn into thumbs; dresses won't button, nor pins keep their place. With all their haste, Katy and Clover were barely ready when the second bell sounded. As they hastened downstairs, Katy fastening her breast-pin, and Clover her cuffs, they met other girls, some looking half asleep, others half dressed; all yawning, rubbing their eyes, and complaining of the early hour.

"Isn't it horrid?" said Lilly Page, hurrying by with no collar on, and her hair hastily tucked into a net. "I never get up till nine o'clock when I'm at home. Ma saves my breakfast for me. She says I shall have my sleep out while I have the chance."

"You don't look quite awake now," remarked Clover.

"No, because I haven't washed my face. Half the time I don't before breakfast. There's that old mattress has to be turned; and when I sleep too long, I just do that first, and then scramble my clothes on the best way I can. Anything not to be marked! "

After prayers and breakfast were done, the girls had half an hour for putting their bedrooms to rights, during which interval it is to be hoped that Lilly found time to wash her face, After that, lessons began, and lasted till one o'clock. Dinner followed with an hour's "recreation; then the bell rang for "silent study-hour," when the girls sat with their books in their bedrooms, but were not allowed to speak to each other. Next came a walk.

"Who are you going to walk with?" asked Rose Red, meeting Clover in Quaker Row.

I don't know. Katy, I guess."

"Are you, really? You and she like each other, don't you? Do you know, you're the first sisters I ever knew at school who did! Generally, they quarrel awfully. The Stearns girls, who were here last term, scarcely spoke to each other. They didn't even sleep together; and Sarah Stearns was always telling tales against Sue, and Sue against Sarah."

"How disgusting! I never heard of anything so mean," cried Clover, indignantly. "Why, I wouldn't tell tales about Katy if we quarrelled ever so much. We never do, though—Katy is so sweet."

"I suppose she is," said Rose, rather doubtfully; "but, do you know, I'm half afraid of her. It's because she's so tall. Tall people always scare me. And then she looks so grave and grown up! Don't tell her I said so though; for I want her to like me."

"Oh, she isn't a bit grave or grown up. She's the funniest girl in the world. Wait till you know her," replied loyal Clover.

I'd give anything if I could walk with you part of this term," went on Rose, putting her arm round Clover's waist. But you see, unluckily, I'm engaged straight through. All of us old girls are. I walk with May Mather this week and next; then Esther Dearborn for a month; then Lilly Page for two weeks; and all the rest of the time with Mary. I can't think why I promised Lilly. I'm sure I don't want to go with her. I'd ask Mary to let me off, only I'm afraid she would not like it. I say, suppose we engage now to walk with each other for the first half of next term."

"Why, that's not till October! " said Clover.

"I know it; but it's nice to be beforehand. Will you?"

"Of course I will—provided that Katy has somebody pleasant to go with," replied Clover, immensely flattered at being asked by the popular Rose. Then they ran downstairs, and took their places in the long procession of girls, who were ranged two and two, ready to start. Miss Jane walked at the head; and Miss Marsh, another teacher, brought up the rear. Rose Red whispered that it was like a funeral and a caravan mixed—"as cheerful as hearses at both ends, and wild beasts in the middle."

The walk was along a wooded road—a mile out and a mile back. The procession was not permitted to stop, or straggle, or take any of the liberties which make walking pleasant. Still, Katy and Clover enjoyed it. There was a spring smell in the air, and the woods were beginning to be pretty. They even found a little trailing arbutus blossoming in a sunny hollow. Lilly was just in front of them, and amused them with histories of different girls whom she pointed out in the long line. That was Esther Dearborn—Rose Red's friend. Handsome, wasn't she? but terribly sarcastic. The two next were Amy Alsop and Ellen Gray. They always walked together, because they were so intimate. Yes; they were nice enough, only so distressingly good. Amy did not get one single mark last term! That child with pig-tails was Bella Arkwright. Why on earth did Katy want to know about her? She was a nasty little thing.

She's just about Elsie's height," replied Katy. "Who's that pretty girl with pink velvet on her hat?"

"Dear me! Do you think she's pretty? I don't. Her name is Louisa Agnew. She lives at Ashburn—quite near U9; but we don't know them. Her family are not at all in good society."

What a pity! She looks so sweet and ladylike."

Lilly tossed her head. "They're quite common people," she said. "They live in a little mite of a house, and her father paints portraits."

But I should think that would be nice. Doesn't she ever take you to see his pictures?"

Take me! cried Lilly, indignantly. "I should think not. I tell you we don't visit. I just speak when we're here, but I never see her when I'm at home."

Move on, young ladies. What are you stopping for?" cried Miss Jane.

"Yes; move on," muttered Rose Red, from behind. Don't you hear Policeman X?

From walking-hour till tea-time was recreation" again. Lilly improved this opportunity to call at No. 6. She had waited to see how the girls were likely to take in the school before committing herself to intimacy; but, now that Rose Red had declared in their favour, she was ready to begin to be friendly.

How lovely!" she said, looking about. "You got the

end room, after all, didn't you? What splendid times you'll have! Oh, how plainly you can see Berry Searles's window! Has he spoken to you yet?"

"Spoken to us? Of course not! Why should he?" replied Katy. He doesn't know us, and we don't know him."

That's nothing. Half the girls in the school bow, and speak, and carry on with young men they don't know. You won't have a bit of fun if you're so particular."

"I don't want that kind of fun," replied Katy, with energy in her voice; "neither does Clover. And I can't imagine how the girls can behave so. It isn't lady-like at all."

Katy was very fond of this word, "lady-like." She always laid great stress upon it. It seemed in some way to be connected with Cousin Helen, and to mean everything that was good, and graceful, and sweet.

"Dear me! I'd no idea you were so dreadfully proper," said Lilly, pouting. "Mother said you were as prim and precise as your grandmother; but I didn't suppose——"

"How unkind!" broke in Clover, taking fire, as usual, at any affront to Katy. Katy prim and precise! She isn't a bit! She's twice as much fun as the rest of you girls; but it's nice fun—not this horrid stuff about students. I wish your mother wouldn't say such things.

"I didn't—she didn't—I don't mean exactly that, stammered Lilly, frightened by Clover's indignant eyes. "All I meant was, that Katy is dreadfully dignified for her age, and we bad girls will have to look out. You needn't be so mad, Clover; I'm sure it's very nice to be proper and good, and set an example."

"I don't want to preach to anybody, said Katy, colouring, "and I wasn't thinking about examples. But really and truly, Lilly, wouldn't your mother, and all the girls'

girls' mothers, be shocked if they knew about these performances here?"

"Gracious! I should think so; Ma would kill me. I wouldn't have her know of my goings on for all the world."

Just then Rose pulled out a drawer, and called through to ask if Clover would please come in and help her a minute. Lilly took advantage of her absence to say—

"I came on purpose to ask you to walk with me for four weeks. Will you?"

"Thank you; but I'm engaged to Clover."

"To Clover! But she's your sister, you can get off."

"I don't want to get off. Clover and I like dearly to go together."

Lilly stared. "Well, I never heard of such a thing, she said; "you're really romantic. The girls will call you 'The Inseparables'."

"I wouldn't mind being inseparable from Clover," said Katy.

Next day was Saturday. It was nominally a holiday; but so many tasks were set for it, that it hardly seemed like one. The girls had to practise in the gymnasium, to do their mending, and have all their drawers in apple-pie order, before afternoon, when Miss Jane went through the rooms on a tour of inspection. Saturday, also, was the day for writing home letters; so, altogether, it was about the busiest of the week.

Early in the morning Miss Jane appeared in Quaker Row with some slips of paper in her hand, one of which she left at each door. They told the hours at which the girls were to go to the bath-house.

"You will carry each a bath towel, a sponge, and soap," she announced to Katy, "and will be in the entry, at the foot of the stairs, at twenty-five minutes after nine precisely. Failures in punctuality will be punished by a mark." Miss Jane always delivered her words like a machine, and closed her mouth with a snap at the end of the sentence.

"Horrid thing! Don't I wish her missionary would come and carry her off. Not that I blame him for staying away," remarked Rose Red, from her door; making a face at Miss Jane as she walked down the entry.

"I don't understand about the bath-house," said Katy. "Does it belong to us? And where is it?"

"No, it doesn't belong to us. It belongs to Mr. Perrit, and anybody can use it; only on Saturday it is reserved for us nuns. Haven't you ever noticed it when we have been out walking? It's in that street by the bakery, which we pass to take the Lebanon Road. We go across the green, and down by Professor Seccomb's, and we are in plain sight from the college all the way; and, of course, those abominable boys sit there with spy-glasses, and stare as hard as ever they can. It's perfectly horrid. 'A bath towel, a sponge, and soap,' indeed! I wish I could make Miss Jane eat the pieces of soap which she has forced me to carry across this village."

"Oh, Rose!" remonstrated Mary Silver.

"Well, I do." And the bath towels afterwards, by way of a dessert," replied the incorrigible Rose. "Never mind! Just wait! A bright idea strikes me."

"Oh! what?" cried the other three; but Rose only pursed up her mouth, arched her eyebrows, and vanished into her own room, locking the door behind her. Mary Silver, finding herself shut out, sat down meekly in the hall till such time as it should please Rose to open the door. This was not till the bath hour. As Katy and Clover went by, Rose put her head out, and called that she would be down in a minute.

The bathing party consisted of eight girls, with Miss Jane for escort. They were half way across the common before Miss Jane noticed that everybody was shaking with stifled laughter, except Rose, who walked along demurely, apparently unconscious that there was anything to laugh at. Miss Jane looked sharply from one to another for a moment, then stopped short and exclaimed, "Rosamund Redding how dare you?"

"What is it, ma'am?" asked Rose, with the face of a lamb.

"Your bath towel! your sponge!" gasped Miss Jane.

"Yes, ma'am, I have them all," replied the audacious Rose, putting her hand to her hat. There, to be sure, was the long towel, hanging down behind like a veil, while the sponge was fastened on one side like a great cockade; and in front appeared a cake of pink soap, neatly pinned into the middle of a black velvet bow.

Miss Jane seized Rose and removed these ornaments in a twinkling. "We shall see what Mrs. Florence thinks of this conduct," she grimly remarked. Then, dropping the soap and sponge in her own pocket, she made Rose walk beside her, as if she were a criminal in custody.

The bath-house was a neat place, with eight small rooms, well supplied with hot and cold water. Katy would have found her bath very nice, had it not been for the thought of the walk home. They must look so absurd with their sponges and damp towels.

Miss Jane was as good as her word. After dinner, Rose was sent for by Mrs. Florence, and had an interview of two hours with her; she came out with red eyes, and shut herself into her room with a disconsolate bang. Before long, however, she revived sufficiently to tap on the drawers and push through a note with the following words:—

"My heart is broken!

"R. R."

Clover hastened in to comfort her. Rose was sitting on the floor, with a very clean pocket-handkerchief in her hand. She wept, and put her head against Clover's knee.

"I suppose I'm the nastiest girl in the world," she said. "Mrs. Florence thinks so. She said I was an evil influence in the school. Wasn't that unkind?" with a little sob.

"I meant to be so good this term," she went on; "but what's the use? A codfish might as well try to play the piano! It was always so, even when I was a baby. Sylvia says I have got a little fiend inside of me. Do you believe I have? Is it that makes me so horrid?

Clover purred over her. She could not bear to have Rose feel unhappy. "Wasn't Miss Jane funny?" went on Rose, with a sudden twinkle; "and did you see Berry, and Alfred Seccomb?"

"No; where were they?"

"Close to us, standing by the fence. All the time Miss Jane was unpinning the towel, they were splitting their sides, and Berry made such a face at me that I nearly laughed out. That boy has a perfect genius for faces. He used to frighten Sylvia and me into fits, when we were little tots, up here on visits."

"Then you knew him before you came to school?"

"Oh dear, yes! I know all the Hillsover boys. We used to make mud pies together. They're grown up now, most of them, and in college; and when we meet we're very dignified, and say, 'Miss Redding', and 'Mr. Seccomb', and 'Mr. Searles'; but we're just as good friends as ever. When I go to take tea with Mrs. Seccomb, Alfred always invites Berry to drop in, and we

65

have the greatest fun. Mrs. Florence won't let me go this term, though, I guess, she's so mad about the towel."

Katy was quite relieved when Clover reported this conversation. Rose, for all her wickedness, seemed to be a little lady. Katy did not like to class her among the girls who flirted with students whom they did not know.

It was wonderful how soon they all settled down, and became accustomed to their new life. Before six weeks were over, Katy and Clover felt as if they had lived at Hillsover for years. This was partly because there was so much to do. Nothing makes time fly like having every moment filled, and every hour set apart for a distinct employment.

They made several friends, chief among whom were Ellen Gray and Louisa Agnew; this last intimacy Lilly resented highly, and seemed to consider as an affront to herself. With no one, however, was Katy so intimate as Clover was with Rose Red. This cost Katy some jealous pangs at first. She was so used to considering Clover her own exclusive property that it was not easy to share her with another; and she had occasional fits of feeling resentful, and injured, and left out. These were but momentary, however. Katy was too good of heart to let unkind feelings grow, and by and by she grew fond of Rose and Rose of her, so that in the end the sisters shared their friend as they did other nice things, and neither of them was jealous of the other.

But, charming as she was, a certain price had to be paid for the pleasure of intimacy with Rose. Her overflowing spirits, and "the little fiend inside her," were always provoking scrapes in which her friends were apt to be more or less involved. She was very penitent and afflicted after these scrapes, but it didn't make a bit of difference; the next time she was just as naughty as ever.

"What are you doing?" said Katy one day, meeting her in the hall with a heap of black shawls and aprons on her arm.

"Hush!" whispered Rose, mysteriously; "don't say a word. Senator Brown is dead—our senator, you know. I'm going to put my window into mourning for him, that's all. It's a proper token of respect."

Two hours later, Mrs. Nipson, walking sedately across the common, noticed quite a group of students in the President's side yard, looking up at the Nunnery. She drew nearer. They were admiring Rose's window, hung with black, and decorated with a photograph of the deceased senator, suspended in the middle of a wreath of weeping-willow. Of course she hurried upstairs, and tore down the shawls and aprons; and, equally of course, Rose had a lecture and a mark. But, dear me! what good did it do? The next day but one, as Katy and Clover sat together in silent-study hour, their lower drawer was pushed open very noiselessly and gently, till it came out entirely, and lay on the floor, and in the aperture thus formed appeared Rose's saucy face, flushed with mischief. She was crawling through from her own room.

"Such fun!" she whispered; "I never thought of this before! We can have parties in study hours, and all sorts of things."

"Oh, go back, Rosy" whispered Clover, in agonized entreaty, though laughing all the time.

"Go back? Not at all! I'm coming in," answered Rose, pulling herself through a little farther. But at that moment the door opened: there stood Miss Jane! She had caught the buzz of voices as she passed in the hall, and had entered to see what was going on.

Rose, dreadfully frightened, made a rapid movement to withdraw. But the space was narrow, and she had wedged herself, and could move neither backward nor forward. She had to submit to being helped through by Miss Jane, in a series of pulls, while Katy and Clover sat by, not daring to laugh or offer assistance. When Rose was on her feet, Miss Jane released her with a final shake, which she seemed unable to refrain from giving.

"Go to your room," she said. "I shall report all of you young ladies for this flagrant act of disobedience.

Rose went, and in two minutes the drawer, which Miss Jane had replaced, opened again, and there was this note:—

"If I am never heard of more, give my love to my family, and mention how I died. I forgive my enemies, and leave Clover my band bracelet.

"My blessings on you both.

"With the deepest regard,

"Your afflicted friend,

"R. R."

Mrs. Florence was very angry on this occasion, and would listen to no explanations, but gave Katy and Clover a "disobedience mark" also. This was very unfair, and Rose felt dreadfully about it. She begged and entreated, but Mrs. Florence only replied, "There is blame on both sides, I have no doubt."

"She's entirely changed from what she used to be," declared Rose. "I don't know what's the matter; I don't like her half so much as I did."

The truth was, that Mrs. Florence had secretly determined to give up her connection with the school at Midsummer; and, regarding it now rather as Mrs.

Nipson's school than her own, she took no pains to study character or mete out justice carefully among scholars with whom she was not likely to have much to do.

CHAPTER 6

THE S. S. U. C.

It was Saturday afternoon, and Clover, having finished her practising, dusting, and mending, had settled herself in No. 6 for a couple of hours of quiet enjoyment. Everything was in beautiful order to meet Miss Jane's inspecting eye; and Clover, as she sat in the rocking-chair, writing-case in lap, looked extremely cosy and comfortable.

A half-finished letter to Elsie lay in the writing-case; but Clover felt lazy, and instead of writing was looking out of the window, in a dreamy way, to where Berry Searles and some other young men were playing ball in the yard below. She was not thinking of them or of anything else in particular. A vague sense of pleasant idleness possessed her, and it was like the breaking of a dream when the door opened and Katy came in, not quietly, after her wont, but with a certain haste and indignant rustle, as if vexed by something. When she saw Clover at the window she cried out hastily, "Oh, Clover, don't! "

"Don't what? asked Clover, without turning her head.

"Don't sit there looking at those boys."

"Why? why not? They can't see me. The blinds are shut.

"No matter for that. It's just as bad a if they could see you. Don't do it. I would much rather that you did not."

Well, I won't then," said Clover, good-humouredly, facing round with her back to the window. I wasn't looking at them either —not exactly. I was thinking about Elsie and John, and wondering——But what's the matter, Katy? What makes you fire up so about it? You've watched the ball-playing yourself, plenty of times."

I know I have, and I didn't mean to be cross, Clover. The truth is, I am very much put out. These girls, with their incessant talk about the students, make me absolutely sick. It is so unladylike and so bad, especially for the little ones. Fancy that mite of a Carrie Steele informing me that she is 'in love' with Harry Crosby. In love! A baby like that! She has no business to know that there is such a thing."

"Yes," said Clover, laughing; "she wrote his name on a wintergreen lozenge, and bored a hole and hung it round her neck on a blue ribbon. But it melted and stuck to her frock, and she had to take it off.

"Whereupon she ate it," added Rose, who came in at that moment. The girls shouted, but Katy soon grew grave. "One can't help laughing," she said; "but isn't it a shame to have such things going on? Just fancy our Elsie behaving so, Clover! Why, papa would have a fit. I declare I've a great mind to get up a society to put down flirting."

"Do," said Rose. "What fun it would be! Call it 'The Society for the Suppression of Young Men.' I'll join."

"You, indeed!" replied Katy, shaking her head. "Didn't I see Berry Searles throw a bunch of syringa into your window only this morning?"

"Dear me! did he? I shall have to speak to Mary again. It's quite shocking to have her go on so. But really and truly do let us have a Society. It would be so jolly. We could meet on Saturday afternoons, and write pieces and have signals and a secret, as Sylvia's Society did when she was at school. Get one up, Katy—that's a dear."

"But," said Katy, taken aback by having her random idea so suddenly adopted, "if I did get one up, it would be in real earnest, and it would be a society against flirting. And you know you can't help it, Rosy."

"Yes, I can. You are doing me great injustice. I don't behave like those girls in Attic Row. I never did. I just bow-to Berry and the rest whom I really know—never to anybody else. And you must see, Katherine darling, that it would be the height of ingratitude if I didn't bow to boys who made mud pies for me when I was little, and lent me their marbles, and did all sorts of kind things. Now wouldn't it?n—coaxingly.

"Per—haps," admitted Katy, with a smile. "But you're such a witch! "

"I'm not—indeed I'm not. I'll be a pillar of society if only you'll provide a society for me to be a pillar of. Now, Katy, do—ah, do, do!

When Rose was in a coaxing mood, few people could resist her. Katy yielded, and between jest and earnest the matter was settled. Katy was to head the plan and invite the members.

"Only a few at first," suggested Rose. "When it is proved to be a success, and everybody wants to join, we can let in two or three more as a great favour. What shall the name be? We'll keep it a secret, whatever it is. There's no fun in a society without a secret."

What should the name be? Rose invented half a dozen, each more absurd than the last. "The Anti-Jane Society" would sound well, she insisted. Or, no!—the "Put-him-down Club" was better yet! Finally they settled upon The Society for the Suppression of Unladylike Conduct."

Only we'll never use the whole name," said Rose; "we'll say, 'The S.S.U.C.' That sounds brisk and snappy, and will drive the whole school wild with curiosity. What larks! How I long to begin!"

The next Saturday was fixed upon for the first meeting. During the week Katy proposed the plan to the elect few.

Lilly Page was the only person who declined. She said it would be stupid; that for her part she didn't set up to be good or better than she was, and that in any case she shouldn't wish to be mixed up in a society of which "Miss Agnew" was a member. The girls did not break their hearts over this refusal. They had felt obliged to ask her for relationship's sake, but everybody was a little relieved that she did not wish to join.

No. 6 looked very full indeed that Saturday afternoon when the S.S.U.C. came together for the first time. Ten members were present. Mary Silver and Louisa were two; and Rose's crony, Esther Dearborn, another. The remaining four were Sally Alsop and Amy Erskine; Alice Gibbons, one of the new scholars, whom they all liked, but did not know very well; and Ellen Gray, a pale, quiet girl, with droll blue eyes, a comical twist to her mouth, and a trick of saying funny things in such a demure way that half the people who listened never found out that they were funny. All Rose's chairs had been borrowed for the occasion. Three girls sat on the bed, and three on the floor. With a little squeezing, there was plenty of room for everybody.

Katy was chosen President, and requested to take the rocking-chair as a sign of office. This she did with much dignity, and proceeded to read the Constitution and Bye-Laws of the Society, which had been drawn up by Rose Red, and copied on an immense sheet of blue paper.

They ran thus:—

CONSTITUTION OF THE SOCIETY FOR THE SUPPRESSION OF
UN-LADYLIKE CONDUCT, KNOWN TO THE UNINITIATED AS
THE S.S.U.C.

ARTICLE I

The object of this Society is two-fold: it combines
having a good time with the pursuit of VIRTUE.

ARTICLE II

The good time is to take place once a week in No. 6,
Quaker Row, between the hours of four and six p.m.

ARTICLE III

The nature of the good time is to be decided upon by
a Committee to be appointed each Saturday by the
members of the Society.

ARTICLE IV

VIRTUE is to be pursued at all times and in all seasons,
by the members of the Society setting their faces
against—" windowpanes," put in Rose Red—"No, the
practice of bowing and speaking to College students
who are not acquaintances, read on Katy, shaking her
head at naughty Rose—"waving handkerchiefs, signals
from windows, and every species of unladylike
conduct."

ARTICLE V

The members of the Society pledge themselves to use
their influence against these practices, both by precept
and example.

In witness whereof we sign,

KATHERIN CARR, President.
ROSAMUND REDDING, Secretary.
CLOVER E. CARR.
MARY L. SILVER

ESTHER DEARBORN.
SALLY P. ALSOP.
AMY W. ERSKINE.
ALICE GIBBONS.
ELLEN WHITWORTH GRAY.

Next followed the Bye-Laws. Katy had not been able to see the necessity of having any Bye-Laws, but Rose had insisted. She had never heard of a Society without them, she said, and she didn't think it would be "legal" to leave them out. It had cost her some trouble to invent them, but at last they stood thus:—

BYE-LAW No. 1

The members of the S.S.U.C. will observe the following signals:—

1st. *The Grip.*—This is given by inserting the first and middle finger of the right hand between the thumb and fourth finger of the respondent's left, and describing a rotatory motion in the air with the little finger. N.B.— Much practice is necessary to enable members to exchange this signal in such a manner as not to attract attention.

2nd. *The Signal of Danger.*—This signal is for use when Miss Jane, or any other foe-woman, heaves in sight. It consists in rubbing the nose violently, and at the same time giving three stamps on the floor with the left foot. It must be done with an air of unconsciousness.

3rd.*The Signal for Consultation.*—This signal is for use when immediate communication is requisite between members of the Society. It consists of a pinch on the back of the right hand, accompanied by the word "Holofernes" pronounced in a low voice.

BYE-LAW No. 2

The members of the S.S.U.C. pledge themselves to inviolable secrecy about all Society proceedings.

BYE-LAW No. 3

The members of the S.S.U.C. will bring their Saturday corn-balls to swell the common entertainment.

BYE-LAW No. 4

Members having boxes from home are at liberty to contribute such part of the contents as they please to the aforementioned common entertainment.

Here the Bye-Laws ended. There was much laughter over them, especially over the last.

"Why did you put that in, Rosy?" asked Ellen Gray; "it strikes me as hardly necessary. "

"Oh," replied Rose, "I put that in to encourage Silvery Mary there! She's expecting a box soon, and I knew that she would pine to give the Society a share, but would be too timid to propose it; so I thought I would just pave the way."

How truly kind!" laughed Clover.

Now," said the President, "the entertainment of the meeting will begin by the reading of 'Trailing Orbits,' a poem by C. E. C.

Clover had been very unwilling to read the first piece, and had only yielded after much coaxing from Rose, who had bestowed upon her in consequence the name of Quintia Curtia She felt very shy as she stood up with her paper in her hand, and her voice trembled perceptibly; but after a minute she grew used to the sound of it, and read steadily.

TRAILING ARBUTUS

I always think, when looking
At its mingled rose and white,
Of the pink lips of children
Put up to say good-night.

Cuddled its green leaves under,
Like babies in their beds,
Its blossoms shy and sunny
Conceal their pretty heads.

And when I lift the blanket up,
And peep inside of it,
They seem to give me smile for smile,
Nor be afraid a bit.

Dear little flower, the earliest
Of all the flowers that are
Twinkling upon the bare, brown earth
As on the clouds a star.

How can we fail to love it well
Or prize it more and more!
It is the first small signal
That winter time is o'er!

That Spring has not forgotten us,
Though late and slow she be,
But is upon her flying way,
And we her face shall see.

This production caused quite a sensation among the girls. They had never heard any of Clover's verses before, and thought these wonderful.

"Why, cried Sally Alsop, "it is almost as good as Tupper!"

Sally meant this for a great compliment, for she was devoted to the "Proverbial Philosophy.

"A Poem by E. D." was the next thing on the list. Esther Dearborn rose with great pomp and dignity, cleared her throat, put on a pair of eyeglasses, and began—

MISS JANE

Who ran to catch me on the spot
If I the slightest rule forgot,
Believing and excusing not?

Miss Jane

Who lurked outside my door all day,
In hopes that I would disobey,
And some low whispered word would say?

Miss Jane.

Who sternly bade me come and go,
Do this, do that, or else forego
The other thing I longed for so?

Miss Jane.

Who caught our Rose-bud half-way through
The wall which parted her from two
Friends, and that small prank made her rue?

Miss Jane.

Who is our bane, our foe, our fear?
Who's always certain to appear
Just when we do not think her near?

Miss Jane.

"Who down the hall is creeping now
    With stealthy step, but knowing not how
        Exactly to discover—"

broke in Rose, improvising rapidly. Next moment came
a knock at the door. It was Miss Jane.

"Your drawers, Miss Carr—your cupboard," she said,
going across the room, and examining each in turn.
There was no fault to be found with either, so she
withdrew, giving the laughing girls a suspicious glance,
and remarking that it was a bad habit to sit on beds—it
always injured them.

"Do you suppose she heard?" whispered Mary Silver.

"No, I don't think she did, replied Rose. "Of course
she suspected us of being in some mischief or other—
she always does that. Now, Mary, it's your turn to give
us an intellectual treat. Begin."

Poor Mary shrank back, blushing and protesting.

"You know I can't," she said, "I'm too stupid."

Rubbish! cried Rose. You're the dearest girl that ever
was. She gave Mary's shoulder a reassuring pat.

"Mary is excused this time," put in Katy. "It is the first
meeting, so I shall be indulgent. But, after this, every
member will be expected to contribute something for
each meeting. I mean to be very strict."

Oh, I never, never can! cried Mary.

Rose was down on her at once.

"Nonsense! hush! she said. "Of course you can. You
shall, if I have to write it for you myself."

Order! said the President, rapping on the table with
a pencil. Rose has something to read to us."

Rose stood up with great gravity. "I would ask for a
moment's delay, that the Society may get out its pocket-
handkerchiefs," she said My piece is an affecting one. I

79

didn't mean it, but it came so. We cannot always be cheerful. Here she heaved a sigh, which set the S.S.U.C. to laughing, and began—

A SCOTCH POEM

Wee, crimson-tippet Willie Wink,
　Wae' s me, drear, dree, and dra,
A waeful thocht, a fearsome flea,
　A wuthering wind, and a'.

Sair, sair thy mither sabs her lane,
　Her een, her mou, are wat;

Her cauld kail hae the corbies ta'en,
　And grierously she grat.

Ah, me, the suthering of the wind
　Ah, me, the waesome mither!
Ah, me, the bairnies left ahind,
　The hither, hither, blither!

"What does it mean? cried the girls, as Rose folded up the paper and sat down.

"Mean?" said Rose; "I'm sure I don't know, it's Scotch, I tell you. It's the kind of thing that people read, and then they say, 'One of the loveliest gems that Burns ever wrote!' I thought I'd see if I couldn't do one too. Anybody can, I find; it's not at all difficult."

All the poems having been read, Katy now proposed that they should play "Word and Question." She and Clover were accustomed to the game at home, but to some of the others it was quite new.

Each girl was furnished with a slip of paper and a pencil, and was told to write a word at the top of the paper, fold it over, and pass it to her next left-hand neighbour.

"Dear me! I don't know what to write," said Mary Silver.

Oh, write anything!" said Clover.

So Mary obediently wrote Anything," and folded it over.

What next?" asked Alice Gibbons.

"Now a question, said Katy. "Write it under the word, and fold over again. No, Amy, not on the fold. Don't you see, if you do, the writing will be on the wrong side of the paper when we come to read?r

The questions were more troublesome than the words, and the girls sat frowning and biting their pencil-tops for some minutes before all were done. As the slips were handed in, Katy dropped them into the lid of her work-basket, and thoroughly mixed and stirred them.

Now, she said, passing it about, "each draw one, read, and write a rhyme in which the word is introduced and the question answered. It needn't be more than two lines, unless you like. Here, Rose, it's your turn first!

Oh, what a hard game! cried some of the girls; but pretty soon they grew interested, and began to work over their verses.

"I should uncommonly like to know who wrote this abominable word, said Rose, in a tone of despair. "Clover, you witch, I believe it was you."

Clover peeped over her shoulder, nodded, and laughed.

"Very well, then!" snatching up Clover's slip, and putting her own in its place, "you can just write on it yourself—I shan't! I never heard of such a word in my life! You made it up for the occasion, you know you did!"

"I didn't! it's in the Bible," replied Clover, setting to work composedly on the fresh paper.

But when Rose opened Clover's slip, she groaned again.

"It's just as bad as the other," she cried. "Do change back again, Clovy, that's a dear. "

"No, indeed!" said Clover, guarding her paper; "you've changed once, and now you must keep what you have."

Rose made a face, chewed her pencil awhile, and then began to write rapidly. For some minutes not a word was spoken.

"I've done," said Esther Dearborn at last, flinging her paper into the basket-lid.

"So have I," said Katy.

One by one the papers were collected and jumbled into a heap. Then Katy, giving all a final shake, drew out one, opened it, and read.

Word.—Radishes.
Question.—How do you like your clergymen done?

How do I like them done? Well, that depends.
I like them done on sleepy, drowsy Sundays!
I like them under-done on other days!
Perhaps a little over-done on Mondays,
But always I prefer them old as pa.
And not like radishes, all red and raw.

"Oh, *what* a rhyme!" cried Clover.

"Well, what is one to do?" said Ellen Gray. Then she stopped and bit her lip, remembering that no one was supposed to know who wrote the separate papers.

"Aha! it's yours, is it, Ellen?" said Rose. "You're an awfully clever girl, and an ornament to the S.S.U.C. Go on, Katy."

Katy opened the second slip.

Word.—Anything.

Question.—Would you rather be a greater fool than you seem, or seem a greater fool than you are?

I wouldn't seem a fool for anything, my dear,
If I could help it; but I can't, I fear.

"Not bad," said Rose, nodding her head at Sally Alsop, who blushed crimson.

The third paper ran—

Word.—Mahershahalhashbaz.

Question.—Does your mother know you're out?

Rose and Clover exchanged looks.

> Why, of course my mother knows it,
>   For she sent me out herself, and
> She told me to run quickly, for
>   It wasn't but a mile;
> But I found it was much farther
>   And my feet grew tired and weary,
> And I couldn't hurry greatly,
>   So it took a long, long while.
> Beside, I stopped to read your word,
>   A stranger one I never heard!
> I've met with Pa-pistical,
>   That's pat;
> But *Ma*-hershahalhashbaz,
>   What's that?

"Clovy, you bright little thing!" cried Rose, in fits of laughter.

But Mary Silver looked quite pale.

"I never heard of anything so awful!" she said. "If that word had come to me, I should have fainted away on the spot—I know I should! "

Next came—

Word.—Buttons.

Question.—What is the best way to make home happy?

To me 'tis quite clear I can answer this right:
Sew on the buttons, and sew them on tight.

"I suspect that is Amy's", said Esther; "she's such a model for mending and keeping things in order."

"It's not fair guessing aloud in this way," said Sally Alsop. Sally always spoke for Amy, and Amy for Sally. "Voice and Echo" Rose called them; only, as she remarked, nobody could tell which was Echo and which Voice.

The next word was "Mrs. Nipson", and the question, "Do you like flowers?"

Do I like flowers? I will not write a sonnet,
    Singing their beauty as a poet might do:
I just detest those on Aunt Nipson's bonnet,
    Because they're just like her—all grey and blue,
    Dusty and pinched, and fastened on askew!
And as for heaven's own buttercups and daisies,
I am riot good enough to sing their praises.

Nobody knew who wrote this verse. Katy suspected Louisa, and Rose suspected Katy.

The sixth slip was a very brief one.

Word.—When?

Question.—Are you willing?

> If I wasn't willing, I would tell you;
> But when—Oh, dear, I can't.

What an extraordinary rhyme!" began Clover; but Rose spied poor Mary blushing and looking distressed, and hastily interposed—

It's very good, I'm sure. I wish I'd written it. Go on, Katy."

So Katy went on.

Word.—Unfeeling.

Question.—Which would you rather, do, or go fishing?

> I don't feel up to fishing, or sich;
> And so, if you please, I'd rather do—which?

"I don't seem to see the word in that poem," said Rose. "The distinguished author will please write another."

"The distinguished author made no reply to this suggestion; but, after a minute or two, Esther Dearborn, "quite disinterestedly", as she stated, remarked that, after all, to "don't feel" was pretty much the same as unfeeling. There was a little chorus of groans at this, and Katy said she should certainly impose a fine if such dodges and evasions were practised again. This was the first meeting, however, and she would be merciful. After this speech she unfolded another paper. It ran—

Word.—Flea

Question.—What would you do, love?

What would I do, love? Well, I do not know.
How can I tell till you are more explicit?
If 'twere a rose you held me, I would smell it;
If 'twere a mouth you held me, I would kiss it;
If 'twere a frog, I;d scream than furies louder;
If 'twere a flea, I'd fetch the Lyons powder.

Only two slips remained. One was Katy's own. She knew it by the way in which it was folded, and had almost instinctively avoided and left it for the last. Now, however, she took courage and opened it. The word was "Measles," and the question, "Who was the grandmother of Invention?n These were the lines:—

The night it was horribly dark,
The measles broke out in the Ark:
Little Japhet, and Shem, and all the young Ham,
Were screaming at once for potatoe and clams.
And "What shall I do," said poor Mrs. Noah,
"And alone by myself in this terrible shower?
I know what I'll do :1'11 step down in the hold,
And wake up a lioness grim and old,
And tie her close to the children's door,
And give her a ginger-cake to roar
At the top of her voice for an hour or more;

86

And I'll tell the children to cease their din,
Or I'll let that grim old party in,
To stop their squeazles and likewise their measles".—
She practised this with the greatest success
She was every one's grandmother, I guess

"That's much the best of all!" pronounced Alice Gibbons. "I wonder who wrote it?

"Dear me! did you like it so much?r said Rose, simpering, and doing her best to blush.

"Did you really write it?" said Mary; but Louisa laughed, and exclaimed, "No use, Rosy you can't take us in—we know better!n

"Now for the last," said Katy. "The word is 'Buckwheat,' and the question, 'What is the origin of dreams?'

When the nuns are sweetly sleeping,
Mrs. Nipson comes a-creeping,
Creeping like a kitty-cat from door to door;
And she listens to their slumbers,
And most carefully she numbers,
Counting for every nun a nunlet snore !
And the nuns in sweet forgetfulness who lie,
Dreaming of buckwheat cakes, parental love,
and—pie,
Moan softly, twist and turn, and see
Black cats and fiends, who frolic in their glee;
And nightmares prancing wildly do abound
While Mrs. Nipson makes her nightly round.

"Who did write that?" exclaimed Rose. Nobody answered. The girls looked at each other, and Rose scrutinised them all with sharp glances.

"Well! I never saw such creatures for keeping their countenances," she said. "Somebody is as bold as brass. Didn't you see how I blushed when my piece was read?"

"You monkey!" whispered Clover, who at that moment caught sight of the handwriting on the paper. Rose gave her a warning pinch, and they both subsided with an unseen giggle.

"What! The tea-bell! cried everybody. "We wanted to play another game."

"It's a complete success!" whispered Rose, ecstatically, as they went down the hall. "The girls all say they never had such fun in their lives. I'm so glad I didn't die with the measles when I was little! "

"Well, demanded Lilly, "so the high and mighty Society has had a meeting! How did it go off?"

"Delicious! replied Rose, smacking her lips as at the recollection of something very nice. But you mustn't ask any questions, Lilly. Outsiders have nothing to do with the S.S.U.C. Our proceedings are strictly private." She ran downstairs with Katy.

"I think you're real mean!" called Lilly after them. Then she said to herself, "They're just trying to tease. I know it was stupid."

CHAPTER 7

INJUSTICE

Summer was always slow in getting to Hillsover, but at last she arrived, and woods and hills suddenly put on new colours and became beautiful. The sober village shared in the glorifying process. Vines budded on piazzas. Wisteria purpled whitewashed wall. The brown elm boughs which hung above the common turned into trailing garlands of fresh green. Each walk revealed some change, or ended in some delightful discovery, trilliums, dog-tooth violets, apple-trees in blossom, or wild strawberries turning red. The wood flowers and mosses, even the birds and bird-songs, were new to our Western girls. Hillsover, in summer, was a great deal prettier than Burnet, and Katy and Clover began to enjoy school very much indeed.

Towards the end of June, however, something took place which gave them quite a different feeling—something so disagreeable that I hate to tell about it; but, as it really happened, I must.

It was on a Saturday morning. They had just come back from the bath-house, and were going upstairs, laughing, and feeling very merry; for Clover had written a droll piece for the S.S.U.C. meeting, and was telling Katy about it, when, just at the head of the stairs, they met Rose Red. She was evidently in trouble, for she looked flushed and excited, and was under the escort of Miss Barnes, who marched before her with the air of a policeman. As she passed the girls, Rose opened her eyes very wide, and made a face expressive of dismay.

"What's the matter?" whispered Clover. Rose only made another grimace, clawed with her fingers at Miss Barnes' back, and vanished down the entry which led to Mrs. Florence's room. They stood looking after her.

"Oh dear!" sighed Clover, "I'm so afraid Rose is in a scrape."

They walked on toward Quaker Row. In the washroom was a knot of girls, with their heads close together, whispering. When they saw Katy and Clover, they became silent, and gazed at them curiously.

"What has Rose Red gone to Mrs. Florence about?" asked Clover, too anxious to notice the strange manner of the girls. But at that moment she caught sight of something which so amazed her that she forgot her question. It was nothing less than her own trunk, with C. E. C." at the end, being carried along the entry by two men. Miss Jane followed close behind, with her arms full of clothes and books. Katy's well-known scarlet pincushion topped the pile; in Miss Jane's hand were Clover's comb and brush.

"Why, what does this mean?" gasped Clover, as she and Katy darted after Miss Jane, who had turned into one of the rooms. It was No. 1, at the head of the row—a room which no one had wanted, on account of its smallness and lack of light. The window looked out on a brick wall not ten feet away; there was never a ray of sun to make it cheerful; and Mrs. Nipson had converted it into a store-room for empty trunks. The trunks were taken away now, and the bed was strewn with Katy's and Clover's possessions.

"Miss Jane, what is the matter? What are you moving our things for?" exclaimed the girls in great excitement.

Miss Jane laid down her load of dresses, and looked at them sternly.

"You know the reason as well as I do," she said icily.

"No, I don't. I haven't the least idea what you mean!" cried Katy. "Oh, please be careful!" as Miss Jane flung a pair of boots on top of Cousin Helen's vase, you'll break it! Dear, dear! Clover, there's your Cologne bottle tipped over, and all the Cologne spilt! What does it mean? Is our room going to be painted, or what?"

"Your room," responded Miss Jane, "is for the future to be this— No. 1. Miss Benson and Miss James will take No. 6; and, it is to be hoped, will conduct themselves more properly than you have done."

"Than we have done!" cried Katy, hardly believing her ears.

"Do not repeat my words in that rude way!" said Miss Jane, tartly. "Yes, than you have done!"

"But what have we done? There is some dreadful mistake! Do tell us what you mean, Miss Jane! We have done nothing wrong, so far as I know."

"Indeed!" replied Miss Jane, sarcastically. "Your ideas of right and wrong must be peculiar! I advise you to say no more on the subject, but be thankful that Mrs. Florence keeps you in the school at all, instead of dismissing you. Nothing but the fact that your home is at such a distance prevents her from doing so."

Katy felt as if all the blood in her body were turned to fire as she heard these words, and met Miss Jane's eyes. Her old, hasty temper, which had seemed to die out during years of pain and patience, flashed into sudden life, as a smouldering coal flashes, when you least expect it, into flame. She drew herself up to her full height, gave Miss Jane a look of scorching indignation, and, with a rapid impulse, darted out of the room and along the hall towards Mrs. Florence's door. The girls she met scattered from her path right and left. She

91

looked so tall and moved so impetuously that she absolutely frightened them.

"Come in," said Mrs. Florence, in answer to her sharp, quivering knock. Katy entered. Rose was not there, and Mrs. Florence and Mrs. Nipson sat together, side by side, in close consultation.

"Mrs. Florence," said Katy, too much excited to feel in the least afraid, "will you please tell me why ur things are being changed to No. 1?'

Mrs. Florence flushed with anger. She looked Katy all over for a minute before she answered; then she said, in a severe voice, "It is done by my orders, and for good and sufficient reasons. What those reasons are, you know as well as I.

"No, I do not!" replied Katy, as angry as Mrs. Florence. "I have not the least idea what they are, and I insist on knowing!

"I cannot answer questions put in such an improper manner," said Mrs. Florence, with a wave of the hand, which meant that Katy was to go, but Katy did not stir.

"I am sorry if my manner was improper," she said, trying to speak quietly, "but I think I have a right to ask what this means. If we are accused of doing wrong, it is only fair to tell us what it is.

Mrs. Florence only waved her hand again; but Mrs. Nipson, who had been twisting uneasily in her chair, said, Excuse me, Mrs. Florence, but perhaps it would be better—would satisfy Miss Carr better—if you were to be explicit.

"It does not seem to me that Miss Carr can be in need of any explanation," replied Mrs. Florence. "When a young lady writes underhand notes to young gentlemen, and throws them from her window, and they are

92

discovered, she must naturally expect that persons of correct ideas will be shocked and disgusted. Your note to Mr. Abernethy Searles, Miss Carr, was found by his mother while mending his pocket, and was handed by her to me. After this statement, you will hardly be surprised that I do not consider it best to permit you to room longer on that side of the house. I did not suppose I had a girl in my school capable of such conduct.

For a moment Katy was too much stunned to speak. She took hold of a chair to steady herself, and her colour changed so quickly from red to pale and back again to red, that Mrs. Florence and Mrs. Nipson, who sat watching her, might be pardoned for thinking that she looked guilty. As soon as she recovered her voice, she stammered out, "But I didn't! I never did! I haven't written any note! I wouldn't for the world! Oh, Mrs. Florence, please believe me!

"I prefer to believe the evidence of my eyes, replied Mrs. Florence, as she drew a paper from her pocket. "Here is the note. I suppose you will hardly deny your own signature."

Katy seized the note. It was written in a round, unformed hand, and ran thus:—

Dear Berry,

"I saw you last night on the Green. I think you are splendid. All the nuns think so. I look at you very often out of my window. If I let down a string, would you tie a cake to it, like that kind which you threw to Mary Andrews last term? Tie two cakes, please; one for me, and one for my room-mate. The string will be at the end of the Row.

"Miss Carr."

In spite of her agitation, Katy could hardly keep back á smile as she read this absurd production. Mrs. Florence saw the smile, and her tone was more severe than ever, as she said—

Give that back to me, if you please. It will be my justification with your father if he objects to your change of room."

"But, Mrs. Florence, cried Katy, "I never wrote that note. It isn't my handwriting; it isn't my——Oh, surely, you can't think so! It's too ridiculous. "

Go to your room at once," said Mrs. Florence, "and be thankful that your punishment is such a mild one. If your home were not so distant, I should write to ask your father to remove you from the school; instead of which, I merely put you on the other side of the entry, out of reach of farther correspondence of this sort."

But I shall write him, and he will take us away immediately, cried Katy, stung to the quick by this obstinate injustice. "I will not stay, neither shall Clover, where our word is disbelieved, and we are treated like this. Papa knows! Papa will never doubt us a moment when we tell him that this is not true."

With these passionate words she left the room. I do not think that either Mrs. Florence or Mrs. Nipson felt very comfortable after she was gone.

That was a dreadful afternoon. The girls had no heart to arrange No. 1. or do anything toward making it comfortable, but lay on the bed in the midst of their belongings, crying and receiving visits of condolence from their friends. The S.S.U.C. meeting was put off. Katy was in no humour to act as president, or Clover to read her funny poem. Rose and Mary Silver sat by, kissing them at intervals, and declaring that it was a shame, while the other members dropped in one by one to re-echo the same sentiments.

"If it had been anybody else! said Alice Gibbons; "but Katy— Katy of all persons! It is too much!"

"So I told Mrs. Florence, sobbed Rose Red. "Oh, why was I born so bad? If I'd always been good, and a model to the rest of you, perhaps she'd have believed me, instead of scolding harder than ever.

The idea of Rose as a "model made Clover smile in the midst of her dolefulness.

"It's an outrageous thing, said Ellen Gray, "if Mrs. Florence only knew it, you two have done more to keep the rest of us steady than any girls in school. "

"So they have, blubbered Rose, whose pretty face was quite swollen with crying. I've been getting better and better every day since they came." She put her arms round Clover as she spoke, and sobbed harder than ever.

It was in the midst of this excitement that Miss Jane saw fit to come in and inspect the room. When she saw the crying girls and the general confusion of everything, she was very angry.

"I shall mark you both for disorder, she said. "Get off the bed, Miss Carr. Hang your dresses up at once, Clover, and put your shoes away. I never saw anything so disgraceful All these things must be in order when I return, fifteen minutes from now, or I shall report you to Mrs. Florence.

"It's of no consequence what you do. We are not going to stay," muttered Katy. But soon she was ashamed of having said this. Her anger was melting, and grief taking its place. Oh, papa! papa! Elsie! Elsie!" she whispered to herself, as she slowly hung up the dresses; and, unseen by the girls, she hid her face in the folds of

Clover's grey alpaca, and shed some hot tears. Till then she had been too angry to cry.

This softer mood followed her all through the evening. Clover and Rose sat by, talking over the affair, and keeping their wrath warm with discussion. Katy said hardly a word. She felt too weary and depressed to speak.

Who could have written the note? asked Clover again and again. It was impossible to guess. It seemed absurd to suspect any of the older girls; but then, as Rose suggested, the absurdity as well as the signature might have been imitated to avoid detection.

"I know one thing, "remarked Rose, "and that is that I should like to kill Mrs. Searles. Horrid old thing!— peeping and prying into pockets. She has no business to be alive at all.

Rose's ferocious speeches always sounded specially comical when taken in connection with her pink cheeks and her dimples.

"Shall you write to papa to-night, Katy?" asked Clover.

Katy shook her head. She was too heavy-hearted to talk. Big tears rolled down unseen and fell upon the pillow. After Rose was gone, and the candle out, she cried herself to sleep.

Waking early in the dim dawn, she lay and thought it over, Clover slumbering soundly beside her meanwhile. Morning brings counsel, says the old proverb. In this case it seemed true. Katy, to her surprise, found a train of fresh thoughts filling her mind, which were not there when she fell asleep. She recalled her passionate words and feelings of the day before. Now that the mood had passed, they seemed to her worse than the injury which provoked them. Quick-tempered and generous people often experience this. It was easier for Katy to forgive Mrs. Florence, because it was needful also that she should forgive herself.

"I said I would write to papa to take us away," she thought. "Why did I say that? What good would it do? It wouldn't make anybody disbelieve this horrid story. They'd only think I wanted to get away because I was found out. And papa would be so worried and disappointed. It has cost him a great deal to get us ready and send us here, and he wants us to stay a year. If we went home now, all the money would be wasted. And yet how horrid it is going to be after this! I don't feel as if I could ever bear to see Mrs. Florence again. I must write."

"But then," her thoughts flowed on, home wouldn't seem like home if we went away from school in disgrace, and knew that everybody here was believing such things. Suppose, instead, I were to write to papa to come on and make things straight. He'd find out the truth, and force Mrs. Florence to see it. It would be very expensive, though; and I know he oughtn't to leave home again so soon. Oh, dear! How hard it is to know what to do!"

"What would Cousin Helen say? she continued, going in imagination to the sofa-side of the dear friend who was her like a second conscience. She shut her eyes and invented a long talk—her questions, Cousin Helen's replies. But, as everybody knows, it is impossible to play croquet by yourself and be strictly impartial to all the four balls. Katy found that she was making Cousin Helen play (that is, answer) as she herself wished, and not, as something whispered, she would answer were she really there.

"It is just the 'Little Scholar' over again," she said, half aloud, "I can't see. I don't know how to act. She remem-

97

bered the dream she once had; of a great beautiful face and a helping hand. "And it was real," she murmured, "and just as real, and just as near, now as then.

The result of this long meditation was that, when Clover woke up, she found Katy leaning over, ready to kiss her for good morning, and looking bright and determined.

"Clovy," she said, "I've been thinking; and I'm not going to write to papa about this affair at all!"

"Are you not? Why not?" asked Clover, puzzled.

Because it would worry him,-and be of no use. He would come on and take us right away, I'm sure; but Mrs. Florence and all the teachers, and a great many of the girls, would always believe that this horrid, ridiculous story is true. I can't bear to have them. Let's stay, instead, and convince them that it isn't. I think we can.
n
I would a great deal rather go home," said Clover. "It won't ever be nice here again. We shall have this nasty room, and Miss Jane will be more horrid than ever, and the girls will think you wrote that note, and Lilly Page will say hateful things!" She buttoned her boots with a vindictive air.

Never mind," said Katy, trying to feel brave. "I don't suppose it will be pleasant, but I'm pretty sure it's right. And Rosy and all the girls we really care for know how it is.

"I can't bear it," sighed Clover, with tears in her eyes. "It is so cruel that they should say such things about you."

"I mean that they shall say something quite different before we go away," replied Katy, stroking her hair. Cousin Helen would tell us to stay, I'm pretty sure. I was thinking about her just now, and I seemed to hear her voice in the air, saying over and over, 'Live it down! Live it down! Live it down!' " She half sang this, and took two or three dancing steps across the room.

"What a girl you are!" said Clover, consoled by seeing Katy look so bright.

Mrs. Florence was surprised that morning, as she sat in her room, by the appearance of Katy. She looked pale, but perfectly quiet an gentle.

"Mrs. Florence," she said, "I've come to say that I shall not write to my father to take us away, as I told you I should."

Mrs. Florence bowed stiffly, by way of answer.

"Not," went on Katy, with a little flash in her eyes, that he would hesitate, or doubt my word one moment, if I did. But he wished us to stay here a year, and I don't wish to disappoint him. I'd rather stay. And, Mrs. Florence, I'm sorry I spoke as I did yesterday. It was not right; but I was angry, and felt that you were unjust."

"And to-day you own that I was not?"

"Oh, no!" replied Katy, I can't do that. You were unjust, because neither Clover nor I wrote that note. We would not do such a horrid thing for the world, and I hope some day you will believe us. But I ought not to have spoken so."

Katy's face and voice were so truthful as she said this, that Mrs. Florence was almost shaken in her opinion.

"We will say no more about the matter," she remarked in a kinder tone. "If your conduct is perfectly correct in future, it will go far to make this forgotten."

Few things are more aggravating than to be forgiven when one has done no wrong. Katy felt this as she walked away from Mrs. Florence's room. But she would not let herself grow angry again. Live it down!" she whispered, as she went into the school-room.

She and Clover had a good deal to endure for the next two or three weeks. They missed their old room with its sunny window and pleasant outlook. They missed Rose, who, down at the far end of Quaker Row, could not drop in half so often as had been her custom. Miss Jane was specially grim and sharp; and some of the upstairs girls, who resented Katy's plain speaking, and the formation of a society against flirting, improved the chance to be provoking. Lilly Page was one of these. She didn't really believe Katy guilty, but she liked to tease her by pretending to believe it.

Only to think of the President of the Saintly Stuck-up Society being caught like this!n she remarked, maliciously. "What are our great reformers coming to? Now if it had been a sinner like me, no one would be surprised!"

All this naturally was vexatious. Even sunny Clover shed many tears in private over her mortifications. But the girls bore their trouble bravely, and never said one syllable about the matter in the letters home. There were consolations, too, mixed with the annoyances. Rose Red clung to her two friends closely, and loyally fought their battles. The S.S.U.C. to a girl rallied round its chief. After that sad Saturday the meetings were resumed with as much spirit as ever. Katy's steadiness and uniform politeness and sweet temper impressed even those who would have been glad to believe a tale against her, and in a short time the affair ceased to be a subject for discussion,—was almost forgotten, in fact, except for a sore spot in Katy's heart, and one page in Rose Red's album, upon which, under the date of that fatal day, were written these words, headed by an appalling skull and cross-bones in pen-and-ink:—

N B.—Pay Miss Jane off."

CHAPTER 8

CHANGES

"Clover, where's Clover?" cried Rose Red, popping her head into the school-room, where Katy sat writing her composition. "Oh, Katy! there you are. I want you too. Come down to my room right away. I've such a thing to tell you."

"What is it? Tell me too" said Bella Arkwright. Bella was a veritable "little pitcher," of the kind mentioned in the Proverb, and had an insatiable curiosity to know everything that other people knew.

Tell you, miss? I should really like to know why!" replied Rose, who was not at all fond of Bella.

You're real mean, and real unkind, whined Bella. "You think you're a great grown-up lady, and can have secrets. But you ain't! You're a little girl too—most a little as me. So there!"

Rose made a face at her, and a sort of growling rush, which had the effect of sending Bella screaming down the hall. Then, returning to the schoolroom—

Do come, Katy, she said; find Clover, and hurry! Really and truly I want you. I feel as if I should burst if I don't tell somebody right away what I've found out.

Katy began to be curious. She went in pursuit of Clover, who was practising in one of the recitation-rooms, and the three girls ran together down Quaker Row.

"Now," said Rose, locking the door, and pushing forward a chair for Katy and another for Clover, "swear that you won't tell, for this is a real secret—the greatest secret that ever was, and Mrs. Florence would flay me alive if she knew that I knew!" She paused to enjoy the effect of her words, and suddenly began to snuff the air in a peculiar manner.

"Girls," she said, solemnly, "that little wretch of a Bella is in this room. I am sure of it."

"What makes you think so?" cried the others, surprised.

"I smell that dreadful pomatum that she puts on her hair! Don't you notice it? She's hidden somewhere." Rose looked sharply about for a minute, then made a pounce, and from under the bed dragged a small kicking heap. It was the guilty Bella.

"What were you doing there, you bad child?" demanded Rose, seizing the kicking feet and holding them fast.

"I don't care," blubbered Bella, "you wouldn't tell me your secret. You're a real horrid girl, Rose Red. I don't love you a bit."

"Your affection is not a thing which I particularly pine for," retorted Rose, seating herself, and holding the culprit before her by the ends of her short pig-tails. "I don't want little girls who peep and hide to love me. I'd rather they wouldn't. Now listen. Do you know what I shall do if you ever come again into my room without leave? First, I shall cut off your hair, pomatum and all, with my pen-knife"—Bella screamed—"and then I'll turn myself into a bear—a great brown bear—and eat you up!" Rose pronounced this threat with tremendous energy, and accompanied it with a snarl which showed all her teeth. Bella roared with fright, twitched away her pig-tails, unlocked the door and fled, Rose not pursuing her, but sitting comfortably in her chair and growling at intervals, till her victim was out of hearing. Then she rose and bolted the door again.

"How lucky that the imp is so fond of that smelly pomatum!" she remarked; "one always knows where to look for her. It's as good as a bell round her neck! Now for the secret. You promise not to tell? Well, then, Mrs. Florence is going away week after next, and, what's more—she's going to be married!"

"Not really!" cried the others.

"Really and truly. She's going to be married to a clergyman."

"How did you find out?"

"Why, it's the most curious thing. You know my blue lawn, which Miss James is making? This morning I went to try it on, Miss Barnes with me of course, and while Miss James was fitting the waist Mrs. Seccomb came in and sat down on the sofa by Miss Barnes. They began to talk, and pretty soon Mrs. Seccomb said, 'What day does Mrs. Florence go?'

"'Thursday week,' said Miss Barnes. She sort of mumbled it, and looked to see if I were listening. I wasn't; but of course after that I did—as hard as I could.

"'And where does the important event take place?' asked Mrs. Seccomb. She's so funny with her little bit of a mouth and her long words. She always looks as if each of them was a big pill, and she wanted to swallow it and couldn't.

"'In Lewisberg, at her sister's house,' said Miss Barnes. She mumbled more than ever, but I heard.

"'What a deplorable loss she will be to our limited circle' said Mrs. Seccomb. I couldn't imagine what they meant. But don't you think, when I got home there was this letter from Sylvia, and she says, 'Your adored Mrs. Florence is going to be married. I'm afraid you'll all break your hearts about it. Mother met the gentleman at a party the other night. She says he looks clever, but isn't at all handsome, which is a pity, for Mrs. Florence is a raving beauty in my opinion. He's an excellent preacher, we hear; and won't she manage the parish to perfection? How shall you like being left to the tender mercies of Mrs. Nipson?' Now did you ever hear anything so droll in your life? went on Rose, folding up her letter. "Just think of those two things coming together the same day! It's like a sum in arithmetic, with an answer which 'proves' the sum, isn't it?"

Rose had counted on producing an effect, and she certainly was not disappointed. The girls could think and talk of nothing else for the remainder of that afternoon.

It was a singular fact that before two days were over, every scholar in the school knew that Mrs. Florence was going to be married! How the secret got out nobody could guess. Rose protested that it wasn't her fault—she had been a miracle of discretion, a perfect sphinx; but there was a guilty laugh in her eyes, and Katy suspected that the sphinx had unbent a little. Nothing so exciting had ever happened at the Nunnery before. Some of the older scholars were quite inconsolable. They bemoaned themselves, and got together in corners to enjoy the luxury of woe. Nothing comforted them but the project of getting up a "testimonial" for Mrs. Florence.

What this testimonial should be caused great discussion in the school. Everybody had a different idea, and everybody was sure that her idea was better than anybody else's. All the school contributed. The money collected amounted to nearly forty dollars, and the question was, what should be bought?

Every sort of thing was proposed. Lilly Page insisted that nothing could possibly be so appropriate as a bouquet of wax flowers and a glass shade to put over it. There was a strong party in favour of spoons. Annie Silsbie suggested "a statue; somebody else a clock. Rose Red was for a cabinet piano, and Katy had some trouble in convincing her that forty dollars would not buy one. Bella demanded that they should get " an organ. n

"You can go along with it as monkey," said Rose, which remark made Bella caper with indignation.

At last, after long discussion and some quarrelling, a cake-basket was fixed upon. Sylvia Redding happened to be making a visit in Boston, and Rose was commissioned to write and ask her to select the gift and send it up by express. The girls could hardly wait.

"I do hope it will be pretty, don't you?" they said over and over again.

When the box arrived, they all gathered to see it opened. Esther Dearborn took out the nails, half-a-dozen hands lifted the lid, and Rose unwrapped the tissue-paper and displayed the basket up to general view.

"Oh, what a beauty!" cried everybody.

It was woven of twisted silver wire. Two figures of children with wings and garlands supported the handle on either side. In the middle of the handle were a pair of silver doves, billing and cooing in the most affectionate way, over a tiny shield, on which were engraved Mrs. Florence's initials.

"I never saw one like it!n "Doesn't it look heavy?" "Rose Red, your sister is splendid!" cried a chorus of voices, as Rose, highly gratified, held up the basket.

"Who shall present it?" asked Louisa Agnew. "Rose Red," said some of the girls.

"No, indeed, I'm not tall enough," protested Rose, "it must be somebody who'd kind of sweep into the room and be impressive. I vote for Katy."

"Oh, no! said Katy, shrinking back, "I shouldn't do it well at all. Suppose we put it to vote?"

Ellen Gray cut some slips of paper, and each girl wrote a name and dropped it into a box. When the votes were counted, Katy's name appeared on all but three.

"I propose that we make this vote unanimous," said Rose, highly delighted.

The girls agreed; and Rose, jumping on a chair, exclaimed—

"Three cheers for Katy Carr! Keep time, girls,—one, two, hip, hip, hurrah! "

The hurrahs were given with enthusiasm, for Katy, almost without knowing it, had become popular. She was too much touched to speak at first. When she did, it was to protest against her election.

"Esther would do it beautifully," she said, "and I think Mrs. Florence would like the basket better if she gave it. You know ever since——" she stopped. Even now she could not refer with composure to the affair of the note.

"Oh, cried Louisa, "she's thinking of that ridiculous note Mrs. Florence made such a fuss about. As if anybody supposed you wrote it, Katy! I don't believe even Miss Jane is such a goose as that. Any way, if she is, that's one reason more why you should present the basket, to show that we don't think so." She gave Katy a kiss by way of period.

"Yes, indeed, you're chosen, and you must give it," cried the others.

"Very well," said Katy, extremely gratified, "what am I to say?"

"We'll compose a speech for you," replied Rose. Sugar your voice, Katy, and, whatever you do, stand up straight. Don't crook over, as if you thought you were tall. It's a bad trick you have, child, and I'm always sorry to see it," concluded Rose, with the air of a wise mamma giving a lecture.

It is droll how much can go on in a school unseen and unsuspected by its teachers. Mrs. Florence never dreamed that the girls had guessed her secret. Her plan was to go away as if for a visit, and leave Mrs. Nipson to explain at her leisure. She was therefore quite unprepared for the appearance of Katy holding the beautiful basket, which was full of fresh roses, crimson, white, and pink. I am afraid the rules of the S.S.U.C. had been slightly relaxed to allow of Rose Red's getting these flowers; certainly they grew nowhere in Hillsover except in Professor Seccomb's garden.

"The girls wanted me to give you this, with a great deal of love from us all," said Katy, feeling strangely embarrassed, and hardly venturing to raise her eyes. She set the basket on the table. "We hope so much that you will be happy," she added in a low voice, and moved towards the door.

Mrs. Florence had been too much surprised to speak, but now she called, "Wait! Come back a moment."

Katy came back. Mrs. Florence's cheeks were flushed. She looked very handsome. Katy almost thought there were tears in her eyes.

"Tell the girls that I thank them very much. Their present is beautiful. I shall always value it!"

She blushed as she spoke, and Katy blushed too. It made her shy to see the usually composed Mrs. Florence so confused.

"What did she say? what did she say?" demanded the others, who were collected in groups round the school-room door to hear a report of the interview.

Katy repeated the message. Some of the girls were disappointed.

"Is that all?" they said. "We thought she would stand up and make a speech."

"Or a short poem," put in Rose Red—"a few stanzas thrown off on the spur of the moment, like this, for instance—

> "Thank you, kindly, for your basket,
> Which I didn't mean to ask it;
> But I'll very gladly take it,
> And when 'tis full of cake, it
> Will frequently remind me
> Of the girls I left behind me ! "

There was a universal giggle, which brought Miss Jane out of the school-room.

"Order!" she said, ringing the bell. "Young ladies, what are you about? Study hour has begun."

"We're-so sorry Mrs. Florence is going away," said some of the girls.

"How did you know that she is going?" demanded Miss Jane sharply.

Nobody answered.

Next day Mrs. Florence left. Katy saw her go with a secret regret.

"If only she would have said that she didn't believe I wrote that note!" she told Clover.

"I don't care what she believes! She's a stupid, unjust woman!" replied independent little Clover.

Mrs. Nipson was now in sole charge of the establishment. She had never tried school-keeping before, and had various pet plans and theories of her own, which she had only been waiting Mrs. Florence's departure to put into practice.

One of these was that the school was to dine three times a week on pudding and bread and butter. Mrs.

Nipson had a theory—very convenient and economical for herself, but highly distasteful to her scholars—that it was injurious for young people to eat meat every day in hot weather.

The puddings were made of batter, with a sprinkling of blackberries or raisins. Now, rising at six, and studying four hours and a half on a light breakfast, has a wonderful effect on the appetite, as all who have tried it will testify. The poor girls would go down to dinner as hungry as wolves, and eye the large, pale slices on their plates with a wrath and dismay which I cannot pretend to describe. Very thick the slices were, and there was plenty of thin, sugared sauce to eat with them, and plenty of bread and butter; but somehow, the whole was unsatisfying, and the hungry girls would go upstairs almost as ravenous as when they came down. The second-table-ites were always hanging over the balusters to receive them, and when to the demand, "What did you have for dinner?n Pudding!" was answered, a low groan would run from one to another, and a general gloom seemed to drop down and envelop the party.

It may have been in consequence of this experience of starvation that the orders for Fourth of July were that year so unusually large. It was an old custom in the school that the girls should celebrate the National Independence by buying as many goodies as they liked. There was no candy shop in Hillsover, so Mrs. Nipson took the orders, and sent to Boston for the things, which were charged on the bills with other extras. Under these blissful circumstances, the girls felt that they could afford to be extravagant, and made out their lists regardless of expense. Rose Red's, for this Fourth, ran thus:—

"Two pounds of Chocolate Caramels.
Two pounds of Sugar Almonds.
Two pounds of Lemon Drops.
Two pounds of Mixed Candy.
Two pounds of Macaroons.
A dozen Oranges.
A dozen Lemons.
A drum of Figs.
A box of French Plums.
A loaf of Almond Cake."

The result of this liberal order was that, after the great wash-baskets of parcels had been distributed, and the school had rioted for twenty-four hours upon these unaccustomed luxuries, Rose was found lying on her bed, ghastly and pallid.

"Never speak to me of anything sweet again so long as I live!" she gasped. "Talk of vinegar or pickles, or sour apples; but don't allude to sugar in any form, if you love me! Oh, why, why did I send for those fatal things?"

In time all the candy was eaten up, and the school went back to its normal condition. Three weeks later came College Commencement.

"Are you and Clover Craters or Symposiums?" demanded Lilly Page, meeting Katy in the hall, a few days before this important event.

"What do you mean?"

"Why, has nobody told you about them? They are the two great College Societies. All the girls belong to one or the other, and make the wreaths to dress their halls. We work up in the Gymnasium; the Crater girls take the east side, and the Symposium girls the west, and when the wreaths grow too long we hang them out of the windows. It's the greatest fun in the world! Be a Symposium, do! I'm one!

"I shall have to think about it before deciding," said Katy, privately resolving to join Rose Red's Society, whichever it was. The Crater it proved to be, so Katy and Clover enrolled themselves with the Craters. Three days before Commencement wreath-making began. The afternoons were wholly given up to the work, and, instead of walking, or piano practice, the girls sat plaiting oak-leaves into garlands many yards long. Baskets of fresh leaves were constantly brought in, and there was a strife between the rival Societies as to which should accomplish most.

It was great fun, as Lilly had said, to sit there amid the green boughs, and pleasant leafy smells, a buzz of gay voices in the air, and a general sense of holiday. The Gymnasium would have furnished many a pretty picture for an artist during those three afternoons, only, unfortunately, no artist was let in to see it.

One day, Rose Red, emptying a basket, lighted upon a white parcel, hidden beneath the leaves.

"Lemon drops!" she exclaimed, applying a finger and thumb with all the dexterity of Jack Horner. "Here, Crater girls, here's something for you! Don't you pity the Symposiums?"

But next day a big package of peppermints appeared in the Symposium basket, so neither Society could boast advantage over the other. They were pretty nearly equal, too, in the quantity of wreath made—the Craters' measuring nine hundred yards, and the Symposiums' nine hundred and two. As for the Halls, which they were taken over to see the evening before Commencement, it was impossible to say which was most beautifully trimmed. Each faction preferred its own, and President Searles said that both did the young ladies credit.

They all sat in the gallery of the church on Commencement Day, and heard the speeches. It was very hot, and the speeches were not exactly interesting, being on such subjects as "The Influence of a Republic on Men of Letters," and "The Abstract Law of Justice, as applied to Human Affairs"; but the music, and the crowd, and the spectacle of six hundred ladies all fanning themselves at once, were entertaining, and the girls would not have missed them for the world. Later in the day another diversion was afforded them by the throngs of pink and blue ladies and white-gloved gentlemen who passed the house on their way to the President's Levee; but they were not allowed to enjoy this amusement long, for Miss Jane, suspecting what was going on, went from room to room, and ordered everybody summarily off to bed.

With the close of Commencement Day, a deep sleep seemed to settle over Hillsover. Most of the Professors' families went off to enjoy themselves at the mountains or at the sea-side, leaving their houses shut up. This gave the village a drowsy and deserted air. There were no boys playing ball on the Common, or swinging on the College fence; no look of life in the streets. The weather continued warm, the routine of study and exercise grew dull, and teachers and scholars alike were glad when the middle of September arrived, and with it the opening of the autumn vacation.

CHAPTER 9

THE AUTUMN VACATION

The last day of the term was one of confusion. Every part of the house was given over to trunks and packing. Mrs. Nipson sat at her desk, making out bills, and listening to requests about rooms and room-mates. Miss Jane counted books and atlases, taking note of each ink-spot and dog-eared page. The girls ran about, searching for missing articles, deciding what to take home and what to leave, engaging each other for the winter walks. All rules were laid aside. The sober Nunnery seemed turned into a hive of buzzing bees. Bella slid twice down the baluster of the front stairs without being reproved; and Rose Red threw her arm round Katy's waist, and waltzed the whole length of Quaker Row.

"I'm so happy, that I should like to scream!n she announced, as their last whirl brought them up against the wall. "Isn't vacation just lovely? Katy, you don't look half glad."

"We're not going home, you know," replied Katy, in rather a doleful tone. She and Clover were not so enraptured at the coming of vacation as the rest of the girls. Spending a month with Mrs. Page and Lilly was by no means the same thing as spending it with papa and the children.

Next morning, however, when the big stage drove up, and the girls crowded in; when Mrs. Nipson stood in the doorway, blandly waving farewell, and the maids flourished their dusters out of the upper windows, they found themselves sharing the general excitement, and joining heartily in the cheer which arose as the stage moved away. The girls felt so happy and good-natured, that some of them even kissed their hands to Miss Jane.

Such a wild company is not often met with on a railroad train. They all went together as far as the Junction; and Mr. Gray, Ellen's father, who had been put in charge of the party by Mrs. Nipson, had his hands full to keep them in any sort of order. He was a timid old gentleman, and, as Rose suggested, his expression resembled that of a sedate hen who suddenly finds herself responsible for the conduct of a brood of ducklings.

"My dear, my dear!" he feebly remonstrated, "would you buy any more candy? Do you not think so many pea-nuts may be bad for

you?"

"Oh, no, sir!" replied Rose; "they never hurt me a bit; I can eat thousands!n Then, as a stout lady entered the car, and made a motion toward the vacant seat beside her, she rolled her eyes wildly, and said, "Excuse me, but perhaps I had better take the end seat, so as to get out easily in case I have a fit. n

"Fits! " cried the stout lady, and walked away with the utmost dispatch. Rose gave a wicked chuckle, the girls tittered, and Mr. Gray visibly trembled.

"Is she really afflicted in this way? " he whispered.

"Oh, no, papa! it's only Rose's nonsense!" apologised Ellen, who was laughing as hard as the rest. But Mr. Gray did not feel comfortable, and he was very glad when they reached the Junction, and half of his troublesome charge departed on the branch road.

At six o'clock they arrived in Springfield. Half-a-dozen papas were waiting for their daughters; trains stood ready; there was a clamour of good-byes. Mr. Page was absorbed by Lilly, who kissed him incessantly, and chattered so fast that he had no eyes for anyone else. Louisa was borne away by an uncle, with whom she was to pass the night; and Katy and Clover found themselves left alone. They did not like to interrupt Lilly, so they retreated to a bench, and sat down feeling rather left out and homesick; and, though they did not say so, I am sure that each was thinking about papa.

It was only for a moment. Mr. Page spied them, and came forward with such a kind greeting, that the forlorn feeling fled at once. They were to pass the night at the Massasoit, it seemed; and he collected their bags, and led the way across the street to the hotel, where rooms were already engaged for them.

"Now for waffles," whispered Lilly, as they went upstairs; and when, after a few minutes of washing and brushing, they came down again into the dining-room, she called for so many things, and announced herself starved in such a tragical tone, that two amused waiters at once flew to the rescue, and devoted themselves to supplying her wants. Waffle after waffle—each hotter and crisper than the last—did those long-suffering men produce, till even Lilly's appetite gave out, and she was forced to own that she could not swallow another morsel. This climax reached, they went into the parlour; and the girls sat down in the window to watch the people in the street—which, after quiet Hillsover, looked as brilliant and crowded as Broadway.

There were not many persons in the parlour. A grave-looking couple sat at a table at some distance, and a pretty little boy in a velvet jacket was playing around the room. He seemed about five years old; and Katy, who was fond of children, put out her hand as he went by, caught him, and lifted him into her lap. He did not seem shy, but looked her in the face composedly, like a grown person.

"What is your name, dear?" she asked.

Daniel D'Aubigny Sparks," answered the little boy. His voice was prim and distinct.

"Do you live at this hotel?"

"Yes, ma'am. I reside here with my father and mother."

"And what do you do all day? Are there some other little boys for you to play with?"

"I do not wish to play with any little boys," replied Daniel D'Aubigny, in a dignified tone. "I prefer to be with my parents. Today we have taken a walk. We went to see a beautiful conservatory outside the city. There is a Victoria Regia there. 1 had often heard of this wonderful lily; and in the last number of the London 'Musèe' there is a picture of it, represented with a small negro child standing upon one of its leaves. My father said that he did not think this possible; but when we saw the plant, we perceived that the print was not an exaggeration. Such is the size of the leaf, that a small negro child might very easily be supported upon it."

"Oh, my!" cried Katy, feeling as if she had accidentally picked up an elderly gentleman, or a college professor. "Pray, how old are you?"

"Nearly nine, ma'am," replied the little fellow, with a bow.

Katy, too much appalled for farther speech, let him slide off her lap. But Mr. Page, who was much diverted, continued the conversation; and Daniel, mounting a chair, crossed his short legs, and discoursed with all the gravity of an old man. The talk was principally about himself—his tastes, his adventures, his ideas about art and science. Now and then he alluded to his papa and mamma, and once to his grandfather.

"My maternal grandfather," he said, was a remarkable man. In his youth he spent a great deal of time in France. He was there at the time of the French Revolution, and, as it happened, was present at the execution of the unfortunate Queen Marie Antoinette. This, of course, was not intentional. It chanced thus. My grandfather was in a barber's shop, having his hair cut. He saw a great crowd going by, and went out to ask what was the cause. The crowd was so immense that he could not extricate himself; he was carried along against his will, and not only so, but was forced to the front and compelled to witness every part of the dreadful scene. He has often told my mother that, after the execution, the executioner held up the queen's head to the people: the eyes were open, and there was in them an expression, not of pain, not of fear, but of great astonishment and surprise.

This anecdote carried "great astonishment and surprise" into the company who listened to it. Mr. Page gave a sort of chuckle, and saying, "By George!" got up and left the room. The girls put their heads out of the window that they might laugh unseen. Daniel gazed at their shaking shoulders with an air of wonder, while the grave couple at the end of the room, who for some moments had been looking disturbed, drew near and informed the youthful prodigy that it was time for him to go to bed.

"Good-night, young ladies," said the small condescending voice. Katy alone had "presence of countenance enough to return this salutation. It was a relief to find that Daniel went to bed at all.

Next morning at breakfast they saw him seated between his parents, eating bread and milk. He bowed to them over the edge of the bowl.

"Dreadful little prig! They should bottle him in spirits of wine as a specimen. It's the only thing he'll ever be fit for," remarked Mr. Page, who rarely said so sharp a thing about anybody.

Louisa joined them at the station. She was to travel under Mr. Page's care, and Katy was much annoyed at Lilly's manner to her. It grew colder and less polite with every mile. By the time they reached Ashburn it was absolutely rude.

"Come and see me very soon, girls," said Louisa, as they parted in the station. "I long to have you know mother and little Daisy. Oh, there's papa! " and she rushed up to a tall, pleasant-looking man, who kissed her fondly, shook hands with Mr. Page, and touched his hat to Lilly, who scarcely bowed in return.

"Boarding-school is so horrid, she remarked, "you get all mixed up with people you don't want to know—people not in society at all"

How can you talk such nonsense?" said her father; "the Agnews are thoroughly respectable, and Mr. Agnew is one of the cleverest men I know."

Katy was pleased when Mr. Page said this, but Lilly shrugged her shoulders and looked cross.

"Papa is so democratic," she whispered to Clover, "he don't care a bit who people are, so long as they are respectable and clever.

"Well, why should he?" replied Clover. Lilly was more disgusted than ever.

Ashburn was a large and prosperous town. It was built on the slopes of a picturesque hill, and shaded with fine elms. As they drove through the streets, Katy and Clover caught glimpses of conservatories and shrubberies, and beautiful houses with bay windows and piazzas.

"That's ours," said Lilly, as the carriage turned in at a gate. It stopped, and Mr. Page jumped out.

"Here we are," he said. "Gently, Lilly, you'll hurt yourself. Well, my dears, we're very glad to see you in our home at last."

This was kind and comfortable, and the girls were glad of it, for the size and splendour of the house quite dazzled and made them shy. They had never seen anything like it before. The hall had a marble floor, and busts, and statues. Large rooms opened on either side; and Mrs. Page, who came forward to receive them, wore a heavy silk with a train and laces, and looked altogether as if she were dressed for a party.

"This is the drawing-room," said Lilly, delighted to see the girls so impressed. "Isn't it splendid? And she led the way into a stiff, chilly, magnificent apartment, where all the blinds were closed, and all the shades pulled down, and all the furniture shrouded in linen covers. Even the picture-frames and mirrors were sewed up in muslin to keep off flies; and the bronzes and alabaster ornaments on the chimney-piece and *étagère* gleamed through the dim light in a ghostly way. Katy thought it very dismal. She couldn't imagine anybody sitting down there to read or sew, or do anything pleasant, and probably it was not intended that any one should do so; for Mrs. Page soon showed them out, and led the way into a smaller room at the back of the hall.

"Well, Katy, she said, "how do you like Hillsover?"

"Very well, ma'am," replied Katy; but she did not speak enthusiastically.

"Ah!n said Mrs. Page, shaking her head, "it takes time to shake off home habits, and to learn to get along with young people after living with older ones and catching their ways. You'll like it better as you go on."

Katy privately doubted whether this was true, but she did not say so. Pretty soon Lilly offered to show them upstairs to their room. She took them first into three large and elegant chambers, which she explained were kept for grand company, and then into a much smaller one in a wing.

Mother always puts my friends in here," she remarked; "she says it's plenty good enough for school-girls to thrash about in!"

"What does she mean?n cried Clover indignantly, as Lilly closed the door. "We don't thrash!"

"I can't imagine," answered Katy, who was vexed too. But pretty soon she began to laugh.

"People are so funny," she said. "Never mind, Clovy, this room is good enough, I'm sure."

"Must we unpack, or will it do to go down in our alpacas?n asked Clover.

"I don't know," replied Katy, in a doubtful tone. "Perhaps we had better change our gowns. Cousin Olivia always dresses so much! Here's your blue muslin right on top of the trunk. You might put on that, and I'll wear my purple.

The girls were glad they had done this, for it was evidently expected, and Lilly had dressed her hair and donned a fresh white pique. Mrs Page examined their dresses, and said that Clover's was a lovely blue, but that ruffles were quite gone out, and everything must be made with basques. She supposed they needed quantities of things, and she had already engaged a dressmaker for them.

"Thank you," said Katy, abut I don't think we need anything. We had our winter dresses made before we left home."

"Winter dresses! last spring! My dear, what were you thinking of? They must be completely out of fashion."

"You can't think how little Hillsover people know about fashions," replied Katy, laughing.

"But, my dear, for your own sake!" exclaimed Mrs. Page, distressed by these lax remarks. "I'll look over your things to-morrow and see what you need."

Katy did not dare to say "No," but she felt rebellious. When they were half through tea, the door opened, and a boy came in.

"You are late, Clarence," said Mr. Page, while Mrs. Page frowned, and observed, "Clarence makes a point of being late. He really deserves to be made to go without his supper. Shut the door, Clarence. O mercy! don't bang it in that way. I wish you would learn to shut a door properly. Here are your cousins, Katy and Clover Carr. Now let me see if you can shake hands with them like a gentleman, and not like a ploughboy."

Clarence, a square, freckled boy of thirteen, with reddish hair, and a sort of red sparkle in his eyes, looked very angry at this address. He did not offer to shake hands at all, but elevating his shoulders said, "How d'you do?" in a sulky voice, and sitting down at the table buried his nose without delay in a glass of milk. His mother gave a disgusted sigh.

"What a boy you are!" she said. "Your cousins will think that you have never been taught anything, which is not the case; for I'm sure I've taken twice the pains with you that I have with Lilly. Pray excuse him, Katy. It's no use trying to make boys polite!"

"Isn't it?" said Katy, thinking of Phil and Dorry, and wondering what Mrs. Page could mean.

"Hullo, Lilly!" broke in Clarence, spying his sister as it seemed for the first time.

"How d'you do?" said Lilly, carelessly. "I was wondering how long it would be before you would condescend to notice my existence."

"I didn't see you."

121

"I know you didn't. I never knew such a boy! You might as well have no eyes at all."

Clarence scowled, and went on with his supper. His mother seemed unable to let him alone. "Clarence, don't take such large mouthfuls! Clarence, pray use your napkin! Clarence, your elbows are on the table sir! Now, Clarence, don't try to speak until you have swallowed all that bread"—came every other moment. Katy felt very sorry for Clarence. His manners were certainly bad, but it seemed quite dreadful that public attention should be thus constantly called to them.

The evening was rather dull. There was a sort of put-in-order-for-company air about the parlour, which made everybody stiff. Mrs. Page did not sew or read, but sat in a low chair looking like a lady in a fashion-plate, and asked questions about Hillsover, some of which were not easy to answer, as, for example, "Have you any other intimate friends among the school-girls beside Lilly?" About eight o'clock a couple of young, very young, gentlemen came in, at the sight of whom Lilly, who was half asleep, brightened and became lively and talkative. One of them was the Mr. Hickman, whose father married Mr. Page's sister-in-law's sister, thus making him in some mysterious way a "first cousin" of Lilly's. He was an Arrowmouth student, and seemed to have so many jokes to laugh over with Lilly that before long they withdrew to a distant sofa, where they conversed in whispers. The other youth, introduced as Mr. Eels, was left to entertain the other three ladies, which duty he performed by sucking the head of his cane in silence while they talked to him. He too was an Arrowmouth Sophomore.

In the midst of the conversation, the door,.which stood

ajar, opened a little wider, and a dog's head appeared, followed by a tail, which waggled so beseechingly for leave to come farther that Clover, who liked dogs, put out her hand and said, "Come here, poor fellow!" The dog ran up to her at once. He was not pretty, being of a pepper-and-salt colour, with a blunt nose and no particular sort of a tail, but he looked good-natured; and Clover fondled him cordially, while Mr. Eels took his cane out of his mouth to ask, "What kind of a dog is that, Mrs. Page?"

"I'm sure I don't know," she replied; while Lilly, from the distance, added affectedly, "Oh, he's the most dreadful dog, Mr. Eels! My brother picked him up in the street, and none of us know the least thing about him, except that he's the commonest kind of a dog— a sort of cur, I believe."

That's not true!" broke in a stern voice from the hall, which made everybody jump; and Katy, looking that way, was aware of a vengeful eye glaring at Lilly through the crack of the door. He's a very valuable dog, indeed—half mastiff and half terrier, with a touch of the bull-dog—so there, miss! "

The effect of this remark was startling. Lilly gave a scream; Mrs. Page rose, and hurried to the door; while the dog, hearing his master's voice, rushed that way also, got before her, and almost threw her down. Katy and Clover could not help laughing, and Mr. Eels meeting their amused eyes, removed the cane from his mouth, and grew conversable.

"That Clarence is a droll little chap!" he remarked, confidentially. "Bright, too! He'd be a nice fellow if he wasn't picked at so much. It never does a fellow any good to be picked at—now does it, Miss Carr?"

"No; I don't think it does."

"I say," continued Mr. Eels, "I've seen you young ladies up at Hillsover, haven't I? Aren't you both at the Nunnery?"

"Yes. It's vacation now, you know."

"I was sure I'd seen you. You had a room on the side next the President's, didn't you? I thought so. We fellows didn't know your names, so we called you 'The Real Nuns.' n

Real Nuns?"

"Yes, because you never looked out of the window at us. Real nuns and sham nuns—don't you see? Almost all the young ladies are sham nuns, except you, and two pretty little ones in the storey above, fifth window from the end."

"Oh, I know!" said Clover, much amused. "Sally Alsop, you know, Katy, and Amy Erskine. They are such nice girls."

"Are they?" replied Mr. Eels, with the air of one who notes down names for future reference. "Well, I thought so. Not so much fun in them as some of the others, I guess; but a fellow likes other things as well as fun. I know if my sister was there I'd rather have her take the dull line than the other."

Katy treasured up this remark for the benefit of the S.S.U.C. Mrs. Page came back just then, and Mr. Eels resumed his cane. Nothing more was heard of Clarence that night.

Next morning Cousin Olivia fulfilled her threat of inspecting the girls' wardrobe. She shook her head over the simple, untrimmed merinos and thick cloth coats.

There's no help for it," she said; "but it's a great pity. You would much better have waited and had things fresh. Perhaps it may be possible to match the merino, and have some sort of basque arrangement added on. I will talk to Madame Chonfleur about it. Meantime I shall get one handsome thick dress for each of you, and have it stylishly made. That, at least, you really need. n

Katy was too glad to be so easily let off to raise objections. So that afternoon she and Clover were taken out to "choose their material," Mrs. Page said, but really to sit by while she chose it for them. At the dressmaker's it was the same; they stood passive while the orders were given, and everything decided upon.

"Isn't it funny?" whispered Clover; "but I don't like it a bit, do you? It's just like Elsie saying how she'll have her doll's things made."

"Oh, this dress isn't mine! it's Cousin Olivia's!" replied Katy. "She's welcome to have it trimmed just as she likes."

But when the suits came home she was forced to be pleased. There was no over-trimming, no look of finery; everything fitted perfectly, and had the air of finish which they had noticed and admired in Lilly's clothes. Katy almost forgot that she had objected to the dresses as unnecessary.

"After all, it is nice to look nice," she confessed to Clover.

Excepting to go to the dressmaker's, there was not much to amuse during the first half of vacation.

Mrs. Page took them to drive now and then, and Katy found some pleasant books in the library, and read a good deal. Clover meantime made friends with Clarence. I think his heart was won that first evening by her attentions to Guest, the dog, that mysterious animal, "half mastiff and half terrier, with a touch of the bull-dog." Clarence loved Guest dearly, and was gratified that Clover liked him; for the poor animal had few friends in the household. In a little while Clarence became quite sociable with her, and tolerably so with Katy. They found him, as Mr. Eels had said, "a bright fellow," and pleasant and good-humoured enough when taken in the right way. Lilly always seemed to take him wrong, and his treatment of her was most disagreeable, snappish, and quarrelsome to the last degree.

"Much you don't like oranges!" he said, one day at dinner, in answer to an innocent remark of hers. Much! I've seen you eat two at a time, without stopping. Pa, Lilly says she don't like oranges! I've seen her eat two at a time, without stopping! Much she doesn't! I've seen her eat two at a time, without stopping! " He kept this up for five minutes, looking from one person to another, and repeating, Much she don't! Much!" till Lilly was almost crying from vexation, and even Clover longed to box his ears. Nobody was sorry when Mr. Page ordered him to leave the room, which he did with a last vindictive "Much," addressed to Lilly.

"How can Clarence behave so?" said Katy, when she and Clover were alone.

"I don't know," replied Clover. "He's such a nice boy sometimes; but when he isn't nice, he's the horridest boy I ever saw. I wish you'd talk to him, Katy, and tell him how dreadfully it sounds when he says such things."

No, indeed. He'd take it much better from you. You're nearer his age, and could do it nicely and pleasantly, and not make him feel as if he were being scolded. Poor fellow, he gets plenty of that!"

Clover said no more about the subject, but she meditated. She had a good deal of tact for so young a girl, and took care to get Clarence into a specially amicable mood before she began her lecture. Look here, you bad boy, how could you tease poor Lilly so yesterday? Guest, speak up, sir, and tell your massa how naughty it was!"

Oh, dear! now you're going to nag!" growled Clarence, in an injured voice.

No, I'm not—not the least in the world. I'll promise not to. But just tell me"—and Clover put her hand on the rough, red-brown hair, and stroked it—"just tell me why you 'go for to do' such things? They're not a bit nice.

Lilly's so hateful! " grumbled Clarence.

Well, she is sometimes, I know," admitted Clover, candidly. "But because she is hateful is no reason why you should be unmanly."

""manly" cried Clarence, flushing.

Yes, I call it unmanly to tease and quarrel, and contradict like that. It's like girls. They do it sometimes, but I didn't -think a boy would. I thought he'd be ashamed."

Doesn't Dorry ever quarrel or tease?" asked Clarence, who liked to hear about Clover's brother and sisters.

Not now, and never in that way. He used to sometimes, when he was little, but now he's real nice. He wouldn't speak to a girl as you speak to Lilly for anything. He'd think it wasn't being a gentleman."

"Stuff about gentleman, and all that!" retorted Clarence. "Mother dings the word into my ears till I hate it"

"Well, it is rather teasing to be reminded all the time, I admit; but you can't wonder that your mother wants you to be a gentleman, Clarence. It's the best thing in the world, I think. I hope Phil and Dorry will grow up just like papa, for everybody says he's the most perfect gentleman, and it makes me so proud to hear them.

"But what does it mean, anyway? Mother says it's how you hold your fork, and how you chew, and how you put on your hat. If that's all, I don't think it amounts to much."

"'Oh, that isn't all. It's being gentle, don't you see? Gentle and nice to everybody, and just as polite to poor people as to rich ones," said Clover, talking fast, in her eagerness to explain her meaning—and never being selfish, or noisy, or pushing people out of their place. Forks, and hats, and all that are only little ways of making one's self more agreeable to other people. A gentleman is a gentleman inside, all through. Oh, I wish I could make you see what I mean!"

"Oh, that's it, is it?" said Clarence.

Whether he understood or not, Clover could not tell, or whether she had done any good or not; but she had the discretion to say no more; and certainly Clarence was not offended, for after that day he grew fonder of her than ever. Lilly became absolutely jealous. She had never cared particularly for Clarence's affection, but she did not like to have anyone preferred above herself.

"It's pretty hard, I think," she told Clover. "Clare does everything you tell him, and he treats me awfully. It isn't a bit fair! I'm his sister, and you're only a second cousin."

All this time the girls had seen almost nothing of Louisa Agnew. She called once, but Lilly received the call with them, and was so cool and stiff that Louisa grew stiff also, and made but a short stay; and when the girls returned the visit she was out. A few days before the close of the vacation, however, a note came from her.

"Dear Katy,—

"I am so sorry not to have seen more of you and Clover. Won't you come and spend Wednesday with us? Mamma sends her love, and hopes you will come early, so as to have a long day, for she wants to know you. I long to show you the baby and everything. Do come. Papa will see you home in the evening. Remember me to Lilly. She has so many friends to see during vacation that I am sure she will forgive me for stealing you for one day."

"Yours affectionately,
"LOUISA."

Katy thought this message very politely expressed; but Lilly, when she heard it, tossed her head, and said she "really thought Miss Agnew might let her name alone when she wrote notes". Mrs. Page seemed to pity the girls for having to go. They must, she supposed, as it was a school-mate; but she feared it would be stupid for them. The Agnews were queer sort of people, not in society at all. Mr. Agnew was clever, people said; but really, she knew very little about the family. Perhaps it would not do to decline.

Katy and Clover had no idea of declining. They sent a warm little note of acceptance, and on the appointed day set off bright and early with a good deal of pleasant anticipation. The vacation had been rather dull at Cousin Olivia's. Lilly was a good deal with her own friends, and Mrs. Page with hers; and there never seemed any special place where they might sit, or anything in particular for them to do.

Louisa's home was at some distance from Mr. Page's, and in a less fashionable street. It looked pleasant and cosy as the girls opened the gate. There was a small garden in front with gay flowerbeds; and on the piazza, which was shaded with vines, sat Mrs. Agnew, with a little work-table by her side. She was a pretty and youthful-looking woman, and her voice and smile made them feel at home immediately.

"There is no need of anybody to introduce you," she said. "Lulu has described you so often that I know perfectly well which is Katy and which Clover. I am so glad you could come! Won't you go right in my bedroom by that long window and take off your things!' Lulu has explained to you that I am lame and never walk, so you won't think it strange that I do not show you the way. She will be here in a moment. She ran upstairs to fetch the baby."

The girls went into the bedroom. It was a pretty and unusual looking apartment. The furniture was simple as could be, but bed and toilet and windows were curtained and frilled with white, and the walls were covered thick with pictures, photographs, and pen-and-ink sketches, and water-colour drawings, unframed, most of them, and just pinned up without regularity, so as to give each the best possible light. It was an odd way of arranging pictures; but Katy liked it, and would gladly have lingered to look at each one, only that she feared Mrs. Agnew would expect them and would think it strange that they did not come back.

Just as they went out again to the piazza, Louisa came running downstairs with her little sister in her arms.

"I was curling her hair," she explained, "and did not hear you come in. Daisy, give Katy a kiss. Now another for Clover. Isn't she a darling?" embracing the Child rapturously herself; "now isn't she a little beauty?"

"Perfectly lovely! cried the others, and soon all three were seated on the floor of the piazza, with Daisy in the midst, passing her from hand to hand, as if she had been something good to eat. She was used to it, and submitted with perfect good nature to being kissed, trotted, carried up and down, and generally made love to. Mrs. Agnew sat by and laughed at the spectacle. When Baby

130

was taken off for her noonday nap, Louisa took the girls into the parlour, another odd and pretty room, full of prints and sketches, and pictures of all sorts, some with frames, others with a knot of autumn leaves or a twist of ivy around them by way of a finish. There was a bowl of beautiful autumn roses on the table; and, though the price of one of Mrs. Page's damask curtains would probably have bought the whole furniture of the room, everything was so bright, and homelike and pleasant-looking, that Katy's heart warmed at the sight. They were examining a portrait of Louisa with Daisy in her lap, painted by her father, when Mr. Agnew came in. The girls liked his face at once. It was fine and frank; and nothing could be prettier than to see him pick up his invalid wife as if she had been a child, and carry her into the dining-room to her place at the head of the table.

Katy and Clover agreed afterward that it was the merriest dinner they had had since they left home. Mr. Agnew told stories about painters and painting, and was delightful. No less so was the nice gossip upstairs in Louisa's room which followed dinner, or the afternoon frolic with Daisy, or the long evening spent in looking over books and photographs. Altogether the day seemed only too short. As they went out of the gate at ten o'clock, Mr. Agnew following, lo! a dark figure emerged from behind a tree and joined Clover. It was Clarence!

"I thought I'd just walk this way," he explained, "the house has been dreadfully dull all day without you."

Clover was immensely flattered, but Mrs. Page's astonishment next day knew no bounds.

"Really," she said, "I have hopes of Clarence at last. I never knew him volunteer to escort anybody anywhere before in his life."

"I say," remarked Clarence, the evening before the girls went back to school, "I say, suppose you write to a fellow sometimes, Clover?

"Do you mean yourself by 'a fellow'?" laughed Clover.

"You don't suppose I meant George Hickman, or that donkey of an Eels, did you?" retorted Clarence.

"No, I didn't. Well, I've no objection to writing to a fellow, if that fellow is you, provided the fellow answers my letters. Will you?"

"Yes," gruffly, "but you mustn't show 'em to any girls, or laugh at my writing, or I'll stop. Lilly says my writing is like beetle-tracks. Little she knows about it, though! I don't write to her. Promise, Clover! "

"Yes, I promise," said Clover, pleased at the notion of Clare's proposing a correspondence of his own accord.

Next morning they all left for Hillsover. Clarence's friendship, and the remembrance of their day with the Agnews, were the pleasantest things that the girls carried away with them from their autumn vacation.

CHAPTER 10

A BUDGET OF LETTERS

Hillsover, October 21st.

"Dear Elsie,—I didn't write you last Saturday, because that was the day we came back to school, and there hasn't been one minute since when I could. We thought, perhaps, Miss Jane would let us off from the abstracts on Sunday, because it was the first day, and school was hardly begun; and if she had, I was going to write to you instead; but she didn't. She said the only way to keep girls out of mischief was to keep them busy. Rose Red is sure that something has gone wrong with Miss Jane's missionary during the vacation—she's so dreadfully cross. Oh, dear, how I do hate to come back and be scolded by her again!

"I forget if I told you about the abstracts. They are of the sermons on Sunday, you know; and we have to give the texts, and the heads, and as much as we can remember of the rest. Sometimes Dr. Prince begins, 'I shall divide my subject into three parts,' and tells what they are going to be. When he does that, most of the girls take out their pencils and put them down, and then they don't listen any more. Katy and I don't, for she says it isn't right to act in that way. Miss Jane pretends that she reads all the abstracts through, but she doesn't; for once, Rose Red, just to try her, wrote in the middle of hers, 'I am sitting by my window at this moment, and a red cow is going down the street. I wonder if she is any relation to Mrs. Seccomb's cow?' and Miss Jane never noticed it, but marked her 'perfect' all the same. Wasn't it funny?

"But I must tell you about our journey back. Mr. Page came all the way with us, and was ever so nice. Clarence rode down in the carriage to the depot. He gave me a real pretty india-rubber and gold pencil for a good-bye present. I think you and Dorry would like Clarence, only just at first you might say he was rather rude and cross. I did; but now I like him ever so much. Cousin Olivia gave Katy a worked collar and sleeves, and me an embroidered pocket-handkerchief with clover leaves in the corner. Wasn't it kind? I'm sorry I said in my last letter that we didn't enjoy our vacation. We didn't much; but it wasn't exactly Cousin Olivia's fault. She meant we should, but she didn't know how. Some people don't, you know. And don't tell any one I said so, will you?

"Rose Red got into the train before we did. She was so glad when we came that she cried. It was because she was home-sick waiting four hours at the Nunnery without us, she said. Rose is such a darling! She had a splendid vacation, and went to three parties and a picnic. Isn't it queer?—her winter bonnet is black velvet trimmed with pink, and so is mine. I wanted blue at first, but Cousin Olivia said pink was more stylish; and now I am glad, because I like to be like Rose.

Katy and I have got No. 2 this term. It's a great deal pleasanter than our old room, and the entry-stove is just outside the door, so we shall keep warm. There is sun, too, only Mrs. Nipson has nailed thick cotton over all the window except a little place at the top. Every window in the house is just so. You can't think how mad the girls are about it. The first night we had an indignation meeting, and passed resolutions, and some of the girls said they wouldn't stay— they should write to their fathers to come and take them home. None of them did, though. It's perfectly forlorn, not being able to look out. Oh, dear, how I wish it were spring!

We've got a new dining-room. It's a great deal bigger than the old one, so now we all eat together, and don't have any first and second tables. It's ever so much nicer, for I used to get so dreadfully hungry waiting that I didn't know what to do. One thing is horrid, though; and that is, that every girl has to make a remark in French every day at dinner. The remarks are about a subject. Mrs. Nipson gives out the subjects. To-day the subject was 'Les oiseaux,' and Rose Red said, 'J'aime beaucoup les oiseaux, especialement ceux qui sont rôtis,' which made us all laugh. That ridiculous little Bella Arkwright said, 'J'aime beaucoup les oiseaux qui sing.' She thought sing was French! Every girl in school began, 'J'aime beaucoup les oiseaux'! To-morrow the subject is 'Jules César.' I'm sure I don't know what to say. There isn't a word in Ollendorf about him.

"There are not so many new scholars this term as there were last. The girls think it is because Mrs. Nipson isn't so popular as Mrs. Florence used to be. Two or three of the new ones look pleasant, but I don't know them yet. Louisa Agnew is the nicest girl here next to Rose. Lilly Page says she is vulgar, because her father paints portraits, and they don't know the same people that Cousin Olivia knows; but she isn't a bit. We went to spend the day there just before we left Ashburn, and her father and mother are splendid. Their house is just full of all sorts of queer, interesting things, and pictures; and Mr. Agnew told us ever so many stories about painters, and what they did. One was about a boy who used to make figures of lions in butter, and afterwards he became famous. I forget his name. We had a lovely time. I wish you could see Lou's little sister Daisy. She's

135

only two, and a perfect little beauty. She has got ten teeth, and hardly ever cries.

"Please ask Papa—

Just as Clover had got to this point, she was interrupted by Katy, who walked in with her hat on, and a whole handful of letters.

"See here!" she cried. "Isn't this delightful? Miss Marsh took me with her to the post office, and we found these. Three for you, and two for me, and one for Rose. Wait a minute till I give Rose hers, and we'll read them together.

In another moment the two were cozily seated, with their heads close together, opening their budget. First came one from Papa.

"MY DEAR DAUGHTERS,"—

"It's for you, too, you see," said Katy.

"Last week came your letter of the 31st, and we were glad to hear that you were well, and ready to go back to school. By the time this reaches you, you will be in Hillsover, and your winter term begun. Make the most of it, for we all feel as if we could never let you go from home again. Johnnie says she shall rub Spalding's Prepared Glue all over your dresses when you come back, so that you cannot stir. I am a little of the same way of thinking myself. Cecy has returned from boarding-school, and set up as a young lady. Elsie is much excited over the party dresses which Mrs. Hall is having made for her, and goes over every day to see if anything new has come. I am glad, on this account, that you are away just now; for it would not be easy to keep steady heads and continue your studies, with so much going on next door. I have sent Cousin Olivia a cheque to pay for the things she bought for you, and am much obliged to her for seeing that you were properly fitted out. Katy was very right to consider expense, but I wish you to have all things needful. I enclose two ten-dollar bills, one for each of you, for pocket-money; and, with much love from the children, am,

> "Yours affectionately,
> "P. Carr"

"PS.—Cousin Helen has had a sharp attack, but is better"

"I wish Papa would write longer letters," said Katy. "He always sends us money, but he don't send half enough words with it." She folded the letter, and fondled it affectionately.

"He's always so busy," replied Clover. "Don't you remember how he used to sit down at his desk, and scribble off his letters; and how somebody always was sure to ring the bell before he got through? I'm very glad to have some money, for now I can pay the sixty-two cents I owe you. It's my turn to read. This is from Elsie, and a real long one. Put away the bills first, Katy, or they'll be lost. That's right; now we'll begin together.

"Dear Clover,—You don't know how glad I am when my turn comes to get a letter all to myself. Of course I read Papa's, and all the rest you write to the family; but it never seems as if you were talking to me unless you begin, 'Dear Elsie'. I wish some time you'd put in a little note marked 'private,' just for me, which nobody else need see. It would be such fun! Please do. I should think you would have hated staying at Cousin Olivia's. When

I read what she said about your travelling-dresses looking as if they had come out of the ark, I was just as mad as fire. But I shouldn't think you'd want much to go back to school either, though sometimes it must be splendid. John has named her old stockinette doll, which she used to call 'scratch-face', 'Nippy', after Mrs. Nipson; and I made her a muslin cap, and Dorry drew a pair of black spectacles round her eyes. She is a perfect fright, and John plays all the time that dreadful things happen to her. She pricks her with pins, and pretends she has the ear-ache, and lets her tumble down and hurt herself, till sometimes I nearly feel sorry, though it's all make-believe. When you wrote us about only having pudding for dinner, I didn't a bit. John put her into the rag-closet that very day, and has been starving her to death ever since; and Phil says it serves her right. You can't think how awfully lonely I sometimes get without you. If it wasn't for Helen Gibbs, that new girl I told you about, I shouldn't know what to do. She is the prettiest girl in Miss McCrane's school. Her hair curls just like mine, only it is four times as long, and a million times as thick; and her waist is really and truly not much bigger round than a bed-post. We're the greatest friends. She says she loves me just exactly as much as if I was her sister, but she never had any real sisters. She was quite mad the other day because I said I couldn't love her quite so well as you and Katy; and all recess-time she wouldn't speak to me, but now we've made up. Dorry is so awfully in love with her, that I never can get him to come into the room when she is here, and he blushes when we tease him about her. But this is a great secret. Dorry and I play chess every evening. He almost always beats, unless Papa comes behind and helps me. Phil has learned, too, because he always wants to do everything that we do. Dorry gives him a castle, and a bishop, and a knight, and four pawns, and then beats him in six moves. Phil gets so mad that we can't help laughing. Last night he buttoned his king up inside his jacket, and said, 'There! you can't checkmate me now any way!'

"Cecy has come home. She is a young lady now. She does her hair up quite different, and wears long dresses. This winter she is going to parties, and Mrs. Hall is going to have a party for her on Thursday, with real, grown-up young ladies and gentlemen at it. Cecy has got some beautiful new dresses—a white muslin, a blue tarlatan, and a pink silk. The pink silk is the prettiest, I think. Cecy is real kind, and lets me see all her things. She has got a lovely breast-pin, too, and a new fan with ivory sticks, and all sorts of things. I wish I was grown-up. It must be so nice. I want to tell you something, only you mustn't tell anybody except Katy. Don't you remember how Cecy used to say that she never was going out to drive with young gentlemen, but was going to stay at home and read the Bible to poor people? Well, she didn't tell the truth; for she has been out three times already with Sylvester Slack in his buggy. When I told her she ought not to do so, because it was breaking a promise, she only laughed, and said I was a silly girl. Isn't it queer?

"I want to tell you what an awful thing I did the other night. Maria Avery invited me to tea, and Papa said I might go. I didn't want to much, but I didn't know what to tell Maria, so I went. You know how poor they are, and how Aunt Lizzie used to say that they were 'touchy', so I thought I would take great care not to hurry home right after tea, for fear they would think I was not enjoying myself. So I waited, and waited, and waited, and got so sleepy that I had to pinch my fingers to keep awake. At last I was sure that it might be almost nine, so I asked Mr. Avery if he'd please take me home; and don't you believe, when we got there, it was a quarter past ten, and Papa was just coming for me! Dorry said he guessed I must be enjoying myself to stay so late. I didn't tell anybody about it for three days, because I knew they'd laugh at me, and they did. Wasn't it funny? And old Mrs. Avery looked as sleepy as I felt, and kept yawning behind her hand. I told Papa if I had a watch of my own I shouldn't make such mistakes, and he laughed and said, 'We'll see.' Oh, do you suppose that means that he's going to give me one?

"We are so proud of Dorry's having taken two prizes at the examination yesterday. He took the second Latin prize, and the first mathematics. Dr. Pullman says he thinks Dorry is one of the most thorough boys he ever saw. Isn't that nice? The prizes were books: one was the life of Benjamin Franklin, and the other the life of General Butler. Papa says he doesn't think much of the life of Butler; but Dorry has begun it, and says it is splendid. Phil says when he takes a prize he wants candy and a new knife; but he'll have to wait a good while unless he studies harder than he does now. He has just come in to tease me to go up into the garret and help him to get down his sledge, because he thinks it is going to snow; but there isn't a sign of it, and the weather is quite warm. I asked him what I should say for him to you, and he said, 'Oh, tell her to come home, and anything you please!' I said, 'shall I give her your love, and say that you are very well?' and he says, 'Oh, yes, Miss Elsie, I guess you'd think yourself mighty well if your head ached as much as mine does every day!' Don't be frightened, however, for he's just as fat and rosy as can be; but almost every day he says he feels sick about school-time. When

Papa was at Moorfield, Miss Finch believed him, and let him stay at home two mornings. I don't wonder at it, for you can think what a face he makes up; but he got well so fast that she pays no attention to him now. The other day, about eleven o'clock, Papa met him coming along the road, shying stones at the birds, and making lots of noise. He told Papa he felt so sick that his teacher had let him go home; but Papa noticed that his mouth looked sticky, so he opened his dinner-basket, and found that the little scamp had eaten up all his dinner on the road, corned beef, bread and butter, a great piece of mince pie, and six pears. Papa couldn't help laughing, but he made him turn round and go right back to school again.

"I told you, in my last, about Johnnie's going to school with me now. She is very proud of it, and is always talking about 'Elsie's and my school.' She is twice as smart as the other little girls of her age. Miss McCrane has put her into the composition class, where they write compositions on their slates. The first subject was, 'A Kitten'; and John's began, 'she's a dear, little, soft, scratching thing, only you'd better not pull her by the tail, but she's real cunning.' All the girls laughed, and Johnnie called out, 'Well, it's true, anyhow.'

"I can't write any more, for I must study my Latin. Besides, this is the longest letter that ever was. I have been four days writing it. Please send me one just as long. Old Mary and the children send lots of love, and Papa says, 'Tell Katy, if a pudding diet sets her to growing again, she must come home at once, for he couldn't afford it.' Oh, dear, how I wish I could see you! Please give my love to Rose Red. She must be perfectly splendid.

"Your affectionate,
"ELSIE"

"Oh, the dear little duck! Isn't that just like her?" said Clover. "1 think Elsie has a real genius for writing, don't you? She tells all the little things, and is so droll and cunning. Nobody writes such nice letters. Who's that from, Katy?"

"Cousin Helen, and it's been such a long time coming. Just look at this date! September 22nd—a whole month ago!" Then she began to read.

"DEAR KATY,—It seems a long time since we have had a talk, but I have been less well lately, so that it has been difficult to write. Yesterday, I sat up for the first time in several weeks; and to-day I am dressed and beginning to feel like myself. I wish you could see my room this morning—I often wish this—but it is so particularly pretty, for little Helen has been in with a great basket full of leaves and flowers, and together we have dressed it to perfection. There are four vases of roses, a bowl full of chrysanthemums, and red leaves round all my pictures. The leaves are Virginia creeper. It doesn't last long, but is lovely while it lasts. Helen also brought a bird's nest which the gardener found in a hawthorn-tree on the lawn. It hangs on a branch, and she has tied it to one side of my bookshelves. On the opposite side is another nest quite different—a great, grey hornet's nest, as big as a band-box, which came from the mountains a year ago. I wondered if any such grow in the woods about Hillsover. In spite of the red leaves, the day is warm as summer, and the windows stand wide open. I suppose it is cooler with you, but I know it is delicious cold. Now that I think of it, you must be in Ashburn by this time. I hope you will enjoy every moment of your vacation.

"Oct. 19th.—I did not finish my letter the day it was begun, dear Katy, and next morning it proved that I was

142

not so strong as I fancied, and I had to go to bed again.
I am still there, and, as you see, writing with a pencil;
but do not be worried about me, for the doctor says I
am mending, and soon I hope to be up and in my chair.
The red leaves are gone, but the roses are lovely as ever,
for little Helen keeps bringing me fresh ones. She has
just been in to read me her composition. The subject was
'stars', and you can't think how much she found to say
about them. She is a bright little creature, and it is a
great pleasure to teach her. I am hardly ever so sick that
she cannot come for her lessons, and she gets on fast.
We have made an arrangement that when she knows
more than I do, she is to give me lessons, and I am not
sure that the time is so very far off.

"I must tell you about my Ben. He is a new canary
which was given me in the summer, and lately he has
grown so delightfully tame that I feel as if it were not a
bird at all, but a fairy prince come to live with me and
amuse me. The cage door is left open always now, and
he flies in and out as he likes. He is a restless, inquisitive
fellow, and visits any part of the room, trying each fresh
thing with his bill to see if it is good to eat, and then
perching on it to see if it is good to sit upon. He mistakes
his own reflection in the looking-glass for another canary,
and sits on the pincushion twittering and making love to
himself for half an hour at a time. To watch him is one of
my greatest amusements, especially just now when I am
in bed so much. Sometimes he hides and keeps so still
that I have not the least idea where he is. But the moment
I call, 'Ben, Ben', and hold out my finger, wings begin to
rustle, and out he flies and perches on my finger. He isn't
the least bit in the world afraid, but sits on my head or
shoulder, eats out of my mouth, and kisses me with his
beak. He is on the pillow at this moment making runs at

143

my pencil, of which he is mortally jealous. It is just so with my combs and brushes, if I attempt to do my hair; he cannot bear to have me do anything but play with him. I do wish I could show him to you and Clover.

"Little Helen, my other pet, has just come in with a sponge cake which she frosted herself. She sends her love, and says when you come to see me next summer she will frost you each one just like it. Good-bye, my Katy. I had nothing to write about, and have written it; but I never like to keep silent too long, or let you feel as if you were forgotten by your loving cousin,

"HELEN.

"P.S.—Be sure to wear plenty of warm wraps for your winter walks. And, Katy, dear, you must eat meat every day. Mrs. Nipson will probably give up her favourite puddings now that the cold weather has begun; but, if not, write to Papa."

"Isn't that letter Cousin Helen all over?" said Katy. "So little about her illness, and so bright and merry, and yet she has really been sick. Papa says 'a sharp attack'. Isn't she the dearest person in the world, next to Papa, I mean?"

"Yes, indeed. There's nobody like her. I do hope we can go to see her next summer. Now it's my turn. I can't think who this letter is from. Oh, Clarence! Katy, I can't let you see this. I promised Clare that I wouldn't show his letters to anybody, not even you."

"Oh, very well. But you've got another. Dorry, isn't it? Read that first, and I'll go away and leave you in peace."

So Clover read:—

DEAR CLOVER,—Elsie says she is going to write to you to-day; but I won't stop, because next Saturday I'm going out fishing with the Slacks. There are a great many trout now in Blue Brook. Eugene caught six the other day—no, five, one was a minnow. Papa has given me a splendid rod; it lets out as tall as a house. I hope I shall catch with it. Alexander says the trout will admire it so much that they can't help biting; but he was only funning. Elsie and I play chess most every night. She plays a real good game for a girl. Sometimes Pa helps, and then she beats. Miss Finch is well. She don't keep house quite like Katy did, and I don't like her so well as I do you; but she's pretty nice. The other day we had a nutting picnic, and she gave me and Phil a loaf of Election cake and six quince turnovers to carry. The boys gave three cheers for her when they saw them. Did Elsie tell you that I have invented a new machine? It is called 'The Intellectual Peach Parer'. There is a place to hold a book while you pare the peaches. It is very convenient. I don't think of anything else to tell you. Cecy has got home, and is going to have a party next week. She's grown up now, she says, and she wears her hair quite different. It's a great deal thicker than it used to be. Elsie says it's because there are rats in it; but I don't believe her. Elsie has got a new friend. Her name is Helen Gibbs. She's quite pretty.

> "Your affectionate brother,
> "DORRY"

"PS.—John wants to put in a note."

John's note was written in a round hand, as easy to read as print.

"DEAR CLOVER,—I am well, and hope you are the same. I wish you would write me a letter of my own. I go to school with Elsie now. We write compositions.

They are hard to write. We don't go up into the loft half so much as we used to when you ware at home. Mrs. Worrett came to dinner last week. She says she ways two hundred and atey pounds. I should think it would be dredful to way that. I only way 76. My head comes up to the mark on the door where you ware mesured when you ware twelve—isn't that tal? Good-bye. I send a kiss to Katy.

"Your loving,
"JOHN"

After they had finished this note, Katy went away, leaving Clover to open Clarence's letter by herself. It was not so well written or spelt as Dorry's by any means.

"DEAR CLOVER,—Don't forget what you promised. I mene about not showing this. And don't tell Lilly I rote. If you do, she'll be as mad as hops. I haven't been doing much since you went away. School begun yesterday, and I am glad; for it's awfully dull now that you girls have gone. Mother says Guest has got flees on him, so she won't let him come into the house any more. I stay out in the barn with him insted. He is well, and sends you a wag of his tail. Jim and me are making him a collar. It is black, with G.P. on it, for Guest Page, you know. A lot of the boys had a camping out last week. I went. It was really jolly; but ma wouldn't let me stay all night, so I lost the best part. They rosted scullpins for supper, and had a bonfire. The camp was on Harstnet Hill. Next time you come I'll take you out there. Pa has gone to Mane on bizness. He said I must take care of the house, so I've borrowed Jim's gun, and if any robers come I mean to shoot them. I always go to sleep with a broom agenst the door, so as to wake up when they open it. This morning I thought they had come, for the broom was gone, and the gun, too; but it was only Briget. She opened the door, and it fell down; but I didn't wake up, so she took it away, and put the gun in the closset. I was mad, 1 can tell you.

"This is only a short letter, but I hope you will answer it soon. Give my love to Katy, and tell Dorry that if he likes I'll send him my compas for his machenery, because I've got two.

> "Your affectionate Cousin,
> "CLARENCE PAGE"

This was the last of the budget. As Clover folded it up, she was dismayed by the tinkle of the tea-bell.

"Oh, dear!" she cried, "there's tea, and I have not finished my letter to Elsie. Where has the afternoon gone? How splendid it has been! I wish I could have four letters every day as long as I live."

CHAPTER 11

CHRISTMAS BOXES

October was a delightful month, clear and sparkling; but early in November the weather changed, and became very cold. Thick frosts fell, every leaf vanished from the woods, in the gardens only blackened stalks remained to show where once the summer flowers had been. In spite of the stove outside the door, No. 2 began to be chilly. More than once Katy found her tooth-brush stiff with ice in the morning. It was a foretaste of what winter was to be, and the girls shivered at the prospect.

Toward the end of November Miss Jane caught a heavy cold. Unsparing of herself as of others, she went on hearing her classes as usual; and nobody paid much attention to her hoarseness and flushed cheeks, until she grew so much worse that she was forced to go to bed. There she stayed for nearly four weeks. It made a great change in the school, and the girls found it such a relief to have her sharp voice and eyes taken away, that I am afraid they were rather glad of her illness than otherwise.

Katy shared in this feeling of relief. She did not like Miss Jane; it was pleasant not to have to see or hear of her. But as day after day passed, and still she continued ill, Katy's conscience began to prick. One night she lay awake a long time, and heard Miss Jane coughing violently. Katy feared she was very sick, and wondered who took care of her all night and all day. None of the girls went near her. The servants were always busy. And Mrs. Nipson, who did not love Miss Jane, was busy too.

In the morning, while studying and practising, Katy caught herself thinking over this question. At last she asked Miss Marsh—

"How is Miss Jane to-day?"

"About the same. She is not dangerously ill, the doctor says; but she coughs a great deal, and has some fever."

"Is anybody sitting with her?"

"Oh, no! there is no need of anyone. Susan answers the bell, and she has her medicine on the table within reach."

It sounded forlorn enough. Katy had lived in a sick-room so long herself that she knew just how dreary it is for an invalid to be left alone with medicine within reach," and some one to answer a bell. She began to feel sorry for Miss Jane, and almost without intending it went down to the entry, and tapped at her door. The "Come in!" sounded very faint; and Miss Jane as she lay in bed looked weak and dismal, and quite unlike the sharp, terrible person whom the girls feared so much. She was amazed at the sight of Katy, and made a feeble attempt to hold up her head and speak as usual.

"What is it, Miss Carr?"

"I only came to see how you are," said Katy, abashed at her own daring, "you coughed so much last night that I was afraid you were worse. Isn't there something I could do for you?"

"Thank you," said Miss Jane, "you are very kind.

Think of Miss Jane's thanking anybody, and calling anybody kind!

"I should be very glad. Isn't there anything? repeated Katy, encouraged.

Well, I don't know; you might put another stick of wood on the fire," said Miss Jane, in an ungracious tone.

149

Katy did so; and seeing that the iron cup on top of the stove was empty, she poured some water into it. Then she took a look about the room. Books and papers were scattered over the table; clean clothes from the wash lay on the chairs; nothing was in its place; and Katy, who knew how particular Miss Jane was on the subject of order, guessed at the discomfort which this untidy state of affairs must have caused her.

"Wouldn't you like to have me put these away? she asked, touching the pile of clothes.

Miss Jane sighed impatiently, but she did not say no; so Katy, taking silence for consent, opened the drawers, and laid the clothes inside, guessing at the right places with a sort of instinct, and making as little noise and bustle as possible. Next she moved quietly to the table, where she sorted and arranged the papers, piled up the books, and put the pens and pencils in a small tray which stood there for the purpose. Lastly, she began to dust the table with her pocket handkerchief, which proceeding roused Miss Jane at once.

"Don't," she said, "there is a duster in the cupboard.

Katy could not help smiling; but she found the duster, and proceeded to put the rest of the room into nice order, laying a fresh towel over the bedside table, and arranging watch, medicine, and spoon within reach. Miss Jane lay and watched her. I think she was as much surprised at herself for permitting all this as Katy was at being permitted to do it. Sick people often consent because they feel too weak to object. After all, it was comfortable to have some one come in and straighten the things which for ten days past had vexed her neat eyes with their untidiness.

Lastly, smoothing the quilt, Katy asked if Miss Jane wouldn't like to have her pillow shaken up?

150

I don't care," was the answer.

It sounded discouraging; but Katy boldly seized the pillow, beat, smoothed, and put it again in place. Then she went out of the room as noiselessly as she could, Miss Jane never saying, Thank you, or seeming to observe whether she went or stayed.

Rose Red and Clover could hardly believe their ears when told where she had been. They stared at her as people stare at Van Amburgh when he comes safely out of the lion's den.

"My stars!" exclaimed Rose, drawing a long breath. You didn't really? And she hasn't bitten your head off!"

"Not a bit," said Katy, laughing. "What's more, I'm going again. n

She was as good as her word. After that she went to see Miss Jane very often. Almost always there was some little thing which she could do—the fire needed mending, or the pitcher to be filled with ice-water, or Miss Jane wanted the blinds opened or shut. Gradually she grew used to seeing Katy about the room. One morning she actually allowed her to brush her hair; and Katy's touch was so light and pleasant that afterwards Miss Jane begged her to do it every day.

"What makes you such a good nurse?" she asked one afternoon, rather abruptly.

Being sick myself," replied Katy, gently.

Then, in answer to further questioning, she told of her four years' illness, and her life upstairs, keeping house and studying lessons all alone by herself. Miss Jane did not say anything when she got through; but Katy fancied that she looked at her in a new and kinder way.

So time went on till Christmas. It fell on a Friday that year, which shortened the holidays by a day, and disappointed many of the girls. Only a few went home, the rest were left to pass the time as best they might till Monday, when lessons were to begin again.

"It isn't much like merry Christmas," sighed Clover to herself, as she looked up at the uncottoned space at the top of the window, and saw great snowflakes wildly whirling by. No. 2 felt cold and dreary, and she was glad to exchange it for the schoolroom, round whose warm stove a cluster of girls was huddling. Everybody was in bad spirits; there was a tendency to talk about home, and the nice time which people were having there, and the very bad time they themselves were having at the Nunnery.

"Isn't it mis-e-ra-ble? I shall cry all night, I know I shall, I am so homesick," gulped Lilly, who had taken possession of her roommate's shoulder and was weeping ostentatiously.

"I declare, you're just Mrs. Gummidge in 'David Copperfield' over again," said Rose. "You recollect her, girls, don't you? When the porridge was burnt, you know—'All of us felt the disappointment, but Mrs. Gummidge felt it the most'. Isn't Lilly a real Mrs. Gummidge girls?"

This observation changed Lilly's tears into anger. "You're as hateful and as horrid as you can be, Rose Red!" she exclaimed, angrily. Then she flew out of the room, and shut the door behind her with a bang.

"There! she's gone upstairs cross," said Louisa Agnew.

"I don't care if she has," replied Rose, who was in a perverse mood.

"I wish you hadn't said that, Rosy," whispered Clover. "Lilly really felt badly."

"Well, what if she did? So do I feel badly, and you, and the rest of us. Lilly hasn't taken out a patent for bad feelings, which nobody must infringe. What business

152

has she to make us feel badder by setting up to be so much worse off than the rest of the world?"

Clover said nothing, but went on with a book she was reading. In less than ten minutes, Rose, whose sun seldom stayed long behind a cloud, was at her elbow, dimpling and coaxing.

"I forgive you," she whispered, giving Clover's arm a little pinch.

"What for?"

"For being in the right. About Lilly, I mean. I was rather hateful to her, I confess. Never mind. When she comes downstairs, I'll make up for it. She's a crocodile, if ever there was one; but, as she's your cousin, I'll be good to her. Kiss me quick to prove that you're not vexed."

"Vexed, indeed!" said Clover, kissing the middle of the pink cheek. "I wonder if anybody ever stayed vexed with you for ten minutes together, you Rosy-Posy you!"

"Bless you, yes! Miss Jane, for example. She hates me like poison, and all the time. Well, what of it? I know she's sick, but I 'can't tell a lie, pa', on that account. Where's Katy?"

"Gone in to see her, I believe."

"One of these days," prophesied Rose, solemnly, "she'll go into that room, and she'll never come out again! Miss Jane is getting back into biting condition. I advise Katy to be careful. What's that noise? Sleigh-bells, I declare! Girls"—mounting a desk, and peeping out of the window—"somebody's got a big box—a big one! Here's old Joyce at the door, with his sledge. Now whose do you suppose it is?"

"It's for me! I'm sure it's for me!" cried half a dozen voices.

"Bella, my love, peep over the balusters, and see if you can't see the name," cried Louisa; and Bella, nothing loath, departed at once on this congenial errand.

"No, I can't," she reported, coming back from the hall. "The name's tipped up against the wall. There's two boxes! One is big, and one is little!"

"Oh, who can they be for?" clamoured the girls. Half the school expected boxes, and had been watching the storm all day, with a dreadful fear that it would block the roads, and delay the expected treasures.

At this moment Mrs. Nipson came in.

"There will be the usual study-hour this evening," she announced. "All of you will prepare lessons for Monday morning. Miss Carr, come here for a moment, if you please."

Clover, wondering, followed her into the entry.

"A parcel has arrived for you, and a box," said Mrs. Nipson. "I presume that they contain articles for Christmas. I will have the nails removed, and both of them placed in your room this evening, but I expect you to refrain from examining them until to-morrow. The vacation does not open until after study-hour to-night, and it will then be too late for you to begin."

"Very well, ma'am," said Clover, demurely. But the minute Mrs. Nipson's back was turned, she gave a jump, and rushed into the schoolroom.

"o girls," she cried, "what do you think? Both the boxes are for Katy and me."

"Both!" cried a disappointed chorus.

"Yes, both. Mrs. Nipson said so. I'm so sorry for you. But isn't it nice for us? We never had a box from home before, you know; and I didn't think we should, it's so far off. It's too lovely! But I do hope yours will come to-night."

Clover's voice was so sympathising, for all its glee, that nobody could help being glad with her.

"You little darling! said Louisa, giving her a hug. "I'm rejoiced that the box is yours. The rest of us are always getting them, and you and Katy never had a thing before. I hope it's a nice one!"

"Oh, it's sure to be nice! It's from home, you know," responded Clover, with a happy smile. Then she left the room to find Katy, and tell the wonderful news.

Study-hour seemed unusually long that night. The minute it was over, the sisters ran to No. 2. There stood the boxes, a big wooden one, with all the nails taken out of the lid, and a small paper one, carefully tied up and sealed. It was almost more than the girls could do to obey orders and not peep.

"I feel something hard," announced Clover, inserting a finger-tip under the lid.

Oh, do you?" cried Katy. Then, making an heroic effort, she jumped into bed.

"It's the only way," she said, "you'd better come, too, Clovy. Blow the candle out, and let's get to sleep as fast as we can, so as to make morning come quicker."

Katy dreamed of home that night. Perhaps it was that which made her wake so early. It was not five o'clock, and the room was perfectly dark. She did not like to disturb Clover, so she lay perfectly still, for hours as it seemed, till a faint grey dawn crept in, and revealed the outlines of the big box standing by the window. Then she could wait no longer, but crept out of bed, crossed the floor on tiptoe, and raising the lid a little put in her hand. Something crumb and sugary met it, and when she drew it out, there, fitting on her finger like a ring, was a round cake with a hole in the middle of it.

"Oh! it's one of Debby's jumbles!" she exclaimed.

"Where? What are you doing? Give me one too!" cried Clover, starting up. Katy rummaged till she found another, then, half frozen, she ran back to bed; and the two lay nibbling the jumbles, and talking about home,

155

till dawn deepened into daylight, and morning was fairly come.

Breakfast was half an hour later than usual, which was comfortable. As soon as it was over, the girls proceeded to unpack their box. The day was so cold that they wrapped themselves in shawls, and Clover put on a hood and thick gloves. Rose Red, passing the door, burst out laughing, and recommended that she should add india-rubber boots and an umbrella.

"Oh, come in," cried the sisters, "come in, and help us open our box! "

" Oh, by the way, you have a box, haven't you?" said Rose, who was perfectly aware of the important fact, and had presented herself with the hope of being asked to look on. "Thank you, but perhaps I would better come some other time. I shall be in your way."

"You impostor!" said Clover, while Katy seized Rose and pulled her into the room. "There, sit on the bed, you ridiculous goose, and put on my grey cloak. How can you be so absurd as to say you won't? You know we want you, and you know you came on purpose!"

"Did I? Well perhaps I did," laughed Rose. Then Katy lifted off the lid, and set it against the door. It was an exciting moment.

"Just look here!ⁿ cried Katy.

The top of the box was mostly taken up with four square paper boxes, round which parcels of all shapes and sizes were wedged and fitted. The whole was a miracle of packing. It had taken Miss Finch three mornings, with assistance from old Mary, and much advice from Elsie, to do it so beautifully.

Each box held a different kind of cake. One was full of jumbles, another of ginger-snaps, a third of crullers, and the fourth contained a big square loaf of frosted plum-cake, with a circle of sugar almonds set in the frosting. How the trio exclaimed at this!

"I never imagined anything so nice," declared Rose, with her mouth full of jumble. "As for those snaps, they're simply perfect. What can be in all those fascinating bundles? Do hurry and open one, Katy."

Dear little Elsie! The first two bundles opened were hers—a white hood for Katy, and a blue one for Clover, both of her own knitting, and so nicely done. The girls were enchanted.

"How she has improved!" said Katy. "She knits better than either of us, Clover."

"There never was such a clever little darling!" responded Clover; and they patted the hoods, tried them on before the glass, and spent so much time in admiring them that Rose grew impatient.

"I declare," she cried, "it isn't any of my funeral, I know, but if you don't open another parcel soon, I shall certainly fall to myself. It seems as if, what with cold and curiosity, I couldn't wait."

"Very well," said Katy, laying aside her hood, with one final glance. "Take out a bundle, Clover. It's your turn."

Clover's bundle was for herself, "Evangeline" in blue and gold, and pretty soon the "Golden Legend," in the same binding, appeared for Katy. Both these were from Dorry. Next came a couple of round packages of exactly the same size. These proved to be inkstands, covered with Russia leather—one marked, "Katy, from Johnnie," and the other "Clover, from Phil." It was evident that the children had done their shopping together, for presently two long, narrow parcels revealed carved penhandles, precisely alike; and these were labelled, "Katy, from Phil," and "Clover, from Johnnie."

What fun it was opening those bundles! The girls made a long business of it, taking out but one at a time, exclaiming, admiring, and exhibiting to Rose, before they began upon another. They laughed, they joked, but I do not think it would have taken much to make either of them cry. It was almost too tender a pleasure—these proofs of loving remembrance from the little ones; and each separate article seemed full of the very look and feel of home.

"What can this be?" said Katy, as she unrolled a paper and disclosed a pretty round box. She opened. Nothing was visible but pink cotton wool. Katy peeped beneath, and gave a cry.

"Oh, Clovy! such a lovely thing! It's from papa—of course, it's from papa! How could he? It's a great deal too pretty."

The "lovely thing" was a long slender chain for Katy's watch, worked in fine yellow gold. Clover admired it extremely; and her joy knew no bounds when farther search revealed another box with a precisely similar chain for herself. It was too much. The girls fairly cried with pleasure.

There never was such a papa in the world," they said.

"Yes, there is; mine is just as good," declared Rose, twinkling away a little tear-drop from her own eyes. Now, don't cry, honeys. Your papa's an angel, there's no doubt about it. I never saw such pretty chains in my life—never. As for the children, they're little ducks. You certainly are a wonderful family. Katy, I'm dying to know what is in that blue parcel."

The blue parcel was from Cecy, and contained a pretty blue ribbon for Clover. There was a pink one also, with a pink ribbon for Katy. Everybody had thought of the girls. Old Mary sent them each a yard measure; Miss Finch, a thread-case, stocked with differently coloured cottons. Alexander had cracked a bag full of hickory nuts.

"Did you ever? said Rose, when this last was produced. "What a thing it is to be popular! Mrs. Hall! Who's Mrs. Hall?" as Clover unwrapped a tiny carved easel.

"She's Cecy's mother," explained Clover. "Wasn't she kind to send me this, Katy? And here's Cecy's photograph in a little frame for you."

Never was such a wonderful box. It appeared to have no bottom whatever. Under the presents were parcels of figs, prunes, almonds, raisins, candy; under those, apples and pears. There seemed no end to the surprises.

At last all were out.

"Now," said Katy, "let's throw back the apples and pears, and then I want you to help me divide the other things, and make up some packages for the girls. They are all so disappointed not to have their boxes. I should like to have them share ours. Wouldn't you, Clover?"

"Yes, indeed; I was just going to propose it."

So Clover cut twenty-nine squares of white paper, Rose and Katy sorted and divided, and pretty soon ginger-snaps and almonds and sugar-plums were walking down all the entries, and a gladsome crunching showed that the girls had found pleasant employment. None of the snowed-up boxes got through till Monday, so except for Katy and Clover the school would have had no Christmas treat at all.

They carried Mrs. Nipson a large slice of cake, and a basket full of the beautiful red apples. All the teachers were remembered, and the servants. The S.S.U.C. was convened and feasted; and as for Rose, Louisa, and other special cronies, dainties were heaped upon them with such unsparing hand that they finally remonstrated.

"You're giving everything away. You'll have none left for yourselves.

"Yes, we shall—plenty," said Clover. 4Oh, Rosy! here's such a splendid pear! You must have this."

"No, no!" protested Rose; but Clover forced it into her pocket.

"The Carrs' Box" was always quoted in the Nunnery afterwards, as an example of what papas and mammas could accomplish, when they were of the right sort, and really wanted to make schoolgirls happy. Distributing their treasures kept Katy and Clover so busy that it was not until after dinner that they found time to open the smaller box. When they did so, they were sorry for the delay. The box was full of flowers—roses, geranium-leaves, heliotrope, beautiful red and white carnations, all so bedded in cotton that the frost had not touched them. But they looked chilled, and Katy hastened to put them in warm water, which she had been told was the best way to revive drooping flowers.

Cousin Helen had sent them; and underneath, sewed to the box, that they might not shake about and do mischief, were two flat parcels, wrapped in tissue paper, and tied with white ribbon, in Cousin Helen's dainty way. They were glove-cases, of quilted silk, delicately scented, one white, and one lilac; and to each was pinned a loving note, wishing the girls a Merry Christmas.

"How awfully good people are! said Clover. 4I do think we ought to be the best girls in the world.

Last of all, Katy made a choice little selection from her stores, a splendid apple, a couple of fine pears, a handful of raisins and figs, and, with a few of the freshest flowers in a wine-glass, she went down the Row and tapped at Miss Jane's door.

Miss Jane was sitting up for the first time, wrapped in a shawl, and looking very thin and pale. Katy, who had almost ceased to be afraid of her, went in cheerily.

"We've had a splendid box from home, Miss Jane, full of all sorts of things. It has been such fun unpacking it. I've brought an apple, and some pears, and this little bunch of flowers. Wasn't it a nice Christmas for us?

"Yes," said Miss Jane, "very nice indeed. I heard some one saying in the entry that you had a box. Thank you,q as Katy set the basket and glass on the table. "Those flowers are very sweet. I wish you a Merry Christmas, I'm sure."

This was much from Miss Jane, who could not help speaking shortly, even when she was pleased. Katy withdrew in high glee.

But that night, just before bed-time, something happened so surprising that Katy, telling Clover about it afterward, said she half fancied that she must have dreamed it all. It was about eight o'clock in the evening: she was passing down Quaker Row, and Miss Jane called and asked her to come in. Miss Jane's cheeks were flushed, and she spoke fast, as if she had resolved to say something, and thought the sooner it was over the better.

"Miss Carr," she began, I wish to tell you that I made up my mind some time since that we did you an injustice last term. It is not your attentions to me during my illness which have changed my opinion—that was done before I fell ill. It is your general conduct, and the good influence which I have seen you exert over other girls, which convinced me that we must have been wrong about you. That is all. I thought you might like to hear me say this, and I shall say the same to Mrs. Nipson."

161

"Thank you," said Katy, "you don't know how glad I am!" She half thought she would kiss Miss Jane, but somehow it didn't seem possible; so she shook hands very heartily instead, and flew to her room, feeling as if her feet were wings.

"It seems too good to be true. I want to cry, I am so happy," she told Clover. "What a lovely day this has been!"

And of all that she had received, I think Katy considered this explanation with Miss Jane as her very best Christmas box.

CHAPTER 12

WAITING FOR SPRING

School was a much happier place after this. Mrs. Nipson never alluded to the matter, but her manner altered. Katy felt that she was no longer watched or distrusted, and her heart grew light.

In another week Miss Jane was so much better as to be hearing her classes again. Illness had not changed her materially. It is only in novels that rheumatic fever sweetens tempers, and makes disagreeable people over into agreeable ones. Most of the girls disliked her as much as ever. Her tongue was just as sharp, and her manner as grim. But for Katy, from that time forward, there was a difference. Miss Jane was not affectionate to her—it was not in her nature to be that—but she was civil and considerate, and, in a dry way, friendly; and gradually Katy grew to have an odd sort of liking for her.

Do any of you know how incredibly long winter seems in climates where for weeks together the thermometer stands at zero? There is something hopeless in such cold. You think of summer as of a thing read about somewhere in a book, but which has no actual existence. Winter seems the only reality in the world.

Katy and Clover felt this hopelessness growing upon them as the days went on, and the weather grew more and more severe. Ten, twenty, even thirty degrees below zero, was no unusual register for the Hillsover thermometers. Such cold half-frightened them, but nobody else was frightened or surprised. It was dry, brilliant cold. The December snows lay unmelted on the ground in March, and the paths cut then were crisp and hard still, only the white walls on either side had risen higher and higher, till only a moving line of hoods and tippets was visible above them, when the school went out for its daily walk. Morning after morning the girls woke to find thick crusts of frost on their window-panes, and every drop of water in wash-bowl or pitcher turned to solid ice. Night after night, Clover, who was a chilly little creature, lay shivering and unable to sleep, notwithstanding the hot bricks at her feet, and the many wraps which Katy piled upon her. To Katy herself the cold was more bracing than depressing. There was something in her blood which responded to the sharp tingle of frost, and she gained in strength in a remarkable way during this winter. But the long storms told upon her spirits. She pined for spring and home more than she liked to tell, and felt the need of variety in their monotonous life, where the creeping days appeared like weeks, and the weeks stretched themselves out, and seemed as long as months do in other places.

The girls resorted to all sorts of devices to keep themselves alive during this dreary season. They had little epidemics of occupation. At one time it was "spattering", when all faces and fingers had a tendency to smudges of India ink; and there was hardly a fine comb or tooth-brush fit for use in the establishment. Then a rage for tatting set in, followed by a fever of fancy-work, every one falling in love with the same pattern at the same time, and copying and re-copying, till nobody could bear the sight of it. At one time Clover counted eighteen girls all at work on the same bead and canvas pin-cushion. Later there was a short period of *decalcomanie*; and then came the grand album craze, when thirty-three girls out of the thirty-nine sent for blank books bound in red morocco, and began to collect signatures and sentiments. Here, also, there was a tendency toward repetition.

Sally Austin added to her autograph these lines of her own composition:—

"When on this page your beauteous eyes you bend,
Let it remind you of your absent friend,

SALLY J. AUSTIN,
Galveston, Texas."

The girls found this sentiment charming, at least a dozen borrowed it, and in half the albums in the school you might read,—

"When on this page your beauteous eyes," &c.

Esther Dearborn wrote in Clover's book: "The better part of valour is discretion." Why she wrote it nobody knew, or why it was more applicable to Clover than to any one; but the sentiment proved popular, and was repeated over and over again, above various neatly-written signatures. There was a strife as to whom should display the largest collection. Some of the girls sent home for autographs of distinguished persons, which they pasted in their books. Rose Red, however, outdid them all.

"Did I ever show you mine?" she asked one day, when most of the girls were together in the school-room.

"No, never!" cried a number of voices. "Have you got one? Oh, do let us see it!"

"Certainly, I'll get it right away, if you like," said Rose, obligingly.

She went to her room, and returned with a shabby old blank book in her hand. Some of the girls looked disappointed.

"The cover of mine isn't very nice," explained Rose. "I'm going to have it re-bound one of these days. You see it's not a new album at all, nor a school album; but it's very valuable to me." Here she heaved a sentimental sigh. "All my friends have written in it," she said.

The girls were quite impressed by the manner in which Rose said this. But, when they turned over the pages of the album, they were even more impressed. Rose had evidently been on intimate terms with a circle of most distinguished persons. Half the autographs in the book were from gentlemen, and they were dated all over the world.

"Just listen to this! " cried Louisa, and she read—

"Thou may'st forget me, but never, never shall I forget thee!

"ALPHONSO OF CASTILE"

"THE ESCURIAL, April Ist."

"Who's he?" asked a circle of awe-struck girls.

"Didn't you ever hear of him? Youngest brother of the King of Spain," replied Rose, carelessly.

"Oh, my! and just hear this," exclaimed Annie Silsbie—

"If you ever deign to cast a thought in my direction, Miss Rose, remember me always as

Thy devoted servitor,
POTEMKIN MONTMORENCY

"And this!" shrieked Alice White—

"They say love is a thorn. I say it is a dart,
And yet I cannot tear thee from my heart.

"ANTONIO COUNT OF VALAMBROSA."

"Do you really and truly know a count?" asked Bella, backing away from Rose, with eyes as big as saucers. "Know Antonio de Valambrosa? I should think I did," replied Rose. "Nobody in this country knows him so well, I fancy."

"And he wrote that for you?"

"How else could it get into my book, goosey?"

This was unanswerable, and Rose was installed from that time forward in the minds of Bella and the rest as a heroine of the first water. Katy, however, knew better, and the first time she caught Rose alone she attacked her on the subject.

"Now, Rosy-Posy, confess. Who wrote all those absurd autographs in your book?"

"Absurd autographs! What do you mean?"

"All those counts and things. No, it's no use; you shan't wriggle away till you tell me."

"Oh, Antonio and dear Potemkin, do you mean them?"

"Yes, of course I do."

"And you really want to know?"

"Yes."

"And will you swear not to tell?"

"Yes."

"Well, then," bursting into a laugh, "I wrote every one of them myself."

"Did you really? When?"

167

"Day before yesterday. I thought Lilly needed taking down, she was so set up with her autographs of Wendell Phillips and Mr. Seward, so I just sat down and wrote a book full. It only took me half an hour. I meant to write some more; in fact, I had one all ready,—

"I am dead, or pretty near:
David's done for me I fear.

"Goliath of Gath";

but I was afraid even Bella wouldn't swallow that, so I tore out the page. I'm sorry I did now, for I really think the geese would have believed it. Written in his last moments, you know, to oblige an ancestor of my own," added Rose, in a tone of explanation.

"You monkey!" cried Katy, highly diverted. But she kept Rose's counsel, and I dare say some of the Hillsover girls believe in that wonderful album to this day.

It was not long after that a sad piece of news came for Bella. Her father was dead. Their home was in Sorra, too far to allow of her returning for the funeral; so the poor little girl stayed at school, to bear her trouble as best she might. Katy, who was always kind to children, and had somewhat affected Bella from the first on account of her resemblance to Elsie in height and figure, was specially tender to her now, which Bella repaid with the gift of her whole queer little heart. Her affectionate demonstrations were rather of the monkey order, and not infrequently troublesome; but Katy was never otherwise than patient and gentle with her, though Rose, and even Clover, remonstrated on what they called this singular intimacy."

"Poor little soul! it's so hard for her, and she's only eleven years old," she told them.

"She has such a funny way of looking at you sometimes," said Rose, who was very observant. "It is just the air of a squirrel who has hidden a nut, and doesn't want you to find out where, and yet can hardly help indicating it with his paw. She's got something on her mind, I'm sure."

"Half a dozen things very likely," added Clover; "she's such a mischief."

But none of them guessed what this "something" was.

Early in January Mrs. Nipson announced that in four weeks she proposed to give a "soiree," to which all young ladies whose records were entirely free from marks during the intervening period would be allowed to come. This announcement created great excitement, and the school set itself to be good; but marks were easy to get, and gradually one girl after another lost her chance, till by the appointed day only a limited party descended to join the festivities, and nearly half the school was left upstairs to sigh over past sins. Katy and Rose were among the unlucky ones. Rose had incurred a mark by writing a note in study-hour, and Katy by being five minutes late to dinner. They consoled themselves by dressing Clover's hair, and making her look as pretty as possible, and then stationed themselves in the upper hall at the head of the stairs to watch her career, and get as much fun out of the occasion as they could.

Pretty soon they saw Clover below on Professor Seccomb's arm. He was a kindly, pleasant man, with a bald head, and it was a fashion among the girls to admire him.

"Doesn't she look pretty?" said Rose. "Just look at Mrs. Searles, Katy. She's grinning at Clover like the Cheshire cat. What a wonderful cap that is of hers. She had it when Sylvia was here at school, eight years ago."

"Hush! she'll hear you."

"No, she won't! There's Ellen beginning her piece. I know she's frightened by the way she plays. Hark! how she hurries the time! n

"There! they're going to have refreshments, after all!r cried Esther Dearborn, as trays of lemonade and cake-baskets appeared below on their way to the parlour. "Isn't it a shame to have to stay up here?"

"Professor Seccomb! Professor!" called Rose, in a daring whisper. "Take pity upon us. We are starving for a piece of cake."

The Professor gave a jump, then retreated, and looked upward. When he saw the circle of hungry faces peering down, he doubled up with laughter. Wait a moment, n he whispered back, and vanished into the parlour. Pretty soon the girls saw him making his way through the crowd with an immense slice of pound-cake in each hand.

"Here, Miss Rose," he said, "catch it." But Rose ran half-way downstairs, received the cake, dimpled her thanks, and retreated to the darkness above, whence sounds proceeded which sent the amused Professor into the parlour convulsed with suppressed laughter. Pretty soon Clover stole up the backstairs to report.

Are you having a nice time? Is the lemonade good? Who have you been talking with?" inquired a chorus of voices.

"Pretty nice. Everybody is very old. I haven't been talking to anybody in particular, and the lemonade is only cream-of-tartar water. I think it's joliier up here with you," replied Clover. I must go now; my turn to play comes next." Down she ran.

"Except for the glory of the thing, I think we're having more fun than she," answered Rose.

Next week came St. Valentine's Day. Several of the girls received valentines from home, and they wrote them to each other. Katy and Clover both had one from Phil, exactly alike, with the same purple bird in the middle of the page, and "I love you" printed underneath; and they joined in fabricating a gorgeous one for Rose, which was supposed to come from Potemkin de Montmorency, the hero of the album. But the most surprising valentine was received by Miss Jane. It came with the others, while all the household were at dinner. The girls saw her redden and look angry, but she put the letter in her pocket, and said nothing.

In the afternoon, it came out through Bella that "Miss Jane's letter was in poetry, and that she was just as cross as possible about it." Just before tea, Louisa came running down the Row, to No. 5, where Katy was sitting with Rose.

Girls, what do you think? That letter which Miss Jane got this morning was a valentine, the most dreadful thing, but so funny!" she stopped to laugh.

"How do you know?" cried the other two.

"Miss Marsh told Alice Gibbons. She's a sort of cousin, you know; and Miss Marsh often tells her things. She says Miss Jane and Mrs. Nipson are furious, and are determined to find out who sent it. It was from Mr. Hardhack, Miss Jane's missionary—or no, not from Mr. Hardhack, but from a cannibal who had just eaten Mr. Hardhack up; and he sent Miss Jane a lock of his hair, and the recipe the tribe cooked him by. They found him 'very nice,' he said, and 'He turned out quite tender.' That was one of the lines in the poem. Did you ever hear anything like it? Who do you suppose sent it?"

Who could it have been?" cried the others. Katy had one moment's awful misgiving; but a glance at Rose's face, calm and innocent as a baby's, reassured her. It was impossible that she could have done this mischievous thing. Katy, you see, was not privy to that entry in Rose's journal, "Pay Miss Jane off," nor aware that Rose had just written underneath, "Did it. Feb. 14,1869."

Nobody ever found out the author of this audacious valentine. Rose kept her own counsel, and Miss Jane probably concluded that "the better part of valour was discretion," for the threatened inquiries were never made.

And now it lacked but six weeks to the end of the term. The girls counted the days, and practised various devices to make them pass more quickly. Esther Dearborn, who had a turn for arithmetic, set herself to a careful calculation of how many hours, minutes, and seconds must pass before the happy time should come. Annie Silsbie strung forty-two tiny squares of cardboard on a thread, and each night slipped one off and burned it up in the candle. Others made diagrams of the time, with a division for each day, and every night scored off one with a sense of triumph. None of these devices made the time hasten. It never moved more slowly than now.

But though Katy's heart bounded at the thought of home till she could hardly bear the gladness, she owned to Clover, "Do you know, much as I long to get away, I am half sorry to go! It is parting with something which we shall never have any more. Home is lovely, and I would rather be there than anywhere else; but if you and I live to be a hundred, we shall never be girls at boarding-school again.

CHAPTER 13

"PARADISE REGAINED

"Only seven days more to cross Off," said Clover, drawing her pencil through one of the squares on the diagram pinned beside her looking-glass, "seven more, and then—oh, joy!—papa will be here, and we shall start for home."

She was interrupted by the entrance of Katy, holding a letter, and looking pale and aggrieved.

"Oh, Clover," she cried, "just listen to this! Papa can't come for us. Isn't it too bad?" And she read:—

"*Burnet, March 20th.*

MY DEAR Girls,,—

"I find that it will not be possible for me to come for you next week, as I intended. Several people are severely ill, and old Mrs. Barlow struck down suddenly with paralysis, so I cannot leave. I am sorry, and so will you be; but there is no help for it. Fortunately, Mrs. Hall has just heard that some friends of hers are coming westward with their family, and she has written to ask them to take charge of you. The drawback to this plan is, that you will have to travel alone as far as Albany, where Mr. Peters (Mrs. Hall's friend) will meet you. I have written to ask Mr. Page to see you in the train, and under the care of the guard, on Tuesday morning. I hope you will get through without embarrassment. Mr. Peters will be at the station in Albany to receive you; or, if anything should hinder him, you are to drive at once to the Delavan House, where they are staying. I enclose a cheque for your journey. If Dorry were five years older, I should send him after you.

"The children are most impatient to have you back. Miss Finch has been suddenly called away by the illness of her sister-in-law, so Elsie is keeping house till your return.

"God bless you, my dear daughters, and send you safe.

"Yours affectionately,
"P. CARR."

"Oh, dear!" said Clover, with her lip trembling, "now Papa won't see Rosy."

"No," said Katy, "and Rosy and Louisa, and the rest won't see him. That is the worst of all. I wanted them to so much. And just think how dismal it will be to travel with people we don't know. It's too—too bad, I declare."

"I do think old Mrs. Barlow might have put off being ill just one week longer," grumbled Clover. "It takes away half the pleasure of going home."

The girls might be excused for being cross, for this was a great disappointment. There was no help for it, however, as Papa said. They could only sigh and submit. But the journey, to which they had looked forward so much, was no longer thought of as a pleasure, only a disagreeable necessity, something which must be endured in order that they might reach home.

Five, four, three days—the last little square was crossed off, the last dinner was eaten, the last breakfast. There was much mourning over Katy and Clover among the girls who were to return for another year. Louisa and Ellen Gray were inconsolable; and Bella, with a very small pocket-handkerchief held tightly in her hand, clung to Katy every moment, crying, and declaring that she would not let her go. The last evening she followed her into No. 2 (where she was dreadfully in the way of the packing), and after various odd contortions and mysterious half-spoken sentences, she said—

"Say, won't you tell if I tell you something?"

"What is it?" asked Katy, absently, as she folded and smoothed her best gown.

"Something," repeated Bella, wagging her head mysteriously, and looking more like a thievish squirrel than ever.

"Well, what is it? Tell me."

To Katy's surprise, Bella burst into a violent fit of crying.

"I'm very sorry I did it," she sobbed—"very sorry! And now you'll never love me any more."

"Yes, I will. What is it? Do stop crying, Bella, dear, and tell me," said Katy, alarmed at the violence of the sobs.

"It was for fun, really and truly it was. But I wanted some cake too," protested Bella, sniffing very hard.

"What! "

"And I didn't think anybody would know. Berry Searles doesn't care a bit for us little girls, only for big ones. And I knew if I said 'Bella' he'd never give me the cake. So I said 'Miss Carr' instead."

"Bella, did you write that note?" inquired Katy, almost too surprised to speak.

"Yes. And I tied a string to your blind, because I knew I could go in and draw it up when you were practising. But I didn't mean to do any harm; and when Mrs. Florence was so cross, and changed your room, I was very sorry," moaned Bella, digging her knuckles into her eyes. "Won't you ever love me any more?" she demanded.

Katy lifted her into her lap, and talked so tenderly and seriously that her contrition, which was only half genuine, became real; and she cried in good earnest when Katy kissed her in token of forgiveness.

"Of course, you'll go at once to Mrs. Nipson," said Clover and Rose, when Katy imparted this surprising discovery.

"No, I think not. Why should I? It would only get poor little Bella into a dreadful scrape, and she's coming back again, you know. Mrs. Nipson does not believe that story now—nobody does. We have 'lived it down,' just as I hoped we should. That is much better than having it contradicted."

"I don't think so; and I should enjoy seeing that little wretch of a Bella well whipped," persisted Rose.

But Katy was not to be shaken.

"To please me, promise that not a word shall be said about it," she urged; and to please her the girls consented.

I think Katy was right in saying that Mrs. Nipson no longer believed her guilty in the affair of the note. She had been very friendly to both the sisters of late; and when Clover carried in her album and asked for an autograph, she waxed quite sentimental and wrote, "I would not exchange the modest Clover for the most brilliant flower in our beautiful parterre, so bring it back I pray thee, to your affectionate teacher, Marianne Nipson"; which effusion quite overwhelmed "the modest Clover," and called out the remark from Rose— "Don't she wish she may get you!" Miss Jane said twice, "I shall miss you, Katy," a speech which, to quote Rose again, made Katy look as "surprised as Balaam." Rose herself was not coming back to school. She and the girls were half broken-hearted at parting. They lavished

176

tears, kisses, promises of letters, and vows of eternal friendship. Neither of them, it was agreed, was ever to love anybody else so well. The final moment would have been almost too tragical, had it not been for a last bit of mischief on the part of Rose. It was after the stage was actually at the door, and she had her foot upon the step that, struck by a happy thought, she rushed upstairs again, collected the girls, and, each taking a window, they tore down the cotton, flung open sashes, and startled Mrs. Nipson, who stood below, by the simultaneous waving therefrom of many white flags. Katy, who was already in the stage, had the full benefit of this performance. Always after that, when she thought of the Nunnery, her memory recalled this scene—Mrs. Nipson in the doorway, Bella blubbering behind, and overhead the windows crowded with saucy girls, laughing and triumphantly flapping the long cotton strip which had for so many months obscured the daylight for them all.

At Springfield next morning she and Clover said good-bye to Mr. Page and Lilly. The ride to Albany was easy and safe. With every mile their spirits rose. At last they were actually on the way home.

At Albany they looked anxiously about the crowded depot for "Mr. Peters." Nobody appeared at first, and they had time to grow nervous before they saw a gentle, careworn little man coming toward them in company with the conductor.

"I believe you are the young ladies I have come to meet," he said. You must excuse my being late; I was detained by business. There is a great deal to do to move a family out West"; he wiped his forehead in a dispirited way. Then he put the girls into a carriage, and gave the driver a direction.

We'd better leave your baggage at the office as we pass," he said, "because we have to get off so early in the morning."

"How early?"

"The boat goes at six, but we ought to be on board by half-past five, so as to be well settled before she starts."

"The boat?" said Katy, opening her eyes.

"Yes. Erie Canal, you know. Our furniture goes that way, so we judged it best to do the same, and keep an eye on it ourselves. Never be separated from your property, if you can help it, that's my maxim. It's the 'Prairie Belle'—one of the finest boats on the Canal."

"When do we get to Buffalo?" asked Katy, with an uneasy recollection of having heard that canal boats travel slowly.

"Buffalo? Let me see. This is Tuesday—Wednesday, Thursday— well, if we're lucky we ought to be there Friday evening; so, if we're not too late to catch the night boat on the lake, you'll reach home Saturday afternoon. Yes; I think we may pretty safely say Saturday afternoon."

Four days! The girls looked at each other with dismay too deep for words. Elsie was expecting them by Thursday at latest. What should they do?

"Telegraph," was the only answer that suggested itself. So Katy scribbled a dispatch, "Coming by canal. Don't expect us till Saturday," which she begged Mr. Peters to send; and she and Clover agreed in whispers that it was dreadful, but they must bear it as patiently as they could.

Oh, the patience which is needed on a canal! The motion which is not so much motion as standing still! The crazy impulse to jump out and help the crawling boat along by pushing it from behind! How one grows to hate the slow, monotonous glide, the dull banks, and to envy every swift-moving thing in sight, each man on horseback, each bird lying through the air.

Mrs. Peters was a thin, anxious woman, who spent her life anticipating disasters of all sorts. She had her children with her, three little boys, and a teething baby; and such a load of bundles, and baskets, and brown-paper parcels, that Katy and Clover privately wondered how she could possibly have got through the journey without their help. Willy, the eldest boy, was always begging leave to go ashore and ride the towing horses; Sammy, the second, could only be kept quiet by means of crooked pins and fish-lines of blue yarn; while Paul, the youngest, was possessed with a curiosity as to the under side of the boat, which resulted in his dropping his new hat overboard five times in three days, Mr. Peters and the cabin-boy rowing back in a small boat each time to recover it. Mrs. Peters sat on deck with her baby in her lap, and was in perpetual agony lest the locks should work wrongly, or the boys be drowned, or some one fail to notice the warning cry, "Bridge! " and have their heads carried off from their shoulders. Nobody did; but the poor lady suffered the anguish of ten accidents in dreading the one which never took place. The berths at night were small and cramped, restless children woke and cried, the cabins were close, the decks cold and windy. There was nothing to see, and nothing to do. Katy and Clover agreed that they never wanted to see a canal-boat again.

They were very helpful to Mrs. Peters, amused the boys, and kept them out of mischief; and she told her husband that she really thought she shouldn't have lived through the journey if it hadn't been for the Miss Carrs, they were such kind girls, and so fond of children. But the three days were terribly long. At last they ended. Buffalo was reached in time for the lake boat; and once established on board, feeling the rapid motion, and knowing that each stroke of the paddles took them nearer home, the girls were rewarded for their long trial of patience.

At four o'clock the next afternoon Burnet was in sight. Long before they touched the wharf Clover discovered old Whitey and the carriage, and Alexander, waiting for them among the crowd of carriages. Standing on the edge of the dock appeared a well-known figure.

"Papa! Papa!" she shrieked. It seemed as if the girls could not wait for the boat to stop, and the plank to be lowered. How delightful it was to feel Papa again! Such a sense of home and comfort and shelter as came with his touch!

"I'll never go away from you again, never, never!" repeated Clover, keeping tight hold of his hand as they drove up the hill. Dr. Carr, as he gazed at his girls, was equally happy—they were so bright, so affectionate, and loving. No, he could never spare them again, for board-ing-school or anything else, he thought.

"You must be very tired," he said.

"Not a bit. I'm hardly ever tired now," replied Katy.

"Oh, dear! I forgot to thank Mr. Peters for taking care of us," said Clover.

"Never mind. I did it for you," answered her father.

"Oh, that baby!" she continued; "how glad I am that it has gone to Toledo, and I needn't hear it cry any more! Katy! Katy! there's home! We are at the gate!"

The girls looked eagerly out, but no children were visible. They hurried up the gravel path, under the locust boughs just beginning to bud. There, over the front door, was an arch of evergreens, with "Katy" and

"Clover" upon it in scarlet letters; and as they reached the porch, the door flew open, and out poured the children in a tumultuous little crowd. They had been on the roof, looking through a spy-glass after the boat.

"We never knew you had come till we heard the gate," explained John and Dorry; while Elsie hugged Clover, and Phil, locking his arms round Katy's neck, took his feet off the floor, and swung them in an ecstasy of affection, until she begged for mercy.

"How you are grown! Dorry, you're as tall as I am! Elsie, darling, how well you look. Oh, isn't it delicious, delicious, delicious, to be at home again!" There was such a hubbub of endearments and explanations, that Dr. Carr could hardly make himself heard.

"Clover, your waist has grown as small as a pin. You look just like the beautiful princess in Elsie's story," said Johnnie.

"Take the girls into the parlour," repeated Dr. Carr.

"Take 'em upstairs! You don't know what is upstairs!" shouted Phil, whereupon Elsie frowned and shook her head at him.

The parlour was gay with daffodils and hyacinths and vases of blue violets, which smelt delightfully. Cecy had helped to arrange them, Elsie said. And just at that moment Cecy herself came in. Her hair was arranged in a sort of pin-cushion of puffs, with a row of curls on top, where no curls used to grow, and her appearance generally was very fine and fashionable; but she was the same affectionate Cecy as ever, and hugged the girls, and danced round them as she used to do at twelve. She had waited until they had had time to kiss once all round, she said, and then she really couldn't wait any longer.

"Now, come upstairs," suggested Elsie, when Clover had warmed her feet, and the flowers had been admired, and everybody had said ten times over how nice it was to have the girls back, and the girls had replied that it was just as nice to come back.

So they all went upstairs, Elsie leading the way.

"Where are you going?" cried Katy; "that's the blue-room." But Elsie did not pause.

You see," she explained, with the door-knob in her hand, "papa and I thought you ought to have a bigger room now, because you are grown-up young ladies! So we have fixed this for you, and your old one is going to be the spare room instead." Then she threw the door open, and led the girls in.

"See, Katy," she said, "this is your bureau, and this is Clover's."

"And see what nice drawers papa has had put in the closet—two for you, and two for her. Aren't they convenient? Don't you like it? And isn't it a great deal pleasanter than the old room?"

"Oh, a great deal!" cried the girls. "It is delightful, everything about it." All Katy's old treasures had been transferred from her old quarters to this. There was her cushioned chair, her table, her book-shelf, the pictures from the walls. There were some new things too—a blue carpet, fresh paper on the walls, window curtains of fresh chintz; and Elsie had made a tasteful pin-cushion for each I bureau, and Johnnie crocheted mats for the wash-stand. Altogether, I it was as pretty a bower as two sisters just grown into young ladies could desire.

"What are those lovely things hanging on either side of the bed?" asked Clover.

They were two illuminated texts, sent as a "welcome home," by Cousin Helen. One was a morning text, and the other an evening text, Elsie explained. The evening text, which bore the words, I will lay me down to sleep, and take my rest, for it is Thou, Lord, only Who makest me dwell in safety," was painted in soft purples and greys, and among the poppies and silver lilies which wreathed it appeared a cunning little downy bird, fast asleep, with his head under his wing. The morning text, "When I awake, I am still with Thee," was in bright colours, scarlet and blue and gold, and had a frame of rose garlands and wide-awake-looking butterflies and hummingbirds. The girls thought they had never seen anything so pretty.

Such a gay supper as they had that night! Katy would not take her old place at the tea-tray. She wanted to know how Elsie looked as housekeeper, she said.

"I'll begin to-morrow," said Katy.

And with that morrow, when she came out of her pretty room and took her place once more as manager of the household, her grownup life may be said to have begun. So it is time that I should cease to write about her. Grown-up lives may be very interesting, but they have no rightful place in a child's book. If little girls will forget J to be little, and take it upon them to become young ladies, they must

bear the consequences, one of which is, that we can follow their fortunes no longer.

I wrote these last words sitting in the same green meadow where the first words of "What Katy Did" were written. A year had passed, but a cardinal-flower which seemed the same stood looking at itself in the brook, and from the bulrush-bed sounded tiny voices. My little goggle-eyed friends were discussing Katy and her conduct, as they did then, but with less spirit; for one voice came seldom and faintly, while the other, bold and defiant as ever, repeated over and over again, "Katy didn't! Katy didn't! She didn't, didn't, didn't.

"Katy did! " sounded faintly from the farther rush.

"She didn't, she didn't," chirped the undaunted partisan.

"Katy didn't." The words repeated themselves in my mind, as I walked homeward. How much room for 'Didn'ts' is in the world, I thought. What an important part they play. And how glad I am that, with all her own and other people's doings, so many of these very 'Didn'ts' were included among the things which my Katy did at school

CHILDREN'S CLASSICS

Heidi

JOHANNA SPYRI

Heidi

PARRAGON

Heidi
A Parragon Classic

This is a Siena book
Siena is an imprint of Parragon

This edition published in 1998 by
Parragon
13 Whiteladies Road
Clifton
Bristol BS8 1PB

Printed and bound in the UK

CHAPTER 1

UP TO THE ALM-UNCLE

From the old and pleasantly situated town of Mayenfeld a path leads through green, shady meadows to the foot of the mountains which look down from their majestic heights upon the valley below. As the footpath begins to slope gently upwards, the fragrance of the nearby heath, with its short grass and vigorous mountain plants, fills the air; then the way becomes more rugged and the path rises steeply towards the Alps.

One bright, sunny morning in June, a tall, sturdy-looking girl of this mountainous country climbed the narrow mountain path, leading a child by the hand. The little girl's cheeks were aglow and the bright crimson shone even through her brown, sunburnt skin. This was not surprising, for in spite of the scorching sun the child was wrapped up as though for protection against bitter frost. She wore two, if not three frocks, one on top of the other, and, in addition, a big red shawl was tied all round her body so that her little five-year-old figure was scarcely discernible. In her heavy, nailed mountain shoes, she toiled laboriously up the slope. The two figures had been climbing from the valley for about an hour when they reached the hamlet called Dörfli which is situated half-way up the Alm. Here they were greeted with friendly calls from every doorway, for this was the girl's birthplace. But she hurried on until she had reached the last of the scattered little houses, and as she passed, a voice called from the doorway, "Wait for me, Dete, if you are going up and I will come too!"

She stood still, and the child let go of her and sat down on the ground. "Are you tired, Heidi?" asked the older girl.

"No, I am hot, though," answered Heidi.

"We shall soon reach the top now. If you can be brave and walk strongly for a little longer we shall get there in an hour," said Dete encouragingly.

5

The stout pleasant-looking woman who had hailed them, came out of her house and joined them, chattering and laughing with Dete, who was an old acquaintance.

"Where are you taking the child, Dete?" she asked. "I suppose it is your sister's child—the orphan?"

"Yes," answered Dete. "I am taking her to stay with the Alm-Uncle."

"Surely you aren't going to leave the child with *him*. You must be out of your mind, Dete! The old man is sure to turn you away, in any case!"

"He can't do that! He is her grandfather. I have looked after the child up till now, and I can tell you, Barbel, I am not going to turn down the offer of a good job on her account. From now on the grand-father will have to do his bit."

"Oh, well, if he were like other people—" replied Barbel, "but you know him as well as I do. How can he look after a child, and especially such a little one? Oh, she will never stay with him! But where are *you* going, Dete?"

"To a very good job in Frankfurt," explained Dete. "I looked after the people I am going to at the Baths last summer. They wanted me to go away with them then, but of course I could not go. Now they have asked me again you can be sure that I am not going to let the opportunity pass!"

"Well, I wouldn't like to be the child," said Barbel disapprovingly. "Nobody knows anything about the old man up there. He never speaks to anybody, and he never goes to church. If he is seen, occasionally, everyone keeps away from him and his stick. With his bushy eyebrows and terrible beard he looks a positive savage. The whole village is afraid of him and not many people would want to be alone with him."

"Still," Dete persisted, "he is the grandfather and it's up to him to look after the child."

"They say all sorts of terrible things about the old man," said Barbel, glancing keenly at her companion. "There must be something on his conscience, that he should live such an isolated life up there. You must surely have heard his history from your sister, eh, Dete?"

6

"Perhaps I have, but I shan't say. It would be a fine thing for me if he found out I had been talking!"

Barbel had been eager for a long time to learn something about the old man whom everybody referred to as the Alm-Uncle. She wanted to know why he seemed to hate everybody and why he lived all by himself up on the mountain. Besides, she wondered why the villagers in Dörfli called him Alm-Uncle. He was obviously not everyone's uncle. Barbel was much the same as all the others though, and referred to him by the same name.

Barbel had married and come to Dörfli quite recently, so she was not familiar with local history. Dete, on the other hand, had spent her childhood and youth in Dörfli, until she had gone into service in the large hotel at Ragatz Baths the previous year.

This morning Dete had come all the way from Ragatz on this special journey with little Heidi. Barbel was quite determined not to miss this golden opportunity to find out as much as she could about the strange old man. Confidentially she took Dete's arm. "Do tell me more about him, now! You have nothing to fear," she coaxed.

"I can't be expected to tell you much about an old fellow who is nearly fifty years older than me. He must be at least seventy! However, if I could be absolutely certain that whatever I told you would be kept completely confidential, then I dare say I could tell you a few things I have found out about him, as he came from Domleschg, where my mother was born."

"Whatever do you mean, Dete?" retorted Barbel, red in the face. "I am not one of those village gossips and you can take my word that I know how to keep a secret."

"All right then, I'll tell you," said Dete, lowering her voice, "but I don't want the child to hear." She looked round to see whether Heidi were nearby and might hear what she had to say, but the little one was not in sight. Dete stopped in some consternation, and looked back. There was no sign of the child.

"Now I see her!" cried Barbel at last. "Over there!" She pointed far away from the path. "She is climbing the slopes

7

with Peter, the goat-herd, and his goats. He can look after the child, and you will be able to go on with your story."

"She's good enough at looking after herself," said Dete, "and perhaps it's a good thing, for the old man will not be able to provide for her very well. He has nothing now but his two goats and the Alm cottage."

"Did he have more in his younger days?" asked Barbel.

"Yes, I should think he did!" replied Dete with conviction. "He was brought up on one of the finest farms in Domleschg. He was the eldest son. But he lost the farm with his gambling and drinking, and, when the whole story of his wild extravagance came out, his parents died of grief. He disappeared after that and at first nobody knew where he had gone. Some said he joined the army in Naples. No more news came for about twelve to fifteen years. Then, suddenly, he appeared again in Domleschg with an almost grown-up boy and tried to find a home for him with relations. But every door was closed against him."

"That so embittered him that he vowed he would never again set foot in Domleschg and came with the boy to Dörfli to live. His wife must have been a native of the Grisons. He probably met and married her there and she died shortly afterwards. It seems he still had a little money left—enough for the boy, Tobias, to be apprenticed to a carpenter. He was a good boy and well liked by everyone in Dörfli. But nobody trusted the old man. There was a rumour that he had to get out of Naples to avoid serious trouble, because it was said that he had killed a man—of course, not in the war, you understand, but in some brawl. But we did not break our connection with him since we were closely related. My great-grand-mother on my mother's side was his grandmother's sister, you know. We called him 'Uncle', and as we are related on my father's side to almost everybody in Dörfli, the whole village called him 'Uncle', too. And because he lived on the Alm he was called the 'Alm-Uncle'."

"But what happened to Tobias?" asked Barbel eagerly.

"Wait a moment, I am coming to that," replied Dete. "Tobias served his apprenticeship in Mels, and as soon as he had finished he came home to Dörfli and married my sister, Adelheid. They were very happy together, but their happiness was short-lived. Two years later, while Tobias was working at the building of a house, a beam fell on him and killed him, and when his mutilated body was brought home, Adelheid fell into a violent fever as a result of the shock, and never recovered. In any case, she was not very strong and sometimes took strange fits when we couldn't tell whether she was asleep or awake."

"Only a few weeks after Tobias died, Adelheid too was buried. Some said it was the uncle's punishment for the wicked life he had led, and they even told him so to his face. The pastor, too, begged him to repent of his past sins, but the uncle only grew more fierce and embittered. He would not speak to anyone, and everyone, in turn, kept clear of him. Then we heard he had come to live on the Alm and he has remained up there in solitude ever since, at war with God and the world."

"Mother and I took in Adelheid's little child. She was only a year old then. When Mother died last summer and I had to go and work at the health resort, I took the child with me and left her in charge of old Ursel up in Pfaferserdorf. I was kept on at the health resort during the winter, for I could knit and sew and plenty of people gave me work to do, and early in the spring some Frankfurt people I had served during the summer came back. They offered me a job, and I am going away with them to Frankfurt. We leave the day after tomorrow."

"And you are going to leave the poor child with that terrible old man!" said Barbel reproachfully.

"Well, what else can I do?" replied Dete defensively. "I have done what I can for the child, and can't take her with me. But, goodness! Where are you going, Barbel? We are already half-way up the Alm."

"I have almost come as far as I need," answered Barbel. "I want to speak to Peter's grandmother. She spins for me in winter. Goodbye, then, Dete! And good luck!"

Dete shook her friend's hand and stopped while Barbel

walked towards the little brown Alm hut which was situated in a sheltered spot some yards off the path. The hut was more than half-way up the Alm from the village. It was fortunate it stood in such a sheltered place, for it looked dilapidated beyond repair. Even situated as it was, it was hardly safe to live in when gales swept the mountains. Then everything in the hut, doors and windows and all the old beams, would shake and crack.

The goat-herd lived here with his mother and his old blind grand-mother. Peter was eleven years old. Every morning he collected goats from the village and drove them up to the Alm where they grazed till evening. At sunset, Peter would go running nimbly down the mountainside with his goats, until, on reaching Dörfli he would whistle through his fingers. The piercing sound summoned the owners of the goats, who then took them home. Usually the little boys and girls came to collect the animals, for they were not in the least frightened of the gentle goats, and this hour of the day, during the long summer, was the time when Peter could see his little friends. For the rest of the day he was alone on the mountain with only the goat for company. He often got home very late from Dörfli, for he stayed as long as possible to play with his friends. So he was left with just enough time to eat his bread and milk, sleep and get up again early the next morning. His father had been killed in a wood-cutting accident several years before. His mother, Brigitta, was always called the goat-herd's wife, and his blind grandmother was just "grandmother" to all and sundry.

Dete stood looking impatiently in all directions to catch a glimpse of the children and the goats; but they had taken a very roundabout way. At first the little girl had toiled hard to climb with the goat-herd, panting in the heat and making a great effort under her heavy encumbrance of clothes. She did not say a word but looked steadily, now at Peter who jumped about on his bare feet, now at the goats who climbed still more easily on their slender little legs. Suddenly the child sat down on the ground and quickly removed her shoes and stockings. Then, standing up, she began to take off her hot red shawl,

10

then her Sunday frock and her everyday frock, which Dete had also made her wear, until, clad only in her light little petticoat, she stood with her bare arms stretched happily into the air. Then she put everything neatly into a little pile and jumped and climbed behind the goats. As she came skipping along in her new garb, Peter grinned broadly. He looked back, and when he saw the little pile of clothes lying on the path he grinned even more, but he said nothing. The child, feeling free at last, began to chatter to the boy, asking him how many goats he had, where he was going with them and what he would do there. So at last the children arrived at the cottage and caught sight of Aunt Dete. She no sooner spotted the group than she cried, "Heidi! What a sight you are! Where are your clothes? And the new shoes I bought you, and the stockings I knitted? Where have you put them?"

The child quietly pointed down the hill.

The aunt followed the direction of her finger. There was, indeed, something lying on the ground. "You dreadful child!" she cried in great annoyance. "What's the meaning of this? Why have you taken everything off?"

"I didn't need them," said the child, not looking at all penitent.

"Oh, have you no sense?" lamented the aunt. "Who is to go back down for them? It's all of half an hour's walk." Then turning to Peter, she ordered, "Peter! Run back and fetch the clothes!"

"I am late already," said Peter slowly, and remained motionless, both hands in his pockets.

"Don't just stand there staring!" Aunt Dete cried. "This will never do! Come here! I will give you something good. Look!" And she held up a bright new coin. The boy's eyes shone at the sight of it. Suddenly he jumped up and made off down the Alm by the shortest way. Soon he reached the little pile of clothes, gathered them up and sped back so quickly that the aunt could not but be pleased, and at once gave him the coin. Peter put it in his pocket, his face wreathed in smiles for he didn't often come by such a prize.

"You can take the clothes up to the uncle's since you are

going that way," Aunt Dete said as she started to climb the steep slope which rose just behind Goat Peter's cottage. Readily Peter carried out the order and followed as she walked ahead; his left arm round the bundle, the goats' stick swinging in his right hand. Heidi and the goats leaped joyously at his side. Thus, in three quarters of an hour, the little group reached the top of the Alm where the old uncle's cottage stood on a ledge of the mountain. Behind the hut were three ancient fir trees, and beyond these, the mountain rose in an almost sheer wall, the lower parts still overgrown with grasses and flowers, with stonier slopes above leading to the black, bare, jagged peaks. Along the side of the cottage facing the valley, the uncle had made himself a bench, and here he now sat puffing his pipe, both hands on his knees, calmly watching the children, the goats and Aunt Dete as they climbed. Heidi arrived first. She went straight up to the old man, stretched out her hand towards him and said, "Good evening, Grandfather!"

"Well, well! What is the meaning of this?" asked the old man gruffly. He took the child's hand abruptly and as he did so a long, piercing glance shot from beneath his bushy eyebrows. Heidi returned his look without blinking. The grandfather presented a fearsome aspect. His face seemed covered in beard and eyebrows, and Heidi could not take her fascinated gaze away from him.

In the meantime, the aunt and Peter had arrived.

"I wish you good day!" said Dete shortly. "This is Tobias' and Adelheid's child. You will hardly recognise her because you have not seen her since she was a year old."

"What have I to do with the child?" asked the old man brusquely. "And you, there!" he called to Peter. "Take yourself off with your goats! You are late as it is."

Peter obeyed at once, for the uncle had given him an angry look which did not make him wish to linger.

"The child just has to stay with you, Uncle," said Dete. "I have done my bit for four years. Now it is your turn."

"Indeed!" mumbled the old man, his glance flashing at Dete. "And if the child starts fretting for you as children do, being such difficult things, what shall I do with her then?"

12

"That's up to you," replied Dete. "No one told me what to do with the little one when she was left in my care, and only one year old, too. Now I have to make my own living and you are the child's nearest relative. If you can't look after her it's your responsibility and you must answer for any harm that comes to her. And I shouldn't think you can afford to add another to your list of wicked deeds."

At that point Dete realised she had said more than she should have.

At her words, the old man got up. He looked so threatening that she took a step backwards. Flinging out his arm, he shouted at her, "Be off! And don't be in a hurry to show your face here again!"

Dete did not need a second telling. "Good-bye, then!" she said hurriedly. "And you, too, Heidi!" And with that she turned and ran down the mountain, and didn't stop until she reached Dörfli.

This time, people were even more eager to stop and question her, wondering what had become of the child. They all knew Dete well, and also the history of the child. When voices called from every door and window, "Where is the child, Dete? What have you done with her?" she replied angrily, "With the Alm-Uncle, of course! I left her with the Alm-Uncle, just as I said." The women of the village began to cry out at her: "Shame on you for leaving a little girl up there! What a terrible thing to do."

Dete ran through the village as fast as she could go. Her one thought was to get away from Dörfli and to avoid speaking to any one, for she was far from easy in her conscience about what she had done. The child's dying mother had asked Dete to take care of Heidi, and here she was, abandoning the girl to an unknown fate. However, she consoled herself with the thought of being better able to provide for the child with her newly earned money, and with the wonderful prospect of soon being free to enjoy her new position far away from all the village talk.

CHAPTER 2

THE GRANDFATHER'S HUT

Long after Dete had gone, the grandfather went back to his seat outside the hut, and sat silently blowing clouds of smoke from his pipe while Heidi began to inspect her new surroundings. She found a shed, attached to one side of the hut, which housed the goats. She peeped in and then walked round to the other side of the cottage where there stood three old fir trees. A strong wind shook their thick branches and the child stood still, listening to the moaning of the wind in the ancient trees. Then she completed the circuit of the cottage and returned to where the grandfather sat. He hadn't moved an inch since she'd left him, so she went across and stood in front of him, her hands clasped behind her back, her steady eyes looking at him.

The old man raised his head. Heidi stayed where she was and continued to gaze at him. "Well, what are we going to do now" he said.

"I would like to see inside the cottage."

"Come, then!" The grandfather got up. "And bring your bundle of clothes!"

"I don't need them any more," declared Heidi.

The old man turned and looked searchingly at the child. Heidi's dark eyes were shining with delight at the prospect of seeing inside the cottage. "She doesn't lack sense, anyway," he said quietly to himself. Then, "Why don't you need them any more?" he asked aloud.

"I would rather be dressed like the goats with their bare legs."

"All right, then, but bring the things!" commanded the grandfather. "We will put them in the cupboard."

Heidi obediently picked up her bundle and followed the old man inside. The door opened directly on to a big room which was the full breadth of the cottage. The only furniture in the room was a table and a chair. In one corner stood the grandfather's bed and in the opposite wall the fireplace above which hung a big kettle. On the same side as the bed, in the middle of the wall, there was a door which the grandfather now opened. This was the cupboard where he kept his belongings. On a shelf lay a couple of shirts, socks and some rough sackcloth sheets. On another stood plates, cups and glasses, and on the top shelf there was a round loaf, a sausage, ham and cheese. Everything that Alm-Uncle possessed in the way of food and clothing was kept in this cupboard. As soon as the door was opened Heidi came forward and pushed her own clothes as far behind the grandfather's as possible so that they would be well out of the way. Then she turned her attention to the room and asked, "Where shall I sleep, Grandfather?"

"Wherever you want to."

This seemed to please the child and she began to inspect every corner. By the grandfather's bed, wooden steps went up, and when the child climbed the little ladder she found herself in the hayloft. A bale of hay, fresh and sweet-smelling, lay on the floor, and from a little window in the roof she could see far down into the valley.

"Oh, this is where I want to sleep!" she cried joyfully. "It is lovely! Come and see how lovely it is, Grandfather!"

"I have seen it before!" came from below.

"I am going to make my bed," the child called again and ran busily to and fro. "You must bring me a sheet to lie upon, Grandfather!"

"Indeed!" remarked the grandfather, and after a while he went to the cupboard and raked about amongst the clothes. Presently he pulled out a long, coarse piece of sack-cloth which might serve as a sheet. He carried it up to the loft and there he saw that a very nice little bed had been made amongst the hay, with extra hay piled up into a pillow at one end, and arranged in such a way that whoever lay on the improvised bed would be able to look up at the little window.

"Well done!" exclaimed the grandfather. "Now the sheet goes on. But wait——I" and here he took a big bunch of hay and made the bed twice as thick so that the hardness of the floor would not come through.

"Now bring it here!"

Heidi quickly grasped the sheet but it was so thick and heavy, she staggered under the weight, It was just as well though, as the thickness of the cloth would prevent the sharp stalks of hay from sticking into her. Together they spread the sheet and now the bed looked very trim and tidy; but Heidi stood back and regarded it critically.

"There is still something we have forgotten, Grandfather."

"Now what?" he asked.

"A top sheet. When you get into bed you need something to pull over you."

"Oh, indeed! But what if I haven't got any?"

"Don't worry, Grandfather," Heidi consoled him. "We can use more hay for a cover," and she began to gather another bundle.

"Wait a moment!" The old man went down the steps to his own bed. Back he came presently with a big, heavy, linen sack which he laid on the floor.

"Isn't that better than hay?" he asked, helping her to spread it on the bed, for Heidi's little frame couldn't manage to lift and spread the heavy cover out smoothly.

Heidi stood admiringly before her new sleeping-place. "The cover is beautiful!" she declared ecstatically, "and the bed is just perfect! I wish it were night-time already so that I could go to sleep on it!"

"I think we should eat first," the grandfather advised.

In her eagerness, Heidi had forgotten everything except the new bed, but now, when she thought of it, she did indeed feel very hungry, for she had had nothing to eat since that morning before the journey, when she had breakfasted meagerly on a piece of bread and a small cup of watery coffee. "Yes, I think so, too!" she agreed.

"Well, then, since we are in such complete agreement, let's go down," said the old man, guiding the child towards the stairs.

In the room below he went over to the fireplace, pushed

back the big kettle and brought a little one forward on the chain. Then he sat down on a three-legged stool and blew up the fire. It was soon blazing merrily and the little kettle began to boil. Next the old man cut a big piece of cheese, and piercing it with a long, iron fork, he held it over the fire, turning it constantly to and fro until it was golden brown all over. Heidi had watched all these operations with the closest attention and apparently some new ideas had entered her head for suddenly she jumped up and went to the cupboard. When the grandfather had decided that the cheese was nicely toasted and took it to the table, there was the round loaf, two plates and two knives neatly laid, for Heidi had been quick to see what was wanted and had brought everything from the cupboard.

"So you can think for yourself! That's good!" said the grandfather and spread the toasted cheese on the bread. "But there is still something missing."

Heidi's eyes alighted on the steaming pot by the fire and she knew at once what it was. Quickly she ran back to the cupboard but could find only one little bowl. She hesitated only a moment for right at the back were two glasses. Presently she came back and put the little bowl and glasses on the table.

"Very good! Very good!" said the old man. "You have found a way out of the difficulty. But now, where are *you* going to sit?" and he drew his own chair up to the table.

Heidi ran to the hearth and brought back the little three-legged stool.

"You have got a seat, at any rate," said the grandfather, "though it is rather low! Even on my chair you would be too small to reach the table. But now you must eat. Come along!"

He filled the little bowl with milk and placing it on his own chair pushed it near the stool so that Heidi had a little table of her own. Then he filled a plate with a big piece of bread and some of the yellow, toasted cheese and laid it also on the chair. He himself sat on the corner of the table and began his meal. Heidi lifted her little bowl and drank without stopping. Then she drew a deep breath—for she had been so thirsty that she hadn't even stopped to breathe—and put down the empty bowl.

17

"Do you like the milk?" the grandfather asked.

"It is the best milk I have ever tasted!" replied Heidi.

"You can have more," said the grandfather, filling the little bowl again and putting it before her. She spread the bread with her slice of golden cheese and began eating hungrily.

The cheese was soft as butter and tasted good. From time to time Heidi took a drink from the bowl and looked blissfully happy.

When the meal was finished, the grandfather went out to the goat-house where there was work to be done. Heidi watched him attentively, observing how he first swept everything clean with the broom then spread fresh straw for the little animals to sleep on. At last the goat-house was finished and he went into the shed which was close by. Here he chopped several round sticks to equal lengths; then he carefully shaped a flat piece of wood and drilled four holes into one side. He put the round sticks into the holes—and there was a chair like the grandfather's, only much higher! Speechless with admiration, Heidi gazed at it.

"What do you think it is, Heidi?" asked the grandfather.

"It is *my* chair, because it is so high. But you made it so quickly, Grandfather!" said the little girl in amazement.

"She has eyes in her head all right," thought the grandfather as he walked round the cottage, fixing a loose board at the door and repairing anything that needed attention. Heidi followed close behind. Nothing escaped her notice, and everything she saw gave her new pleasure.

Evening came, and the old fir trees behind the cottage began to rustle more loudly as a strong wind swept along, roaring amongst the branches. Heidi's heart beat faster. She thought she had never heard anything so beautiful and went skipping and running for sheer joy under the trees. All the while the grandfather watched the child from the doorway.

There was the sound of a shrill whistle. Heidi stood still and the grandfather stepped out of the cottage. From above, the goats came jumping like wild creatures and in the midst of them was Peter. With a joyful cry, Heidi rushed to welcome her old friends of the morning. At the cottage, children and animals came to a halt and two pretty, slender goats, one

18

brown, one white, ran from the herd towards the grandfather. Eagerly they licked his hands for in the palms he held a little salt which the goats liked very much. Peter disappeared with the rest of the flock and Heidi fell to caressing first one and then the other of the goats and jumped gaily round them.

"Do they belong to us, Grandfather? Do they really belong to us?" she asked. "Will they stay in the little shed? Do they always stay with us?" Heidi scarcely gave the grandfather a chance to put in his steady, "Yes! Yes!" between one question and the next.

When the goats had finished licking the salt from his hands, the old man commanded, "Go and fetch your little bowl and the bread!"

Heidi obeyed at once. Then the grandfather milked the white goat into the little bowl which was soon full to the brim. He cut a piece of bread and handing it to the child said, "Eat now, and then go upstairs to sleep. I suppose your night things are in the bundle Aunt Dete made up, which I put in the cupboard. Get it out if you need it. I have to tie up the goats for the night. Sleep well!"

"Good night, Grandfather! But what are the goats' names? Tell me, Grandfather!" cried the child, running behind the old man's receding figure.

"The white one is called 'Little Swan' and the brown one is 'Little Bear'," the grandfather called over his shoulder.

"Good night, Little Swan! Good night, Little Bear!" cried Heidi happily as all three disappeared into the goat-house.

Heidi went back to the bench outside the cottage where she sat and took her bread and milk. The wind was so strong she was almost blown from her seat, so she finished hurriedly and went into the house and upstairs to bed where she was soon fast asleep, as soundly and happily as though on the best feather-bed. Not long after, and before the darkness had come completely, the grandfather, too, had gone to bed, for he always rose at sunrise, which was at a very early hour during the long summer months. All night long the wind blew strongly so that the whole cottage seemed to shake and every beam cracked and groaned.

In the middle of the night the grandfather rose, saying half aloud to himself, "Perhaps she is afraid." He climbed the steps and stood by Heidi's bed. At intervals the moon shone brightly, then as clouds were chased across it everything became dark again. At that moment a shaft of moonlight came through the little window, falling directly on Heidi's bed. Her cheeks were flushed from sleep and her head rested quietly and peacefully on her little round arm. Her dreams appeared to be happy ones for a smile played about her mouth. The grandfather gazed at the sleeping child until the moon was again overshadowed. Then he went back to his bed.

CHAPTER 3

ON THE ALM

Early in the morning, Heidi was awakened by a loud whistle. As she opened her eyes, a gleam of sunshine came through the little window on to her bed and shone on the hay nearby so that everything was bathed in golden light. Then, from outside, she heard the grandfather's deep, quiet voice and she remembered that she was up on the Alm. She no longer lived with old Ursel who was almost stone deaf and always wanted to have Heidi by her side, so that sometimes the child had felt like a prisoner and would have liked to run away from the stuffy room where she had to sit all day. For Ursel was always too cold and insisted on keeping the room unbearably hot. So Heidi was very glad when she awoke and found herself in her new home. She remembered all the exciting things she had seen the previous day and wondered what this new day had in store for her. Above all she looked forward to seeing Little Swan and Little Bear again. Quickly she jumped out of bed and in a few minutes had dressed herself. Then she climbed down the steps and ran out to the front of the cottage. Peter, the goat-herd, was already there with his flock and the grandfather was leading out Little Swan and Little Bear to join them. Heidi ran forward to say good-morning to him and the goats.

"How would you like to go with them to the pasture?" asked the grandfather.

Heidi was overjoyed. That was the thing she would like best of all.

"But first you must wash yourself or the sun, shining brightly up there, will laugh at you when he looks down and sees how dirty you are! See! This is where you wash." The grandfather pointed towards a big flat tub filled with water which stood in the sun before the cottage door. Heidi jumped towards it and splashed and scrubbed until she was perfectly clean. In the meantime the grandfather went into the cottage, calling to Peter, "Come here, goat-general, and bring your rucksack!"

Amazed, Peter answered the call and laid down the rucksack in which he carried his meagre lunch.

"Open it!" ordered the old man, and then put in a big piece of bread and an equally big piece of cheese. Peter opened his round eyes very wide for this food was twice as much as he had for his own lunch.

"And now the little bowl has to go in, too," the old man continued. "At lunch-time you will milk for her two little bowlfuls, for she is going, too, and can stay with you until you come back in the evening. Take care she doesn't fall over the precipice!"

Now Heidi came running towards them. "Grandfather, the sun can't laugh at me now!" For fear of the sun's mockery she had rubbed her face, neck and arms so vigorously with the rough cloth which the grandfather had hung up beside the water-tub, that she was almost as red as a lobster.

The old man smiled. "No, he has no reason to laugh now," he agreed. "But do you know what happens when you come home in the evening? You go right into the tub like a fish because if you run like the goats your feet will get dirty. Now, off you go!"

Happily the children climbed up the Alm. The high winds during the night had blown away the last little cloud and now the sky was a vast expanse of deep blue out of which the sun shone and glittered on the green slopes. The little blue and yellow mountain flowers opened their cups and seemed to nod merrily at Heidi who romped everywhere. Here and there were big patches of pretty red primroses, and china-blue gentians, and enchanted by this sparkling, waving sea of flowers, she forgot all about Peter, even about the goats. All along the way she picked flowers until she had a big bunch which she wrapped in her pinafore, for she wanted to take them home and put them in her bedroom, so that it would look as pretty as the fields themselves.

Peter was quite dazed trying to look in every direction at once, for the goats, like Heidi, were jumping from one place to another. He had to whistle and shout and brandish his stick to bring the goats together again.

"Where are you now, Heidi?" came the boy's exasperated and rather angry cry.

"Here!" came the reply, but Peter could see no one. Heidi was sitting, hidden from view, behind a little hillock which was covered with sweet-smelling prunella. The air was filled with the perfume of these beautiful flowers, and Heidi was sitting taking in deep breaths of the scented air and thinking how wonderful it all was.

"Come here!" Peter called again. "You are not to go near the precipice—the uncle said so!"

"Where is that?" asked Heidi, still not moving from her hiding-place.

"Up there! Right on the top the old eagle sits on the look-out for his prey."

That did the trick.

At once Heidi jumped up and ran to Peter with her apronful of flowers.

"That is enough flower-picking for now," he said as they climbed up together, "if you are going to keep pace with me. And if you pick all the flowers to-day there will be none left for to-morrow."

Heidi was convinced. Moreover, her pinafore was so full that it could hardly hold another one. So she now walked quietly beside Peter. The goats were also quieter, as they were anxious to reach their delicious pasture, and climbed unhesitatingly towards their grazing ground. The pasture which Peter usually chose and where he spent the day was situated at the foot of the high rocks. Bushes and fir trees covered the lower parts but nearer the summit the rocks rose bare and rugged towards the sky. On one side of the mountain, jagged clefts stretched far down and the grandfather had been right to warn Peter of the danger. When they had reached the pasture, Peter carefully put his rucksack into a little hollow in the ground, for the wind often blew with great violence across this part of the country and Peter did not want to see his precious possessions rolling down the mountainside. Then the boy, tired after the strenuous climb, stretched himself out at full length on the sunny pasture.

Heidi, by this time, had undone her pinafore and rolled it neatly round the flowers which she laid beside Peter's rucksack in the hollow. Then she sat down beside him and looked around. The valley lay far below, bathed in the sparkling morning sunshine. In front of Heidi a big, broad snowfield rose up to the dark blue sky and on the left stood a huge pile of rocks above which a bare rocky peak reached towards the sky, towering majestically above the child. Heidi sat motionless. A great silence was all around and only the delicate blue harebells and yellow cistus swayed softly in the gentle breeze, nodding joyfully on their slender little stems. Peter had fallen asleep and the goats were climbing high up amongst the bushes. Heidi had never been so happy. The golden sunlight, the fresh breezes and the delicate perfume of the flowers filled her with delight and she only wished that she might stay there for ever. She gazed so long at the mountains that it seemed to her that each had a face and that these mountain faces were as familiar to her as old friends.

Suddenly Heidi heard a loud, harsh cry and when she looked up she saw, circling overhead, a huge bird, larger than she had ever seen before. His large wings were outspread and he flew in a wide circle, coming back again and again and uttering loud, piercing shrieks above Heidi's head.

"Peter! Peter! Wake up!" cried Heidi. "Look! There is a big bird just above us!"

Peter got up and watched the bird, too, as it rose higher and higher and at last disappeared behind the grey rocks.

"Where has he gone to?" asked Heidi who had been watching the bird with keen interest.

"Home to his nest," replied Peter.

"Is his home up there? Oh, how nice to live so high up! How terrible he cries! Let's climb up there and see where his nest is!"

"Oh, no!" replied Peter emphatically. "Even the goats can't climb so high and the uncle said you were not to climb the rocks."

Suddenly Peter started to whistle and call loudly. Heidi could not think what this meant, but the goats apparently understood, for, one after another, they came springing down until they were all gathered together on the green slope. Some continued to nibble and others ran about, playfully pushing each other with their horns. Heidi jumped up and ran amongst them. She delighted in their individual antics and quickly made friends with each of them in turn, for to her they were like separate people with their own personalities. While she played with the goats Peter fetched the rucksack and laid out the four pieces of bread on the ground, the big ones on Heidi's side and the small ones on his own. Then he took the little bowl, drew some milk into it from Little Swan and placed it in the centre. "Stop skipping now! It is time to eat," he said. But he had to shout again, for Heidi was so absorbed in her games with the goats that she was oblivious to everything else. So Peter called until the rocks themselves echoed his voice, and then Heidi appeared and ran to join Peter and the feast spread out on the ground before him.

She sat down. "Is the milk for me?" she asked.

"Yes," replied Peter, "and the two big pieces of bread and cheese are yours too, and when you have finished you get another bowlful from Little Swan." "And where do you get your milk?" asked Heidi. "From my own goat. Go on and eat," urged Peter.

Heidi began to drink her milk and as soon as she put down her empty bowl Peter filled it again. Then Heidi gave a big piece of her bread to Peter and all the cheese as well, saying, "You can have it all. I have had enough."

Peter gazed at her, speechless with surprise. Never in his life could he have given away as much as that. He hesitated a little, for he could not believe that Heidi meant it seriously. She held out the pieces, but as Peter still did not take them she laid the food on his knees. Peter had never before had such a satisfying lunch.

The animals had begun to climb up again towards the bushes; some skipping gaily over everything, others stopping to taste the tender herbs. Heidi watched the goats, and after a while she said, "Tell me their names, Peter."

Peter knew them all, of course, and told Heidi the name of each, pointing them out as he did so. Heidi listened carefully and very soon she had learnt their names of by heart and could call to each one, for they all had distinguishing characteristics.

Turk was the big one, with enormous horns with which he was always trying to butt the others. So he was mostly left on his own as the rest of them were frightened of his bullying.

Only one, little Goldfinch, would face him without fear, and would rush at him nimbly, several times, so that Turk simply stood still in bewilderment, not knowing which way to turn, for her little horns were sharp.

There was also a sad little goat called White Snowflake, who bleated plaintively, and Heidi had frequently to go and comfort it and stroke its little soft head. Just then, it cried again, and Heidi ran over, and clasping her arms around it, beseeched it to tell her what was wrong. The goat snuggled to Heidi and stopped bleating.

Peter called out, between mouthfuls of bread and cheese, "She is missing her mother, an old goat who was sold at Mayenfeld the other day."

"Hasn't she a grandfather or a grandmother?" called back Heidi.

"She has neither," replied Peter.

"Oh, poor Snowflake," cried Heidi. "Please don't cry any more; I will come with you every day, and I will never leave you alone again, I promise."

The young goat nuzzled Heidi's shoulder and seemed more content.

Peter now joined Heidi, who had come to the conclusion that the best and most distinctive goats by far were the two which were owned by her grandfather. They even treated the arrogant Turk with total indifference.

"Peter," Heidi said presently, "the prettiest of all are Little Swan and Little Bear." These two were light on their feet, and always seemed to find the best leaves to nibble. Heidi watched them with pleasure.

"I know," Peter replied. "The uncle brushes and washes them, and gives them salt, and has the nicest shed."

Suddenly Peter jumped up and bounded after the goats. Heidi followed. Something must have happened and she simply could not stay behind. Peter forced his way through the middle of the herd to that side of the Alm where the bare and jagged rocks fell away steeply. Here, a heedless little goat might easily tumble down and break his legs. Peter had noticed inquisitive little Goldfinch jumping in that direction. The boy arrived just in time, for the little goat was just about to jump towards the edge of the precipice. Peter, lunging towards the goat, fell down and only managed to seize one of its legs as he fell. Goldfinch gave an angry cry at finding herself caught and tried desperately to free herself. Peter could not get up and shouted for Heidi to help because he was afraid Goldfinch might wrench her leg. Heidi was already there and at once saw the danger. She quickly gathered some sweet-smelling plants from the ground and held them out towards Goldfinch, saying coaxingly, "Come along, Goldfinch, and be good! Look! You might fall down and hurt yourself."

The little goat turned quickly and ate the herbs from Heidi's outstretched hand. In the meantime Peter got to his feet again and held Goldfinch by the cord with which her little bell was fastened to her neck. Heidi grasped the goat in the same way

26

at the other side of its head and together they led the truant back to the peacefully grazing flock. As soon as Peter got her back to safety, he raised his stick and started to give her a good beating. Goldfinch, however, knowing what was in store, timidly shrank back, and Heidi cried, "No, Peter! No! You mustn't beat her! Look how frightened she is!"

"She deserves it," Peter muttered, about to strike; but Heidi threw herself against his arm, crying indignantly, "Don't touch her! You will hurt her! Leave her alone!"

Peter turned surprised eyes on the fierce little girl and his stick dropped to his side. "All right, then, I'll let her off—if you give me some of your cheese to-morrow again," he bargained.

"You can have it all, to-morrow and every day. I don't want it," Heidi consented. "And I'll give you the bread, too, the same as today, but you must promise never to beat Goldfinch or Snowflake, or any of the goats."

"Suits me," said Peter, and that was as good as a promise. He let Goldfinch go and the little goat leapt joyously towards the herd.

So the day passed quickly and the sun began to sink behind the mountains. Heidi was sitting quietly on the ground, gazing at the cistus and the harebells which glistened in the evening sunshine; rocks and grass shimmered in a golden glow. Suddenly she jumped up and cried, "Peter! Peter! They are on fire! They are all on fire! All the mountains are burning! And the great snow mountain also, and the sky! Oh, look at the lovely fiery snow! Peter, get up and look! The fire is at the great bird's nest, too. Look at the rocks and the grass and the fir trees! Everything is on fire!"

"It is always like that," replied Peter with great unconcern, continuing to peel his stick, "but it is not real fire."

"What is it, then?" asked Heidi, gazing eagerly around. She ran back and forth looking from side to side, as if she could not take in enough of the majestic sight. "What is it, Peter?"

"It just gets like that," Peter tried to explain.

"Oh, look, look, Peter!" cried Heidi again in great excitement. "Everything is turning a rosy pink colour. Look at the snow and the high rocks! What are their names Peter"

"Mountains don't have names," replied Peter.

"Oh, how beautiful. Crimson snow! Oh, now all the rocks are turning grey—now the colour is all gone. Now it is all over, Peter."

Heidi sat down, looking as distressed as if everything really had come to an end.

"To-morrow it will be the same," said Peter. "Get up now. We must go home."

"Will it be like this every day we are on the pasture?" asked Heidi insistently, as she walked down the Alm at Peter's side. She waited breathlessly for his answer, hoping that he would be able to set her mind at rest.

"Mostly," he replied. "But will it definitely be like that again tomorrow" Heidi persisted. "Yes, yes; it will certainly come tomorrow," Peter replied.

Heidi was very happy. She had absorbed so many new impressions . . . had so many new things to think about that she was quite silent until they reached the hut and saw the grandfather sitting on the bench under the fir trees. Here he sat in the evenings, waiting for his goats.

Heidi ran up to him, followed by Little Swan and Little Bear, for the goats knew their master.

"Good night!" Peter called after Heidi, and then added, "come again, tomorrow!" because he was very anxious for her to go with him. Heidi ran back and gave her hand to Peter, promising him that she would go with him, and then ran over to little Snowflake, whom she clasped gently round the neck, saying, "Sleep well, and don't forget that I will be back tomorrow, so you needn't be sad." Snowflake looked at her happily and then leapt off after the other goats.

Heidi raced towards her grandfather.

"Oh, Grandfather, it was wonderful" she cried long before she reached him. "The fire on the snow and the rocks and the blue and yellow flowers, and look what I have brought for you!" Heidi unfolded her pinafore and all the flowers fell at the grandfather's feet. But what a sight the poor flowers were! Heidi did not recognise them. They were like withered grass and not a single little cup was open. "Grandfather, what is the matter with the flowers?" cried Heidi, quite alarmed. "They weren't like that before. What is wrong with them?"

"They would rather be out in the sun than tied up in a pinafore," explained the grandfather.

"Then I will never gather any more. But Grandfather, why did the eagle screech so?" Heidi asked.

"You had better have your bath now," said the grandfather, "and I shall fetch some milk from the shed. Afterwards, when we are having our supper, I will tell you about everything."

Later, when Heidi sat in her high chair, the little bowl of milk in front of her and the grandfather at her side, she again asked her question.

"Why did the great bird scream at us, Grandfather?"

"He screams in mockery of the people in the villages down in the valley where they sit gossiping together. He wants to say, 'If you would all mind your own business or climb up into the heights like me you would be much happier!'"

The grandfather spoke these words with such vehemence that Heidi seemed to hear again the croaking of the great bird.

"Why don't the mountains have names, Grandfather?" asked Heidi again.

"They have names," he answered, "and if you can describe one to me so that I can recognise it, then I will tell you its name."

Heidi tried to describe the rocky mountain with the two high peaks exactly as she had seen it. Presently the grandfather interrupted, "Yes, I know that one. Its name is Falknis. Did you notice any others?"

Then Heidi recalled the mountain with the large snowfield which looked at first as if it were on fire and then turned rose-coloured, then pale pink, and at last faded back to its own grey colour.

"I know that one, too," said the grandfather. "That is the Scesaplana. Did you like being on the pasture?"

Now Heidi told him everything: how wonderful it had been and particularly about the fire in the evening. Heidi wanted the grandfather to explain why this had happened, since Peter had been unable to do so.

"You see," the grandfather instructed her, "that's what the sun does when he says good night to the mountains. He throws his most beautiful rays over them so that they won't forget him before morning."

Heidi was delighted. She could hardly wait for the next day when she would again be allowed to go to the pasture, to watch how the sun said good night to the mountains. But first she had to go to bed, and how soundly she slept all night on her hay bed and dreamt of nothing but glistening mountains tinged with red, and Little Snowflake running happily about!

CHAPTER 4

PETER'S GRANDMOTHER

Next morning, the sun shone brightly as Peter appeared with the goats and they all went up together to the pasture. And so it continued every day. Heidi grew stronger and sturdier with living so much in the open and her little sunburnt face shone with health. When autumn came and the wind blew with greater force over the mountains, the grandfather would sometimes say, "To-day you had better stay at home, Heidi. A little one like you might easily be swept down the mountainside by the wind."

But when Peter heard this in the morning he would look very miserable. He found it dull now without Heidi; and, of course, he got less to eat. On such days the goats would become so stubborn that he had twice as much trouble with them. They, too, had grown so accustomed to Heidi that they would hardly move off without her.

Heidi herself was never bored because she always saw something new and exciting to take up her attention. Best of all she liked to go up the Alm with the goats to where the great bird was, where there was such a lot to see, and so much to experience with the little goats and their different personalities. But she also liked to watch the grandfather at work, helping him all she could at the carpenter's bench.

Then a very special treat for Heidi was to watch the grandfather prepare the lovely round goat's milk cheese. But even in the midst of such exciting activities she would sometimes steal away when the wind blew strongest to stand and listen beneath the old fir trees, catching her breath as the wind roared amongst the branches. Nothing sounded so strange and mysterious to her as the stirring of the tree-tops. She would stand directly beneath them and look up at the bending, swaying, roaring branches, bowing to the mighty wind sweeping through them.

As the season changed, the sun lost the fierce heat of summer and Heidi looked out her warm stockings and shoes and her wool dress. Gradually the weather grew colder and as Heidi stood beneath the trees, she would feel as if the wind were blowing straight through her, but she could never tear herself away and go indoors while the stirring branches beckoned her. As it grew ever colder, Peter would appear early in the morning blowing on his hands to warm them. Then one morning they awoke to find the whole Alm covered in snow. Not one blade of grass was visible. Peter and the goats did not appear and Heidi watched from the window of the hut as the big snowflakes fell. The snow fell thickly until it reached above the window so that it was impossible to open it and Heidi and the Alm-Uncle were imprisoned in the hut. This amused Heidi and she ran from one window to another expecting the hut to be covered right over at any moment. The next day it had stopped snowing and the grandfather forced his way out and shovelled the snow away from around the hut. Soon the snow was heaped up around the cottage and they were able to open the window again. In the afternoon, as Heidi and the grandfather sat together by the fire there came a great thumping outside the door. At last the door opened and there stood Peter, knocking the snow from his boots. He had struggled through deep snowdrifts and he still had great lumps of frozen snow clinging to his clothes.

"Good evening!" he said coming in and at once getting as near as possible to the fire. After this salutation the boy lapsed into complete silence but nevertheless his whole face beamed with joy.

Heidi looked at him in amazement for the snow which had covered him from head to foot was beginning to melt and ran from him in rivulets.

"Well, General, and how are things going?" called the grandfather. "Now that the goat army has been disbanded you will have to turn to nibbling at the slate pencil."

"Why must he nibble the slate pencil?" asked Heidi at once.

"In winter the boy has to go to school," explained the grandfather. "There he learns to read and write and that is sometimes difficult; and then it helps a little if one can nibble the slate pencil, isn't that so, General?"

"Yes, that's true," acknowledged Peter.

Now Heidi's interest was thoroughly aroused. She asked Peter many questions about school and everything to be seen and heard there. Since conversation with Peter was inclined to be a slow business he had ample opportunity to get thoroughly dry. He always had great difficulty in putting his thoughts into words and on the subject of school this was particularly hard. By the time he had managed to think of the answer to one question Heidi had already thought of two or three more to ask and they were all of a kind which required much answering. The grandfather kept silent during this dialogue but an occasional twitch of amusement at the corners of his mouth showed that he was listening.

"Well, General, now you have been under fire and must be in need of some refreshment!" As he spoke, the old man rose and got the supper from the cupboard and Heidi brought the chairs up to the table. The grandfather had also made a bench for two people, hinged into the wall, and several different seats here and there, so that he and Heidi could sit together, as she had a way of staying close beside him whatever he was doing. So there was plenty of room for all of them to sit in comfort.

32

Peter's round eyes opened wider when he saw what a large piece of delicious meat the grandfather put on his plate. He had not enjoyed himself so much for a long time. As they finished the meal it began to grow dark and Peter prepared to go home. He had already bade them good night, but turned again at the door and said, "I'll come back again on Sunday, a week to-day, but the grandmother said she would like you to come to see her some time."

This new idea of going to visit somebody appealed to Heidi at once and on the following morning her first words were, "Grandfather, I must go down and see the grandmother today. She will be expecting me."

"The snow is too deep," replied the grandfather to put her off. But Heidi was determined to go since she had got the grandmother's message. Not a day passed without her pleading, "Grandfather, I must go now! The grandmother is waiting for me!"

On the fourth day a hard frost had set in and the ground cracked at every step. But the bright sun peeped in at the window and fell on Heidi where she sat on her high chair at the table. Soon she had begun her customary little speech, "Today I must go to the grandmother or she will be tired of waiting for me."

The grandfather rose and going up to the hayloft brought down the thick sack which was Heidi's bedcover. "Come, then!" he said. Joyously the child skipped out into the glittering snow world. The old fir trees were silent now and on every branch the snow lay thickly.

The grandfather went into the shed and brought out a large sleigh. There was a pole fixed at the side and from the low seat the sleigh could be guided by the feet pressing against the ground and with the help of the pole.

The grandfather took his seat on the sleigh and placed the child on his knee, wrapping her carefully in the sack to keep her warm. His left arm held her secure and this was necessary for the long drive ahead. Then he grasped the pole with his right hand and gave a push with his feet. The sleigh shot down the Alm with such rapidity that Heidi felt she was flying through the air like a bird. She shouted aloud with joy.

By and by the sleigh stopped with a jerk just outside Goat Peter's cottage. The grandfather lifted the child and unwrapped her, saying, "Now in you go and when it starts to get dark come straight home!" Then he turned and pulled the sleigh back up the mountain.

Heidi opened the cottage door and found herself in a small, rather dark room. She could see a fireplace and a shelf with some dishes so she concluded that this was the kitchen. Then she saw a door and she found that it led into another, narrower room. This cottage was quite different from her grandfather's and everything looked very poor and shabby. When Heidi entered the room she saw a table, and at the table a woman was sitting patching a jacket which Heidi recognised at once as Peter's. In the corner, an old bent woman sat spinning. Heidi went straight to her. "Good day, Grandmother!" she said. "Here I am to see you. Did you think I was long in coming?"

The old woman lifted her head and groped for the hand which Heidi held out to her. When she had found it she held it for a while, thoughtfully. Then she said, "Are you the child who stays with the Alm-Uncle? Are you Heidi?"

"Yes," said Heidi. "I have just come down in the sleigh with Grandfather."

"How can it be? Your hands are quite warm. Brigitta, did the Alm-Uncle himself come with the child?"

Peter's mother, Brigitta, who had been mending at the table got up and looked curiously at the little girl. "I don't know, Mother," she said. "I suppose the child knows if the Alm-Uncle came himself."

Heidi looked at the woman and said firmly, "I know very well who wrapped me in the cover and brought me down in the sleigh. It was Grandfather."

"Then there must be something in what Peter said about the Alm-Uncle although we didn't believe him at the time," said the grandmother. "Who could believe it possible! I didn't think the child would stay up there more than three weeks. How does she look, Brigitta?"

By this time Brigitta had carefully inspected Heidi from every angle so she was able to report: "She is as finely built as Adelheid was, but she has the dark eyes and curly hair of Tobias and the old man. I think she resembles both her parents."

During this time, Heidi's attention had not been idle. She had looked round carefully at everything in the room. Suddenly she said, "Look Grandmother! One of your shutters is loose. The grandfather would put a nail in and then the shutter would be all right. It will break the window-pane soon. See how it shakes!"

"Ah, my child," said the grandmother, "I can't see but I can hear, and much more than the shutter banging. Everything in this house cracks and rattles as soon as the wind blows. It comes in from all sides. Everything seems to be loose. During the night, when the others are asleep, I often fear that the house is going to fall to pieces and kill us all. Alas, there is no one here to repair things. Peter doesn't know how to."

"But can't you see the shutter banging, Grandmother? Look! There it is, just over there!" said Heidi, pointing towards the shutter.

"Alas, child, I can see nothing, nothing!" lamented the grand-mother.

"But if I go outside and open the shutter properly so that it is lighter, won't you see then, Grandmother?"

"No, not even then. Nobody can ever make it light for me."

"But if you go outside into the white snow then surely it will be light. Come with me, Grandmother, and I will show you." Heidi, beginning to feel very distressed, took the old woman's hand and tried to lead her.

"Just let me sit, child. It will always be dark for me."

"But surely in summer it will be different, Grandmother," comforted Heidi, becoming more and more anxious to help. "Surely then it will be light for you! When the sun shines on the mountains and on the flowers and turns them all to crimson and gold, then everything will be bright and wonderful for you."

"Ah, child, I shall never again see the flaming mountains nor the little golden flowers up there. It will never again be light for me on this earth, never!"

Suddenly, Heidi began to cry. Full of compassion she sobbed, "Who then can help you? Is there no one?"

The grandmother tried to comfort the child. The old woman was touched to hear her sob so bitterly. Heidi rarely cried, but when she did her grief was not easily overcome. At last the grandmother said, "Come, my dear Heidi, come and I will explain something to you. You see, when one can't see one likes to hear a kind word and I like to hear you talking. Come, sit here close to me and tell me what you have been doing up there and all about the grandfather. I knew him very well years ago. But for many years now I have only heard of him from Peter, and Peter doesn't talk much."

Suddenly, Heidi had a new idea. Quickly she wiped away her tears and said comfortingly, "You wait, Grandmother, and I shall tell Grandfather everything. He will make it light for you again and will repair the cottage for you. He can do everything."

The grandmother was silent now and Heidi began to give a lively account of her life, of summer days on the pasture and her present life in winter with the grandfather. She described the things he could make from wood—benches and chairs and beautiful mangers where the hay was put for Little Swan and Little Bear, and a big new tub for bathing in summer, a new milk bowl and a spoon. Heidi was quite carried away describing all the beautiful things which could be made from pieces of wood. The grandmother listened intently and every now and then she would say, "Do you hear, Brigitta? Do you hear what she says about the Alm-Uncle?"

Suddenly the story was interrupted by a loud clatter at the door and in tramped Peter. He stopped abruptly and gaped when he saw Heidi, but managed a friendly grin as she greeted him, "Good evening, Peter!"

"Is the boy back from school already?" asked the grandmother in surprise. "An afternoon has not passed so quickly for me for a long time! Good evening, Peter. How did you get on with your reading to-day?"

"Just as usual," answered Peter.

"Well, well," sighed the grandmother gently. "I thought

36

there might perhaps be a change by this time, especially as you are going to be twelve years old in February."

"What do you mean by change, Grandmother?" Heidi asked with interest.

"I hoped he would be able to learn to read," explained the grand-mother. "Up there on the shelf is an old hymn book with beautiful hymns in it. I have not heard them for a very long time and I can't remember them now. So I had hoped if Peter could learn to read he would be able to read the hymns to me. But he can't learn the letters. It is too difficult for him."

"I think I had better light the lamp. It is getting quite dark," said Peter's mother, who was still busy patching his jacket. "This afternoon has flown by without my noticing."

Heidi jumped up from her chair, stretched out her hand quickly to the grandmother and said, "Good-bye, Grandmother. I have to go home when it gets dark." She said good night to Peter and his mother and went towards the door. But the grandmother called anxiously, "Wait, wait, Heidi! You mustn't go alone. Peter will go with you. Do you hear? Take care of the child, Peter, and see that she doesn't fall down. And don't loiter on the way in case she catches cold, do you hear? Has she got a warm scarf?"

"I haven't got a scarf," replied Heidi, "but I shall not be cold."

With these words she was outside the house and away so quickly that Peter could hardly keep pace. "Run after her, Brigitta!" the grandmother called. The child will be frozen to death on such a night. Take my scarf! Hurry up now and run quickly!"

Brigitta obeyed. The children had only gone a little way up the mountain when they saw the grandfather coming down and soon he stood beside them.

"Good, Heidi! You have kept your word," he praised her. Then wrapping her snugly in the cover he picked her up and turned back up the mountain.

Brigitta saw the old man lift the child, well wrapped up, into his arms. She returned with Peter to the cottage and told the grandmother with amusement what she had seen.

The grandmother was both astonished and glad. "God be thanked that he is good to the child! If only he would allow her to come again! She is a great comfort and what a kind heart she has!" Until the grandmother went to bed she kept repeating, "If only she could come again! Then I might have something to look forward to in this world! She has done me so much good. She has such a loving little heart and how good she is at telling her story."

Brigitta agreed with her mother, and Peter was well pleased, saying, "I told you so," with great satisfaction.

All the way, Heidi chatted to the grandfather although he could not make out a word of the muffled voice coming from inside the sack. So he said, "Wait until we get home, then you can tell me all about it."

As soon as they entered the hut and Heidi was released from her wrapping she said, "Grandfather, to-morrow we must take the hammer and plenty of long nails to fix the grandmother's shutters and all the loose boards because her house rattles and shakes all over!"

"Must we, indeed! And who told you so?" inquired the grandfather.

"Nobody told me but I know myself," replied Heidi, "for everything is loose and the grandmother cannot sleep if she is afraid that any minute the house will fall down on their heads. And for her everything is dark and she thinks that nobody can ever make it light for her again; but you can do it, Grandfather, I am sure. Think how sad it is for her always having to sit in the dark, and being frightened; and only you can help her. To-morrow we will go and help her, won't we, Grandfather?"

Heidi clung tightly to the grandfather and looked up at him with eagerness and confidence. For a little while the old man looked down at the child, then he said, "Yes, Heidi, we will go and see about the repairs. We can do that to-morrow."

The child started to skip round the room, chanting joyfully, "Tomorrow we'll go! To-morrow we'll go!"

The grandfather kept his promise and on the following afternoon they took the same sleigh drive as they had done the previous day. Once again the old man set the child down before the door of Goat Peter's cottage and said, "Go in now and come away again whenever it gets dark!"

Scarcely had Heidi opened the door and skipped into the room when the grandmother called from the corner, "It is Heidi! Here comes the child!" In her eagerness, she let the thread drop from her fingers and the wheel stood still as both her arms stretched out towards the child. Heidi ran to her at once, and drawing the little chair close to her she sat down at her side. Once again there was so much she had to tell the grandmother and so many questions she had to ask. But suddenly such heavy blows sounded against the wall that the grandmother started violently and nearly upset the spinning wheel. "Mercy on us!" she exclaimed, trembling. "What is that? The house must be falling about us!" Heidi grasped her arm firmly and comforted her, "No, no, Grandmother! Don't be afraid! It is only Grandfather hammering. He will fix everything so that you don't need to be afraid any more."

"Is it possible? Then the Lord has not forgotten us!" the grandmother exclaimed. "Did you hear that, Brigitta? If it is the Alm-Uncle, go and tell him to come in so that I can thank him!"

Brigitta went outside. The Alm-Uncle was busy nailing some strong planks to the wall, knocking in the nails with great vigour. Brigitta approached and said, "Good evening, Uncle! Mother and I want to thank you for your kindness and she would like to tell you herself how grateful she is."

"That will do," interrupted the old man. "I know what you think of the Alm-Uncle. Go back inside. I can find out for myself what is needed here."

Brigitta obeyed at once for the Uncle expressed himself in a way which brooked no opposition.

He knocked and hammered his way all round the house and then climbed the narrow little stair up to the roof, and hammered away there until he had used his last nail. By the time he had finished, darkness had fallen and he had no sooner come down and got out the sleigh from behind the shed than Heidi appeared. As on the previous day, the grandfather wrapped her up and took her in his arms, and, dragging the sleigh behind, made his way back up the mountain. For although he had to drag the heavy sleigh, he was afraid that if Heidi sat in it alone, her wrappings would come loose and then she would get very cold; so he carried her snug and warm in his arms.

And so the winter passed. After many lonely years a great happiness had entered the joyless life of the old blind grandmother, and her days were no longer dreary and dark for now she had something to look forward to. From early morning she listened for Heidi's familiar tripping steps. The child became very attached to the old grandmother. And Heidi, sitting beside her, would chat so merrily that the grandmother hardly noticed the passing of time, and never bothered to ask Brigitta whether the day was over, as she used to do. Indeed, as Heidi left, the old lady would remark on how short the afternoon had been. She continually asked Brigitta to say if the child looked well and Brigitta always replied, "She looks the picture of health!" As soon as she understood that nobody, not even the grandfather, could help the old woman, Heidi was very sad; but the grandmother told her again and again that she felt the darkness much less when Heidi was with her. So every fine winter's day Heidi came down on the sleigh. Without any fuss, the grandfather always packed in his tools and he spent many afternoons repairing the cottage. All his good work soon had its effect and the cottage no longer rattled and groaned when the wind blew around it. The grandmother said she had not slept so well for many a year and that she would never forget what the Alm-Uncle had done for her.

CHAPTER 5

TWO VISITORS TO THE ALM-HUT

Quickly the winter passed, and more quickly still the happy days of summer; and now another winter was drawing to its close. Heidi was happy as a bird and each day she looked forward eagerly to the coming of spring when the warm south wind would sweep through the fir trees and across the valley, melting the last patch of snow on the lower slopes. Long days on the pasture would return and this seemed to Heidi the greatest joy of all. She was eight years old now and had learnt a great deal during the time she had lived with the Alm-Uncle. She knew how to manage the goats, and Little Swan and Little Bear would follow her about, bleating at the very sound of her voice.

Twice during this winter Peter had come from the school in Dorfli with a message from the teacher telling the Alm-Uncle that the child he had staying with him should go to school since she was over the age and should, indeed, have attended the previous winter. On both occasions, the Alm-Uncle had replied that he had no intention of sending the child to school.

When the sun had melted all the snow on the mountain, and the snowdrops were appearing and the fir trees had shaken off the weight of snow and were once again waving their green branches in the wind, Heidi ran back and forth with pleasure between the goat shed, the trees and the hut, to show her grandfather how big the area of green grass under the trees had grown. One sunny morning in March, as she ran out of the house, she was startled to come face to face with an old gentlemen dressed in black. He stood regarding her gravely for a time and then, thinking that his unexpected appearance had frightened her, he said kindly, "It is all right. You need not be afraid of me. You are Heidi, are you not? Where is your grandfather?"

"He is sitting at the table, making wooden spoons," replied Heidi and at once led him inside.

It was the old pastor from Dörfli who had known the uncle well in the old days. He walked towards the old man who was bent over his work, and addressed him.

"Good morning, neighbour!"

Astonished, the grandfather looked up, then rose, saying, "Good morning, pastor!" Offering his seat to the visitor, he added, "Pray sit down, if you do not mind a wooden seat."

41

The pastor seated himself. "I have not seen you for a long time, neighbour," he said.

"Nor I you!"

"I have come to-day to discuss something with you," continued the pastor. "I think perhaps you know what it is I want to talk to you about, and that I am anxious to hear what you intend to do about a certain matter."

There was a silence. The pastor glanced quickly towards the child, who stood by the door and watched the newcomer with interest.

"Heidi, go and see how the goats are getting along!" said the grandfather. "You may take them a little salt, and stay with them until I come!"

Heidi disappeared at once.

"The child should have gone to school a year ago," said the pastor now. "The school master reminded you often but you ignored him. What is it you intend should become of the child, neighbour?"

"I intend that she should not go to school!"

The pastor looked with surprise at the old man who sat on his bench with his arms folded determinedly.

"But how is the child going to grow up?" asked the pastor reasonably.

"She will grow up with the goats and birds. That way she will learn nothing evil."

"But the child is neither a goat nor a bird but a human being," pleaded the pastor. "Though she learns nothing evil from her companions, they cannot teach her her A B Cs! Learn she must, and the time has come to begin. I came to speak a word to you in time, neighbour, so that you may think it over at your leisure and make arrangements during the summer. The child must not be allowed to run about another winter without taking lessons. Next winter she must attend school regularly!"

"No, she will not go, pastor!" muttered the old man with unwavering determination.

"Do you really think there is no way of making you see reason if you insist so stubbornly on this decision?" asked the pastor, beginning to lose patience. "You have lived in the world and have seen and learnt a lot. I should have thought you would have had more sense, neighbour."

"You think so? asked the old man, and the tremor in his voice betrayed that he was no longer calm. "And do you really think that next winter I shall send a delicate child on a two hours' walk down the mountain on ice-cold mornings in storm and snow, and allow her to return at night when there may be a wind raging fit to blow a man over, let alone a child? Perhaps the pastor still remembers the child's mother, Adelheid. She was a sleep-walker and had a delicate constitution. Might not the health of this child, who is also finely built, be endangered by so much exertion? I wonder who can force me to send her? I shall take it to the highest law court in the country and then we shall see who can force me!"

"You are quite right, neighbour," agreed the pastor, amicably. "It would not be possible to send the child from here. But I see the child is dear to you. For her sake, do what you ought to have done long ago. Come down into Dörfli and live amongst us! What a life you live here, alone and embittered towards God and men. If anything should happen to you up here in the mountains who would come to your assistance? I cannot understand how you are not frozen to death in this hut of yours in the winter-time. How does this delicate child stand up to it?"

"I see to it that she is not cold, and that she has a good warm bed, I should like the pastor to know. And another thing: I get all the wood I need. If the pastor cares to look into my wood-shed he will soon see! There is plenty there! The fire is never out in my hut all through the winter. As for living down in the valley, it is out of the question. The people down there despise me and I them. For all our sakes, it is better we stay apart."

"No, no, you are quite wrong!" the pastor said warmly. "The people down below don't dislike you half as much as you think. Take my advice, neighbour! Make your peace with God, ask His forgiveness and then come and see how people will change towards you and how happy you will be!"

43

The pastor rose. He held out his hand to the old man and repeated with kindly emphasis, "I am counting on it, neighbour! Next winter you'll come back to live with us in the valley and we'll be good neighbours again, as we used to be. I would be disappointed to think that you were coming back only because of the school business. Promise me that you will live amongst us again, reconciled to God and man!"

The Alm-Uncle shook hands with the pastor but insisted firmly, "I know you mean well, but as to what you expect me to do—no! Once and for all I tell you I will not send the child, nor will I come down to live in the valley."

"Then God help you!" sighed the pastor and sadly made his way back down the mountain to the village.

As a result of the interview, the Alm-Uncle was in a very black mood, and when Heidi asked in the afternoon, "Shall we go down to the grandmother's now?" he replied harshly, "Not to-day!" He was silent the whole day and the following morning, when Heidi asked again, "Shall we go to-day to see the grandmother?" he turned away abruptly, mumbling, "Perhaps."

But before the dinner dishes had been cleared away another visitor had arrived. It was cousin Dete, dressed in a beautiful gown which swept the floor and wearing on her head a very fine hat with feathers. The Alm-Uncle examined her from head to foot in amazement. But Dete was all prepared to make friendly conversation and at once adopted a flattering tone.

"How well the child looks! I hardly recognised her! I can see that she has not had a bad time with the Alm-Uncle, far from it! I have often thought of taking the child back for I can imagine that she is in your way. Day and night I have thought about what to do with her and that's why I am here to-day. I have just heard of something that would be a piece of luck for Heidi. I have fixed everything. It is really a wonderful chance. The people I am in service with have some very wealthy relations. They live in the most beautiful house in Frankfurt and they have an only daughter who is an invalid and has to be wheeled in a chair. She is very much alone and has her lessons with a private teacher, which, of course, is very boring

44

for her. Now she would like a playmate so her people have asked my mistress to help them find a companion. The lady house-keeper thinks that a simple, unspoilt child, one different from the children now-a-days, would be most suitable. Naturally I thought of Heidi and went at once to the lady and told her all about our child's character. She agreed immediately to take her. No one can foresee what good fortune will be in store for Heidi. If the people become fond of her and if something should happen to their own little daughter—and who knows when she is so weak—then in all likelihood they would not want to be without a child—then it would be the most unheard-of luck—"

"Do you think you have just about finished?" interrupted the Alm-Uncle who had held his peace up till now.

"Ugh!" exclaimed Dete, tossing her head. "You behave as though I were telling you something of no consequence. Anybody in Prättigau would thank God if I were to bring such news!"

"You may take your news where you like. I want to hear no more of it," replied the Uncle dryly.

This threw Dete immediately into a passion. "Well!" she stormed, "if that is all you have to say, Uncle, I will speak my mind, too. The child is eight years old now, but she knows nothing. You neither want her to attend school nor to go to church. Oh, I have heard all about it in Dörfli. She is my sister's child and I am responsible for what happens to her. When such a good chance comes her way only one who cared nothing for her welfare would oppose it. But I tell you, I won't give in and people are on my side. There is not a single person who would not take my part—and they are all against you. And if you are thinking of taking it to law, think well, Uncle! There are things that could be brought up against you which you wouldn't like to hear."

"Hold your tongue!" thundered the uncle, his eyes ablaze with anger. "Very well, then. Take the child away and ruin her! And never let me set eyes on you again, with that ridiculous hat on your head and such words on your tongue!" Then the uncle turned from her abruptly and strode from the hut.

"You have made Grandfather angry," said Heidi, fixing dark, smouldering eyes on her aunt.

"Oh, he'll soon get over it," replied Dete impatiently. "Come along now! Where are your clothes?"

"I won't go!" said Heidi defiantly.

"What did you say?" asked the aunt, about to fly into a temper. Then she softened her tone a little and continued more persuasively, "Come, come! You don't know any better. You have no idea how well off you will be." Then, going to the wardrobe, she took out Heidi's things and parcelled them together. "Come now! Here is your hat! What a sight it is! But never mind! It will do for to-day. Put it on, quickly."

"I am going to stay here," repeated Heidi.

"Don't be so silly. You are as obstinate as a goat. I suppose that is what you have learnt from them. But you've got to understand, the grandfather is cross and doesn't want to see us again, you heard him say so. He wants you to go with me, so now you mustn't make him more angry. You have no idea how nice it is in Frankfurt. But, of course, if you don't like it you can always come back here. By that time the grandfather will have recovered himself."

"Can I come straight home again tonight if I want to?" asked Heidi.

"Come along now and don't be silly! I said you can go home when you like. To-day we are only going as far as Mayenfeld but tomorrow we will travel by train, and the train can carry you home again as fast as the wind."

Aunt Dete took the bundle of clothes under one arm, grasped Heidi firmly by the other hand, and together they started to climb down the hill. It was still too early in the spring to take the goats up to the pasture, so Peter was still going to school in Dörfli, but once in a while he took a day's holiday, for learning to read seemed not nearly as attractive a proposition as wandering about looking for thick sticks which might come in useful.

As Dete and Heidi approached the grandmother's hut, Peter appeared from round a corner of the cottage. He was carrying a huge bundle of thick hazel twigs, when the two figures approached. He stopped to stare at them as they passed by; then he called out after them, "Where are you going?"

"I have to go at once to Frankfurt with Aunt," answered Heidi, "but I am going to say good-bye to the grandmother first. She will be waiting for me and I must see her before I go."

"No, no," interrupted the aunt quickly. "It is much too late. You can see her next time you come back. Come along, now!" And she pulled the child along, afraid that she might again take it into her head to stay and that the grandmother would support her wishes.

Peter dashed into the cottage and dropped his bundle of sticks so noisily that the grandmother started up from her spinning, exclaiming fretfully, "What is it now? What is it?" And Peter's mother, who had been sitting by the table, said in her patient way, "What is it, Peter? What is the matter?"

"She is taking Heidi away!" gasped Peter.

"Who?" asked the grandmother in distress. "Taking her where, Peter?" But she soon guessed what had taken place, for her daughter had told her not long ago that she had seen Dete going up to the Alm-Uncle's. The old woman unfastened the window with trembling fingers and called out imploringly, "Dete, Dete, don't take the child away from us! Don't take Heidi away!"

Dete and Heidi heard the voice. Dete had evidently made out the grandmother's words for she grasped the child's hand still more firmly and ran as fast as she could.

Heidi, struggling to get her hand free, cried, "The grandmother is calling! I want to go to her!"

But that was exactly what the aunt did not want. She tried to soothe the child.

"Come quickly now or it will be too late and we will not be able to continue our journey to-morrow. You will soon see how much you will like Frankfurt. Perhaps you will never want to come back again. But if you do it will be quite simple. You could even take something home for the grandmother—something she would like."

This appealed to Heidi and she stopped trying to resist and started to run, too.

47

After a little while she asked, "What could I get for Grandmother?"

"Something nice," said the aunt. "Perhaps some nice soft rolls. She would enjoy that. It would be such a change from the dark bread."

"Oh, yes! She always gives it to Peter and says 'It is too hard for me.' I have heard her myself", admitted Heidi. "Let us hurry, then, Aunt Dete! We may reach Frankfurt to-day and I shall soon be back with the rolls." And Heidi started to run so fast that the aunt with her bundle could hardly keep pace with her. But she was glad to be having no more difficulty with the child for now they had almost reached the first houses in Dörfli and a lot of talk and questions might have made Heidi change her mind again. So Dete strode straight ahead holding Heidi's hand tightly so that every one would see that she had to hurry along because of the child. To every question she merely answered, "I can't stop now. We have a long way to go."

"Are you going away?" Is she fleeing from the Alm-Uncle?" "It's amazing that she has survived!" "But how healthy she looks!" Questions and exclamations came from all sides and Dete was glad that she didn't have to stop and that Heidi didn't say a word but hurried on eagerly.

From that day on the Alm-Uncle looked even more fierce and terrifying when he came down to Dörfli. He spoke to no one and looked more threatening with his cheese-basket on his back and his mountain stick in his hand. The old man ignored everyone as he strode through the village to the valley where he sold cheese and bought bread and meat. After he had gone, the villagers stood around watching his retreating back and everyone commented on his wild appearance and his total lack of response to anyone's greeting.

They all agreed that it was a good thing that the child had been taken from him—they had noticed how Heidi hurried along as though afraid that her grandfather might catch them up. Everybody was of the same opinion; that it was a great blessing that the child had been taken away. Only the blind grandmother took the old man's part. When people came to the house to give her some spinning to do, she would tell them again and again how kind and good he had been to the child and what he had done for herself and her daughter; how he had spent many afternoons repairing the cottage which, without his help, would undoubtedly have collapsed upon them. This story soon got about in Dörfli, but most people thought the grandmother was too old to understand and too blind and hard of hearing to know exactly what went on around her.

It was as well it had been repaired, for the Alm-Uncle never came to Goat Peter's cottage now and the grandmother's days were once more passed in sighing and fretting. "Alas, all the joy and happiness has gone with the child!" she would say, "and the days are long and dreary! If only I might see Heidi again before I die!"

CHAPTER 6

A NEW START FOR HEIDI

In the house in Frankfurt, the little daughter of Herr Sesemann sat in the comfortable invalid chair in which all her life was spent and in which she had to be wheeled from room to room. Now she was in the room which they called the study, and where she had her lessons.

Clara's little face was pale and thin and her soft, gentle blue eyes were fixed at this moment on the door. To-day, time seemed to pass very slowly for her, for she was saying rather impatiently, "But isn't it time yet, Fräulein Rottenmeier?"

The lady thus addressed sat very upright at a small work-table and nodded. Principally because of her rather odd and very severe style of dress, Fräulein Rottenmeier presented an awe-inspiring appearance. Over her shoulders she wore a cape with a stiff collar and on her head a very elaborate cap. Since the death of Frau Sesemann, several years ago, Fräulein Rottenmeier had acted as house-keeper and manager of the domestic staff. Herr Sesemann very often went off on business trips, leaving Fräulein Rottenmeier in sole charge of the house, stipulating only that no decisions should be taken without first consulting his little daughter and that nothing should be done against her wish.

Just as Clara was asking the same question a second time, Dete and Heidi arrived at the door. Dete asked the coachman, who had descended from is box, whether it was too late to see Fräulein Rottenmeier.

"That's nothing to do with me," he muttered. "Ring the bell you'll find in the hall and Sebastian will come."

Dete rang the bell and the butler came down the stairs, the big round buttons of his livery in keeping with his round eyes which stared blankly at the two strangers.

"I wonder if it is too late to see Fräulein Rottenmeier?" Dete asked.

Sebastian stared frostily for a moment, then pressed a bell and disappeared without a word. Next a maid appeared. A spotless white cap was perched on top of her head. Regarding the visitors haughtily from the top of the stairs, "What is it?" she asked.

Dete repeated her request. Tinette disappeared, but very soon came back and called from above, "Come this way! You are expected."

Dete and Heidi went upstairs and followed Tinette into the study. At the door Dete stopped politely, still holding Heidi's hand firmly for there was no knowing what the child might do in strange surroundings.

Fräulein Rottenmeier rose slowly and came forward to examine the new playmate for the daughter of the house. She did not appear to be very pleased with what she saw. Heidi wore her simple little cotton dress and on her head, her old, crushed, straw hat. She gazed innocently from underneath it, staring with unconcealed surprise at the lady's towering headgear.

"What is your name?" asked Fräulein Rottenmeier, after a

lengthy inspection of the child, who had returned her gaze steadily and inquiringly throughout.

"Heidi," the child answered distinctly.

"What? That is not a Christian name! You were surely not baptised so! What name were you given when you were christened?"

"I can't remember now," replied Heidi.

"What a foolish answer!" exclaimed the lady, shaking her head disapprovingly. "Dete, is the child stupid or impertinent?"

"I am so sorry! Would you kindly allow me to speak for the child? She is not accustomed to strangers," said Dete hastily, secretly nudging Heidi for having given such an unsuitable answer. "She certainly is not stupid, nor impertinent. It is just that she always says exactly what she is thinking. This is the first time she has ever been in an upper-class house and she knows nothing about good manners. She is docile and willing to learn if madam will have the patience. She was christened Adelheid for her mother, my late sister."

"Well, at least that's a name one can pronounce," remarked Fräulein Rottenmeier. "But Dete, I must say that for her age the child looks to me a little strange. I told you that a companion for Fräulein Clara had to be of her age to be able to share her lessons and everything. Fräulein Clara is twelve now. What is the age of the child?"

"With your permission," began Dete elaborately, "I am not quite sure myself but I think she is a little younger, but not much. She will be ten, or perhaps a little more."

"I am eight now, the grandfather said," declared Heidi. The aunt gave her another push but Heidi was not in the least embarrassed.

"What! Only eight years old!" cried Fräulein Rottenmeier indignantly. "Four years younger! What use is that? And what have you learnt? Which books did you use for your lessons?"

"None," replied Heidi.

"What? How did you learn to read?"

"I never learnt. Neither did Peter," said Heidi.

"Mercy! You cannot read! Is that true that you cannot read?"

demanded Fräulein Rottenmeier, deeply shocked. What did you learn, then?"

"Nothing," said Heidi.

"Dete!" cried Fräulein Rottenmeier when she had recovered from this shock. "This is not the agreement at all! How dare you bring this child to me!"

But Dete was not easily frightened and replied boldly, "With madam's permission, the child is just what I understood madam wanted. Madam told me she wanted a companion unlike ordinary children. Therefore I chose this one because the older ones are not so unspoilt. But now I am afraid I must go. My mistress will be expecting me. If I may, I shall come again soon to see how the child is getting on."

With a curtsy, Dete left the room and quickly ran downstairs. For a moment Fräulein Rottenmeier was too surprised to speak, then she ran after Dete. There were many things which must be discussed if the child were to stay and the aunt seemed determined that she should.

Heidi still stood by the door where she had remained since she entered the room. So far Clara had watched silently; now she beckoned to Heidi to come nearer.

Heidi went up to her.

"Would you rather be called Heidi or Adelheid?" asked Clara.

"I am always called Heidi," Heidi replied.

"Then I shall always call you that, too," said Clara "I like the name although never before have I heard it or seen a little girl like you. Has your hair always been short and curly like that?"

"Yes, I think so," replied Heidi.

"Did you come to Frankfurt yesterday, and are you pleased to be here?" Clara continued to ask.

"No, we came to-day. But to-morrow I am going home again with some white rolls for the grandmother."

"How strange you are!" Clara burst out. "You have been brought here to stay with me and share my lessons with me. What fun it will be now because you can't read at all. At least it will be a change. It is usually very dull and the mornings are so long! You see, every morning at ten my tutor comes and the lessons go on till two. That is far too long! Sometimes the tutor holds his book close to his face as if he had suddenly become short-sighted but I know quite well it is only because he is yawning; and Fräulein Rottenmeier takes out her handkerchief and holds it to her face as if she were affected by what we are reading, but she too only wants to yawn. But I don't dare, because if I only did it once Fräulein Rottenmeier would fetch the cod liver oil and say I was getting weak again, and the worst thing of all is to take cod liver oil. But it will be much more fun now. I can listen to you learning to read."

Heidi shook her head doubtfully at the mention of her learning to read.

"Of course, Heidi, you have to learn to read. Everybody has to learn to read and my tutor is very kind. He is never cross and he will explain everything to you. But nevertheless, you won't be able to understand what he explains. Don't ask any questions, as you will only encourage him to continue explaining and you'll understand even less. The best thing to do is to wait until you've learnt more and know about everything on your own, then what he says will have some sort of meaning."

Just then Fräulein Rottenmeier came back into the room. She had not succeeded in calling Dete back and was apparently very annoyed about it. She had wanted at least to persuade Dete that Heidi was totally unsuitable to be Clara's companion and to complain at Dete's misleading behaviour. She felt even more annoyed at the thought that she herself had brought the problem on to her own head by agreeing to Heidi being fetched.

What was she going to do about it? She ran to and fro in a bother from the dining room to the study, and then began scolding Sebastian, who was studying the table he had just laid, to make sure nothing had been missed out.

"You can carry on day-dreaming tomorrow morning," she said crossly, "hurry up or we'll get no dinner today."

Then she bustled out, calling Tinette, but in such an irritable voice that the maid came up with even more of a swagger than usual. She looked so pert that Fräulein Rottenmeier did not dare scold her.

"See that a room is made ready for the child who has just

arrived," she said, tight-lipped. "It's all ready; it just needs a duster over it." Sebastian had opened the folding doors of the study and quietly wheeled Clara into the other room. While he adjusted the chair Heidi placed herself before him and stared steadily up at him.

"Well, what is it you are looking at?" he grumbled.

When Fräulein Rottenmeier returned she was just in time to hear Heidi say, "You look like Peter."

She raised her hands in horror. "Really!" she murmured. "She treats the butler as an equal! The child knows absolutely nothing!"

Sebastian helped Clara to her seat at the table and Fräulein Rottenmeier seated herself beside her, motioning Heidi to sit opposite. Beside Heidi's plate lay a lovely white roll. She glanced at it happily. The resemblance Heidi had discovered in Sebastian seemed to have given her confidence in him for she sat as quiet as a mouse until he came to her side to serve the fish, then she pointed to the roll and asked, "May I have it?"

Sebastian nodded, glancing sideways at Fräulein Rottenmeier to see what effect the question had had on her.

Immediately Heidi took the roll and put it into her pocket. Sebastian hid a smile. Motionless and silent, he stood at her side, waiting for her to take her helping of fish for it was not his place to speak or move away until Heidi had helped herself. For a few seconds Heidi looked at him wonderingly, then she asked, "May I have a little of that, too?" Sebastian nodded again. "Then give me some, please," she said, looking calmly at her plate. At this breach of etiquette Sebastian was almost in danger of losing control of his features and the arm which held the dish was beginning to shake.

"You can leave the dish on the table and come back afterwards," ordered Fräulein Rottenmeier, looking very severe, and Sebastian disappeared at once.

"Adelheid, I see I shall have to teach you the first simple rules of good behaviour," said the lady with a deep sigh. "First of all I will show you how to behave at the table and improve your manners."

She instructed Heidi thoroughly and clearly on what she had

to do. "Then," she went on to explain, "I must impress upon you particularly that you are not to speak to Sebastian at table unless the question or remark is absolutely necessary, and even then you must not address him as a friend. Do you understand? And so with Tinette. You will address *me* as you hear others do. Clara will decide for herself what you are to call her."

"Clara, of course!" Clara interrupted.

Then followed a long list of rules about getting up and going to bed, about entering and leaving a room, about being tidy and shutting doors. All of a sudden Heidi's eyes closed, for she had been up since five o'clock that morning and had had a long journey. She leaned back in her chair, fast asleep. When Fräulein Rottenmeier had finished her lecture at last, she said, "Now, remember everything I have said, Adelheid! Have you understood it all?"

"Heidi has been asleep for ever so long," Clara said with amusement. She had not had such an entertaining dinner for a long time!

"It is really shocking how much trouble this child is causing," exclaimed Fräulein Rottenmeier angrily and rang the bell so violently that both Sebastian and Tinette came rushing in. But in spite of all the noise Heidi slept on and it was only with great difficulty that they succeeded in awakening her so that she could be shown to her bedroom which was at the end of a long passage, beyond those of Clara and Fräulein Rottenmeier.

CHAPTER 7

AN EVENTFUL DAY

Heidi awoke in the morning and looked around in bewilderment. She blinked and rubbed her eyes but it did not help her to remember where she was. She was lying in a high white bed in a big room and daylight streamed in between long white curtains. There were two arm-chairs covered in a floral material. A sofa stood against the wall with a round table in front of it and in the corner there was a wash-stand with all sorts of objects on it which were entirely new to Heidi.

Suddenly she remembered that she was in Frankfurt and the events of the previous day came back to her quite clearly. She remembered the long list of instructions given to her by Fräulein Rottenmeier, up to the point at which she must have fallen asleep. Heidi jumped out of bed and dressed; then went from one window to the other to try to get a glimpse of the sky and the countryside outside. Behind the big curtains she felt like a bird in a cage. As she could not manage to pull them aside she crept underneath to get to the window. It was so high that she could only just see over the sill. However, the view was not one of pleasant green fields but only of walls and windows. She ran backwards and forwards from one window to another, but the view was just the same. It frightened her to think that she could not see the sky, for she was used to rising early and running outside straight away to inspect the meadows, the blue sky, the sun and the trees and flowers. Heidi couldn't believe that there might be no green grass or snow on the mountain slopes. She was like a captive bird, trying to fly out into the free air through the bars of its cage. But the windows would not open, and her little fingers were not strong enough to prise them open from the bottom. At last she realised that her efforts were in vain, and she started to consider going outside and round the house until she found the grass. Then she remembered that the previous night when she arrived, she had seen only hard pavements in front of the house. Presently there came a knock at the door and Tinette popped her head round, saying in a bored voice, "Breakfast is ready!"

Heidi failed to understand that this was an invitation, for the sour expression on Tinette's face had suggested rather a warning to stay away. So it seemed to Heidi, at any rate, and she acted accordingly. She took the little stool from under the table, put it in a corner, sat down and waited quietly to see what would happen next. After some time Fräulein Rottenmeier bustled along with a great deal of noise. Once again she seemed to be thoroughly annoyed and shouted at Heidi, "What is the matter with you, Adelheid? Don't you know what breakfast is? Come along!"

This Heidi understood and followed at once. Clara had been seated in the dining-room for some time and she greeted Heidi in a friendly way. Her face wore a much happier expression than usual for she was looking forward to all kinds of unexpected events that day. Breakfast passed without incident. Heidi ate her rolls very nicely and when they had finished Clara was wheeled back to the study. Fräulein Rottenmeier told Heidi to follow and remain with Clara until the tutor arrived to begin lessons. As soon as the children were alone together Heidi asked, "How can I see right down to the ground?"

"You just open the window and look out!" replied Clara, amused.

"But the windows won't open," replied Heidi sadly.

"Oh yes," Clara assured her, "but you can't do it alone. Neither can I. But if you see Sebastian he will open them for you."

Heidi sighed with relief, for the house had begun to make her feel as though she were a prisoner. Then Clara began to ask Heidi about her home and Heidi was delighted to tell her all about the Alm and the goats and the pasture and everything that was dear to her.

In the meantime the tutor had arrived, but Fräulein Rottenmeier did not show him into the study as usual. She wanted to talk to him first and led him to the dining-room. There, in great agitation, she began to describe to him the awkward situation which had arisen and told him how, some time ago, she had persuaded Herr Sesemann to get a companion for Clara as it would help Clara at her lessons and give her some amusement during her leisure hours. In actual fact, Fräulein Rottenmeier had wanted this for her own benefit, as it would no longer necessitate her own continual attendance on the sick child. The father had replied that he was delighted for his daughter to have a companion, as long as she was given exactly the same kindness and care as Clara, for he would not tolerate any tormenting of the child—"a quite unnecessary and tactless remark," added Fräulein Rottenmeier. She recounted how dreadfully she had been deceived and she went on to enlighten the tutor on all the dreadful things of which Heidi had so far been found guilty, and how, in view of Heidi's complete ignorance, the tutor would have to begin at the very beginning with the A B C, and how she herself had had to give the child instruction on the simplest rules of behaviour. There was only one way out of the situation, in Fräulein Rottenmeier's opinion, and that was for the tutor to insist that it was impossible to teach two children so far apart in age without retarding Clara's progress. That would be a very good reason for Herr Sesemann's sending the child back home. Herr Sesemann knew the child had arrived and without his consent Fräulein Rottenmeier could not send her away again.

However, the tutor was cautious and unwilling to commit himself. With many words of comfort he assured Fräulein Rottenmeier that though the child were backward in some things she might be quite advanced in other respects and that regular lessons might very well restore the balance. When Fräulein Rottenmeier at last realised that she would get very little support from the tutor she opened the door to the study and allowed him him to go through to the children. She paced up and down the dining room, silently pondering how the servants should be instructed to address Adelheid. The father had expressly stated that she was to be treated exactly like his own daughter, and this would probably refer particularly to her dealings with the servants. However, her musing was suddenly interrupted, for before many minutes had passed, a dreadful noise came from the study. Then there was a loud cry from Sebastian. Fräulein Rottenmeier rushed in to find the whole room in complete disorder; books, copy-books, inkstand; and across the table, on to the floor and across the carpet there flowed a stream of ink. Heidi was nowhere to be seen.

"What is all this?" cried Fräulein Rottenmeier. "Carpet,

books, work basket, everything covered with ink! I never saw such a mess! I have no doubt that wretched child is to blame!"

The tutor looked very distressed but Clara was following events with obvious amusement.

"Yes, Heidi did it, but not on purpose. She mustn't be punished. It was just that she was in such a hurry to get away that she tugged the tablecloth and then everything fell on the floor. She wanted to see the carriages passing; that's why she rushed out. Perhaps she has never seen one before!"

"What did I tell you? The creature doesn't know the first thing! She has no idea what a lesson is—that she must sit still and listen. But where is the little trouble-maker? Surely she hasn't run away! Whatever will Herr Sesemann say?"

Fräulein Rottenmeier ran downstairs. There stood Heidi in the open doorway looking out into the street in complete bewilderment.

"What is the matter? What are you thinking of to run away like that?" Fräulein Rottenmeier shouted at the child.

"I thought I heard the fir trees rustling but I can't find them and I don't hear them any more," said Heidi disconsolately, turning her head in the direction of the disappearing carriages. The rumbling of their wheels had seemed to her like the howling of the wind in the fir trees at home and she had tried to follow the sound.

"Fir trees! What nonsense! Do you think we live in a wood! Come and see the mess you have made!"

Heidi followed Fräulein Rottenmeier upstairs. She gazed in astonishment at the havoc she had created, for in her haste to get downstairs she had noticed nothing.

"You won't do this a second time," warned Fräulein Rottenmeier. "During lessons you will sit still and pay attention! And if you can't do that I will have to tie you to your chair. Do you understand?"

"Yes," said Heidi. "I shall be good now."

Sebastian and Tinette were called in to restore order and the tutor went away because there could be no more lessons that day— there had not even been time for yawning!

Clara always rested in the afternoons, so Heidi was told she might do as she pleased. This suited her perfectly because there was something she very much wanted to do. But she needed assistance, and for this reason she posted herself in front of the dining-room door, right in the centre of the hall so that she would not miss the person to whom she wished to speak. It was not very long before Sebastian came upstairs carrying a large tray. Heidi addressed him formally, as Fräulein Rottenmeier had instructed her.

"Is there something the little fräulein wants?" inquired Sebastian, carrying the silver into the dining-room. "I only wanted to ask you something—but nothing nasty like this morning," said Heidi, hastily, eager to placate him, for Sebastian appeared to be in a bad mood, and Heidi was sure that it was because she had spilt ink on the floor.

"Oh yes, and why are you talking to me in that manner?" replied Sebastian, in an offended tone, obviously still cross.

"Fräulein Rottenmeier ordered me always to speak to you like that," said Heidi.

Sebastian laughed, to Heidi's astonishment, and added in a friendly way, "What is it that the little fräulein wants?"

"My name is Heidi, not fräulein," replied Heidi, now put out herself.

"Exactly, but the lady in question has ordered me to call you fräulein," he explained.

"Oh, well, I had better accept it," said Heidi quietly, for she had realised that whatever Fräulein Rottenmeier said was to be obeyed absolutely. "So now I have three names," she sighed.

"What was it the little fräulein wanted to ask?" said Sebastian kindly as he went through to the dining room to put away the cutlery.

"How do you open a window, Sebastian?"

"Like this!" And he opened one of the large windows in the dining-room.

Heidi crossed over to the window but she was not tall enough to be able to see out.

"Here you are!" said Sebastian, bringing a high stool. "Now the little fräulein can see everything that is going on in the street down below."

Cheerfully Heidi climbed up and at last managed to see out of the window. Greatly disappointed, she withdrew her head almost at once. "But I can only see the stony street! Nothing else!" she said sadly. "If you go round the house what do you see on the other side, Sebastian?"

"Just the same!" he replied.

"But where have you to go to see over the whole valley?" she asked.

"Then you must climb a high tower or a church steeple, like that one with the golden ball. From there you can see ever so far."

At that, Heidi quickly jumped down from her stool and raced downstairs into the street. But it was not so easy as she had imagined. When she saw the steeple from the window it looked as though she only had to cross the street to reach it. But although she had walked right down the street she had not come to the steeple and she could not even see it any longer. She walked on and on. Many people passed but they all seemed to be in such a hurry that Heidi did not like to stop any of them to ask the way. Then Heidi saw a boy standing on the street corner with a barrel organ and, perched on his arm, a very strange-looking little animal. Heidi went forward and asked, "Where is the tower with the golden ball on the top?"

"Don't know!" answered the boy.

"Who can tell me, then?" asked Heidi again.

"Don't know."

"Don't you know of any church with a high steeple?"

"Yes, I know one!"

"Well, then, come and show it to me!"

"You show me first what you will give me for it!" said the boy, holding his hand out. Heidi searched in her pocket and found a pretty little card on which was printed a wreath of red roses. It was not easy to part with it for it had been given to her by Clara only that morning. But she longed to be able to look down over the green slopes into the valley. "There," said Heidi, "would you like this?"

The boy withdrew his hand and shook his head.

"What do you want, then?" asked Heidi, cheerfully putting away her little picture.

"Money," said the boy.

"I haven't got any now, but Clara will give me some later. How much do you want?"

"Twopence."

"Well, come along, then!"

They walked down a long street and on the way Heidi asked her companion what he was carrying on his back. He told her it was a barrel organ which played beautiful music when you turned the handle. All at once they found themselves in front of an old church with a high steeple. The boy stood still and pointed at it.

"But how can I get in?" asked Heidi when she saw that the doors were closed.

"Don't know," came the reply.

"Perhaps I could ring the bell as we do for Sebastian." Heidi had discovered a bell in the wall which she now pulled as hard as she could.

"When I go up you must wait here for me for I don't know my way back and you must show it to me."

"What will I get for it?"

"What do you want?"

"Another twopence."

They heard steps inside and the door creaked open. An old man appeared, looking first surprised and then angry when he saw the children. "How dare you ring-the bell like that!" he shouted at them. "Can't you read the notice? 'Visitors wishing to go to the top of the tower, please ring!' "

The boy said nothing but pointed to Heidi.

"But that's just what I want!" said Heidi.

"Why do you want to go up there?" asked the caretaker. "Did somebody send you?"

"No," said Heidi. "I would just like to go up to the top and look down."

"Be off with you! And don't dare to try this trick on me again!" said the old man and was about to close the door; but Heidi grasped his coat and cried beseechingly, "Let me go up just once!"

The imploring look in Heidi's eyes made the old man change his mind. He took her hand and said kindly, "If you really want it so much I will take you up."

The boy sat down on the stone steps and prepared to wait.

Together Heidi and the old man climbed many, many steps which became smaller and smaller as they went up, until at last, a very narrow little stair led up to the top of the tower. The caretaker lifted Heidi up to let her see out of the window. "Now you can look down," he said.

Heidi saw nothing but roofs, steeples and chimneys. She withdrew her head presently and said, very dispiritedly, "It is not at all as I expected."

"There! You see how a little one like you knows nothing about views. Now come down and never ring my bell again!"

The old man put Heidi back down on the floor and went ahead of her down the narrow stair. When the steps got broader they came to the caretaker's little room and beside it, underneath the sloping roof, stood a big basket. In front of it sat a big grey cat which snarled and spat because inside the basket lived her family and she wanted to warn everybody not to meddle with them. Heidi looked at her in amazement. She had never seen such a big cat. There were scores of mice in the old tower and the cat had no difficulty in catching half a dozen every day, for her kittens. The caretaker saw the look of delight on Heidi's face and said, "Come! She won't hurt you when I am here. You can still look at the kittens."

Heidi went over to the basket and exclaimed joyfully, "Oh, what sweet little kittens!"

'Would you like one?" asked the old man as he watched Heidi with amusement.

"For myself? To keep?" whispered Heidi, who could hardly believe her luck.

"Yes, you can have them all if you like," he said, thinking this would be a better way of getting rid of them than drowning.

Heidi was overjoyed. There was certainly plenty of room in the big house and how happy the kittens would make Clara!

"But how can I carry them away?" asked Heidi, picking

some of them up, but the big cat sprang at her arm and hissed at her so fiercely that she shrank back.

"I will bring them if you tell me the address," said the old man.

"Herr Sesemann's. On the door there is a dog's head with a gold ring in its mouth."

The caretaker did not need such a detailed description. He had been in the church for many years and knew every house in the district.

"I know the house."

"If only I could take one or two with me—one for me and one for Clara! May I?"

"Yes! Take them."

Heidi's eyes shone with delight. She chose a white one and a tabby and put one into her right and one into her left pocket. Then they went downstairs.

The boy was still sitting on the steps outside. He jumped up when he saw Heidi but it took Heidi several minutes of detailed description of the house and its surroundings before the boy realised where she had to go and they then quickly reached the house. Heidi rang the bell and Sebastian opened the door. When he saw Heidi he hustled her inside.

"Quickly! Into the dining-room! They are all at table and Fräulein Rottenmeier looks like a loaded cannon. But why did you run away like that?"

Heidi went into the room. Fräulein Rottenmeier did not look up, Clara said nothing and it was an altogether uneasy atmosphere. When Heidi was seated Fräulein Rottenmeier began in a very severe and solemn voice:

"Adelheid! I shall talk to you afterwards. I will only say now that you have behaved exceedingly badly, leaving the house without permission and wandering about the streets until such a late hour without telling anyone. Your conduct is unparalleled!"

"Miaow!" It sounded like an answer.

Now the lady's temper rose, "What Adelheid! You are rude as well as naughty! I warn you!"

"I didn't—," began Heidi. "Miaow! Miaow!"

Sebastian could conceal his amusement no longer and had to leave the room.

"That will do!" Fräulein Rottenmeier tried to say, but her voice cracked with excitement. "Get up and leave the room!"

Heidi, frightened, got up and tried to explain, "I really didn't— Miaow! Miaow!"

"But Heidi," Clara said reproachfully, "when you see it makes Fräulein Rottenmeier angry why do you go on saying 'Miaow'?

"I didn't. It is the kittens!"

"What! Cats!" screamed Fräulein Rottenmeier. "Sebastian! Tinette! Find the horrid animals! Remove them at once!"

The lady rushed into the study and locked the door for she disliked cats more than anything.

Sebastian had to wait outside the door until his face was straight again. When he had served Heidi he had noticed the little kitten's head peeping out of her pocket and had guessed what would happen. When at last he entered the room everything seemed quiet and peaceful again. Clara had the kittens on her lap and Heidi knelt beside her. Both played happily with the two tiny animals.

"Sebastian," said Clara. "You must help us to find a place for the kittens where Fräulein Rottenmeier will not find them, because she is afraid of them and wants to get rid of them. Where can we put them?"

"I shall see to that, Fräulein Clara," replied Sebastian willingly. "I shall prepare a nice bed in a basket and put it in a place where madam is not likely to go; rely on me!" He made ready at once, chuckling to himself, for he realised that there would be a further to-do about this at some time in the future, and Sebastian was by no means unhappy at the thought of Fräulein Rottenmeier being unsettled.

Much later Fräulein Rottenmeier opened the door an inch or two and called through the slit, "Are the horrid animals away?"

"Yes! Yes!" answered Sebastian, quietly collecting the kittens from Clara's lap and disappearing with them.

The lecture for Heidi was put off until the following day as

Fräulein Rottenmeier felt too exhausted, after her ordeal of irritation, anger and fear, through which the innocent Heidi had put her, so she retired quietly. Clara and Heidi went cheerfully to bed, knowing that the kittens were all right.

CHAPTER 8

A COMMOTION IN THE HOUSE

The following morning, shortly after Sebastian had admitted the tutor, the door bell rang again, so loudly this time that the butler thought the master himself had arrived home unexpectedly. He rushed downstairs and threw open the door, and there stood a little ragged boy with a barrel organ on his shoulder.

"What do you want?" asked Sebastian irritably. "I'll teach you to ring the bell like that! Be off with you!"

"I want to see Clara," the urchin replied.

"You cheeky little brat. Don't you know to say *Fräulein* Clara? What could you possibly have to see Fräulein Clara about?" stormed Sebastian.

"She owes me fourpence," said the boy.

"You must be insane! What makes you think Fräulein Clara lives here, anyway?"

"Yesterday I showed her the way for twopence; and back again; that was fourpence."

"You are telling a pack of lies! Fräulein Clara never goes out—she can't walk. Be off with you now before I take my boot to you!"

But the boy was not to be turned away so easily. He stood firm and repeated determinedly, "But I have seen her in the street and can tell you what she looks like. She has short, curly hair and she wears a brown dress. She talks different from us."

"Ho!" thought Sebastian. "So this is more mischief the little fräulein has been up to!" He chuckled to himself as an idea occurred to him, then he said aloud, "Very well. Come with me, but wait outside the door until I call you, and when I let you into the room begin right away to play a tune on your barrel organ for the young lady. That will please her."

Sebastian knocked on the study door and went in. "There is a boy outside who says he has a message for Fräulein Clara," he announced.

This unexpected interruption to the lesson delighted Clara. "Let him come in at once!" she begged, turning to her tutor. "You see, he wants to speak to me particularly."

The boy entered, and at once started to play his organ according to Sebastian's instructions. Fräulein Rottenmeier was busy in the dining-room when the sound came to her ears. Was it in the street? Yet it seemed so much nearer! But who could be playing an organ in the study? And yet . . . She rushed into the study, and there, incredible as it seemed, there stood the ragged organ player. The tutor looked as though he were making an effort to speak, but failed. Clara and Heidi were listening happily.

"Stop! Stop at once!" commanded Fräulein Rottenmeier, but her voice was drowned by the music. She was walking towards the boy when suddenly on the floor between her feet she caught sight of a horrible, dark, crawling animal. It was a tortoise! At the sight of it, Fräulein Rottenmeier leaped into the air, shrieking at the top of her voice, "Sebastian! Sebastian!"

The organ player stopped abruptly. Sebastian stood behind the door, convulsed with laughter. At last he came in.

"Take them away! All of them! Boy, animal and all! At once, Sebastian!"

Sebastian dragged off the boy with the tortoise, at the same time putting something into his hand and whispering, "Fourpence for Fräulein Clara and fourpence for the music. You have done well!"

The door closed behind the little organ player, peace returned to the study and the lesson continued. This time Fräulein Rottenmeier remained in the room, grimly determined to prevent further incident.

Again a knock came to the study door and Sebastian appeared with the news that someone had brought a large basket to be delivered to Fräulein Clara. He carried in a covered basket and then disappeared.

"I think we will finish the lesson first," said Fräulein Rottenmeier, "and then we will see what is inside the basket."

Clara could not imagine what it could be and looked longingly at the basket. She broke off in the midst of her declensions to ask the tutor if she might have just one peep inside. The tutor frowned and was just about to refuse his permission when the lid of the basket lifted of its own accord and out jumped one, two, three, and then another two, and then several more kittens, and they all raced about the room in every direction. They climbed up on to Fräulein Rottenmeier's dress and scampered about her feet. They climbed up on Clara's chair, and, in fact, went into every corner of the room, scratching and maiowing. Clara cried delightedly, "Oh, look at them, Heidi! Aren't they sweet!"

Heidi raced about after them and the tutor, in a dilemma, moved uncomfortably from one foot to the other, at a complete loss to know what to do. At first, Fräulein Rottenmeier was too horror-stricken to utter a word, then she began to scream, "Tinette! Sebastian! Sebastian! Tinette!" She was terrified to move from her chair until Sebastian and Tinette appeared at last and removed the kittens only to put them in the basket with the others.

There had been no yawning during lessons that day.

In the evening, Fräulein Rottenmeier held an inquiry into the affair. She summoned Sebastian and Tinette and it soon became evident that Heidi, on her excursion of the previous day, had been responsible for all these alarming occurrences. Fräulein Rottenmeier was pale with anger. She gave a sign for Sebastian and Tinette to withdraw, then she turned to Heidi who stood beside Clara's chair, not very sure of what crime she had been guilty.

"Adelheid," Fräulein Rottenmeier began in a stern voice, "I know of only one punishment which will make you aware of your frightful misconduct for you are nothing but a little barbarian. We shall see if a spell down in the dark cellar with the rats and black beetles will tame you a little so that you will know not to do such things in future."

Heidi listened in silence and was rather surprised at the threatened punishment for she had never been in such a cellar. The room which the grandfather called the cellar at home was a very pleasant place where the fresh cheese and milk was kept.

But Clara started to cry, sobbing, "No! No! Fräulein Rottenmeier! You must wait till Papa comes home. He said in his letter that he would come back soon and when he does I will tell him everything and he shall decide what is to be done with Heidi."

Fräulein Rottenmeier was obliged to agree and she got up and left the room, grumbling, "Well, Clara, I too will have something to say to Herr Sesemann."

Although a few days passed quietly after this, Fräulein Rottenmeier failed to regain her peace of mind. She was constantly aware of the disappointment that Heidi had been and of the fact that since her arrival the whole household had been upset. But Clara was very happy indeed. She was never bored now, for during lessons something amusing was always happening. Instead of trying to learn the letters, Heidi would cry out, "Oh, it is shaped like a goat's horn!" or "It is like an eagle!" until the poor tutor would completely lose patience. Then, after lessons were over, in the late afternoon, Heidi would sit by Clara and tell her about the Alm and how much she wanted to go back. Indeed, she would talk about her old home until the longing to go back became so great that she would say, "I must go home again! To-morrow I must really go!" But Clara would persuade her to stay, saying, "Just wait until Papa comes home!" And Heidi would remember that each day she stayed meant that she could add another roll to her collection. Every night at supper she found a soft white roll on her plate and she would quietly slip it into her pocket. So she now had quite an amazing quantity of rolls to take back to the grandmother!

Every afternoon, while Clara rested, Heidi found herself

alone and then she would sit by herself and think about the Alm. One day, the memory of the snowcapped peaks, the yellow flowers glittering in the sun, and the green valley made her feel so homesick that she could hardly control her longing to be home again. Dete, after all, had said that she could go home whenever she wanted. She hastily put the rolls into her red scarf, put on her little straw hat and started of for home. But she got no farther than the front door, for there stood Fräulein Rottenmeier, just returned from her walk. Her sharp eyes looked Heidi up and down. "What is the meaning of this? Didn't I forbid you to run about in the streets? And you are surely not going out dressed like a beggar child!"

"I wasn't going to run about, I just wanted to go home," explained Heidi, frightened.

"Wanted to go home, indeed! I wonder what Herr Sesemann would have to say to this? Running away from his beautiful house! What do you find wrong with it, I should like to know? Are you not treated better than you deserve? Have you ever in your life had such a splendid place to live in or had so many servants to wait upon you? Have you?"

"No," said Heidi.

"I should think not," continued the lady. "You are an exceedingly ungrateful child who thinks of nothing but getting into mischief."

This rebuke was too much for Heidi and she began to pour out all the things that she had kept hidden for so long. "I only want to go home because Snowflake will be crying and the grandmother is waiting for me; and Goldfinch gets beaten when Goat Peter doesn't get part of my lunch. Here I can never watch the sun saying good night to the mountains, and if the great bird were to fly over Frankfurt he would croak even louder about so many people huddling together, gossiping, and not living in the mountains where it is so much nicer."

"Mercy! The child has gone out of her mind!" cried Fräulein Rottenmeier, rushing upstairs and colliding with Sebastian. "Take the unfortunate creature upstairs at once!" she called to him.

"What mischief have we been up to now, eh?" said Sebastian good-humouredly. Heidi stood trembling and frightened, and when Sebastian saw the distress on her little face he said kindly, "Now, now! Don't take it so much to heart! Cheer up and everything will be all right! Come! We'd better do as we were told and go upstairs."

Heidi looked such a picture of dejection as she slowly climbed the stairs that Sebastian felt really sorry for her. "Don't you give in!" he said encouragingly. "There's a brave little girl! Never a tear all the time she is with us, and others at her age cry twelve times a day. And the kittens are so happy! You should just see them jumping about in the loft! Afterwards we shall go up and look at them, together, shall we?—when madam is not here."

Heidi nodded, but not very cheerfully, and disappeared into her room.

At supper Fräulein Rottenmeier did not speak but kept casting very odd glances in Heidi's direction as though she expected the child to do something extraordinary at any moment. But Heidi sat silently at the table, neither eating nor drinking although the roll had, as usual, disappeared quickly into her pocket.

Next morning, when the tutor arrived, Fräulein Rottenmeier took him into the dining-room and told him her worries about Heidi and of her attempt to go home the previous day. "I really think the child has gone mad," she concluded. The tutor managed to quieten her fears, explaining that Adelheid was perhaps a little strange but with careful handling and education the balance would soon be restored. He was quite sure of this having now heard Fräulein Rottenmeier's revelation, and having so far failed to teach Heidi the alphabet. He felt that she was perhaps just a little eccentric, but it was nothing that perseverance would not cure.

Fräulein Rottenmeier felt quite relieved after this conversation and during the afternoon she began to recall Heidi's outlandish appearance when she had prepared to set out on her journey. She decided that the child had better have one or two things from Clara's wardrobe before Herr Sesemann arrived. Clara was completely in favour of the plan and the lady went into Heidi's room to inspect her wardrobe. Very soon she returned, wearing an expression of complete disgust. "Adelheid!" she said. "I have never seen anything like it! In a wardrobe of all places, what do I find? Heaps of little rolls! Who ever heard of keeping bread in a wardrobe? Tinette! Go and remove all that stale bread from Heidi's wardrobe—and you can take away the old straw hat, too! "

"No! No!" screamed Heidi. "Not the hat! And the rolls are for Grandmother!" And she began to run after Tinette until Fräulein Rottenmeier stopped her.

"Stay just where you are!" she said. "All that rubbish must be thrown out."

Then Heidi threw herself into Clara's chair, crying in despair. "Now Grandmother won't get her rolls. She has taken them away!" and she sobbed as though her heart would break.

Clara was very much alarmed at this outburst and pleaded, "Heidi! Heidi! Don't cry! Listen to me! I will give you as many rolls as you want when you go home and they will be soft and fresh. Yours were quite stale. Don't cry any more, Heidi!"

It was a long time before Heidi could stop sobbing but Clara's promise had comforted her and when she had assured herself that Clara would indeed give her as many or more rolls than she had collected, she quietened down.

At supper, Heidi's eyes were still swollen with crying and when she looked at her roll she started to sob again; but with a great effort she managed to control herself for she knew that she had to be quiet at table. Whenever Sebastian came near he smiled at her encouragingly as if to say, "I will put everything right for you." He made signs at her all evening, pointing to his head and hers, nodding and smiling.

When it came time for Heidi to go to bed, what did she find under the bed-cover but her old hat! She hugged it with delight, knocking it more out of shape than ever; then she wrapped it in a handkerchief and put it right at the back of the wardrobe. Sebastian had seen Tinette with the hat and had taken it from her quickly, saying, "It's all right. I shall dispose of this." This had been the reason for all the nods and smiles which Sebastian had given Heidi at supper.

CHAPTER 9

NEWS FROM THE MASTER

A few days later there was great excitement in the house because Herr Sesemann had returned. Sebastian and Tinette were kept busy carrying up parcels and suitcases from the carriage. They were packed with all sorts of exciting presents which Clara's father was in the habit of bringing back from his travels.

It was late afternoon when Herr Sesemann arrived and he came straight into the study where Clara and Heidi were sitting together. Father and daughter greeted each other affectionately for they loved each other very much, then Herr Sesemann held out his hand to Heidi and said kindly, "And this is our little Swiss girl? Come and shake hands with me? That's right! Now, you and Clara are great friends, are you not? Or are you always quarrelling with each other?"

"No, Clara is very good to me," answered Heidi.

"And Heidi," interjected Clara, "has never quarrelled with me."

"That's good! I'm delighted to hear it," said Herr Sesemann, rising from his chair. "Now, Clara, you must allow me to go and have something to eat. I have had nothing since breakfast. Later I shall see you again and show you all the things I have brought home."

In the dining-room he found Fräulein Rottenmeier inspecting the table which had been laid for dinner. Herr Sesemann sat down and Fräulein Rottenmeier, looking the picture of gloom, took her place opposite.

"What is the matter, Fräulein Rottenmeier?" asked Herr Sesemann. "You look very dismal. Have you had a stroke of bad luck? Clara seems to be cheerful enough. What is wrong?"

With a very long face, the lady began, "Herr Sesemann, we have been completely deceived—and it concerns Clara."

"In what way?" Herr Sesemann asked calmly.

"You know we decided that Clara should have a companion, and as I knew you were anxious to have a nicely brought up girl, I thought of a little Swiss girl of whom I had heard a great deal. You know what I wanted—the sort of child of whom I often read, who is so at ease living the natural life high in the mountains, that she would be like a pure being from another world!"

"And what do you think Clara would have in common with such a person as you describe, Fräulein?"

"I do not jest, Herr Sesemann. I have been terribly cheated. Completely taken in! Really shockingly!"

"But what is so shocking? I see nothing shocking in the child," remarked Herr Sesemann, still completely unperturbed.

"Oh, if you only knew the type of people—and the animals!— this creature has brought into your house! The tutor can tell you all about it."

"Animals? What am I to understand from that, Fräulein Rottenmeier"

"Herr Sesemann, it is beyond *my* understanding! Her whole behaviour would be beyond comprehension were it not for one thing. She has spells of mental disturbance!" concluded Fräulein Rottenmeier with conviction.

Up till now, Herr Sesemann had not thought the affair of any great importance; but mental disturbance! That could easily have a harmful effect on his little daughter.

He looked quickly at Fräulein Rottenmeier as though to assure himself that it was not she who was the victim of a troubled mind. Just then, the door opened and the tutor entered.

"Ah, here is our tutor! Perhaps he can clear this matter up for us," Herr Sesemann exclaimed. "Come, sit down and have a cup of coffee with us," he said, addressing the tutor. "No need for ceremony. Now tell me what is wrong with this child who has come to be a companion to my daughter. What's this about her bringing animals into the house, and about her mental faculties?"

The tutor began in his usual roundabout way, "Since you

74

ask me for my opinion about this young girl, Herr Sesemann, I should like to direct your attention to the fact that, although there may be a lack of development, caused by more or less neglected education, or rather by somewhat delayed tuition, on the one hand, there is, on the other hand, I think we must admit, a certain benefit to be gained from such a solitary life in the mountains, and we must consider—"

"My dear friend," interrupted Herr Sesemann, "you take too much trouble. Tell me, did her bringing animals to the house alarm you too, and what is your opinion of her as a companion for my little daughter?"

"I have no wish to say anything against the young girl," the tutor began again. "If on the one hand there is a certain inexperience of social custom, owing to the somewhat uncivilised life she led up to the time she came to Frankfurt, on the other hand she has gifts not to be overlooked, and if carefully led—"

"My dear sir, you must please excuse me now. I must speak to my daughter." And with these words Herr Sesemann quickly left the room.

In the study, he sat down beside his little girl and turning to Heidi said, "Listen, little one, will you go and fetch me— ah—fetch me—" Herr Sesemann wanted the child out of the room but was having difficulty in thinking up an excuse. "Fetch me a glass of water?"

Heidi disappeared at once.

"And now, my dear Clara," said Herr Sesemann, pulling his chair closer and taking his daughter's hand, "tell me quite frankly, what kind of animals did your little friend bring into the house? And what makes Fräulein Rottenmeier think that she is sometimes not quite right in her mind?"

Clara had no difficulty in explaining. She told her father the story of the tortoise and the kittens and explained all the remarks which Fräulein Rottenmeier had thought so odd, and which seemed to upset her so much.

Herr Sesemann laughed heartily. "Well, then, you don't want me to send the child home, Clara? You are not tired of her?" asked her father.

"No! No! Papa, Please don't!" exclaimed Clara in alarm.

"The time has passed so quickly since Heidi came. Something happens every day, and it used to be so dull. And she always has so much to tell me."

"Very well, then. Ah! Here is our little friend! Have you brought me nice fresh water?" Herr Sesemann asked as Heidi handed him the glass.

"Yes. It is fresh from the pump," answered Heidi.

"Did you go yourself to the pump, Heidi?" asked Clara.

"Yes, but I had to go a long way because at the first pump there were ever so many people and at the second there were just as many. Then I went into another street and got the water there. The gentleman with the white hair sends his kind regards to Herr Sesemann."

"Well, that was a long expedition," laughed Herr Sesemann. "And who is this gentleman?"

"As he was passing the pump he stopped and said, 'Since you have got a glass would you mind giving me a drink? To whom are you taking the glass of water?' And I said, 'To Herr Sesemann.' And he laughed and gave me the message for you and said 'he hoped Herr Sesemann would enjoy the water."

"And what did this gentleman look like who sends me so many good wishes?" asked Herr Sesemann with a smile.

"He wore a thick gold chain with a big red stone hanging from it; and the top of his stick was a horse's head."

"That is our old friend, the doctor," cried Clara and her father at the same instant. Herr Sesemann smiled to himself as he wondered what their friend would think of the new way in which the Sesemanns went about quenching their thirst.

That very evening, he told Fräulein Rottenmeier that Heidi would remain; that he found the child perfectly normal and that his daughter preferred her company to any other. "I am anxious, therefore," said Herr Sesemann emphatically, "that this child should always be treated in a friendly way and that her little peculiarities should not be treated as crimes. And, by the way, if you find difficulty in managing the child there is a prospect that you will be relieved of this duty. I am expecting my mother very soon for a long visit, and, as you know, she gets along with everybody, Fräulein Rottenmeier," he concluded pointedly.

"Yes, I know," Herr Sesemann," said Fräulein Rottenmeier rather sourly.

Herr Sesemann remained only a short time at home and after a fortnight he set off for Paris, comforting his little daughter with the prospect of the arrival of her grandmother in a day or two.

On the day after Herr Sesemann's departure, a letter came announcing Frau Sesemann's arrival on the following day. Clara was overjoyed and talked so much about her grandmother that Heidi, too, called her Grandmamma.

Later, when Heidi was going to her bedroom, Fräulein Rottenmeier took her into her own room and instructed her that she should never address Frau Sesemann as Grandmamma but always as 'madam'. "Do you understand?" she asked.

Heidi really did not understand at all why she should call the lady by this title but Fräulein Rottenmeier's face wore such a severe expression that Heidi did not dare ask for an explanation.

CHAPTER 10

ANOTHER GRANDMOTHER

The following evening great preparations were afoot in the Sesemann house. It was clear that the lady who was to arrive was held in great esteem by all and presently there was the sound of a carriage stopping at the front door. Sebastian and Tinette rushed downstairs and put footstools everywhere, that the lady might find one wherever she wanted to put her feet. Fräulein Rottenmeier followed, but slowly and with dignity.

She knew that she would have to be there to welcome Frau Sesemann, but was not going to let her authority be undermined by the presence of another woman. Suddenly the carriage rolled up to the door, and the servants ran down the step to assist their important visitor. Heidi, who had been ordered to wait in her room until she was called, sat in a corner and repeated over and over again to herself the little speech which she had been instructed to address to Frau Sesemann.

Before very long Tinette came to call her. Putting her head round the door, she announced in her usual saucy manner "You're to go into the study."

Heidi made her way to the study, still turning the words over in her mind and still hardly able to believe that she should address any one in the peculiar way Fräulein Rottenmeier had told her. As she opened the door, the grandmother said in a kind voice, "Ah, here is the child! Come here and let me look at you!"

Heidi approached, and said very distinctly in her clear voice, "Good evening, Mrs madam!"

"Well," said the grandmother, laughing. "Is that how you address people on the Alm?"

"No. At home nobody has a name like that," said Heidi gravely.

"Neither do they here!" said the grandmother, still smiling, and patted Heidi's cheek. "When I am with children I am always Grandmamma. Can you remember that?"

"Yes, very well," Heidi assured her, "because that's what I used to say."

"I understand," said the grandmother, shaking her head a little. She looked more closely at Heidi and Heidi's steady, serious eyes looked back at her eagerly, for there was a warmth about the old woman which attracted the child. Heidi gazed entranced at the beautiful white hair which was adorned with a lacy frill, ending in two broad ribbons which floated gently about the grandmother's head as though blown by a soft breeze.

"And what is your name, child?"

"It is really Heidi, but if you call me Adelheid I shall try to

78

remember—" Heidi stopped guiltily, remembering that sometimes she failed to answer when Fräulein Rottenmeier called her by this name. Just at that moment, Fräulein Rottenmeier entered.

"Frau Sesemann will agree that I had to choose a name which one could pronounce, and, of course, on account of the servants—"

"Very correct, I have no doubt, Rottenmeier," replied Frau Sesemann, "but if the child is called Heidi and is accustomed to that name, I shall call her by it; so that's settled."

Fräulein Rottenmeier found it very embarrassing to be called by her surname but since the grandmother would have her own way there was nothing she could do about it. She was a very alert old lady and had her wits about her, and she very soon knew exactly what was going on in the house.

The following afternoon, after sitting by Clara's bed until she fell asleep, Frau Sesemann went upstairs and knocked at Fräulein Rottenmeier's door. Fräulein Rottenmeier looked startled at this unexpected visit.

"Where is the Heidi child and what is she doing, I should like to know," said Frau Sesemann, coming straight to the point.

"She is in her room where she could find something useful to do if she had the slightest inclination," replied Fräulein Rottenmeier. "But if Frau Sesemann only knew the queer things she imagines and does—I can hardly bring myself to talk of them."

"And so would I, if I were in her place, I don't doubt. Tell the little one to come to my room. I have some nice books to give her."

"But that's just it!" replied Fräulein Rottenmeier, throwing up her hands in despair. "Of what use are books to her? She does not even know the alphabet yet! It is quite impossible to teach her anything. The tutor will tell you so himself. If he didn't have the patience of a saint he would have given up trying to teach her long ago."

"Well, that is strange. The child does not strike me as being stupid," said Frau Sesemann shortly. "Now go and fetch her. She can look at the pictures for the time being."

Fräulein Rottenmeier was about to say more but Frau Sesemann turned and went quickly into her room. She was very surprised at Fräulein Rottenmeier's remarks and was determined to find out more about the whole matter. Perhaps the tutor would help, although his conversation was so round-about and lengthy that she felt it might be difficult to get to the root of the problem.

Heidi was greatly delighted with the beautiful coloured pictures in the books which the grandmother had brought. Suddenly she cried aloud as the grandmother turned a page, and when the old lady looked at the child she saw that tears were streaming down her cheeks. She looked at once at the picture. It depicted a beautiful green pasture with all sorts of animals grazing. In the midst, the shepherd leant upon his stick and looked happily at his flock. Everything was bathed in a golden light for the sun was just setting on the far horizon.

The grandmother took Heidi's hand gently. "Come, come! child! Don't cry! It has reminded you of something, perhaps. But look, there is a beautiful story about it and I am going to tell it to you tonight. There are many beautiful stories in this book which can be read over and over again. Come now, we must have a chat, so dry your tears and stand in front of me so that I can look at you. That's right. Now we are happy again."

Heidi tried very hard to stop sobbing and when at last she succeeded the grandmother said, "Now I want you to tell me something, child. How are you getting on with your lessons? Do you like them? Are you doing well?"

"Oh, no!" answered Heidi with a sigh. "But I knew it would be impossible."

"What is impossible, Heidi? What do you mean?"

"To learn to read. It is too difficult."

"Well I never! And who told you this?"

"Peter did, and he knows for he has tried and tried but he can't learn. It is too difficult."

"What a boy Peter must be! But listen to me, Heidi. We must never believe what the 'Peters' say but try for ourselves. I am sure you have never paid enough attention to the tutor or looked properly at the letters."

"It is no use," said Heidi with a great sigh of resignation.

"Now, Heidi. Listen to what I say! You have not been able to learn to read because you believed what Peter said. Now you must believe what I say when I tell you that you can learn to read like many other children who are like you and not like Peter, and in a very short time. First you must know what happens when you are able to read. Do you see the shepherd on the beautiful green pasture? Well, as soon as you can read you shall have the book for your own and then you will know the whole story just as if someone were to tell it to you—what the shepherd did with his sheep and goats and the wonderful things that happened to him. Wouldn't you like to know all that, Heidi?"

Heidi had been listening with keen attention and now exclaimed with sparkling eyes "Oh, if only I could read already!"

"You will learn in no time—I can see that, Heidi. But now we must go to Clara. Come, we will take the books with us!"

The grandmother took Heidi's hand and they went together into the study.

From the day Heidi had tried to go home and Fräulein Rottenmeier had scolded her for being so wicked and ungrateful, a change had come over the child. She knew now that she could not go home whenever she liked, as Aunt Dete had told her, but that she had to stay in Frankfurt for a long time, maybe for ever. She also understood that Herr Sesemann would think her very ungrateful, and Clara and the grandmother, too, if she again showed signs of wanting to leave. So there was nobody to whom she could reveal how homesick she was, for she could not face giving the grandmother, who was so kind to her, cause to be angry, as Fräulein Rottenmeier had been.

But the strain of keeping all this to herself became almost more than she could bear. She lost her appetite and every day grew paler and paler. At night she would lie awake for a long time, for as soon as she was alone with everything quiet around her, she would see again in her thoughts the Alm and the sunshine and the flowers; and when at last she fell asleep she would see in her dreams the red summits of the crags and the crimson snowfield in the evening sun. Awakening in the morning she wanted to run out happily into the sun—but she soon realised that she was in the big bed at Frankfurt, far, far away from home. Then Heidi would weep long and quietly, her head pressed into the pillow so that no one could hear.

Heidi's unhappiness did not escape the grandmother. She waited a few days to see if there might be a change. But as Heidi remained subdued and when she noticed that often in the early morning the child looked as though she had been crying, the grandmother took her, one day, into her room and said lovingly, "Now tell me, Heidi, what is the matter? Are you worrying about something?"

But not for the world would Heidi show ingratitude to the grandmother who had been so kind, so she replied:

"Please, I cannot tell you."

"Could you tell Clara, then?"

"Oh, no! Nobody," said Heidi, looking so pitiful that the grandmother was filled with compassion.

"Come here, little one, and I will tell you something. If one is in trouble and can't speak about it to any one, then one tells it to God who is in Heaven and prays to Him for help because he is able to take away all our troubles. Do you know that? Do you pray every night to your Heavenly Father and thank Him for all he has done for you and ask Him to keep you from harm?"

"Oh, no! I never do that," answered Heidi.

"Have you never prayed, Heidi? Don't you know what it is?"

"Sometimes I used to pray with the first grandmother but it is a long time ago and I have forgotten it."

"You see, Heidi, because you have nobody to help you, you are unhappy. Think how wonderful it is when our hearts are heavy with sadness, to be able to go any moment to God and tell Him everything and ask Him for help when no one else can give it. He is always able to help and can give us what makes us happy again."

A gleam of joy came into Heidi's eyes, "May I tell Him everything?"

"Everything, Heidi. Everything."

Heidi drew away the hand which the grandmother held affectionately and asked hastily, "May I go?"

"Certainly, certainly!" answered the grandmother and Heidi

ran off to her room. She sat down on her little stool, folded her hands and told God about everything that made her so unhappy and begged Him with all her heart to let her go home to the grandfather.

A little more than a week after this the tutor asked to see Frau Sesemann as he had something very remarkable to tell her. When he was shown into her room Frau Sesemann held out her hand, saying, "I am pleased to see you. Sit down, won't you? Now tell me why you wish to see me. I hope it is not a complaint."

"On the contrary, madam," the tutor began. "Something has occurred—something which I did not expect. In the light of all my previous experience it was an impossibility and yet it really has happened. It is like a miracle. Contrary to all I had expected—"

"Am I to understand that the child, Heidi, has learned to read after all?" Frau Sesemann guessed.

Speechless with surprise the tutor looked at her.

"It is indeed nothing short of a miracle. In spite of my painstaking explanations, she never seemed to be able to learn the alphabet, and now she has learnt it with such rapidity—overnight, so to say—and so correctly! It is most unusual with a beginner."

"Life is full of miracles," Frau Sesemann smiled. "Of course, there might be such a happy coincidence as a fresh zeal for learning and a new method of teaching. Now we must be glad the child has made such a good beginning and hope for her future progress."

After she had seen the tutor to the door, she went straight to the study to make sure of the good news. Sure enough, Heidi was seated beside Clara and was reading a story to her with great eagerness, evidently surprised herself to find the black letters turning into real people and exciting adventures.

That same evening, at the dinner table, Heidi found by her plate the big book with the lovely pictures and when she looked questioningly at the grandmother the old lady nodded her confirmation, "Yes, it is yours, now."

"Always? Even when I go home?" asked Heidi, flushed with happiness.

"Of course, for ever!" assured the grandmother. "To-morrow we shall start to read it."

"But you are not going home yet, Heidi," Clara put in. "Not for many years. I want you to stay with me, especially when grandmother goes away."

Before she went to bed, Heidi looked at her book, and from that day on, her greatest pleasure was to read over and over again the stories which belonged to the beautiful pictures.

When, in the evening, the grandmother said, "Now Heidi will read to us," the child was delighted and when she read aloud, the stories seemed to be still more beautiful and interesting. The picture she liked best was the one with the green pasture and the shepherd leaning happily on his crook. He was tending his father's fine flock. But the next picture showed how the shepherd had run away from home and had to look after a herd of swine. He had grown quite thin for all he had to eat was husks. In this picture, the sun did not shine so golden and the land was grey and misty. But then there was still another picture to this story. In it the old father was running with outstretched arms to meet his returning and repentant son, welcoming him as he approached timidly, tired and dirty and dressed in rags. This was Heidi's favourite story which she read again and again without ever tiring of hearing the grandmother's explanations of the meaning of the story. There were many other beautiful tales in the book, and with reading and studying the pictures the days passed quickly and the time came for the grandmother's departure.

CHAPTER 11

HEIDI LEARNS A GREAT DEAL

Every afternoon during her visit, the grandmother sat beside Clara for a time while she was resting, and afterwards she would call Heidi into her room and would talk to her and keep her occupied in all sorts of ways. The grandmother had pretty little dolls and showed Heidi how to make little dresses and coats for them so that without knowing it Heidi had learnt to sew. Since Heidi could now read she was allowed to read aloud to the grandmother and this she enjoyed very much, growing more fond of the stories the more she read them. But still, Heidi never looked really happy and her sparkling eyes were never as bright as before.

One afternoon during the last week of the grandmother's visit, when Heidi was paying her customary afternoon call, the grandmother asked, "Tell me, child, why is it you are not happy? Is there still the same grief in your heart?"

"Yes," Heidi nodded.

"Have you told God about it?"

"Yes."

"And do you say your prayers every day so that all will be well and you will be happy again?"

"Oh, no. I don't pray at all now."

"What is this, Heidi? Why don't you pray any more?"

"It is no use. God does not listen, and I can understand it; when there are so many people in Frankfurt all praying to Him, He cannot possibly listen to them all. He certainly has not heard me."

"What makes you so sure, Heidi?"

"I have prayed for the same thing every day for weeks and weeks and God has never done it."

"Oh, Heidi! That is not the way in which to think of Him. You see, God is our Heavenly Father and always knows what is best for us, even when we ourselves do not. If we ask for something which is not good for us, He does not grant it but instead gives us the thing that is best for us. If we go on praying earnestly and never run away or lose faith our prayers will be answered. You see, Heidi, what you asked for was not good for you just at the moment. God has certainly heard you. He can hear every one at the same time because He is God and not a human being like you or me. And because He knows what is good for you He says, 'Yes, Heidi shall have what she wants but only when it is good for her; because if I give her what she wants right away and then, by and by, she sees that it would have been better for her not to have had her own way, she will say, "If only God had not given me what I asked for! It is not so good as I thought."' Since God watched over you, you should have trusted in Him, come with everything to Him and prayed every day; but you ran away, stopped praying and forgot all about Him!

"But you see, when someone behaves like you so that God never hears his voice among those who pray, He lets him go his own way. And when he gets into trouble and then complains, 'There is no one to help me!' God says, 'Why did you run away from Me? I cannot help you when you run away.' Do you want that, Heidi? Or would you rather go and ask Him to forgive you for running away, and pray to Him every day and trust that He will make everything right for you and that you will be happy again?"

Every word the grandmother said had touched the child's heart and she said repentantly, "At once I will ask God to forgive me and I will never forget Him again. I will go and pray now."

"That is a good child. He will help you at the right moment, never fear!" And Heidi ran to her room and prayed to God to forgive her and asked Him not to forget her.

It was a sad time for Clara and Heidi when the day of the grandmother's departure arrived, but the old lady insisted on making it quite a party so that they would not think too much about her going. After the grandmother had driven off in her carriage the house seemed very empty and silent and Clara and Heidi felt quite lost.

The next day, when the children sat together in the afternoon, Heidi suggested to Clara that she should read aloud to her every afternoon. Clara was very pleased with this idea and Heidi began with great enthusiasm. But the first story turned out to be about a dying grandmother and Heidi, who took all the stories very seriously and believed every word was true, at once thought that it was the grandmother on the Alm who was dead and burst into tears. Clara tried to explain that the story was about a quite different grandmother, but the idea that such a thing could happen had entered Heidi's mind and she realised with a great shock that the grandmother and the grandfather also might die while she was so far away and if she did not go home for a very long time everything on the Alm might be silent and dead and she would be all alone and would never see her dear ones again. And these sad thoughts made her sob the louder.

In the midst of Clara's explanation Fräulein Rottenmeier had entered the room and as Heidi still continued to sob she burst out impatiently, "Adelheid! That will do! I warn you, if you continue to give way to these outbursts whenever you read I will take the book away from you for good."

Heidi turned pale at such a thought. The book was her most treasured possession. Hurriedly she dried her tears. The stratagem had worked all right. No matter what the story, Heidi never cried again. But sometimes it was so difficult to keep back the tears that Clara would say, "Heidi, what terrible faces you are making!" But grimaces made no noise and did not attract Fräulein Rottenmeier's attention.

Heidi began to lose her appetite again and grew so pale and thin that Sebastian was extremely perturbed when she refused to take any of the delicious food which he served. Often he would whisper encouragingly as he held out a dish, "Take a little of this, Fräulein Heidi! It is so good! No, not like that! A heaped spoonful, and another one!" and other pieces of fatherly advice. But it was no use. Heidi hardly ate anything and as she lay in bed at night she would begin to think about home and what might be happening there, and she would turn her face into her pillow so that no one would hear, and cry as though her heart would break.

The days went by and Heidi could hardly tell whether it were winter or summer, for all she ever saw of the outside world was the same grey walls and roofs. She was only allowed out when Clara was well enough to go for a short drive (which never took them farther than the neighbouring streets) and never had a glimpse of grass or flowers, let alone fir trees and mountains. Heidi's longing for the beautiful, remembered things grew every day so that she could not speak or think of them without her eyes filling with tears.

Autumn and winter passed and the spring sun shone on the white walls of the house opposite, and Heidi knew it would soon be the time when Peter climbed up to the Alm with his goats, the flowers glittered in the sunshine and in the evening the mountains turned to crimson in the setting sun. Heidi would sit in her lonely little room and press her palms into her eyes so that she would not be able to see the sunshine striking the wall, and so she sat, silently struggling against her homesickness until she heard Clara's voice calling her.

CHAPTER 12

THE HOUSE IS HAUNTED

For some time, very strange things had been happening in the house. Every morning when the servants came down they found the front door wide open. During the first few days when this had happened all the rooms in the house were carefully searched for signs of burglary, but nothing was missing. At night every care was taken. The door was carefully locked and bolted, and to make it even more secure the wooden bar was put across. But all these precautions were of no avail; in the morning, the servants would again find the door wide open. Fräulein Rottenmeier would never go alone to some parts of the house, and would invent some excuse for one of the servants to accompany her. She was especially nervous if she had to visit the upper guest rooms, or go down to the strange, vast council chambers, where every footfall sounded and the ancient senators in their austere robes looked down sternly at her.

The cook meanwhile, would stand by her stove, shaking her head and muttering to herself, "To think that I should live to see such strange goings-on." At last John and Sebastian plucked up courage and promised to sit up all night in the room off the hall and watch to see what took place. Fräulein Rottenmeier, thinking they should be armed against any intruders, got out two of Herr Sesemann's pistols, and brought up a bottle of wine from the cellar with which the watchers might fortify their courage.

On the appointed night, the two installed themselves in the downstairs room and at once felt in need of a little stimulant. At first the wine made them very talkative, and by and by very sleepy, so they both leaned back in their arm-chairs and fell fast asleep. Sebastian awoke as the old church clock struck midnight. He called to his companion but John remained fast asleep. Sebastian did not go to sleep again but sat uneasily in the quietness of the night, only now and then giving John a quiet poke to see if he were awake. The clock struck the hour and John awoke with a start. He jumped to his feet and with a great show of courage said, "Now, Sebastian, we had better go outside and see what is going on. You aren't feeling scared, are you? Come on! I'll go first."

John opened the door wide and stepped into the hall. A sudden draught put out the light which he carried and he turned quickly, pushing against Sebastian, and stumbled back into the room, slamming the door and turning the key in the lock with feverish haste. Then he relit the candle. Sebastian did not know what to make of this odd behaviour and turned a puzzled look on John. In the light of the candle he saw that John was as white as a sheet and trembled all over. "What is it?" Sebastian asked hurriedly. "What did you see?"

"The door wide open," gasped John, "and on the stairs, a white figure—then, poof! and it was gone."

Sebastian shuddered with horror and felt as though his knees were going to give way. For the rest of the night the two sat close together and did not move again until the morning light came streaming through the window and the sound of passers-by came from the street. Then they went out and closed the front door and made their way upstairs to tell their story to Fräulein Rottenmeier. Straight away, she wrote a long letter to Herr Sesemann, telling him all about the open door and the ghostly figure, and insisting upon his immediate return as every one in the house now went in fear of his life and there was no knowing what the dreadful consequences of these incidents might be. But Herr Sesemann replied that it was impossible for him to return home just then, and altogether treated the affair very lightly. He suggested that should the ghost not have already disappeared, the grandmother should be summoned by letter to come and dispense with the nuisance.

Fräulein Rottenmeier was not at all satisfied. She wrote immediately to Frau Sesemann, but received a similarly indifferent reaction, and the tone of the letter, was to her mind, quite uncivil. Frau Sesemann implied that she did not care to undertake the journey from Holstein to Frankfurt, simply because Rottenmeier imagined she saw ghosts. She had never known a ghost in the house, and if there was now one in residence, it must be alive, in which case Rottenmeier should be able to deal with it.

Fräulein Rottenmeier was beginning to feel that she had had quite enough of this particular worry. She had never told the children of the apparition for fear of upsetting them, but now she had an idea. In a hushed voice and with much colourful detail, she told them of the nightly visitations. The story so frightened Clara that she began to scream for her father to come home. She was in such a state of fright that she would not be left alone for a minute. She insisted that everyone should sleep in the same room, and leave the light burning all the time; and Tinette should be next door, and Sebastian and John upstairs in the hall in order to frighten the ghost as soon as it appeared. Fräulein Rottenmeier wrote another letter to Herr Sesemann saying she would not answer for the serious consequences the mysterious occurrences might have on his daughters's delicate constitution. This had the desired effect.

Two days later Herr Sesemann came home. He stood and rang the front door-bell in such a way that everyone rushed down and stood trembling as if they thought the ghost was up to his tricks in broad daylight.

Sebastian peered through a window, and at once there was

another, very human and impatient ring on the bell. Clara was over-joyed to see him, and when she saw in what good spirits she was, a look of great relief spread over his features. Indeed, she was so pleased to see him that she was almost grateful to the ghost, for being responsible for his homecoming.

"And how is the ghost behaving?" he asked Fräulein Rottenmeier with a twinkle in his eye.

"It is no joke," she replied tartly. "I am sure by to-morrow Herr Sesemann will no longer consider it a laughing matter."

"Well, we shall see," replied Herr Sesemann, "but I must request you not to suspect my honourable forefathers. Now send Sebastian to me."

Herr Sesemann knew that Sebastian and Fräulein Rottenmeier were not always on the best of terms and he had his own ideas as to the cause of the disturbances.

"Now, Sebastian," he said, "tell me frankly. Have you been playing ghosts to tease Fräulein Rottenmeier?"

"On my honour, sir, no" replied Sebastian with unmistakable sincerity; "Please don't think that! I have been feeling very uncomfortable myself about this thing."

"Well, if that is so, I will have to show you and the brave John how ghosts look in the daylight. You should be ashamed of yourself, Sebastian, a big strong fellow like you running away from a ghost! But now go at once to my old friend Dr. Classen. Give him my kind regards and ask him to come here to-night at nine o'clock. Tell him I have come specially from Paris to consult him and will he make arrangements to spend the night here. Do you understand?" Sebastian indicated that he understood perfectly, and Herr Sesemann went to reassure Clara, telling her that the ghost would soon be found out and done away with.

Promptly at nine o'clock the doctor arrived after both Fräulein Rottenmeier and the children had gone to bed. He was a grey-haired man with bright, kindly eyes. At first he looked a little worried but presently he burst out laughing. "Well, well! For a patient with whom I am to sit up all night you don't look too bad."

"Not so hasty, my friend. Wait until I tell you this. There's a ghost in the house! This place is haunted."

The doctor laughed uproariously.

"That's a fine way of showing your sympathy I must say," Herr Sesemann continued. "It's a pity my friend Rottenmeier can't enjoy it. She is convinced that some ancient member of the family is prowling about the house."

"And how did she make his acquaintance?" asked the doctor, still chuckling. Herr Sesemann told him how the front door was found open every morning, as everyone in the house was willing to swear, and he had prepared two loaded revolvers in readiness for any untoward event. It could be that an elaborate practical joke was being played by a friend of one of the servants—in which case a pistol shot would frighten him sufficiently, or it was a thief, thinking to create safe access for himself at a future time, by pretending to be a ghost with whom everyone would become familiar and used to seeing in the house.

When the doctor had heard the whole story the two gentlemen went downstairs to the room where Sebastian and John had kept watch. There, a bottle of wine was put at their disposal, and the two revolvers together with two large lamps. They settled themselves comfortably in arm-chairs and smoked and chatted together with such enjoyment that in what seemed no time at all they heard the clock strike twelve.

"The ghost seems to have got wind of us and does not choose to come to-night," said the doctor.

"Hold on! It usually comes before one o'clock," replied his friend.

They resumed their conversation and until one o'clock struck there was not a sound to be heard. Then suddenly the doctor lifted a-finger.

"Hush, Sesemann. Don't you hear something?"

They both listened and heard distinctly the bar on the door being softly pushed aside, the key turning in the lock and the door opening. Herr Sesemann seized one of the pistols which lay ready on the table.

"You are not afraid are you?" whispered the doctor.

"As well to be careful," Herr Sesemann replied, picking up the lamp. The doctor took the other pistol and together they stepped out into the hall.

Moonlight streamed through the open door and fell on a white figure which stood motionless on the threshold.

"Who is there?" the doctor demanded loudly, his voice echoing through the hall. As both gentlemen advanced towards the figure it turned and gave a little cry. In her little white nightgown and with her bare feet, Heidi stood there trembling and blinking at the light and the weapons pointed in her direction.

The gentlemen exchanged surprised glances.

"Well if it isn't the little water-carrier!" said the doctor.

"Child, what does this mean?" asked Herr Sesemann. "Why have you come downstairs?"

Pale and trembling with fright, Heidi stood before him. "I don't know," she whispered.

Then the doctor intervened. "Sesemann, this is something I shall have to deal with. Go and sit by the fire while I take the child up to bed."

The doctor put down his revolver and taking the child in his arms he carried her upstairs, reassuring her gently all the while, and laying her on her bed he covered her carefully with the quilt. Then he sat on the edge of the bed, and taking her hand, he said kindly, "Everything is all right now. Tell me where you wanted to go."

"I didn't want to go at all," said Heidi. "I didn't know I was going downstairs but suddenly I was there."

"Were you dreaming about something which you could see and hear everything as if you were there?"

"Yes, I dream every night and it is always the same. I think I am with Grandfather and outside I hear the fir trees rustling and I think how beautifully the stars will be shining and I run quickly and open the door of the cottage. But when I awake I am still in Frankfurt." Heidi struggled to swallow the lump which rose in her throat.

"And have you a pain anywhere? In your head or in your back?"

"No. Only a feeling as if there were a big stone here."

"As though you had eaten something and it would not go down?"

"No, not like that. But so heavy that it makes me want to cry and cry."

"I see, and then you have a good cry?"

"Oh, no, I mustn't. Fräulein Rottenmeier doesn't allow it."

"Then you just swallow hard, is that it? But you like being in Frankfurt, don't you?"

"Yes," said Heidi in a flat voice which made it sound more like 'no'.

"And where did you live when you were with your grandfather?"

"Always on the Alm."

"And wasn't that rather dull?"

"Oh, no, it was beautiful. It was so beautiful—" Heidi could not go on. Remembrance of the past, the recent excitement and the long-suppressed weeping overwhelmed the child. Tears gushed from her eyes and her little body was shaken with sobs. The doctor rose. Gently he laid Heidi's head on the pillow. "Cry a little. It will do no harm, and then sleep. To-morrow everything will be all right."

The doctor went downstairs and joined his friend. He lowered himself into the opposite arm-chair and looked across at him gravely. "Sesemann, your little protégé is a sleep-walker. Every night, without knowing it, she has been opening the front door and alarming your staff. The child is pining away with homesickness. Didn't you see how pathetically thin she is? Now there is only one remedy for her overstretched nerves, and that is to send her back home at once. My advice is that the child should travel home to-morrow."

Herr Sesemann got up in a great state of agitation and strode up and down the room. "Ill, Homesick! Wasting away! In my house! And nobody seems to have noticed it! And you, doctor, suggest that I should send her back home in that pathetic state. No, doctor, I cannot do it. You take the child in hand and restore her to health; then I shall send her home if she wants to go."

"Sesemann," said the doctor, "consider! This is not an illness that can be cured with pills and powders. The child does not have a strong constitution but if she gets back home to the mountain air she will very quickly recover; if not—wouldn't you rather send the child back ill than not at all?"

Such blunt words alarmed Herr Sesemann and he agreed at once. "Well, if you think that is the only way then we must act at once." They discussed the matter further and after a while the doctor took his leave. When the master of the house opened the door the bright morning light shone in.

CHAPTER 13

BACK TO THE ALM

In great agitation, Herr Sesemann went upstairs to Fräulein Rottenmeier's room. His loud rap on the door awakened the lady and she was startled to hear him say, "Come down to the dining-room quickly, please! We must make preparations for a journey."

Fräulein Rottenmeier had never before been obliged to get up so early. It was only half-past four in the morning. What could possibly have happened? She was so flustered that she could hardly manage to dress. Herr Sesemann proceeded to rouse the whole staff and his urgent cries convinced them that the ghost had attacked the master and he needed their help. But, to their surprise, they found him walking up and down in the dining-room and not looking at all terrified. John was ordered to get the horses and carriage ready; Tinette had to wake Heidi and help her to dress and Sebastian was sent off to the house where Dete was in service, to bring her along.

At last Fräulein Rottenmeier was ready and came downstairs although she had put her cap on back to front in her hurry of preparation. Herr Sesemann instructed her to pack a trunk with the Swiss child's belongings and to add one or two things of Clara's so that the child would have some decent clothes to go home with. All this had to be done at once, Herr Sesemann insisted.

Poor Fräulein Rottenmeier stared in bewilderment at Herr Sesemann. She had expected to hear a hair-raising account of an encounter with a ghost in which she would have revelled in broad daylight and instead she was being given these practical instructions. Unable to believe her ears, she waited silently for Herr Sesemann to say something further; but he had no time for lengthy explanations and bustled off to Clara's room, leaving her standing there. He found Clara lying awake, wondering what could be the cause of such an upheaval in the house. Sitting beside her bed, her father told her all that had happened; about the doctor's verdict and how he thought that as Heidi was in a very overwrought state her sleep walking might take her somewhere dangerous. So they had decided to send Heidi home again at once.

Clara was distressed and made all sorts of suggestions for keeping Heidi with her, but her father remained firm, promising that if she were a good girl and did not make a fuss he would take her to Switzerland the following year. Eventually Clara gave in to him, on condition that Heidi's box would be packed in her room so that it would be possible for Clara to add things to it if she wanted.

In the meantime, Dete had arrived and was waiting downstairs wondering what on earth had happened that she should be summoned at such an early hour. Herr Sesemann told her about Heidi and that she was to go home that very day, accompanied by Dete herself.

Dete was very disappointed for this was the last thing she had expected to hear. She recalled the Uncle saying that he never wished to see her again, and it occurred to her that it would not be a safe undertaking to once again take the child to him, having once already delivered her and taken her away. Quickly she made as many excuses as she could muster, speaking low and fluently, so that Herr Sesemann, sensing her reluctance, told her to go away.

Herr Sesemann told Sebastian that he would have to accompany the child on her journey, the first day as far as Basle and the next day to her destination. He would be furnished with an explanatory letter to the grandfather, after presenting which he could return at once.

"But the main thing is this, Sebastian," concluded Herr Sesemann, "and I want you to see it is carried out. On this card I have written the name of the hotel in Basle. Show it to the manager and you will be given accommodation for the child and yourself. Go into the child's room and see that the windows are securely fastened, and when he has gone to bed, lock the door from the outside, for the child is a sleep-walker."

"Ah, so that was the ghost! I understand!" exclaimed Sebastian in great surprise.

"Yes, you foolish fellow. What cowards you all were," said Herr Sesemann and went off to his room to write a letter to the Alm-Uncle. Sebastian stayed where he was, feeling sheepish, and wishing that he had not let John drag him back into the room, instead of going after the small white figure. "I should certainly follow it if I saw it now," he said to himself. But of course everything was clearly illuminated by daylight.

All this time, Heidi was completely ignorant of what was afoot and was standing dressed in her Sunday best without the faintest notion why. Tinette had helped her to dress without uttering a word, for she considered her a common child and not fit to be spoken to.

The letter written, Herr Sesemann returned to the dining-room where breakfast was ready, and demanded, "Where is the child?"

Heidi was fetched and as she said good morning, Herr Sesemann looked into her sad little face. "Now what do you say to this, little one?" he asked kindly.

Heidi looked at him in surprise.

"Don't you know about it yet?" Herr Sesemann laughed. "You are going home to-day."

"Home?" repeated Heidi faintly, turning pale. For a moment she could hardly breathe, she was so overcome by the news.

"Perhaps you don't want to go," suggested Herr Sesemann.

"Oh, yes, I do want to go home," she replied, her face aglow with pleasure.

"Very well, then, you must take a good breakfast and then off you go in the carriage."

But hard as she tried, Heidi could scarcely swallow a mouthful for excitement. It all seemed like a dream and she thought that at any moment she might wake and find herself at the front door, shivering in her nightgown.

"Tell Sebastian to take plenty of provisions, for naturally the child can't eat just at present," Herr Sesemann told Fräulein Rottenmeier, who just at that moment entered the room. And turning to Heidi, he said kindly, "Go and join Clara until the carriage arrives."

Heidi rose eagerly and ran upstairs to Clara's room. In the middle of the floor was a big trunk which Clara had packed with dresses, pinafores, handkerchiefs and all sorts of clothes. "Look what I have packed for you," said Clara "Aren't you pleased, Heidi? And look, Heidi!" Triumphantly she held up a basket. Heidi peeped in and jumped for joy, for inside were twelve beautiful white rolls for the grandmother.

The children were so happily absorbed in their preparations that they had forgotten completely that the time for parting had come, and when the carriage was ready there was no time left for sadness.

Remembering her favourite book, Heidi ran back quickly to her own room and took it from under the pillow, the place where she always kept it, and racing back she put it into the basket with the rolls. Then she went and had a last look in the wardrobe and, sure enough, there was her old red shawl, which Fräulein Rottenmeier had not thought worth including with the rest of her luggage. Heidi wrapped it up and carefully hid it amongst the other luggage so that it would not be seen.

The children had to say good-bye quickly for Herr Sesemann was waiting to see Heidi to the carriage. Fräulein Rottenmeier was waiting at the top of the stairs and somehow a peep of red amongst Heidi's luggage caught her eye. She at once pulled out the red shawl and threw it aside.

"No, Adelheid," she scolded, "you cannot possibly take that old thing with you. Good-bye, then!"

Heidi did not dare lift up the little bundle but looked

imploringly at the master of the house with an expression which suggested that her greatest treasure had been taken from her.

"No, no," objected Herr Sesemann very firmly. "The child can take home whatever she pleases, whether it be kittens or tortoises and we won't be upset about it either, Fräulein Rottenmeier."

Heidi quickly lifted up her bundle and her eyes beamed with gratitude. Herr Sesemann shook hands with her, wished her a happy journey and said that he and Clara would always remember her. Heidi thanked him for all his kindness and said finally, "And please say good-bye to the doctor for me and thank him very, very much." She had not forgotten his words of the night before when he had said, "And to-morrow everything will be all right." And now these words had really come true and Heidi was convinced that it was all of his doing.

She was lifted into the carriage, and trunk, basket and provisions followed. Finally Sebastian climbed up beside her. Once more Herr Sesemann wished her a good journey and the carriage rolled away.

Very soon Heidi was sitting beside Sebastian in the train, her basket on her lap. She would not let go of it for a second, for inside were the rolls for the Grandmother. For many hours she sat silent. Only now did she fully realise that she was on her way home to the grandfather, the grandmother and Goat Peter; and the familiar scene rose before her eyes. She thought of how beautiful everything would look at home, but then a sudden thought came to her and suddenly she turned anxiously to Sebastian. "Sebastian, are you sure the grandmother on the Alm is not dead?"

"No, no," he replied comfortingly, "I am sure she will still be alive."

Once more Heidi became preoccupied with her own thoughts, occasionally peeping into the basket. After some time she asked again, "Sebastian, if I only knew for certain that grandmother is still alive!"

"Yes, yes," said Sebastian, half asleep. "She will be alive. Why should she be dead?"

After a while Heidi fell asleep, too, and slept so soundly that she did not wake up until Sebastian shook her by the arm and said, "Wake up! Wake up! We are in Basle. This is where we get out!"

The next morning they had to start again on a long train journey, and as they reached their destinations Heidi was too excited to talk and again sat with her basket held tightly. When she least expected it, a voice shouted, "Mayenfeld!" Up she jumped from her seat and Sebastian followed. As they stood on the platform beside Heidi's luggage, Sebastian looked regretfully after the disappearing train, for he much preferred that comfortable mode of transport to the tiring and dangerous climb up into the mountains in this, as he considered it, barbarous country. Cautiously he looked round to see of whom he might inquire the safest road to Dörfli. He spotted a broad-shouldered man loading a cart with big heavy sacks which had just arrived by train. Sebastian addressed his inquiry to him.

"All the roads here are safe," answered the man.

So Sebastian asked which was the best way one could take without being in danger of falling over a precipice, and also how to get a trunk up to Dörfli. The man regarded the trunk and then declared that if it was not too heavy, he would take it on his cart, as he was on his way there. After further conversation, the man agreed to take both the child and the trunk as far as Dörfli and from there somebody would take her up to the Alm.

"I can go by myself. I know the way from Dörfli to the Alm," said Heidi, who had been listening attentively to the conversation.

Sebastian was greatly relieved not to have to do any climbing. He took Heidi aside and gave her a heavy little leather bag and the letter to the grandfather, explaining; "This little bag is a present from Herr Sesemann. It must go to the bottom of the basket, under the rolls, and the little fräulein must be very careful with it for Herr Sesemann would be very angry if she were to lose it."

"I won't lose it," said Heidi confidently and at once put both the bag and the letter at the bottom of her basket.

The trunk was hoisted on to the cart and then Sebastian helped Heidi with her basket on to the driver's seat. He shook hands with her and reminded her once more about the contents of the basket. (Sebastian was rather worried as he knew he was supposed to see the child right to her destination.) The driver swung himself up beside Heidi and the cart moved off. Sebastian, glad to have rid himself of a wearisome duty, sat down in the station to wait for the return train.

The man with the cart was the miller from Dörfli who was taking home his sacks of flour. He had never seen Heidi before but felt sure this must be the much-discussed child whose parents he had known. He began to wonder what had happened that she should be returning here. "Aren't you the little girl who lived with the uncle on the Alm?" he shouted to Heidi above the noise of the cart.

"Yes," replied Heidi.

"You are soon back, aren't you? Didn't they treat you well there?"

"No, it wasn't that. Nobody could have been treated better than I was in Frankfurt."

"What brings you back then?"

"Because Herr Sesemann allowed me."

"But wouldn't you rather have stayed?"

"Oh, I'd rather be with the grandfather on the Alm than anywhere else in the world!"

"Maybe you'll think differently once you're there," muttered the baker, and then said to himself, "It's very odd, she must surely know what it's like up there." Then he started to whistle and said no more.

Heidi looked round and trembled with excitement as she began to recognise the trees on the road and above, the great towering peaks which seemed to welcome her back like old friends. Heidi nodded to them in turn, and at every bend of the road grew more and more happy until she felt she would burst with joy. More than anything she wanted to leap from the plodding cart and run as fast as she could until she reached the Alm. But instead, she sat still and patient, despite her inward excitement. As they drove into Dörfli the clock was striking five. A group of women and children clustered round the cart and wanted to know where they had come from and where they were going. As the baker lifted Heidi down she said quickly, "Thank you. Grandfather will fetch the trunk later," and tried to run off. She was at once stopped by questions from all sides but she pushed her way through the crowd with such a worried expression that the people were compelled to stand aside and let her through. It was certain, in their minds, that she would not go back to the grandfather if she had anywhere else to go, but the baker quickly enlightened them, declaring that although she had had the chance to live in a house where she had everything, it was her own wish to return to the grandfather. "There you are," they said to each other, "you can see she's frightened, and no wonder." They whispered about the Alm-Uncle and how he had deteriorated during the year, never saying one word, and looking like thunder at those he met. This news amazed everybody and it was soon spread around Dörfli that Heidi had given up a luxurious home to return to the hut on the Alm.

As fast as she could, Heidi climbed up from Dörfli. As she reached the top the path got steeper and the basket seemed to get heavier and heavier, so that she was obliged to pause now and then to get her breath. There was only one thought in her mind. Would she find the grandmother still in her usual corner by the spinning wheel? Suddenly she caught sight of the cottage and her heart began to pound. She ran as fast as she could until she reached the door ant trembled so much with excitement that she could hardly open it. But then she was inside and standing in the middle of the little room with no breath left to say a word.

"Dear Lord!" a voice cried from the corner, "that sounded like Heidi. If only I could have her with me again. Who is there?"

"But it *is* Heidi, Grandmother! I am back!" called Heidi and rushed towards the old woman. She put her arms round her and hugged her, unable to speak for joy. At first the grandmother was too overwhelmed to utter a word; then she caressed Heidi's curly head and said, "It is her hair, and her voice. Thank God that He has granted this to me!" Tears of joy spilled from her blind eyes. "Is it really you, Heidi? Have you come back to me?"

"Yes, Grandmother, it is true," assured Heidi. "Don't cry. I am really back and will come to you every day and never go away again. And you won't have to eat hard bread for a while. Look, Grandmother, look!"

Heidi unpacked her basket and piled the twelve rolls in the grandmother's lap.

"Ah, child, what a blessing you bring with you," she said, feeling the rolls, of which there seemed to be a countless number, but the greatest blessing is you yourself," and again she touched Heidi's hair and her hot cheek. "Speak to me, child," she murmured, "so that I can hear your voice again."

Heidi was in the midst of telling the grandmother how she had feared she might never see her again when the door opened and Peter's mother walked in. For a moment she stood perplexed, then she cried, "Can it possibly be you, Heidi?"

Brigitta's quick glance soon took in Heidi's appearance, and with little gasps of admiration she exclaimed to the grandmother, "Mother, if you could only see what a pretty frock she is wearing and how grand she looks! I hardly recognise her. And this hat with the feather, is it yours, too, Heidi? Put it on and let me see how you look in it."

"No, I don't care about it," replied Heidi. "If you like it, please have it. I still have my old one." Heidi opened the little red bundle and took out her own hat which looked more crushed than ever after the long journey. But that did not trouble Heidi. She still remembered all the grandfather had had to say about hats with feathers, on Dete's last visit. This was why she had looked after her old hat so lovingly, for she had always the thought of going home again in the back of her mind. And taking off her pretty frock, she wrapped the red shawl round her shoulders. "But now," she said, taking the grandmother's hand, "I must go home to Grandfather. To-morrow I shall come back. Good night, Grandmother!"

"Yes, come again, Heidi, come again to-morrow," begged the grandmother and pressed the child's hands.

"But why have you taken off your pretty dress?" Brigitta wanted to know.

"Because I would rather go to Grandfather like this in case he shouldn't recognise me. You hardly knew me at first."

Brigitta thought she was silly, and told her not to give it away. Perhaps Heidi should sell it to the schoolmaster's daughter in Dörfli. But Heidi did not change her mind, and later hid the hat behind the grandmother's chair. Brigitta accompanied her to the door and there said to her, "You could have kept the dress, he would have recognised you; but approach him carefully, for Peter says that Alm-Uncle never talks to anyone these days and is very moody."

Heidi said good night and went off up to the Alm. The big snow-field at the Scesaplana sparkled in the evening sun. A red shimmer fell on the grass at Heidi's feet and she turned round. She had not remembered, even in her dreams, how beautiful this picture was. The two peaks of the Falkins rose like twin flames, the snowfield was aglow and above it floated rose-tinted clouds. Far below stretched the valley, and above and around everything glittered and sparkled. Tears crept down Heidi's cheeks at the sight of all this splendour. Earnestly she pressed her hands together and thanked God for bringing her home again. She stood still, her heart full of thankfulness, until the light began to fade, and then all at once she ran up the mountain as fast as she could. Presently the tops of the fir trees waving in the wind and then the hut came into view, and there was the grandfather sitting on his bench and smoking his pipe. Heidi ran faster and before the Alm-Uncle was aware of anything Heidi had thrown her basket to the ground and put her two arms round his neck, unable to say more than, "Grandfather! Grandfather! Grandfather!"

The old man could say nothing. For the first time for many years his eyes were wet with tears and he brushed them roughly away with the back of his hand. Then he lifted Heidi on to his knee and looked at her. "So you have come home again to me, Heidi," he began. "You don't look very much of a lady. Did they send you away?"

"Oh, no, Grandfather. You mustn't think that. They were all

very good to me, Clara and Grandmamma and Herr Sesemann. It was just that I couldn't bear being away from you any longer. Sometimes I felt I would choke, but I never said anything because it would have been ungrateful. Then suddenly one morning Herr Sesemann called for me very early—I think maybe it was the doctor who told him—but perhaps it is all in the letter—" and Heidi jumped down and fetched the letter and the little bag from her basket and handed them both to the grandfather.

"I think that belongs to you," he declared, laying the little leather bag beside him on the bench. Then he read the letter and without a word put it into his pocket.

"Do you think you could still drink milk with me?" he asked Heidi and took her hand to go into the hut. "But take your money! You can buy a proper bed with it and enough clothes to last several years."

"I don't need it, Grandfather," assured Heidi. "I have got a bed already and Clara packed such a lot of clothes in my trunk that I shall never have to buy any ever again. It's wonderful."

"Take the money and put it into the cupboard, then. Some day you will want it."

Heidi obeyed and followed the grandfather into the hut. Joyfully she ran about and looked into every corner. Then she went up the ladder, but she stopped short when she put her head into the loft. "Oh, Grandfather, where is my bed?" she cried reproachfully.

"It will soon be there again," came from below. "How was I to know you were coming back? Come down and drink your milk."

Heidi came down and took her old seat in the high chair. Eagerly she drank her milk as though nothing had ever tasted so delicious. Then she took a deep breath and declared, "There is nothing in the whole world so good as our milk, Grandfather!"

Suddenly a shrill whistle sounded. Quick as lightning Heidi rushed outside, and there were the goats, skipping and jumping down the steep heights with Peter in their midst. Speechlessly he stared at Heidi.

"Good evening, Peter!" she said. "Do you still know me?"

The little goats had evidently recognised her voice, for they rubbed their heads against her eagerly. Heidi was wild with joy to see her old companions once more and called each one by name as they came scampering and leaping down to her. Even shy little Snowflake pushed the Great Turk out of her way in such a sure manner that he was left standing looking very put out by her bravado.

Heidi was thrilled to be back with all her old friends. She threw her arms around Snowflake's neck, stroked Goldfinch, and was pushed and nuzzled on all sides.

Slowly Peter came towards her. "So you are back again!" he managed to say at last. Then, just as in the old days, he asked, "Will you come up to the pasture, to-morrow?"

"No, not to-morrow, but the next day. To-morrow I must go and see the grandmother as I have been worried about her."

"I am glad you are back!" Peter said, beaming with happiness, and began to urge the goats down the mountain.

When Heidi got back into the cottage her bed was already made up for her. With a sigh of contentment she lay down and slept as she had not done for a whole year. During the night the grandfather got up again and again and listened anxiously to hear if Heidi slept quietly. But Heidi never stirred. Now there was nothing to make her wander about in the night-time for her longing was satisfied. She had seen the mountains again and had heard the wind in the fir trees. She was home on the Alm.

CHAPTER 14

THE BELLS RING OUT

Heidi stood under the fir trees and waited for the Alm-Uncle who was going to take her as far as the grandmother's and then go on to Dörfli to fetch her trunk. She was impatient to hear how the grandmother had enjoyed the white rolls and thought the grandfather would never be finished with his tasks, but at the same time she could not listen enough to the whispering of the trees, or breathe in the beautiful flower-filled air of the pastures. At last the old man appeared and announced, "Well, I have finished."

It was a Saturday, which was Alm-Uncle's day for cleaning and tidying the house. He had spent the morning doing this so that he could go with Heidi in the afternoon, and the hut was now shining bright and clean.

At Goat Peter's cottage they parted and Heidi ran inside. The grandmother heard her step and called lovingly, "Are you there, child? Have you come back again?" She took Heidi's hand and told her how much she had enjoyed the rolls and how much stronger she felt already. Brigitta explained how the grandmother would only take one roll each day for fear they would be finished too soon. At that Heidi exclaimed, "I know what I shall do, Grandmother. I shall write to Clara and I am sure she will send as many rolls as you want."

"That is very good of you," said Brigitta, "but I am afraid they would get very hard and stale. If only I had money! The baker in Dörfli makes them too, but I can't afford to buy them. I have hardly enough money for the ordinary black bread."

"Oh, but I have lots of money!" the child cried delightedly. "Now I know how I shall spend it. Every day Grandmother will have a white roll and two on Sundays and Peter will get them in Dörfli."

"No, no, my child," remonstrated the grandmother. "The money you have got is not for that; you must give it to the grandfather and he will tell you what to do with it."

But Heidi took no notice and continued to chatter happily, "Now Grandmother can eat a roll every day and will get quite strong. Perhaps it's only dark for you because you are so weak, Grandmother."

The grandmother said nothing. She did not want to spoil the child's joy.

Suddenly Heidi caught sight of the grandmother's hymn book and a new thought struck her:

"Grandmother, I can read now. Shall I read to you one of the hymns from your old book?"

"Yes, indeed," replied the grandmother, both surprised and delighted. "But do you really know how to read, child?"

Heidi had climbed on a chair and lifted down the dusty book which had lain untouched on the shelf for a very long time.

She blew the dust off and then sat down on the stool beside the old woman, asking which hymn she wanted to hear.

"Whichever you like, child! Whichever you like!" And she waited in eager expectation while Heidi turned over the pages and read softly a line here and there.

"Here is one about the sun. I shall read that one, Grandmother."

And Heidi read the hymn aloud, very touchingly.

The grandmother sat with folded hands while Heidi read and the face of the aged woman shone with an indescribable joy such as Heidi had never seen before, and her eyes glistened with tears. When the child stopped reading, "Once more, Heidi, please. Read it once more," she begged, and Heidi read the hymn again.

The morning breaks,
And warm and bright
The earth lies still
In golden light—
For Dawn has scattered the clouds of night.

God's handiwork
Is seen around
Things great and small
To his praise abound—
Where are the signs of his love not found.

All things must pass
But God shall still
His will fulfill—
Sure and unshaken is His will.

His saving grace
Will never fail
Though grief and fear
The heart assail—
O'er life's wild seas he will prevail.

Joy shall be ours
In that garden blest,
Where after storm
We find our rest—
I wait in peace—God's time is best.

"Oh, Heidi, that is enough to fill my heart with light. How comforting the words are!"

As the grandmother spoke, there was a knock at the window and the grandfather stood outside, beckoning Heidi to come home. She went at once, but not without promising the grandmother that she would come again to-morrow. She was completely happy because she could make the grandmother's life cheerful again. It was an even greater source of happiness to her than the goats and the pasture.

Heidi had so much to tell the grandfather, particularly about the rolls. "Surely, Grandfather," she said, "if Grandmother won't take the money you will give me money from the bag so that I can give it to Peter to buy the rolls every day!"

"What about a bed, Heidi?" asked the grandfather. "A proper bed for you would be nice and there would still be plenty left over for the rolls?"

But Heidi gave him no peace and at last the old man said, "The money is yours to do with as you please. You will be able to buy rolls for the Grandmother with it for many, many years."

Heidi was jubilant. "Oh, Grandfather, isn't everything wonderful!" Then she became serious. "If God had answered when I prayed to come here at once, everything would have been different. I would only have come for a short time and Grandmother would only have got a few rolls and I wouldn't have been able to read to her. But God has thought it out much better than I ever could, just as Grandmamma told me in Frankfurt. Everything has turned out as she said. Oh, how glad I am that God did not let me have my way! Now I shall always pray as Grandmamma taught me and if God does not do what I ask I shall think at once, 'I am sure it is just the same as at Frankfurt and God knows a much better way.' So we will pray every day, please, Grandfather, and we will never forget Him so that He does not forget us."

"And if somebody does forget Him?" murmured the grandfather.

"Oh, it will be the worse for him! Because then God will forget *him*, and nobody will pity him because he ran away from God who could have helped him."

"That is true, Heidi. But how do you know?"

"From Grandmamma She explained it all to me."

The grandfather walked on silently, then, lost in his own thoughts. He said, "But nobody can go back once he has forgotten God and God has forgotten him for ever."

"Oh, no, Grandfather! It's possible to go back. I know that, too, from Grandmamma, and it even says so in the lovely story in my book, but you have not read it yet. As soon as we are home you shall hear what a beautiful story it is."

As soon as they reached the top of the hill Heidi ran into the cottage to get her book and returned presently with it under her arm. The grandfather, busy with his own thoughts, was seated on the bench. Heidi climbed up beside him and opened her book at her favourite story.

Now Heidi began to read the story of the Prodigal Son who, although he had all he could wish for at home tending his father's flock, longed for wealth and riches, and asked for his share of his father's wealth so that he could go out into the world and be his own master. After he had foolishly spent all he had, he was obliged to work as a swine-herd with nothing to wear but rags and nothing to eat but the husks which the pigs left. Then he remembered his father and thought what an ungrateful son he had been, and he wept bitterly. So he decided, 'I shall go to my father and ask forgiveness and say to him, "I am not worthy to be called thy son; make me one of thy day labourers.'" But when he was still a great distance from his father's house, his father recognised him and hastened forward—

"And what do you think happens now, Grandfather?" Heidi could not help stopping to ask. "Do you think the father in still angry and will say to him, 'Go away!' Listen now to what happens next!"

"And when the father saw him coming he had compassion on him and embraced him, and the son said, 'Father, I have sinned against Heaven and in thy sight and am not worthy to be called thy son.' But his father said to his servants, 'Bring the best robe for him. Put a ring on his finger and bring shoes for his feet. And bring forth the fatted calf and kill it and let us eat and be merry, for this, my son, was dead and is alive again; he was lost and is found.'

"Isn't that a beautiful story, Grandfather?" asked Heidi when she saw that he was still absorbed in his thoughts.

"Yes, Heidi, the story is beautiful," answered the grandfather, his face still grave. So Heidi was silent for a while and looked at the pictures in her book. After a while she laid the book on his lap and said, "Look, Grandfather, he is so happy standing there," pointing to the figure of the prodigal son, who was standing by his father in new clothes, as one of the family.

A few hours later when Heidi had been asleep for a long time, the grandfather climbed up the ladder and put his lamp beside her bed so that its light fell on the sleeping child. She was lying with folded hands, as if she had fallen asleep saying her prayers. On her little face was an expression of peace and trust. For a long time the old man stood gazing at the child, then he folded his hands and half aloud he prayed with bent head, "Father, I have sinned against Heaven and in Thy sight and am not worthy to be called Thy son." As he spoke tears rolled down the old man's cheeks.

Early next morning the Alm-Uncle stood in front of his hut, smiling gently as he looked around him. It was a beautiful Sunday morning and he could hear the church bells ringing down in the valley. He went back into the hut and called up

111

to the loft, "Get up, Heidi! Put on your nice frock for we are going to church together."

Heidi was soon dressed in her pretty Frankfurt clothes and came downstairs quickly, her curiosity aroused by this unusual summons from the Alm-Uncle; but great was her surprise when she caught a glimpse of him. "Oh, Grandfather, I have never seen you in this coat with the silver buttons. How nice you look in your Sunday coat!"

The old man smiled and said, "You too, in your pretty dress. Come along now!" He took Heidi's hand in his and they walked down the mountain together. The bells were ringing on every side and the sound of them filled the whole valley and rose up echoing among the mountains. As they descended, the peals sounded louder and richer and Heidi listened rapturously. "Listen, Grandfather! It is like a great festival."

When the grandfather and Heidi entered the church the singing had already begun so they sat down together at the back. But before the hymn was finished there was subdued whispering on all sides, "The Alm-Uncle, did you see the Alm-Uncle?"

Soon everybody knew that the Alm-Uncle was in church and the women, hardly able to believe, kept turning their heads to look. When the sermon began, everybody became more attentive and forgot, for the time being, about the uncle.

As soon as the service was finished the old uncle walked with the child in the direction of the pastor's house. Some of the people followed him curiously and when they saw him and the child go inside, they gathered in excited groups to discuss the extraordinary event, for they could not imagine what had brought the old man down from his mountain-top. It soon became evident that many of them were beginning to change their opinion of the old man. They had noticed what great care he took of the little one and surely, they thought, he cannot be so very wicked or he would be afraid to face the pastor. Then the baker reminded them, "Didn't I tell you? What child would give up a wonderful home with the best life can offer to go back to a grandfather who had been unkind and of whom she is afraid?" And so a friendly feeling for the grandfather began to spread amongst the people and they waited patiently at the pastor's door as though to welcome back an old friend who had been gone a long time.

The uncle knocked at the door of the pastor's study and the pastor greeted him as though he had expected the old man. His appearance in church had not escaped the pastor's notice and he shook hands warmly. At first the Alm-Uncle could not find words, then, pulling himself together, he began, "Pastor, I have come to ask you to forget the words I spoke to you on the Alm and not to hold it against me that I was too obstinate to take your well-meant advice. I see now that you were right and I was wrong, so I am following your advice and I would like to take the house in Dörfli for the winter, for the cold season up there is not good for the child. She is too delicate. Of course, the people here do not trust me and I deserve no better."

The kind eyes of the pastor brightened with joy. Once more he grasped the old man's hand and said with deep emotion, "Neighbour, I am sincerely glad; and you will never have cause to regret coming back to live amongst us. You will always be welcome in my house and I hope to spend many a pleasant winter evening with you for I value your friendship. And we shall also find playmates for the little one."

The pastor laid his hand affectionately on Heidi's curly head, and taking her by the hand, accompanied them both to the door. When they stood outside on the doorstep he bade them good-bye and everybody noticed that the pastor shook hands with the Alm-Uncle as if they were the best of friends.

As soon as the door closed the old man was assailed by friendly greetings from every one, "How nice to see you again, Uncle!" "It's good to see you back, Uncle. I have been wanting to have a talk with you for a long time." And when the Uncle told them that he was going to live again in his old house in Dörfli for the winter months, there was such a chorus of joyful shouts that it seemed as though the Alm-Uncle was the most popular person in Dörfli. The farming people accompanied the old man and the child far up the mountain path and when they said farewell every one invited him to call next time he was down. When they parted, the old man followed them with his eyes and his face reflected an inner light so that Heidi could not take her eyes off him. "Grandfather," she said, "today you look nicer every minute. I have never seen you like this before."

"Do you think so?" asked the old man, smiling. "You see, Heidi, I am so happy to-day. To be at peace with God and man is good! God was good to me when He sent you to the Alm."

When they arrived at Goat Peter's hut, the grandfather opened the door and they walked inside.

"Good morning, Grandmother!" he said. "I think we will have to do some more patching before the autumn winds come."

"Mercy!" exclaimed the grandmother. "That is the uncle!" and her voice was both surprised and pleased. "Now I can thank you for all you have done for us, Uncle. God bless you! God bless you!" And when he held her trembling hand she said, "If I have ever hurt you, don't punish me by taking Heidi away from me. Oh, you do not know what the child means to me." And she held Heidi close to her.

"Have no fear, Grandmother. I shall not punish either you or myself. We shall all stay together now and, if God wills it, for a long time."

Brigitta beckoned the Uncle into a corner, and showed him the hat with the feathers, explaining how it came to be there and insisting that she could not take such a thing from a child. But the grandfather, glancing towards Heidi, replied that Brigitta should indeed take the hat, as Heidi was free to decide if she didn't want it.

Brigitta was thrilled. "It is worth more than ten shillings," she said, displaying it for all to admire. "And what changes for the good Heidi has brought with her from Frankfurt. I've a good mind to send Peter there for a while—I am sure it would benefit him tremendously."

The grandfather's eyes twinkled. He thought it would probably do Peter good, but he meant to wait for the right moment to broach the subject to him.

At that moment, Peter himself rushed in noisily and evidently in a great hurry. He held a letter in his hand which was a rare enough occurrence to account for his excitement. It

114

was a letter for Heidi which had been given to Peter at the post office in Dörfli. Heidi opened her letter and read it aloud. It was from Clara.

She told Heidi how dull it had been since she had gone and how, for this reason, she had persuaded her father to take her to Ragatz next autumn so that she might have a chance of seeing her again. Grandmamma wished to come too, for she also wished to visit Heidi and the grandfather on the Alm; and Grandmamma was sending some coffee so that the grandmother would not have to eat the rolls dry. And she was looking forward to visiting the grandmother herself if Heidi would take her.

There were so many questions to ask and so much to discuss after this news that even the grandfather did not notice how quickly time was passing. Everybody was happy about the news but, as the grandmother said, the greatest delight of all was to see an old friend return like old times. "Come again, soon, Uncle, and you, child, tomorrow!"

They both promised. But now it was time to leave. As in the morning the bells had greeted them, so now the peaceful evening chimes accompanied them on their way up to the sunny Alm cottage which shone with an air of Sunday calm in the red glow of the evening sky. But when Grandmamma arrives next autumn there will be even more surprises for Heidi and for the grandmother; for a proper bed will certainly be put up in the hay loft. If Grandmamma has anything to do with it, everything turns out very well.

CHAPTER 15

PREPARATIONS FOR A JOURNEY

It was a sunny morning in September and the good doctor, who had been the cause of Heidi's going home, was on his way to the Sesemann's house. There was a look of great sadness on his face and he seemed to have aged considerably since the spring. The doctor had had an only daughter in whom, since the death of his wife, he had found his only happiness. A few months before, she had died and, ever since, all the doctor's brightness and cheerfulness had gone.

Sebastian opened the door with marked civility, for the doctor was not only the best friend of the master but also of his little daughter, and because of his warmth and kindness was beloved by everyone in the house.

"Everything all right?" he asked Sebastian in his pleasant voice as he preceded the servant upstairs.

"Ah, I am glad you are here!" exclaimed Herr Sesemann as he stepped forward to welcome his friend. "We must definitely discuss again this Swiss journey. Do you still stick by your decision in spite of the fact that Clara's health shows signs of improvement?"

"My dear Sesemann, what am I to think of you!" replied the doctor. "This is the third time to-day you have called me in to ask the same question."

"Yes, you are perfectly right and I cannot blame you for becoming impatient; but you must understand, my dear friend, how difficult it is for me to deny the child now, at the last minute, something which I promised her so faithfully and to which she has been looking forward for months. It is only the prospect of this journey and the thought of seeing her friend again which has enabled Clara to suffer so patiently these last bad weeks and now, suddenly, I am to deprive the poor child of this joy. I simply cannot do it."

"Sesemann, it has to be done," replied the doctor firmly, and when he saw his friend silent and depressed he continued, "now think it out for yourself. For years Clara hasn't had such a bad summer as this last one. There can be no question of travelling without risk of the worst consequences. And after all, it is September, and although there is a chance that it is still fine up there, it may very easily be cold. The days are getting shorter and the journey from Ragatz to the Alm would take several hours as Clara would have to be carried up the

116

mountain. In short, Sesemann, it is quite impossible. But I shall speak to her myself. She is a sensible child. If she is taken to Ragatz next May for very special care and if she is stronger she will enjoy the excursion up the mountain far more than now. Only with the greatest care and attention can she have a chance of recovery."

Herr Sesemann suddenly turned to the doctor and said bluntly: "Tell me honestly, Doctor: do you really think she may one day recover?"

The doctor shrugged. "I don't hold out much hope," he said quietly. "But think what I have to go through. You still have a loving child to watch for you and to be there when you arrive home. You do not return to a lonely house, and Clara is comfortable there too. Despite all the things she has to miss she has many things for which to be grateful. No, my friend, you have not a great deal to be sorry about."

Herr Sesemann rose and walked up and down the room as was his habit when something occupied his mind.

Suddenly he tapped his friend on the shoulder.

"Doctor, I have a suggestion to make. You don't look well and are not the same as you used to be. You need a change and do you know what has occurred to me? You should go and visit Heidi on the Alm in our name."

This suggestion surprised the doctor very much and he started to make objections, but Herr Sesemann gave him no opportunity. He was so enthusiastic about his new plan that he took his friend by the arm and drew him into Clara's room. Clara was always pleased to see the doctor, for he nearly always had some funny story to tell her. Recently he had been more serious, but Clara knew why, and would have given anything to see him lively and cheerful once more.

Herr Sesemann took Clara's hand in his and began to talk about the Swiss journey and how he himself had looked forward to it. He passed quickly over the main point—that it was impossible now for Clara to go—for he could not bear the thought of the tears which would be bound to fall, and then told her of his latest plan to persuade their good friend, the doctor, to take this holiday.

117

Tears came into Clara's eyes although she tried to hide them for her father's sake, but it was a great disappointment to her to have to give up this journey which had been her only joy and comfort during many lonely hours. She knew, however, that her father would only deny her something which would do her harm; so she swallowed her tears and tuned her thoughts to the only remaining hope. She took the doctor's hand and said imploringly:

"Please, doctor, go and see Heidi and then come back and tell me what it is like there and how Heidi is getting on; and the grandfather, and Peter and the goats. I feel I know them all so well! And then you can take to Heidi all the things I have for her, and something for the grandmother. Please go, doctor, and I'll take as much cod liver oil as you like."

It may not have been this promise which altogether decided the doctor but he certainly replied smilingly: "Then I suppose I must go, Clara, if we are to see you grow plump and strong! And when have you decided I am to start?"

"As soon as possible, doctor. To-morrow morning," replied Clara.

"She is quite right," interrupted her father. "The weather is fine and it would be a pity to miss a single day which you could enjoy on the Alm."

The doctor could not help laughing a little. "Soon you'll reproach me for not being there already, Sesemann. I see I shall have to make haste."

But Clara still detained him. She had to give him lots of messages for Heidi. She would send round the presents later on. The doctor promised to deliver them all faithfully and to bring back a full account of everything that happened.

The servants of a household have a strange capacity for knowing what is going on long before they are informed about it by the master. Tinette, having been rung for, went into Clara's room. Clara asked her to fill a box with the cakes normally served with coffee. Tinette picked it up, and swinging it carelessly, carried it out. "I wouldn't have bothered if I'd been you," she said cheekily as she went out. Sebastian, as he opened the front door for the doctor, said with his usual deference: "May I ask the doctor to give my regards to the little fräulein?"

"Ah, Sebastian," the doctor smiled, "you know already about my going?"

Sebastian looked embarrassed, "Well, I—not exactly—as a matter of fact—well, you see, I just happened to go into the dining-room when I heard the little fräulein's name mentioned, and then I thought—"

"I see! I see!" smiled the doctor. "Good-bye, Sebastian! I'll be sure to remember your message."

The doctor stepped across the threshold, and then jumped back again quickly. The doorway was blocked by Fräulein Rottenmeier returning from her walk which she had been prevented from concluding by the rough wind. It was a very gusty day and the wind blew out her skirts so that she looked like a ship in full sail. The doctor drew aside to let her pass, but the wind was so strong she was blown right into the doorway and, gasping for breath, crashed into the doctor. The poor lady was very much upset by this loss of dignity for she had a great admiration for the doctor, but he very quickly smoothed her down and told her of his plans, asking her in a most amiable voice to pack the parcel for Heidi in the way in which only she could do it. Then off he went.

Clara had expected that Fräulein Rottenmeier would make all sorts of objections to sending the many presents to Heidi, but she was mistaken. Fräulein Rottenmeier was in an exceptionally good temper and everything was laid out on a large table where Clara could watch it all being packed. This was not an easy task, for the presents were all of different shapes and size. There was the little warm coat with the hood which Clara had herself designed for Heidi, so that during the long, cold winter she could be warm enough to visit the grandmother whenever he wanted. Then came a thick warm shawl for the grandmother in which she could wrap herself up and not feel the draught from the cold wind and also a large cake as a change from the rolls. There was the large box full of cakes, also for the grandmother, as a change from bread when she had her coffee. Then there was a delicious sausage which

119

Clara had at first meant for Peter as he never had anything to eat except bread and cheese, but had later decided to send to Brigitta, since there might be a danger of Peter eating it all himself, and Brigitta could be depended upon to divide it up between all of them for supper. There was a packet of tobacco for the grandfather who was so fond of his pipe, and last of all, there were a lot of mysterious little packages which Clara had especially enjoyed putting together, as they had been made up specially to be put in as individual surprises for Heidi.

At last the job was done and an imposing-looking parcel lay on the floor ready for transport. Fräulein Rottenmeier looked at it with a satisfied smile, pleased with her efforts at the art of packing. Clara gazed at it blissfully, imagining Heidi's squeals of delight when it arrived.

Fräulein Rottenmeier rang for Sebastian and with an energetic swing he lifted the parcel on to his shoulder and carried it off to be despatched at once to the doctor's house.

CHAPTER 16

A VISITOR TO THE ALM

The morning sky was all aglow, shedding its light upon the mountains, and a fresh breeze stirred in the fir trees, swaying their ancient branches. Heidi opened her eyes, awakened by the sound of the wind in the trees, and jumping out of bed, dressed herself very quickly. When she came down the ladder, the grandfather was already standing outside and was looking at the sky to see what sort of weather it was going to be. Little pink clouds floated across the sky and gradually more and more blue patches appeared. The sun was just rising and touched the mountain tops with gold.

"Oh, how lovely!" cried Heidi. "Good morning, Grandfather!"

"Are you awake already?" he said, patting the child's head. She ran off to listen to the fir trees, and with every new gust of wind which blew through their old branches, she thrilled with pleasure.

The grandfather went off to milk the goats and brought them out ready for their climb up to the pastures. There came the sound of Peter's whistle and presently Heidi was surrounded by the whole flock who were all bleating, nuzzling and rubbing against her so that she could hardly move. Little Bear pushed rather harder than he should, and was gently reproached by Heidi; whereupon Little Swan lifted her head daintily, as if to imply that she would not stoop to such behaviour. Heidi, meanwhile, had pushed her way through to where Snowflake was standing, for the little goat had tried to reach her and had been pushed aside by the others. Peter at last gave one more piercing blast on his whistle, and the goats moved off.

"Are you coming with us to-day?" he asked and it was clear from the tone of his voice that he was anxious for Heidi to accompany him.

"No, Peter, I can't come to-day," replied Heidi. "The friends from Frankfurt may arrive at any moment and I must be here when they come."

"That's what you always say," grumbled Peter. "And I shall go on saying it until they arrive," returned Heidi. "How could you think that I would not stay here to greet them?" "The uncle is always here. So I can't see that it matters," he muttered.

Just at that point the uncle himself called out, "What's wrong with the army to-day, it isn't on the move? Is it the General's fault or is it the troops'?"

Peter turned at once and cracked his whip in the air, and the goats, who knew the sound well, started off up the mountain with Peter trotting after them.

Since Heidi had come back she thought of all sorts of things to do about the house which had not occurred to her before.

Every morning she made her bed carefully, then she went downstairs and tidied the kitchen. She put the chairs straight and anything which was lying about she put into the cupboard. Next she would get out a duster, and climbing on to a chair, would rub the table until it shone. All this pleased the grandfather and he would look round, saying, "The house is so well kept nowadays it always looks as though it were Sunday! Heidi's trip certainly hasn't been in vain!"

To-day Heidi had begun her chores as usual but the beautiful weather seemed to draw her outside and she was not making much progress with her work. A sunbeam slanting through the open window seemed to be calling: "Come, Heidi! Come out!" She simply could not stay indoors any longer and ran outside. The sunlight sparkled on the mountains and shone down on the valley. Heidi had to sit down for a minute and look about her. However, she soon jumped up and ran back to the hut when she remembered that her stool was still standing in the middle of the floor and that the table had still not been rubbed properly.

Hardly had she set about her tasks again when she heard the fir trees calling her and off she ran again to listen to their song. The grandfather was working in the shed and came out from time to time to look smilingly at the child. He had just gone back to his work when Heidi called out loudly, "Grandfather! Grandfather! Come quickly!" The old man came out at once, afraid that something had happened to the child. He saw Heidi running towards the path, calling as she went, "They are coming! They are coming! The doctor is first!"

Heidi rushed forward to welcome her old friend who stretched out his hand in greeting. As soon as she reached him she clasped his out-stretched arm affectionately. "Good morning, doctor, and thank you, ever so much, I am so grateful to you."

"God bless you, Heidi! And what is it you are grateful to me for?"

"For arranging it so that I could come home to be with Grandfather," explained the child.

The doctor's face brightened with joy. He had not expected

122

such a welcome. He had climbed the steep mountain path feeling lonely and depressed and with never a thought for the beautiful scenery around him. Convinced that Heidi would hardly even recognise him again he had pictured the disappointment his arrival without the expected friends would cause. But instead, here was Heidi beaming with joy and full of love and gratitude, and still clinging to his arm.

With fatherly tenderness the doctor took the child by the hand. "Take me to your grandfather, Heidi, and show me where you live."

But Heidi did not go on. Her gaze was fixed on the path down the mountain and her little face showed disappointment. "Where are Clara and Grandmamma?" she asked.

"I have something to tell you, Heidi, and I know you will be as sorry about it as I am," replied the doctor. "You see, Heidi, I have come alone. Clara has been very ill and could not travel, so the grandmamma did not come either. But in the spring, when the days begin to get warmer and longer, they will certainly come."

Heidi looked perplexed. It was difficult for her to realise that everything she had looked forward to was not to be. She stood frozen for a moment, overwhelmed by the sudden disappointment. The doctor stood silently before her and there was no sound save the sighing of the wind in the fir trees. Then it occurred to Heidi that after all the doctor had come and she looked up at him. The eyes that looked down into hers were sad. Heidi had never seen him look like this in Frankfurt and her heart was at once full of sorrow for him. No doubt, she decided, it was because Clara and the grandmamma could not come and she tried to think quickly of a way to comfort him.

"Oh, it won't be long until the spring and then they'll be sure to come, won't they?" she asked. "The winter is never very long here, and when they do come, they will be able to stay much longer. Clara will certainly like that! Now let's go up to the grandfather."

Hand in hand with the doctor, she climbed up to the cottage and called out cheerfully to the grandfather. "They haven't come yet, but it won't be long."

The doctor was no stranger to the grandfather, for Heidi had talked about him a great deal. The old man welcomed his guest heartily and then the two men sat down on the bench before the cottage and there was still a little place for Heidi beside the doctor. The doctor started to explain:

"Herr Sesemann wanted me to come and I allowed myself to be persuaded because I have not been well for quite a time and I thought the fresh mountain air would do me good. Heidi," said the doctor, stooping towards her, "there will be something coming up here which has travelled with me all the way from Frankfurt—something which will give you more pleasure than the old doctor."

Heidi was intensely interested to know what it could be but the doctor would not give a hint.

The grandfather encouraged the doctor to spend the beautiful autumn days on the Alm, or at least, to come up every fine day. "I cannot invite you to stay here, as I have no accommodation, but if you would take a room down in Dörfli in the pleasant little inn instead of going back to Ragatz you could come up here in the mornings. There are many places round about which I would take pleasure in showing you."

This proposal delighted the doctor and so it was settled.

Time had passed quickly and it was now noon. The wind had dropped and the fir trees were quiet in the sun. The air was beautifully clean up there, but was nevertheless warm and gentle with its fill of sunlight. The Alm-Uncle rose and went into the cottage and brought back a little table which he placed in front of the bench. "Now, Heidi. Fetch everything we need for the meal," he ordered. "The doctor has to be content with our simple fare but he must admit that the dining-room is very pleasant."

"It is, indeed," agreed the doctor, looking down into the sunlit valley, "I gladly accept your kind invitation. Everything is bound to taste good in such surroundings."

Heidi ran to and fro like a busy little squirrel and brought whatever she could find in the cupboard for she wanted to show her pleasure in being able to entertain the doctor. The grandfather prepared the meal and appeared presently with the steaming milk jug and golden-brown toasted cheese. From the meat which he had cured himself he cut nice thin slices and the doctor ate more heartily than he had done for a whole year.

"Yes, Clara must certainly come here," he said. "It will give her new strength, and if her appetite is as good as mine has been to-day she'll grow plump and strong in no time."

As the doctor spoke, a man appeared coming up the path with a big bundle on his back. Panting, he arrived at the hut and put it down with a sigh of relief. "This is what I have brought with me all the way from Frankfurt," said the doctor, rising. The bundle was opened and when the first wrapping had been taken off he said: "Now, child, you go on and get out the treasure for yourself."

Heidi looked with big, astonished eyes at each item as it was unwrapped, speechless with pleasure. The doctor lifted the lid of one of the boxes. "Look, Heidi. Something the grandmother can have with her coffee!"

Heidi picked up the cake and skipped around with it joyfully: "Oh, a cake for the grandmother!" Heidi wanted to go down at once to the grandmother with the presents, but the grandfather persuaded her to wait until the evening when she could accompany the doctor on his way down and take the presents at the same time.

Now Heidi found the packet of tobacco and handed it to the grandfather who started at once to fill his pipe. The two men went back and sat down on the bench, leaving Heidi to continue her inspection of Clara's parcel alone. After she had admired them all sufficiently, Heidi put away the many presents and came back to where the men were sitting. As soon as there was a gap in the conversation she addressed their guest very solemnly:

"No, the parcel did not give me as much pleasure as your visit, doctor."

The two men could not help laughing at her childish gravity.

As the sun set behind the mountains, the guest rose to take his leave and begin his walk down to Dörfli. The grandfather took the presents under his arm, the box with the cake, the big

125

sausage and the shawl; the doctor took Heidi's hand and so all three walked down to Goat Peter's cottage where Heidi was to wait for her grandfather, who would first accompany their guest into Dörfli. Here Heidi said good night to the doctor and asked: "Would you like to come with the goats to-morrow?"

"Very well, Heidi. We'll go together," he replied. Now the two men walked on down the valley and Heidi ran into the cottage; taking first the cake box, then bringing in the big sausage, and last of all the shawl. She put everything very close to the grandmother so that the old woman would be able to touch the presents; and she laid the shawl on her knees.

"It has all come from Clara and the grandmamma in Frankfurt," she told the astonished Brigitta and the grandmother, Brigitta watching in amazement as one heavy package after another was dragged through the door.

"Aren't you delighted with the cake, Grandmother?" Heidi wanted to know again and again.

"Yes, Heidi. What kind people they must be!" Then she felt the warm, soft shawl and said, "How cosy it will be in the winter-time! I never dreamt I would possess anything so luxurious."

Heidi was surprised that the grandmother was more pleased about the shawl than the cake.

Brigitta was gazing at the sausage with a look in her eyes little short of worship. Never in her life had she seen such an enormous sausage, and she had certainly never owned one. She shook her head and looking puzzled, said, "I still have to ask Uncle what we should do with it."

But Heidi replied straight away, "You must eat it! That's what it's for."

Then Peter came rushing in. "The Alm-Uncle is just behind me, Heidi—" Peter stopped and gasped with astonishment as he caught sight of the sausage. Heidi understood immediately that she must leave, for it was getting late and although the grandfather always stopped by nowadays to greet the old lady, they would have a dark climb to the hut tonight. The grandfather never let Heidi go to bed too late, for she was always up at sunrise, so on this occasion he wished everyone

126

goodnight through the open door, and started back with Heidi straight away, climbing to their peaceful home under a star-filled sky.

A COMPENSATION

Early next morning the doctor climbed up to the Alm with Peter and the goats. The man and the boy walked in silence. In vain the kindly doctor had tried to start up a conversation with the boy but Peter remained obstinately silent and would not be coaxed into chatting about himself. Up at the Alm cottage Heidi waited with her two goats looking as sunny and sparkling as the morning.

"Are you coming?" asked Peter as he did every morning.

"Of course, if the doctor is coming, too," replied Heidi.

Peter cast a suspicious glance at the gentleman.

The Alm-Uncle came out of the hut carrying the lunch bag which he flung across Peter's shoulder. It was heavier than usual, for the uncle had put in something extra for the doctor in case he decided to stay long enough on the pasture to have his lunch with the children. When Peter felt the extra weight a grin spread across his face and the sulky look vanished. His thoughts were busy with the special tit-bits which the uncle might have put in the bag.

Now the trip started. The goats came crowding round Heidi as usual, so that she could hardly move forward, and eventually she stopped and told them to go on ahead properly and behave themselves. Gradually she was able to push them on in front of her, leaving her space to walk with the doctor, who took her by the hand. He had no difficulty this time in making conversation, for Heidi had so much to say about the goats,

127

the mountains, the flowers and the birds, that time passed quickly and they soon found themselves at the pasture. All the way up Peter had cast hostile glances at the doctor, which had fortunately gone unnoticed by Heidi and her companion. Heidi led the doctor to her favourite spot where she liked to sit, and the doctor sat down on the grass beside her, casting a contented glance around him at the wide, green, sunlit valley. The snowfield glittered in the clear autumn sunlight, and the two rocky peaks were sharply silhouetted against the deep blue sky. A gentle breeze blew across the valley, gently ruffling the late summer flowers which still waved amongst the grasses. The eagle flew silently above them. Heidi looked around her with delight. Everything was so perfect. Her eyes sparkled with happiness and she glanced round at her friend to see if he too was enchanted with the beautiful scenery. The doctor had been sitting, silent and thoughtful, but when he met Heidi's eager, inquiring eyes, he said, "Yes, Heidi, it is beautiful, but if one's heart is sad how is it possible to enjoy all this beauty? Can you tell me?"

"Oh!" Heidi exclaimed confidently. "No one is ever sad here. That only happens in Frankfurt."

The doctor smiled quietly, then he asked again, "But if somebody brings all the sadness from Frankfurt up here, Heidi, do you know what to do then?"

"When we don't know what to do we have only to tell God about our troubles," said Heidi seriously.

"Well, my dear, that seems to be a good idea," remarked the doctor, "but what if God Himself has sent the sorrow? What can one say to Him, then?"

Heidi had to think about this. "Then, we must wait," she said, "and just keep thinking, 'soon God will make things right.' We have only to have a little patience and not run away; then something will turn up and we will see quite clearly that all the time it was all for the bet. At the time we only think of the sadness."

"You have a wonderful faith, Heidi, and you must never lose it." The doctor was silent, gazing at the towering mountains above them. Then he said again, "You see, Heidi, when someone has a great grief he cannot enjoy anything lovely, and beauty, like this around us, only makes him more sad. Can you understand that?"

Heidi thought sadly of the old grandmother who would never see again the splendour of the sun and the mountains. Every time she thought about darkness Heidi sorrowed anew for the grandmother, and for a while she said nothing. Then, "Yes, I can understand that." Then she said softly, "That's how it was with the grandmother until I read the hymns for her from the old book. She says they made everything light for her again and made her happy."

"Can you remember any of the hymns, Heidi?" asked the doctor.

"Yes, shall I say one to you?" replied Heidi eagerly.

The doctor nodded, and Heidi folded her hands and started to recite the grandmother's favourite hymn.

> Let not your heart be troubled
> Nor fear your soul dismay,
> There is a wise Defender
> And he will be your stay.
> Where you have failed, he conquers,
> See, how the foeman flies
> And all your tribulation
> Is turned to glad surprise.
>
> If for awhile it seemeth
> His mercy is withdrawn,
> That he no longer careth
> For his wandering child forlorn,
> Doubt not His great compassion,
> His love can never tire,
> To those who wait in patience
> He gives their heart's desire.

She stopped. The doctor did not look as though he were listening. He was sitting quite still, with his hand over his eyes. Heidi thought he had perhaps fallen asleep. But he was wide awake, and thinking about a very long time ago, when he had been a little boy, and his mother had read him the very same hymn. He could see his mother's loving gaze and hear her dear voice, and she seemed to be saying many things to him. It was some while before he stirred, to see Heidi looking at him in a puzzled way.

"That was a beautiful hymn, Heidi," he said. "I would like you to read it to me again net time we come here together."

All this time Peter had been standing apart and growing more and more angry because the old gentleman sat beside Heidi all the time so that Peter had not once had a chance to speak to her. He felt so cross, he stood behind the doctor and shook his fist at him. Peter knew by the sun that it was midday and time for lunch, so he called out at the top of his voice, "Dinnertime!"

Heidi got up to bring the rucksack to where they sat, but the doctor said he was not hungry and only wanted a glass of milk and wanted to climb higher. Heidi did not feel very hungry either and she wanted to take the doctor to the spot where Greenfinch had nearly jumped to her death, so she ran to Peter and asked him to fetch two bowls of milk, one for the doctor and one for herself. Peter looked at her in surprise and asked, "What about all the food in the rucksack?"

"You can have it, Peter," replied Heidi, "but bring the milk first."

Peter had never been so quick in all his life and when he opened the rucksack and saw all the good food he was ashamed of making such faces at the doctor's back. So he ran to where he had stood shaking his fist at the doctor. There he held up his unclenched hands to show that he no longer bore any ill-will, then raced back down to his enormous meal, knowing his conscience was clear.

Heidi and the doctor wandered about together and talked for a long time until the doctor decided it was time for him to go home. Heidi accompanied him down the mountain as far as the Alm-hut. She held his hand all the way and chattered to him about the joys of life on the mountain, where the most beautiful flowers grew and so on. Heidi could name every

Alpine flower growing, for her grandfather had taught her well.

At last the doctor insisted on Heidi's returning to the hut, and then he went on alone, turning now and again to see Heidi still standing on the same spot and waving to him just as his own little daughter might have done.

The month remained beautiful throughout. The doctor came up to the Alm every morning and sometimes went out with the Alm-Uncle whose conversation he enjoyed very much, for the old man knew the ways of all the wild animals and had many interesting stories to tell. He knew all kinds of uses for the plants on the mountainside, from the scented pines, to the curling moss which was found everywhere.

He also had marvellous tales to relate of the animals living in holes, caves and trees all over the mountain.

And so the lovely month of September passed. On the finest days, the doctor would climb the Alm with Heidi, and they would sit together whilst Heidi read hymns and talked of things which she had learnt from her life there.

Peter sat some way away from them, but was more or less resigned to the situation, and no longer flew into tantrums. One morning the doctor did not look quite so happy as usual and told them that this would be his last day and that he would have to return to Frankfurt. "I am very sad to go," he admitted, "for I feel now as if the Alm were my home."

The Alm-Uncle was sorry to hear this news of the doctor's departure for he too had enjoyed his companionship. Heidi could hardly believe that her dear friend had to go and she looked at him beseechingly; but the doctor's smile told her that his visit was at an end. She accompanied him a little of the way until the doctor stopped and said lovingly, stroking her curly hair, "Heidi, I have to go away now. How I would love to take you with me to Frankfurt!"

Heidi recalled Frankfurt, with its many houses and long streets. She remembered Fräulein Rottenmeier and Tinette and replied despondently, "I would rather you came back to us."

"You are right. That will be better," said the doctor. "Good-bye, then, Heidi." His kind eyes looked down on her for an instant and then he turned away quickly and continued his walk down the valley.

Heidi did not move. The sight of tears in the doctor's eyes had upset her and suddenly she started to cry. Then she ran after the doctor as fast as she could, and as soon as she was beside him she sobbed, "I want to come with you! Just let me go back and tell Grandfather!"

The doctor tried to soothe the excited child. "Oh, my dear Heidi," he comforted her, "you must stay here among the fir trees or you may become ill again. But you can promise me this: if I should ever become ill and lonely would you come then and stay with me? If I could know that there would be someone to care for me then."

"Oh, yes, I would come at once. I love you nearly as much as the grandfather."

Once again the doctor said farewell and Heidi stood and waved as long as he remained in sight. As he turned for the last time he whispered to himself, "It is good to live up there. One is restored, body and soul, and knows again what it is to be happy."

CHAPTER 18

WINTER IN DÖRFLI

Snow lay high around the Alm cottage until the windows appeared to be level with the ground. If the Alm-Uncle had still been living there he would have to have done the same as Peter did every day. When snow had fallen during the night Peter had to jump out of the window, and if there was no frost he sank so deeply into the snow that he had to struggle with both hands and feet to get out again. Then his mother would hand him a shovel and he would scrape a path to the door.

He had to dig the snow well clear of the house, otherwise the pile of snow would fall inside as soon as the door was opened. But if there was severe frost the house was shut in altogether except for the little window through which only Peter was able to creep. But the great advantage of the frost was that once Peter got through the little window he would be on hard, frozen snow. His mother would hand him his little sleigh through the window and Peter would go where he pleased, for the whole Alm was one huge sledging track.

The Alm-Uncle had kept his word. As soon as the first snows began to fall he had shut up the cottage and the shed and had taken Heidi and the goats down to Dörfli to live. Near the church stood a building which had, once upon a time, been a mansion house. A famous soldier had once lived there; he had been cited for bravery whilst fighting in Spain and had returned home much the richer. On his return he used some of his money to build a beautiful house where he intended to live.

But rural life was too quiet for him, and it was not long before he left again, this time never to return. After many years a relative took over the house, being certain that the soldier must have died. It was in such a poor state of repair that he did not wish to incur the expense of rebuilding it; so it was let for a nominal rent to the poor people of the district. Thus, if part of it fell down, it was not replaced. Although it was now half in ruins it still retained something of its former dignity. When the uncle had come to Dörfli with his son, Tobias, he had lived in this neglected house, and since that time it had been empty, for no one could live in it who did not know how to close up all the gaps and holes to keep out the wind which blew out the candle and made draughts all through the dilapidated old house.

But all this the uncle could fix, and when he had decided to spend the winter in Dörfli he had come down many times in the autumn to repair the house. Then, in October, he and Heidi had taken up their abode.

Entering from the back, one came first into a tumbledown building where, on one side, the wall had collapsed

133

completely. Although the other wall was half in ruins the arch of an old window was still visible but thickly overgrown with ivy. The roof was vaulted and this had apparently been the chapel.

Next one entered a large hall where the walls and the ceiling had partly collapsed, and to prevent further ruin, strong pillars had been put in for support. Here the Alm-Uncle had built a partition and had covered the ground with straw, for this was to be the goat-house.

After going through many passages where in places the broken roof revealed patches of sky, one at last entered, through a heavy oak door, a spacious room which was still in good condition. The four strong walls with dark panelling were unbroken, and in one corner a stove reached to the ceiling. On white tiles big blue pictures were painted, representing old castles buried amidst high trees, huntsmen with their dogs or quiet lakes bordered by shady trees with a fisherman in the foreground. A bench was built all round the stove and here one could sit and study the pictures.

This attracted Heidi at once, and as soon as they entered the room she ran to the stove, sat down on the bench and began to look at the pictures. But as she slid along and round towards the back of the stove she found something else to attract her attention. Between stove and wall four boards had been put up. It might have been a place for storing apples but there were no apples there now and it was, quite obviously, going to be Heidi's bed just like the one on the Alm; a high straw bed with a sheet on it and the sack as a cover. Heidi was overjoyed. "Oh, Grandfather! This is going to be my room. How nice! But where are you going to sleep?"

"Your room has to be near the stove to keep you warm," declared the grandfather. "But you shall see mine, too."

Heidi ran through the huge room behind the grandfather who opened a door on the other side. This led into a small room where the old man had made up his bed. Then there was another door, and Heidi stood amazed when she looked into the spacious kitchen. In this room there were many signs of the grandfather's activity but there still remained a great deal of work to be done to fill up all the holes and crannies through which the wind still whistled. He had already made the old door strong, with the judicious use of screws and nails, and it served well as protection against the elements and the numerous insects which lived in the weeds surrounding the building.

Heidi was delighted with their new home, and the next day when Peter came she showed him all over the house, for she had already explored every corner. She insisted that he inspect each and every thing to be found in it, before he went.

Heidi slept comfortably and well in her warm corner, but every time she woke she thought immediately of the mountain and had to restrain herself from the impulse to rush outside and see why the trees were so quiet. She had to remind herself of her surroundings, and occasionally felt uneasy when she realised that she was not in her real home. But then the comforting sound of her grandfather's voice, and the bleating of the goats would reassure her, and once again Heidi was happy, and would leap out of bed and run to join the animals as quickly as she could.

Four days after they had settled down Heidi announced to the grandfather one morning that she must go and visit the grandmother. "I can't leave her alone any longer," she said. But the grandfather would not agree.

"Not to-day or to-morrow," he said. "The Alm is covered fathom-deep in snow, and it is still falling; Peter can hardly get through. A little one like you would soon be buried and no one would be able to find you. Wait a little until it freezes and then you can walk up quite comfortably."

At first Heidi was impatient at the thought of having to wait, but the days were busy and passed quickly. Every morning and afternoon she went to school and learned eagerly. She hardly ever saw Peter there for he seldom turned up. The teacher was a kind man and would remark tolerantly, "Peter absent to-day again! Ah, well, the snow is lying high, he won't be able to get through."

But in the evening, when school was finished, Peter always seemed able to come down to see Heidi no matter how deep the snow! After a few days the sun came out again and shone strongly on the wintry landscape, but the days were short and at night the moon would take up the vigil, clear and huge and sparkling, so that the whole mountain glittered.

One morning, when Peter, as usual sprang from the window into the snow he found that it had hardened with the strong frost of the previous night. The hard ice came as a surprise to him and he could not stop himself sliding off down the Alm which was frozen over as hard as iron. This delighted Peter because he knew that Heidi would be able to come up now to the cottage. Quickly he rushed back to the house and hurriedly swallowing his breakfast he announced, "I must be off to school!"

"Yes, go and learn as much as you can," said his mother.

Peter climbed through the little window, got on to his sledge and went shooting rapidly down the mountain. He went so fast that when he reached Dörfli he was quite unable to stop and the sledge skimmed along until it reached level ground when it stopped of its own accord. Peter got up and looked about. The headlong drive had taken him some way beyond Mayenfeld. It would take him an hour to climb up again and that would be much too late for school, thought Peter, so he might as well take his time. He arrived back in Dörfli just as Heidi and the grandfather were sitting down to dinner. Peter entered and as he had something special to tell them to-day he began right away.

"It's done it!" he fairly shouted.

"Eh! What has?" asked the old man. "You sound quite warlike to-day, General."

"The snow—frozen!" announced Peter.

"Oh, now I can go to the grandmother!" rejoiced Heidi, who was quick to understand Peter's odd way of expressing himself. "But why didn't you come to school? You could easily have come on the sledge," she added reproachfully, for she felt that it was not the thing to do to stay away if it were possible to attend.

"Took me too far down," said Peter. "So it was too late."

"Now that's what I'd call desertion," said the uncle, "and people who do that get their ears pulled; do you hear?"

Peter fidgeted uncomfortably, for there was no one whom he feared and respected more than the Alm-Uncle.

"And a leader like you should be doubly ashamed of himself," continued the uncle. "What would you do if your goats ran anywhere they liked?"

"Beat them," Peter replied smartly.

"And if a boy behaved like that and got a good beating, what would you say then?"

"Serves him right," was the answer.

"Very well, then, if it should happen again that your sledge passes the school when you should be inside, come to me and get what you deserve!"

At last the meaning of the uncle's little speech was beginning to dawn on Peter. He looked quite thunderstruck and retreated into a corner looking round in a frightened way in case there should be a stick in sight similar to the one he sometimes used on the goats. But the uncle said cheerfully, "Come now and eat with us and then Heidi can go up with you. In the evening you can bring her home again and have your supper here."

This unexpected turn to the conversation cheered Peter immensely. He obeyed at once and sat beside Heidi, who could hardly eat for excitement about going to the grandmother's. She pushed aside her plate of potatoes and toasted cheese, and offered it to Peter, together with the helping which the Uncle was already giving him. He was not put off, however, by the enormous amount of food on his Plate, and started eating heartily straight away.

Heidi ran to the cupboard and brought out the little warm coat with the hood which Clara had given her. Putting it on she stood waiting beside Peter and as soon as he had swallowed his last bite she said, "Come along now!" On the way, Heidi told Peter how unhappy the two goats had been at first in their new surroundings, and how they would not eat nor make any sound. She had asked her grandfather why this was so, and he told her that they were feeling as she had.

When they arrived at the cottage, Peter's mother was alone in the room. She told them that the grandmother was not very well and had had to stay in bed because it was so cold. Heidi had always been accustomed to seeing the grandmother in her place in the corner. She ran to the other room and there lay the old woman in her narrow bed with only a thin coverlet over her, but wrapped in the warm grey shawl . . . .

"Thank God!" exclaimed the old woman when she heard Heidi running in, for she had had a secret fear that the gentleman from Frankfurt, with whom Heidi had been seen out walking on the Alm, would take the child away.

"Are you very ill, Grandmother?" asked Heidi with concern.

"No, no, child!" said the old woman and patted Heidi lovingly. "It is only the frost getting into my bones a little."

"Will you be better as soon as it is warm again?' Heidi persisted.

"Yes, yes, and with God's help before that so that I can get back to my spinning," said the grandmother, noticing how worried the child was.

This cheered Heidi a little, for she had never seen the grandmother ill in bed before, and was greatly upset. "Grandmother, in Frankfurt people put on a shawl when they go for a walk. Did you think it was for going to bed?" she said thoughtfully.

"I have put the shawl on in bed to keep warm, Heidi. You see the cover is rather thin."

"But, Grandmother," Heidi started again, "your pillow goes downhill instead of uphill!"

"Yes, I know, child." The grandmother tried to find a more comfortable place on the thin pillow which looked as hard as a board. "You see, the pillow has never been particularly soft and now I have slept on it for so many years that it has become quite flat."

"If only I had asked Clara if I could take my bed home! I had three big, thick pillows and they were so high I could hardly sleep for my head slipping off them. Could you have slept on them, Grandmother?"

"I am sure I could. One keeps warmer that way and breathes more easily when the head is high. However, don't let's speak about it. I have so much for which to thank God. The nice rolls

I get, and the lovely warm shawl, and you coming to see me, Heidi. Would you care to read some of my favourite hymns to me to-day?"

Heidi got down the old hymn book and chose the most beautiful verses for they were all familiar to her now and she was as pleased as the old lady to hear them again. As the grandmother listened, a joyous smile lightened her face which had looked so worn and tired before.

Heidi stopped. "Grandmother, are you feeling better already? she asked.

"Yes, child, I am much better already. Please read to the end." Heidi read the last lines:—

"As the eyes grow dim, and darkness

Closes round, the soul grows clearer,

Sees the goal to which it travels,

Gladly feels its home is nearer."

As she read them, the grandmother repeated the words softly to herself, with a serene expression on her face. Heidi remembered the beautiful day of her return home and her face lit up with joy.

"Grandmother, I know just what it means to be going home."

The grandmother made no reply but the happy expression stayed on her face.

After a while the child said: "I must go home now, Grandmother. It is getting late. I am so glad you are feeling better." The grandmother held Heidi's hand.

"I feel at peace again, even if I have to stay here. It is dreadful to have to lie alone for days on end, without light or sound. It makes me sad and I sometimes feel that it is too much for me to stand. But to hear you read the hymns to me gives me comfort and peace in my heart once more."

Heidi said good-bye to the grandmother and she and Peter set off quickly, for the darkness was already coming down. As Peter got out his sledge the moon came through and shone brightly on the white snow so that it seemed as if the day were about to break. Peter sat in front, and off they shot down the Alm like two birds.

That night, as Heidi lay in her warm bed behind the stove, she thought about the grandmother and how she would like to visit her every day, for if she could read to her more often, perhaps the peace and light which came to her would help make her better. But Heidi knew one or two weeks might pass before she was allowed to go up again. She thought and thought about how things could be arranged. Suddenly she had an idea and she could hardly wait for daylight to carry out her plan. She suddenly sat upright in bed, for she had been so busy thinking about her plan that in her excitement she had forgotten to say her prayers.

When she had prayed from the bottom of her heart for the grandfather and the grandmother and all the people she knew, she lay down on the soft hay and slept soundly and peacefully until the morning.

CHAPTER 19

WINTER CONTINUES

Next morning, Peter turned up at school in good time. He had brought his lunch with him, as did all the children who lived any distance from the school. They all sat at tables at mid-day and with their lunches on their knees and their feet upon the benches, ate heartily, whilst the other children went home to Dörfli.

They were free to do whatever they liked until one o'clock, when school recommenced. As was his usual habit when he happened to be at school, Peter paid a visit afterwards to the uncle. To-day, immediately he entered the house, Heidi rushed to him."Peter, I have thought of something!" she exclaimed.

"What is it?" he asked.

"You must learn to read now," was her reply.

"I know how to read—a little."

"Yes, yes, Peter, but I mean so well that you can read easily and quickly."

"I'll never be able to do that," remarked Peter gloomily.

"I don't believe that, and neither would anybody else," said Heidi with determination. "Grandmamma told me some time ago that I was not to believe you. I shall teach you. I know quite well how to do it. You must learn now, and then you will be able to read one or two hymns to Grandmother every day."

"Oh, I don't care about *that*!" Peter grumbled.

This obstinacy towards something which she considered was kind and right annoyed Heidi. With flashing eyes she stood before the boy and said threateningly, "Then I will tell you what will happen if you refuse to learn. Your mother has said already that she will send you to Frankfurt to be taught, and I have seen the building where the boys go to school. Clara showed it to me. But they don't go there just when they are boys, but always, even when they are grown up. And don't think there is only one teacher as in our school."

A cold shudder ran down Peter's back.

"And you will have to go there among all the teachers and pupils," Heidi continued, "and if you cannot even read, and make mistakes with your spelling, you'll see how much they will laugh at you; much worse than Tinette, and if you only knew what she was like!"

"All right, then. I will," said Peter reluctantly.

Heidi was mollified at once. "That's right. We can start today," she decided joyfully. She dragged Peter to the table and brought out the necessary books. In Clara's big parcel there had been a book which Heidi thought was just right for teaching Peter, for it was an A B C book with verses.

They both bent over the book and the lesson began. Peter had to spell out the first verse again and again for Heidi wanted him to be able to read it correctly and fluently. At last she said, "You still don't know the verse so I shall read it to you. If you know the meaning it will be easier for you to spell it." And Heidi read:

"Learn A B C without a grudge
Or you'll be brought before the judge."

"I won't," said Peter obstinately.

"What?" asked Heidi.

"Go before the judge," was the answer.

"Hurry up then and learn these three letters and you won't need to."

Peter started again and repeated the three letters until Heidi said, "Now you can read these three! And read them carefully!"

As she noticed the effect this verse had had upon Peter she thought it would be a good idea to prepare him a little for the following lessons.

"Wait! I'll read the other verses to you now," she continued, "and you'll see what else can happen."

And she began to read very slowly and clearly:

"D E F G must smoothly flow
Or you will get a nasty blow.

If you forget H I J K
The fatal blow will fall to-day.

To learn L M is not a strain
And will prevent a lot of pain.

Remember well N O P Q
Or you'll get what's in store for you.

R S T may save a smack
If you will make a quick attack."

Here Heidi stopped because Peter was so quiet. All these secret hints and threats had petrified him with fright and he stared anxiously at Heidi. Her kind heart was touched at once and she said reassuringly, "You don't need to be afraid, Peter. If you come every evening and learn as well as you have done to-day you will soon know the letters and nothing will happen to you. But you must come *every* day and not just sometimes as you did with school—even if it snows. The snow doesn't trouble you anyway."

Peter promised. Fear of punishment had made him quite docile. Then he set off home.

He followed Heidi's advice and arrived promptly every evening. The letters were studied with zeal and the verses taken to heart. Often the grandfather listened to the lessons while he contentedly smoked his pipe. Every now and then his face would twitch with amusement. Peter was usually asked to stay to supper with them which was a great compensation to him for the anxiety which the verses caused.

So the winter passed. Peter appeared regularly and made good progress. He had now got as far as U and Heidi read:

> "Who still mistakes the U for V
> May go where he won't like to be."

This gave Peter an uncomfortable feeling but made him learn all the quicker lest the threat were carried out. The following evening the verse was:

> "If W is still unknown
> The stick may come into its own."

Peter remarked sneeringly, "There isn't one."

But Heidi reminded him that the grandfather had a very big stick in his cupboard, at least as thick as Peter's arm and this made him bend over his W in a feverish effort to memorise it. Next was:

> "X is a cross you may recall
> And this is easiest of them all."

And Heidi quickly prompted him to learn another letter as well so that only the last one remained for the following day. Although Peter tried to object, Heidi read out:

"To stop at Y will never do
And all the world will laugh at you."

Peter at once attacked the Y with energy, imagining the gentlemen of Frankfurt in their tall black hats, jeering at him and scorning his inadequacy. He did not give up until he could close his eyes and still remember what it looked like.

Peter arrived the next day feeling very jaunty because there was only one more letter to be learnt and when Heidi read the verse:

"Who still forgets the Z you know
Straight to the Hottentots will go,"

he said sarcastically, "Who knows where they live?"

"Grandfather does. Wait! I shall ask him at once. He is only across the road with the pastor."

Heidi was about to run to the door when Peter exclaimed in alarm, "Wait a moment!" In his imagination he saw both the pastor and the uncle carrying him off and sending him away to the Hottentots—because he really had forgotten completely what Z was like.

"What is the matter?" Heidi asked in surprise.

"Nothing! Come back! I shall learn now," muttered Peter.

Heidi, though, wanted to know just where the Hottentots were to be found, and persisted in her suggestion that she should ask the grandfather, but Peter seemed so desperately anxious that she should not, that she eventually changed her mind. Instead, she made him repeat the letter until it was engraved on his brain, and in addition she began to teach him spelling, at which Peter made a very good start indeed. And from day to day Peter made progress with his reading.

The ice had thawed and new snow had fallen every day so that about three weeks had passed since Heidi's visit to the grandmother. This made her work all the harder with Peter so that he would be able to take her place and read to the old woman.

One evening Peter went home and announced, "I can do it now!"

"What can you do, Peter?" asked his mother.

"Read," he answered.

"Did you hear that, Grandmother?" Brigitta exclaimed.

Grandmother did hear and was wondering how this had come about.

"I have to read a hymn now. Heidi said so."

Brigitta quickly fetched the book and the grandmother smiled in anticipation of hearing the comforting words once more. Peter sat down ant began to read and his mother sat beside him, listening, and saying after each verse, in a voice full of astonishment and admiration, "Who would have thought it!"

The grandmother, too, followed the verses with the greatest attention but she did not say anything.

The following day at school when it was Peter's turn to read, the teacher said, "Well, Peter, must we pass you again or would you like to try?"

Without hesitation, Peter read three lines. The teacher laid down his book and stared at Peter as if he had never see him before. Then he said, "Peter, this is a miracle! With all the patience in the world I did not succeed in teaching you even your letters and here you are reading beautifully. How did this come about?"

"It was Heidi," Peter answered.

In surprise the teacher turned towards Heidi who sat on her bench looking as though nothing out of the ordinary had happened.

The teacher continued, "I have noticed a change in you altogether. You have been attending school very regularly lately. What can have brought about this change for the better?"

"The uncle," came the reply.

With ever-growing astonishment the teacher looked at Heidi, then back again at Peter.

As soon as school was over, the teacher hastened to tell the pastor what had happened and what a good influence the uncle and Heidi had been.

Every night now Peter read a hymn in obedience to Heidi's instructions, but he refused to read a second one and indeed the grandmother never encouraged him to do so.

145

Brigitta was always delighted that her Peter had achieved so much but the grandmother said, "Yes, it is good that he has learnt so well but still I shall be glad when it is spring and Heidi can come up again. When Peter reads there always seem to be some words missing in the hymn so that I don't understand them so well as when Heidi reads them."

The reason was, of course, that Peter was rather lazy about reading for the grandmother and if a word was too difficult or too long, he just skipped over it thinking it would not matter very much to the grandmother, seeing there were so many words! Thus it was that most of the important words in the hymns were missing altogether when Peter read them.

CHAPTER 20

NEWS FROM CLARA

May had come again and from the heights the streamlets rippled eagerly down into the valley. The last snow had melted and the golden sun had dried up the last traces of winter. The spring breeze was rustling the tops of the old fir trees and last year's dark green pine needles were being replaced by bright, shiny light green ones. The great eagle flew high above, lazily circling in the blue air, and the warmth of the sunshine seeped into the ground beneath, and warmed the ancient timbers of the grandfather's hut. Heidi was happy to be on the Alm again and jumped about for joy, and it seemed to her that the little wild creatures which started about were as happy as she and all were humming and singing, "On the Alm! On the Alm!" At one moment she would stand listening to the strange sounds of the wind blowing down from the mountain tops and bending the fir trees until they strained with its force. Then she would rush round to the front of the hut, and sitting on the ground in the sunshine she would watch the tiny flowers gradually opening in the warmth of the sun. Joyfully, she followed the antics of all the thousands of little insects going about their lives in the glorious spring weather, All the, while, she could not stop thinking how beautiful the mountain looked.

Familiar sounds came from the carpenter's shed. Heidi knew what the sounds meant, for they had been familiar to her ever since her first arrival on the Alm. The grandfather was busy finishing a beautiful new chair and another one, already finished, stood outside.

"Oh, I know what these are for!" cried Heidi. "We will need them when they come from Frankfurt. This one is for Grandmamma and the one you are making now is for Clara. Will there be another one, Grandfather?" she asked hesitantly. "Perhaps Fräulein Rottenmeier is coming too."

"Well, I am not sure at the moment," replied the grandfather, "but it is best to make an extra one just in case she does come."

Heidi gazed at the simple wooden chair, and couldn't imagine Fräulein Rottenmeier actually sitting down on it. After a few moments' contemplation she said doubtfully, "Grandfather, I really don't think that Fräulein Rottenmeier would be suitable for that chair."

"In that case she can enjoy the comfortable bed with the mattress of green grass," was the grandfather's reply.

Suddenly there was a great whistling and shouting and Heidi knew immediately it was Peter. She rushed outside and immediately found herself crowded on all sides by her animal friends. They too were delighted to be on the mountain once more, for they were frolicking and bleating with joy, nudging and pushing Heidi in their anxiety to show her how pleased they were to see her. A harsh command from Peter sent them scattering, however, for he had something to deliver to Heidi. There he stood brandishing a letter. It was addressed to Heidi.

"How did you get this?" she asked in surprise.

"I found it inside my dinner bag," replied Peter. This was only partly true. The letter had been handed to him the previous

147

evening by the postman at Dörfli, and Peter had put it at the bottom of his bag. This fine morning he had filled the bag with his bread and cheese and had completely forgotten about the letter when he collected the grandfather's two goats. He only remembered it when he had finished his lunch and was checking for any additional food which might have been missed. Carefully Heidi read the address, then ran towards the grandfather, holding out her letter. "From Frankfurt! From Clara! Do you want to hear it?"

Of course, both he and Peter wanted to hear it, so Heidi began to read:

"DEAR HEIDI,

Everything is packed and ready and in two or three days we shall be on our way. Papa will not be coming with us as he has to go to Paris first. The doctor comes to see me every day and as he comes into the room he always calls, 'Off you go now! Off to the Alm as quickly as you can!' He says everybody must become healthy and happy there. He, too, is his own self again after being with you. He has come almost every day during the winter, and has spent long hours telling me everything about life up there. He tells me of all he did with you two, and talks of the flowers and the light and the peacefulness of the mountains, high above the noise of the towns and villages. And he takes a deep breath, as though he were breathing your pure mountain air, and says that no-one can fail to get better up there. He is altogether changed since he saw you, and looks much younger and happier. Oh, how I am looking forward to seeing everything, to being with you and also to getting to know Peter and the goats! I have to go to Ragatz first, for six weeks, as the doctor has ordered. Then we will go to Dörfli, and every day, if the weather is good, I shall be carried up to see you. Grandmamma is coming with me and is looking forward greatly to seeing you. But what about this: Fräulein Rottenmeier has adamantly refused to join us. Grandmamma often asks her if she would not like to accompany us, but she always refuses, very politely of course. Apparently Sebastian gave her a fright by emphasising the dangers of the mountains and the precipices, and she quite lost interest in the idea of a journey. Tinette is just as frightened, so Sebastian will come with us as far as Ragatz, and we will finish the journey alone. I can hardly bear to wait. Good-bye, Heidi! Grandmamma sends her love,

Your affectionate friend,
CLARA."

Peter was not at all thrilled with the news of the arrival of the guests from Frankfurt. It made him very cross indeed and he ran outside, waving his stick in the air so wildly that he frightened the goats, and they scrambled down the mountain ahead of him. Peter tore after them, brandishing his stick as though he would strike someone.

He was furious at the thought of the prospective visitors, who would again take Heidi's company away from him. Heidi was overflowing with happiness. As soon as possible she called at the grandmother's to tell her the good news. She knew the grandmother would be interested in all she had to tell, for Heidi had talked to her of all the people who were to arrive, and she had sympathised with the troubles which had beset her life at Frankfurt. Heidi called on her in the afternoon, while the sun was high in the sky, and she raced down the mountain, with the breeze blowing her along. The grandmother was sitting spinning once more in her usual corner. She was no longer confined to bed, but although she was so much better her face wore an expression of sadness. Peter had told her the news about the people who were coming from Frankfurt and the grandmother had her own ideas of what might come to pass. She could not help dreading that they might take Heidi away again. Heidi rushed in, and sitting on her little stool began a stream of excited chatter about the events which were about to happen.

As she was in the midst of telling the grandmother the great news, she had to stop suddenly and ask with concern, "What is the matter, Grandmother? Aren't you happy about all this?"

"Yes, yes, I am glad for you, Heidi," said the old woman, trying to put on a more cheerful expression. "Is it that you think Fräulein Rottenmeier may come after all?" asked Heidi nervously.

"No, Heidi, don't worry," said the old lady. "Hold my hand, and I'll know that you're here with me. Perhaps it would be a good thing if you went, although I doubt if I could bear the parting."

"Grandmother, nothing would give me pleasure if you could not bear it," said Heidi, and her voice was so positive that the grandmother thought that perhaps even if the Frankfurt people did want to take Heidi, she might refuse to go. But, oh dear, that too would be all wrong. She was anxious to hide her fears and suggested, "I know something, Heidi, that would calm my thoughts. Read the hymn for me which begins: 'All things will work for good.'"

Heidi quickly found the hymn and read:—

> All things will work for good
> To those who trust in Me;
> I come with healing in my wings
> To save and set thee free.

When she had finished reading the grandmother said, "Yes, that is right! If one trusts in God one knows that whatever happens is for our good. Read it once more so that we won't forget." Heidi repeated the verse, reassuring herself as well as her grandmother.

Heidi returned home as evening descended, and rejoiced to see the stars glittering overhead. Eventually, entranced by the vast sparkling sky she said to herself, "I understand now why we should be happy and go bravely on our way; it is because God knows what is best for us, and what will bring us most happiness." The stars twinkled back at her all the way home, where she found her grandfather also star-gazing, overwhelmed by the beauty of the night sky.

The month of May had seldom before been so beautiful and sunny.

The sky was clear blue day after day and the grandfather exclaimed repeatedly, "This is indeed a good year. The sun will make the plants grow strong and nourishing. Take care, Peter, that your flock doesn't get out of hand from overfeeding!"

Peter's answer could be clearly read in his face.

"I can manage them!"

May had passed and June arrived, bringing hot, long days filled with the scent of the flowers carpeting the mountainside. The month was drawing to its close when one morning Heidi ran out of the hut. She had intended to visit the fir trees and then climb up to see if the rock roses were in bloom. Just as she turned the corner she gave a loud cry which brought the uncle hurrying to see what had happened.

"Grandfather! Grandfather!" the child called excitedly, "Come over here! Come and look!"

He came, and his eyes followed the direction of her outstretched arm. A strange procession could be seen coming up the mountain path. In front came two men carrying a sedan chair in which a young girl sat, wrapped in many shawls. A horse followed, mounted by a stately lady who looked about her with keen interest. Another man pushed an empty wheelchair, for it was easier and safer to carry the invalid up the mountain in the sedan.

"Here they are! Here they are!" cried Heidi joyfully.

When the eagerly expected guests reached the Alm, Heidi sprang forward and the two children embraced each other lovingly. Grandmamma, too, was welcomed with the greatest affection. Then Grandmamma turned to the Alm-Uncle who came forward to bid them welcome. They all felt like old friends, as they had heard so much about each other.

Grandmamma was delighted with the beautiful situation. "What a marvellous place to live, Uncle. I would never have believed it could be so very beautiful. You would be envied by the richest of men. And how well my little Heidi is looking!" she remarked, patting the child's rosy cheeks. "What do *you* think, Clara? Isn't it delightful here?"

Clara was entranced. Never in her life before had she seen or imagined anything so beautiful. "Oh, how lovely it is! How I wish I could always live here with Heidi, Grandmamma!"

Meantime the uncle had pushed the invalid chair nearer and now he suggested, "Wouldn't it be better to put the little daughter into her accustomed seat?" And without waiting for assistance he lifted Clara in his strong arms and very gently placed her in her own comfortable chair, putting some of the wraps over her knees and doing it all as expertly as if he had looked after invalids all his life. Grandmamma was greatly impressed by his care and attention.

"If I knew where you had come by your skill, I would pack every nurse I know off to learn to handle their patients as gently as you. How on earth do you know what should be done?"

Alm-Uncle smiled sadly and said, "I know from my own experience." He saw again a painful scene of many years before, of a crippled man lying helpless and unable to move. It was his captain, who had been mortally wounded during some fierce fighting in Sicily. The Uncle had carried him from the battlefield and nursed him until his death.

Thus it had seemed easy and natural to him to adopt the role of nurse once again. Clara could not find words to express her delight in everything around her. "Oh, Heidi," she said, "if only I could go about and see all the things you have described to me!"

With a great effort Heidi succeeded in wheeling the chair on to the grass so that Clara could see the magnificent old fir trees which had gazed down undisturbed for so many years on the valley below. The sky extended a clear blue for as far as the eye could see, and Clara was fascinated. She had never seen such trees before. The grandmamma had followed them and was equally amazed at the appearance of strength of the magnificent great firs, which had seen so much change beneath their spreading branches. Heidi wheeled Clara to the goat-house next, and opened the door so that Clara could see inside.

"If only I could wait till Peter comes with the goats!" Clara said regretfully. "How I should love to see Little Swan and Little Bear! If we must always leave as early as you say, Grandmamma, we shall never see them!"

"My dear child, let us enjoy the things we can and not think of those we may miss."

"Oh, how pretty the flowers are! If only I could get up and pick some!"

Heidi ran and gathered a big bunch. "But that is nothing, Clara," she said. "If you come with us up to the pasture you will see ever so many. There are flowers of every colour you can think of, and they smell so lovely. There are so many there is hardly room to move amongst them. They are as thick as a carpet and if you sit down amongst them you never want to get up again."

Heidi's eyes sparkled with longing to be able to show it all to her friend, and Clara's soft blue eyes reflected Heidi's enthusiasm.

"Oh, Grandmamma! Do you think I shall ever be allowed to go up as high as that?" she asked. "If only I could go with you, Heidi! I should like to climb all over the Alm."

"I shall push your chair," said Heidi stoutly, and to show how easy it was she made a rush at the chair which nearly sent it rolling down the slope. But the grandfather was near at hand and stopped it in time.

Grandfather had been busy preparing the meal and he had brought the table and the chairs outside beside the bench. Soon the meal was ready and the whole company sat down merrily. Grandmamma was delighted with this dining-room under the blue sky where she could sit and enjoy the magnificent view far down into the valley. "Can I believe my eyes?" she exclaimed when she saw Clara taking a second helping of toasted cheese which she was eating with a great appetite.

"Yes, Grandmamma. It tastes so good. Better than the whole menu at Ragatz," Clara assured her.

"That's right. Eat all you can," encouraged the uncle. "Our mountain air makes up for the deficiency of the kitchen."

Grandmamma and the uncle chatted together as though they had known each other for years. They had much in common and the time passed quickly in lively conversation. But suddenly Grandmamma remembered, "We will have to go presently, Clara. The sun will be going down soon and the men with the chair will be here."

"Just let's stay another hour, Grandmamma," pleaded Clara.

"We haven't seen inside the cottage yet and we must see Heidi's bed."

Grandmamma wanted to see inside the cottage, too, and the uncle invited them to go in. Clara's chair, however, was too broad to pass through the door, but without hesitation, the uncle lifted Clara out of the chair and carried her inside.

Grandmamma looked around with interest and was very much impressed by the tidiness and cosy atmosphere of the house. "Is your bed up there, Heidi" she asked and started to climb up to the loft. "Oh, what a lovely scent! This should be a healthy bedroom," she exclaimed.

Grandfather followed, carrying Clara, and Heidi came after. They all stood around Heidi's bed. "Heidi, how jolly!" exclaimed Clara. "From your bed you can look straight up into the sky! And you will always have the lovely smell of the hay and will be able to listen to the fir trees rustling! It is quite the loveliest bedroom I have ever seen."

The uncle looked at Grandmamma. "I have an idea," he said. "I think if we could agree to have your little grand-daughter staying here with us for a while, she would be bound to get strong and well. With all the rugs you have brought we could make a fine soft bed and I myself would look after her."

Clara and Heidi were as happy as two birds let out of their cage at this suggestion and the Grandmamma's face beamed. "My dear Uncle, you are kindness itself," she said. "I have just been thinking how good a holiday so high up in the mountains would be for the child. But the nursing, the trouble and the inconvenience for you! And you make the offer as if it were nothing at all. I thank you from the bottom of my heart." The old lady took his hand and the uncle nodded happily. He carried Clara back to her chair outside, with Heidi skipping along after them. Then he picked up a huge pile of shawls and furs which had been carried up the mountain for Clara and said, "What a good thing Grandmamma brought all these with her; they will be most useful."

He at once started to get Clara's bed ready and he and the Grandmamma spread the rugs over it. When they had finished, the bed was so smooth and thick, not a single bit of hay could penetrate. Satisfied, Grandmamma climbed down the ladder and joined the children who were already discussing how they would spend their time. But, how long would Clara be allowed to stay, was the great question. Grandmamma replied, "Grandfather knows best. You must ask him."

The grandfather thought four weeks would be just right to decide if the mountain air was agreeing with the child. The prospect of being together for so long surpassed the children's expectations and they both shouted for joy.

The chair-bearers appeared at the cottage but they were immediately sent down the mountain again.

"It is not farewell, Grandmamma," said Clara as they parted. "You will come and visit us here on the Alm and see what we are doing and how we are getting on, won't you?"

Heidi could only express her happiness with a high jump.

Grandmamma mounted her horse and the Alm-Uncle set off to lead her down the mountain path. She tried to persuade him to go back, but he insisted on seeing her safely to Dörfli for it was a rocky and dangerous path for those who did not know it well.

She decided to return to Ragatz rather than stay alone in Dörfli. From there she could equally well pay occasional visits to the Alm.

Peter and the goats arrived while the Uncle was escorting Grandmamma, and as soon as they saw Heidi the animals rushed towards her. She and Clara were soon in the midst of a pushing, nudging, bleating crowd. Clara made acquaintance with each and every one as Heidi introduced them, including little Snowflake, and Goldfinch, about whom she had heard so much.

Peter, meanwhile, stood sullenly to one side, not looking at all pleased at the attention being given Clara.

The two girls greeted him in a friendly way, but he turned on his heel, and waving his stick in the air, rushed off, with the goats following him.

The day closed for Clara with the most overwhelming experience of all. She lay in the big soft bed in the loft with

Heidi near, and looked through the round open window right into the middle of the starlit sky. "Oh, Heidi!" she exclaimed. "It seems as if we were riding through the sky!"

"Do you know why the stars twinkle so happily?" asked Heidi.

"No, why do you think?"

"Because they see how well God has arranged everything for men so that nobody needs to be afraid and can be quite sure that everything will turn out for the best. But we must not forget to pray, Clara, and to ask God to remember us."

The children sat up and said their prayers together; then Heidi put her head on her arm and fell asleep at once. But Clara lay awake a long time. She had never been able to see the stars at home because she had never been outside the house at night, and inside, the heavy curtains were always drawn long before the stars came out. So she could not gaze long enough at the sparkling heavens and lay looking out of the little round window until at last her eyes closed of their own accord and she saw the stars in her dreams.

CHAPTER 21

LIFE ON THE ALM

The Alm-Uncle had been standing outside the hut as was his habit, watching the early mists rising and the new day awakening. The morning clouds grew brighter and brighter until the sun appeared in its full glory and flooded the rocks, woods and mountains with golden light.

The uncle went back into the hut and quietly climbed up the little ladder. Clara had just opened her eyes and did not know at first where she was. Then she saw the sleeping Heidi beside her and heard the kindly voice of the grandfather whispering, "Did you sleep well?"

Clara assured him that she had slept soundly all night. The grandfather was pleased and straight away began to attend to her so gently and sympathetically that one would think that he had been looking after sick children all his life. Now Heidi was awake and watched the grandfather carry Clara downstairs. Quickly she got up and dressed and ran down the ladder after them and out into the open air.

There a surprise awaited her, for the grandfather had not been idle after the children had retired for the night. He had noticed that it was impossible for Clara's chair to be carried through the hut door. So he loosened two boards at one side, which would allow for the chair to go through whenever required. Clara was just being wheeled into the sunshine. There he left her while he went to attend to the goats, and Heidi joined her friend.

The soft morning breeze touched their faces, and Clara could smell the fresh scent of the fir trees. She took a deep breath of pleasure and noticed how well and comfortable she felt.

She had never before been out in the country so early in the day, and it was sheer delight for her to breathe the clear mountain air and feel the warm sun caressing her face and hands. It was better than Clara had ever imagined it could be.

"Oh, Heidi, if only I could stay in the mountains with you always!" she exclaimed.

"Do you understand now why I said that the best place in the world is on the Alm with Grandfather?"

Just at that moment the grandfather appeared with two bowls of foaming milk. "This will give you strength," he said to Clara. "It is from Little Swan, and will help you regain your health."

Clara had never tasted goats' milk before and she smelt it first. But when she saw Heidi drinking hers to the last drop, she did the same. It tasted sweet and strong, as though it contained sugar and cinnamon. Soon her bowl was empty, too.

"To-morrow we may be able to take two," the grandfather suggested, observing with satisfaction how Clara had followed Heidi's example.

Soon Peter arrived with his flock and the uncle took him

aside to tell him to be sure to take Little Swan high up where she would get the best grass. "She knows where the best food is, and if it should mean going a little higher, never mind. Follow her; a bit of extra climbing won't do you any harm. I want the best possible milk from her and you can ensure that she eats well. Why are you staring over there as though you wanted to eat somebody?" the grandfather exclaimed in the midst of his instructions. "Now be off! And remember what I have said!"

Peter marched off at once, but it was obvious that there was something going on in his mind. When Heidi appeared amongst the goats he said to her threateningly, "You had better come with me because Little Swan has to get special attention and someone will have to stay with the others."

"No, I can't," replied Heidi. "I can't come so long as Clara is with me. But Grandfather has promised that some time we shall come together."

As she said this she ran back to Clara and Peter made threatening gestures towards the invalid chair. Then he quickly climbed up until he was out of sight for he was afraid the uncle might have seen him.

Clara and Heidi had so many plans that they hardly knew what to do first. Heidi suggested that they should first write to Grandmamma for they had promised to write every day and tell her all their experiences.

"Must we write the letter inside the cottage?" asked Clara who preferred to stay outside and enjoy the lovely scenery.

Heidi went into the cottage to get all the things they needed and then they both settled down to write the letter. After almost every sentence Clara had to stop and look around. It was far too beautiful for writing. The wind was no longer cool, and gently caressed her face. Insects danced and hummed in the air and a deep silence lay on the sunny fields. The whole, broad valley lay peacefully below and only now and then was the silence broken by the yodelling of a shepherd boy, and the sound echoed softly amongst the rocks.

The morning passed so quickly, the children were surprised to see the uncle bringing the lunch which they took out of doors just as they had done the day before. He had decided that as long as there was a ray of light from the sun, the little daughter should have the benefit of the fresh air. In the afternoon they sat in the shadow of the fir trees and Clara related all the things that had happened at Frankfurt since Heidi left. The greater their animation as they talked, the louder chorused the birds above, as if they, too, wished to join in the conversation. Time flew past, and they hardly realised that the afternoon was nearly over.

Evening was approaching and the goats came rushing down the mountain, their keeper following them with a not very pleasant expression on his face. He did not even answer the children's friendly call but went on chasing the goats.

When Clara saw that the grandfather had taken Little Swan away for milking she suddenly felt very impatient to taste the milk. "Isn't it strange!" she said. "I never used to like to eat. Everything tasted like cod liver oil, and now I can hardly wait until supper-time when Grandfather brings the milk." Heidi understood—she remembered the dreadful times in Frankfurt, when she had felt unable to eat. Clara though, was puzzled. She did not realise that it was simply that she had never ever spent a complete day out-of-doors, let alone in the pure, healthy mountain air.

This time, when the milk arrived, Clara even finished hers before Heidi and asked the grandfather for a second helping. He nodded cheerfully, and taking both bowls, went back into the cottage. When he returned with the milk he brought two large slices of bread, spread with plenty of butter which he had got fresh from a herdsman's cottage that afternoon. It tasted delicious and the grandfather smiled with satisfaction to see the two children eat so heartily.

That night, when they went to bed, Clara wanted to look up again at the stars but her eyes would not stay open and she was soon fast asleep like Heidi and slept as she had never done before in her life.

So the days passed happily. One day the children were surprised to see two porters climbing up the mountain. Each of them carried a bed on his back, complete with sheets and mattress. The men also brought a letter from Grandmamma in which she said that the beds were for Clara and Heidi. She instructed Heidi to sleep in the proper bed, and to take it with her to Dörfli in winter, leaving the other behind, so that there would always be a bed for Clara if she visited. She also thanked the children for their letters and encouraged them to continue to write and tell her about everything that happened. The grandfather moved all the hay out of Heidi's room, and then enlisted help in moving the two beds up to the loft. There they were set close enough for both the children to be able to watch the stars.

Grandmamma was very pleased that Clara was enjoying the Alm so much and she was quite content to wait a little before she repeated her visit to the Alm because the ride up the steep mountain was rather trying for her.

Clara had now spent three weeks on the Alm and was enjoying life more every day. She could not praise sufficiently the love and care with which the grandfather nursed her. As for Heidi, her cheerful chatter and amusing companionship made her presence even more enjoyable than in Frankfurt. Every morning Clara expressed her delight in the good fortune which had brought her there.

Grandmamma decided, on the basis of the optimistic reports coming daily from the mountain, that she would postpone her visit for a while, for it was by no means an easy journey for her. During the last few days, when Grandfather carried Clara downstairs to put her into her chair he asked her, "Wouldn't the little daughter like to try to stand on the ground?" Clara had always tried to please him but had soon been forced to cry out, "Oh, it hurts!" and had clung to him; but each day he allowed her to stand just a little longer without her noticing.

For years they had not had such a splendid summer on the Alm. Every day the sun shone brilliantly out of a cloudless sky.

Heidi never tired of describing the high pasture to her friend. She talked of the golden light from the setting sun, and the myriads of beautiful flowers carpeting the ground. As she told Clara about the lovely rock roses and the vivid blue harebells she longed suddenly to be up there once again, and she sprang up and asked the grandfather, "Will you come to the pasture with us to-morrow?"

He consented. "But the little daughter must do me a favour too. To-night she must try her very best to stand."

Cheerfully Heidi ran with this news to Clara who promised to try to stand on her feet as much as ever Grandfather wanted, for she was looking forward immensely to this excursion.

As soon as Heidi caught sight of Peter in the evening she exclaimed, "Peter! Peter! To-morrow we shall come up too and stay all day on the pasture."

But Peter just grumbled like a bear in a temper and was about to give Goldfinch a hefty whack out of sheer bad feeling, but nimble Goldfinch saw what was coming and leaped out of the way in time.

That night Clara and Heidi went to their new beds full of anticipation of the next day. They agreed to stay awake all night to talk about their plans, but hardly had their heads touched the pillows when the conversation suddenly ceased. Clara saw in her dreams a big pasture thickly covered with flowers and Heidi heard the eagle crying, "Come! Come! Come!"

CHAPTER 22

AN UNEXPECTED EVENT

Early next morning the old man looked out to see what sort of day it would be. The dark shadows in the valley lifted and gradually a rosy light spread across the mountains until above and below were bathed in colour. The sun had risen. A gentle breeze was moving the branches of the fir trees back and forth as the sun caught the tips of the trees in its warm glow.

The uncle brought the invalid chair from the shed and

placed it in front of the house, and then went inside to tell the children what a beautiful morning it was.

Peter came lumbering up the hill. All the jealousy and temper in him had reached a climax. For weeks he had not had Heidi to himself. Even the goats avoided him as much as they could, for he would brandish his stick and hit them hard without any justification, and they no longer trusted him as they had in former days. When he came in the morning the strange child was carried out to her chair and Heidi's attention was completely taken up with her. In the evening, the invalid was still there and again Heidi had no time for him. Not once, all during the summer, had Heidi come up to the pasture, and though she came to-day she would still be accompanied by her friend and would still have no time for him. Peter anticipated this and it made him quite wild with rage.

When he caught sight of the chair, standing so proudly on its wheels, it seemed to him that here was the enemy who had done all this harm to him and would, to-day, hurt him still more. There was no one about and everything was quiet. Wildly he rushed forward, and, seizing the chair, he pushed it with all his might down the slope. He pushed with such violence that it disappeared almost at once. Peter then rushed up the Alm and took cover behind a big black-berry bush. Here he was hidden from the uncle's sight but could watch the chair's progress down the mountain. Far below, he saw it gather speed, bouncing off the rocks until it turned over and over and flew into a hundred pieces. The sight filled Peter with such an indescribable joy that he laughed aloud and stamped his feet. The boy raced round in circles, completely beside himself at the destruction of his enemy.

And now he thought of all the pleasant things for him which would result from the disaster. The stranger would have to leave because she could not get about without her chair; then Heidi would be free again to come with him up to the pasture. Everything would be as it had been in days gone by. It did not occur to Peter that if we do something wrong, trouble is sure to follow.

Presently Heidi came out and ran to the shed. The door was

wide open. She looked everywhere, puzzled to know what had become of the chair.

"Did you move the chair, Heidi?" asked the grandfather.

"I have looked everywhere for it. You said it was by the door," replied Heidi.

The wind suddenly grew stronger and rattled the door of the shed, blowing it back against the wall with a bang.

"Grandfather, it must have been the wind," called Heidi. "Oh, if it has blown the chair down the valley we will never get it back in time."

"If it has rolled a far as that we will never get it back at all," said the grandfather. "By now it will be in a thousand pieces," and he went round the corner of the hut to look down the path. "It is very odd," he said to himself. "The chair would have had to have turned the corner outside the shed."

"Oh, what a pity! Now we can't go," lamented Clara "If I have no chair I am sure I shall have to go home. Oh, what a pity!" Heidi, however, looked confidently at her grandfather, and said, "You will help, won't you, Grandfather, so that Clara doesn't have to go home?"

"We will go to-day as we intended," replied the uncle. "Then we shall see what else can be done."

The children were delighted.

The uncle then went back into the hut and bringing out some of the rugs, spread them out on the sunniest spot for Clara to sit on. Then he brought the milk for the children and led Little Swan and Little Bear out of the shed.

"I wonder why the boy is not here yet?" thought the uncle, for Peter had not greeted them with his usual whistle that morning.

He picked up Clara and, carrying her on one arm and the rugs on the other he said, "Now, let's be off! The goats will come with us."

With one arm round Little Swan's neck and the other round Little Bear's, Heidi walked behind the grandfather. The little goats were so pleased to be with her again that they almost pushed her over with their loving nudges and squeezes.

When they arrived on the pasture they saw here and there

on the slopes, goats peacefully grazing, and in the midst of them, on the ground, Peter was lying.

"I'll teach you to pass my house another time, you lazy fellow!" called the uncle "What does this mean?"

Peter shot up at the sound of the familiar voice. "There was nobody up," he answered.

"Did you see anything of the chair?" the uncle continued.

"Of what?" Peter answered back obstinately.

The uncle said no more but spread the rugs on the sunny slope and set Clara down upon them, asking if she was comfortable.

"As comfortable as in the chair," she said gratefully, "and I think this most be the most beautiful spot on earth. Oh, Heidi, how lovely it is!"

The grandfather got ready to leave them. "Enjoy yourselves!" he said. "When dinner-time comes, Heidi will get the food from the rucksack which I have put in the shade. Peter will provide the milk but Heidi must see that it is milk from Little Swan, and in the evening I will come back to fetch you. Now I must go and look for the chair and see what has happened to it." It was a truly beautiful day. The sky was a deep, clear, azure blue, and the high snowfields glittered as though covered in a thousand jewels. The great mountain summits rose majestically to the sky, and the great eagle hovered above. The wind blew down from the mountains and swept cool draughts of air around the children sitting in the sun.

The children had never been so happy together. The goats would gather round them in a friendly way and they had even got to know Clara well enough to rub their heads affectionately against her shoulder. Little Snowflake came to see Heidi most often, laying her head in Heidi's lap, and only going away when another goat pushed her out of the way.

So the hours went by, and Heidi thought she would like to go to her favourite spot where the flowers grew so profusely, and see if the cups were open now and as beautiful as last year. Clara could only be taken there in the evening when the grandfather came back, but by that time the flower bells would have closed again. Heidi could not resist the temptation to go and look. Hesitatingly she asked Clara, "Do you mind, Clara, if I leave you for a few minutes? I would so much like to go and see the flowers. But wait!" Heidi had an idea She led Snowflake up to Clara. "There, now! You won't be lonely."

Clara encouraged Heidi to go. She was quite content to be with the little goat. Heidi had thrown some leaves into Clara's lap and Clara held them out to Snowflake one by one. The little goat ate the leaves slowly from her hands and seemed contented and trusting in her new-found friend. As she sat alone on the mountain and looked at the little animal which seemed to look up to her for protection, she thought how wonderful it would be to be able, one day, to help others instead of always being dependent as she was now. A great many thoughts came into her mind and she longed to be able to go on living in the sun and to lead a useful life.

She suddenly felt extraordinarily happy, as if she saw everything in a new and beautiful light, and in a fit of gaiety she threw her arms round Snowflake's neck and cried, "Oh, Snowflake—it is so wonderful here; I would so like to stay here for ever with you."

Heidi reached the lovely flower patch and the ground seemed to be completely covered with sparkling gold. It was more beautiful than ever and she breathed in the sweet fragrance. Suddenly she turned and ran back to Clara, out of breath with excitement. "You must come and see it!" she called from a distance. "The flowers are so beautiful now and in the evening they may have changed. I can carry you, don't you think, Clara?"

Clara shook her head. "No, no, Heidi! You are much smaller than I. Oh, if only I could walk!"

Heidi looked about as if searching for something. Up above, Peter sat staring at the children, as if he couldn't believe his eyes. Didn't he destroy the hated chair so that the stranger would not be able to move about and here she sat beside Heidi? Heidi spotted Peter and called, "Come down, Peter!"

"No, I don't want to," was the reply.

"But you must! Come! I can't carry Clara by myself. You have to help me. Come quickly!" Heidi urged him.

"I don't want to," he shouted again.

Heidi came up the hill towards him. With flaming eyes she stood before him and said, "Peter, if you don't come at once I shall do something which you won't like at all, I can tell you!"

Fear seized Peter. He knew he had done something wicked which he did not want anybody to know about and here was Heidi speaking as though she knew all about it. What if she told the uncle! Peter feared nobody so much as him. Tortured with anxiety, he got up and went down to Heidi.

"I am coming, but you mustn't do what you said," he pleaded timidly so that Heidi felt quite sorry for him.

"There's nothing to be afraid of. Come with me now."

Heidi told him to take Clara's arm and she would support her from the other side. But the difficulty was how to make her walk when she could not even stand. So Heidi ordered Peter to give her his arm to lean on and asked her to put her other arm firmly round Heidi's neck. "Then we can carry you."

But Peter had never in his life before given his arm to anybody and kept it stiffly by his body.

"That's not the way," said Heidi and showed him how to do it.

But in spite of it all they did not get on very well. Clara was not light and the team was too unequal—down on the one side and up on the other. Clara tried to help by putting forward first one foot and then the other but she always drew them back quickly again.

"Put your foot down firmly," Heidi suggested.

"Do you think—" Clara hesitated.

But she obeyed, and ventured first one step on the ground and then another. The pain made her moan a little. Then she put a foot out again and cried joyfully that it was less painful already.

"Try again!" urged Heidi eagerly.

Clara went on trying, again and again, and suddenly she exclaimed, "I can do it, Heidi! Oh, I can! Look! I can make steps—one after the other!"

"Can you really walk now? Can you really walk all by yourself? Oh if only Grandfather were here!" cried Heidi. "You can walk, you can walk!"

166

Clara had still to hold on to both Peter and Heidi, but with every step she felt safer, and it was less and less uncomfortable.

Heidi was quite beside herself with joy. "Now we will b able to come here every day and you will be able to walk like me and you will be healthy! Oh, this is the most marvellous thing that could have happened."

Clara joyfully agreed. She could think of nothing in the world more wonderful than being able to walk around like normal people and never again to have to lie all day in her invalid chair.

It was not far to the slope where the beautiful flowers grew. The children could already see the yellow and blue patches. Soon they reached it.

"Let's sit down here," said Clara. They sat down in the midst of the flowers. Heidi thought she had never seen it so beautiful before. Clara was silent, overcome with happiness at the beauty around her and at the wonderful prospect which had opened up before her . . . the joy of being able to walk about like other people. Surrounding her were the many colours of the flowers waving in the grass, and their mixed perfumes enveloped her in an aura of fragrance, so that she could hardly believe the beauty of it all.

Heidi thought of Clara's cure, and the thought made everything so perfect that she wanted to shout aloud with pleasure. Clara could not speak, she was so totally overwhelmed by the prospect of new life which had opened before her, and the perfection of her situation. Peter was quiet, too, and lay quite still on the ground. He was fast asleep. Occasionally, Heidi ran to and fro to look more closely at the groups of flowers, and whichever way she turned they seemed to smell sweeter and to grow in greater abundance.

The children remained there for a long time. It was long past noon when some of the goats approached the slope and started to bleat loudly. They did not care to eat flowers, and they looked like a small deputation with Goldfinch as their spokesman, who had come to protest at the absence of their companions. The chorus awoke Peter and he remembered with a pang of misgiving his wicked deed of the morning. He willingly obeyed Heidi's every command in the hope that she would not report him to the uncle. The three of them went back to the pasture and had their meal, Heidi running to get the bag, for unknown to Peter, her threat to him had been related to Peter's dinner. She had noticed the lovely things which her grandfather had packed for them, and had been pleased at the thought of Peter sharing them, and she had originally intended that he should pay for his moodiness by going without dinner. Since he had, after all, complied with her wish to help Clara, she now divided the food equally into large helpings. They all three ate well, but although Peter ate up every bit as usual he did not enjoy it very much, tortured as he was by the fear of punishment.

Soon after they had finished, the grandfather appeared, climbing up the slope, and Heidi rushed towards him to tell him the good news. The grandfather's face brightened and he smiled happily at Clara. "You have made the effort and you have won," he said.

He lifted Clara up and with his left arm behind her she walked, with his strong support, much more confidently than before. Heidi skipped happily beside them. Then the grandfather lifted Clara into his arms. "We mustn't overdo it," he said. "In any case it is time to go home."

Later in the evening, when Peter arrived in Dörfli with his goats, a crowd of people had gathered. They were looking at something which lay on the ground. Peter wanted to see too, and eventually elbowed his way through. There lay the pitiful remains of Clara's chair. There was a part of the back and some red padding and a few shiny nails; it was clearly the same chair and although it was broken beyond repair it was easy to see that it had once been a beautiful piece of workmanship.

"I saw them carry it up," said the baker. "I bet it's worth a lot of money. I wonder if somebody did this deliberately? When the gentleman from Frankfurt hears of this he is sure to investigate. Suspicion is going to fall on all those who have been up on the Alm lately. I'm glad I haven't been up there for two years at least." "Alm-Uncle said that it may have been the wind," said one of the women, admiring the shiny red upholstery.

"Just as well," returned the baker, "for whoever else might have been responsible for such a deed would surely be in trouble if he were found."

Peter had heard enough. Stealthily he crept away from the crowd and ran up the mountain path as though the devil were after him.

He was in a terrible state by the time he reached home. He would not answer when he was spoken to, refused to eat, and went up to bed as soon as he could, only to put his head under the sheets and torture himself with fears about what was to happen to him.

As the children lay in bed that night, looking out at the stars, Heidi said, "I have been thinking all day how good it is that God does not give us just what we ask. He always knows of something better for us."

"Why do you think that, Heidi?" asked Clara.

"Because when I was in Frankfurt I prayed to be allowed to go home at once and when it did not happen I thought God did not hear. But, you see, if I had run away at once you would never have come here and would never have got well."

Clara thought hard. "But, Heidi," she said, "that would mean that we must never pray for anything because God knows better than we do."

"Yes, Clara, but we must do it like this," Heidi replied eagerly. "Every day we must thank God for everything to let Him know that we haven't forgotten that it all comes from Him. But, you know, if we don't get what we have asked for we must not think that God has not heard, and stop praying. We must say then, 'Now I know, dear Father, that you have something better in mind and I am glad that you will make it right in the end, no matter what happens now.'"

"How well you can explain it, Heidi," remarked Clara.

"Grandmamma explained it all to me and it turned out to be true. But I think we have to thank God particularly to-day because He has given us this great happiness—that you can walk now." They each silently prayed and thanked God from the bottom of their hearts for His goodness to Clara.

The following morning, the grandfather suggested that they should invite the grandmamma to the Alm because they had something new to show her. But the children wanted to give Grandmamma a great surprise and wanted to wait until Clara could go for a little walk supported only by Heidi. They thought it would be about a week before this could happen and in their next letter Grandmamma was eagerly invited to come for a visit; but they did not give away the secret.

Every day walking became easier and less painful for Clara and longer walks were undertaken. The exercise gave her such an appetite that the grandfather had to cut the bread a little bit thicker every day, and he was very pleased when he saw it disappearing.

So another week went by, and the day of the grandmamma's visit approached.

CHAPTER 23

PROMISES TO MEET AGAIN

The Grandmamma wrote to announce the day of her arrival and Peter brought the letter up from Dörfli that morning. Everyone was already up and about and the goats were waiting for him in their customary high spirits. The grandfather stood looking with pleasure at his happy healthy brood. As Peter approached he slowed his pace, and handing the letter apprehensively to the Alm-Uncle he then turned quickly and fled back down the mountain.

"Grandfather," asked Heidi. "Why does Peter always behave now as if he expected to be punished for something? He is like the goats running away for fear of the stick."

"Maybe he, too, is afraid of the stick which he sometimes thoroughly deserves," replied the grandfather. Peter ran without stopping until he was out of sight. Then he stopped. He was nervous and jumpy, as if he expected someone to leap on him and arrest him at any moment.

Heidi tidied the hut in preparation for the grandmamma's arrival, and when everything was in order the children sat down on the bench outside the cottage, ready to welcome her. The grandfather came and sat down beside them. He held in his hands a lovely bunch of gentians which he had picked that morning. Heidi ran forward every now and then to see if there was any sign of their guest's arrival. Soon she saw a group of people toiling up the mountain path. First there came a guide, and then a white horse on which rode the grandmamma, and last of all a porter with grandmamma's luggage. At last the procession arrived and the old lady caught sight of the children.

"Why, what is this?" she cried out. "Clara, you aren't in your chair! I can't believe my eyes!" And before even shaking hands with any one she still exclaimed, "Clara, is this really you? Your cheeks have become quite round and rosy. I hardly recognise you, child."

She came forward to embrace Clara, but Heidi quickly slipped from the bench, and, with Clara leaning on her shoulder, they walked slowly towards the grandmamma.

The old lady stood transfixed. Then she embraced her little grandchild, then Heidi, then Clara again. She gazed at them both speechlessly. At last she saw the Alm-Uncle who had been watching the proceedings with a broad smile. With Clara on her arm she walked with her to the bench, and, letting Clara sit down, she grasped the old man's hand.

"My dear Uncle! How can I thank you? This is your doing! Your care and nursing—"

"And God's sunshine and mountain air," interrupted the grandfather, smiling.

"And also Little Swan's good milk," put in Clara. "Grandmamma, you should have seen how much milk I have been drinking!"

"I can see it, Clara, by your cheeks! What a change! You have become plump and strong and taller, too. I simply can't take my eyes off You! But now we must send a telegram to my son in Paris. He must come at once—but I shan't tell him why. This will be the most wonderful surprise he has ever had. Uncle, have the men gone? How can we send a telegram?"

"They have gone, but, if you are in a hurry, I will call Peter. He will do it."

A piercing whistle summoned Peter and he came running down from the high rocks. His face was pale and drawn, for he was convinced that the moment of truth had arrived and that Uncle was about to hand him over to the police. He was given a piece of paper on which the message was written and the uncle told him to take it to the post office at Dörfli. Peter hurried away, quite relieved to see that no policeman had arrived so far.

So now, everyone sat down to a delicious meal outside the hut, and grandmamma was regaled with elated accounts from all sides of the progress made with Clara, and the way in which her cure had come about. They told her how grandfather had persuaded Clara to do a little every day, first standing, then taking a few steps, and how, finally, after the chair had blown down the mountain, they had managed to take Clara up to the pasture. Grandmamma could hardly believe all that had taken place, and exclaimed with delight at every turn of events.

Clara and Heidi were of course beside themselves at Grandmamma's reaction.

In Paris, Herr Sesemann had finished his business and he also had a surprise in store. Without giving any warning, he took the train to Basle, for he had a great longing to see his little daughter from whom he had been separated all summer. He arrived at Ragatz a few hours after his mother's departure, and this fitted in nicely with his plans. He took a coach to Mayenfeld, where he learned that he could drive as far as Dörfli. The climb from there seemed to him very long and fatiguing, and when the cottage failed to come into view he began to wonder uneasily if he had chosen the right path or if the hut was on the other side of the mountain. He looked around, but no human being was to be seen of whom he could ask the way. He was beginning to wonder uneasily if he was on the right track. Just then, a boy came running from above; it was Peter with the telegram. He did not keep to the footpath but ran straight down the mountainside. Herr Sesemann beckoned to him and reluctantly Peter came forward.

"Come here, boy!" Herr Sesemann encouraged him. "Tell me, is this the way to the hut where the old man lives with the child, Heidi, and where the people from Frankfurt are staying now?"

A gasp was the only answer that came from Peter, and in his haste to get away, the boy fell head over heels and catapulted down the mountainside, just as the chair had done—except that Peter did not break up into pieces! The telegram, however, was torn to scraps.

"What a timid boy!" exclaimed Herr Sesemann, thinking that the appearance of a stranger had had this extraordinary effect on the simple boy of the mountains. And he continued on his way.

Peter had been convinced that this was the policeman from Frankfurt. He was overcome with terror at the sight of the visitor and was utterly certain that he had been sent to collect him and take him away to Frankfurt. He tumbled on down the mountainside until at last he managed to catch hold of a bush. He had to lie still for a moment or two to recover, and then he picked himself up.

"Well, well, and what is this that comes hurtling down the mountain?" said a voice behind him. Peter jumped, and saw the baker standing there chuckling. He had been most amused to see Peter tumbling down the mountain just like the chair had done.

Peter did not answer but began to scramble back up the slope. He wanted to go home and hide, but the goats were still up there waiting for him, and he dared not delay for fear of fresh recriminations from the Uncle. He was in a sorry state: bruised and shaken from his fall, and in an agony of fear and apprehension about the fate that was to befall him.

Shortly after meeting Peter, Herr Sesemann reached the first hut and knew that he was on the right road. So he climbed higher and higher and at last, after a long, strenuous walk, his goal came in sight. There stood the Alm hut.

Herr Sesemann joyfully climbed the last steep path. Before he had reached the top he was recognised by the party outside the cottage and quickly a surprise was prepared for him. As he left the path to approach the hut, two figures came towards him. A tall girl with fair hair and rosy cheeks leaned on her smaller companion. Herr Sesemann stood still and stared at them.

"Papa don't you know me?" called Clara "Have I changed so much?"

At once Herr Sesemann rushed to embrace his little daughter.

"Yes, you have changed indeed! Is it possible? Can this be my little Clara?" he exclaimed repeatedly.

Grandmamma had come forward. "My dear son, what do you think of this?" she cried. "You had prepared a pleasant surprise for us but I think we have an even pleasanter one for you! But now you must meet the Alm-Uncle who is our greatest benefactor."

"Gladly, and also our dear little Heidi," replied Herr Sesemann, shaking hands with Heidi. "I don't need to ask if you are well and happy. No alpine rose could look more blooming."

Heidi looked up with sparkling eyes at the kind Herr Sesemann who had always been so good to her. How glad she was that he could find such happiness on the Alm.

Then the grandmamma led her son to the Alm-Uncle. As the two men shook hands, Herr Sesemann expressed his heartfelt thanks and his great astonishment at the miracle.

Her eyes filled with tears, and the grandmamma turned away and looked towards the ancient fir trees. A patch of blue caught her eye. It was a beautiful bouquet of blue gentians. "How exquisite!" she exclaimed. "Heidi, did you pick them for me?"

"No," replied Heidi, "but I think I know who did."

Suddenly, a slight rustling sound came from behind the trees. It was Peter. At the sight of the strange gentleman with the Alm-Uncle, he had tried to slip away unobserved. But the grandmamma recognised him. She thought that perhaps it was he who had brought her the flowers, and that he was sidling along in the background from shyness at the possibility of her discovering them. She felt that she should reward him for his kindness. "Come here, my boy," she said loudly. "Don't be afraid."

Paralysed with fright, Peter looked out from behind the trees. "It is all up now!" he thought. His face distorted with terror, he began to creep forward.

"Come along now," encouraged the grandmamma. "Now tell me, boy, did you do this?"

Peter never lifted his eyes and, of course, did not see where the grandmamma's finger pointed. All he had noticed was the uncle standing at the corner of the hut, looking piercingly at him, and, what was most terrifying of all, beside him stood the policeman from Frankfurt. Trembling all over, Peter could only mutter something which sounded like "Yes."

"Well, what is so dreadful about that?" asked the grandmamma.

"That it is broken to pieces and can't be put together again." With great difficulty Peter managed to stammer the words and his legs shook so much he could hardly stand.

Grandmamma went over to the Alm-Uncle. "My dear Uncle, is there something seriously wrong with the poor boy?" she asked sympathetically.

"Nothing," replied the uncle, "but I think the lad may have been the 'wind' which chased the invalid chair down the mountain and now he is expecting his well-deserved punishment."

Grandmamma could hardly believe this for she did not think he looked such a bad boy; and there seemed no reason for him to destroy the chair. But to the uncle, Peter's confession only confirmed the suspicion which he had had from the beginning. The angry looks Peter had cast on Clara and the signs of resentment towards the newcomers to the Alm had not escaped the uncle. He had put two and two together and explained it all now to grandmamma. When he had finished, the lady said, "No, no, my dear Uncle, we don't want to punish the poor boy any more. One must be fair. We strangers have, for weeks, taken Heidi away from him, so he sits, day after day, and broods all by himself. No, no, we must be fair. Anger and resentment drove the boy to his revenge which was, perhaps, a little foolish; but we are all foolish when we are angry."

Grandmamma went over to Peter and sat down on the bench under the fir trees. In a kind voice she said, "Come, my boy, stand in front of me. I want to speak to you. Stop trembling and listen. You pushed the chair down the slope to destroy it; that was wicked and you knew that you deserved to be punished. So to avoid that you took a lot of trouble to hide the truth; but you see, he who does something wrong and thinks nobody will find out is always mistaken. God sees and hears everything and when He notices that somebody wants to hide a wrong deed He wakes up the little watchman whom He has placed inside us from our birth and who sleeps inside us until we do something wrong. This little watchman has a little prong in his hand and he prods us with it all the time so that we do not have a minute's peace. His voice torments us, too, for it keeps calling. 'Soon you will be found out! Now they'll come and drag you away!' So we live in terror and anxiety and never have a moment's happiness. Did you feel something like that, Peter?"

Peter nodded penitently, for that was exactly how he had felt.

"In still another way you miscalculated, for you wanted to do something wrong and something good came out of it. Because Clara had no chair and she wanted to see the beautiful flowers she tried hard to walk; and she succeeded, and in the end, was able to go every day to the pasture—much more frequently than she would have done in the chair. You see, Peter, God can turn evil into good for the one who was meant to be harmed; harm comes to the evil-doer instead. Do you understand, Peter? If so, don't forget; and if you ever again

176

want to do something wrong, remember the little watch-man inside with his prong and unpleasant voice, will you?"

"Yes, I will," answered Peter, very depressed for he still did not know how the affair would end.

"Then everything is all right and the whole matter is settled," finished the grandmamma. "But now you shall have a souvenir from the Frankfurt visitors. Tell me, my boy, what would you like?"

Slowly Peter lifted his head and gazed at the grandmamma in astonishment.

He had expected some awful punishment and now he was being asked what he would like. He was completely confused.

"Yes, I am quite serious," continued the grandmamma "You shall have something as a remembrance and as a token that the people from Frankfurt think no more than that you did something wrong. Do you understand, my boy?"

Now it began to dawn on Peter that he need not fear any punishment and that the kind lady had saved him from arrest by the police. It was a great weight off his mind. Now he saw, too, that it was better to confess at once if one had done something wrong and suddenly he stammered, "And I also lost the paper."

The grandmamma had to think for a moment what this meant but soon she recalled the telegram and said kindly:

"That is right. Always confess at once what you have done and everything will be all right. And now have you any special wish?"

Peter felt quite giddy at the thought of being able to have anything he wanted. The annual fair at Maienfeld flashed before his eyes with all the beautiful things he had admired so often and never hoped to possess. There were the red whistles, which he could use for his goats; and the fascinating knives. Peter was deeply absorbed in his thoughts and he could not decide which of the two he would like the better. Suddenly he had a brainwave. "A penny," he said.

The grandmamma laughed. "That is not an extravagant wish," she said. "Come here!" She pulled out her purse and took from it four bright round shillings and on top of them she put four pennies. "Well, we want to settle our accounts," she said. "I will explain it to you. Here are just as many pennies as there are weeks in the year and so you will be able to spend a penny every week for a whole year."

"All my life?" asked Peter innocently.

Now the grandmamma could not help laughing heartily so that the gentlemen interrupted their talk to hear what was going on.

"Yes, my boy, that's a passage for my will," said the old lady. "I will put down, 'A penny a week to Peter as long as he lives.'" Herr Sesemann nodded his agreement and laughed too.

Peter looked once more at the present in his hand. He still could hardly believe his eyes. Then he said, "God bless you!" and off he went, running and leaping, all fear and anxiety gone. His joy sent him flying over the rocks and boulders with twice his usual agility. He was forgiven, and he was to have a penny every week for the rest of his life.

After dinner, Clara took her father aside and said to him, "If you only knew, Papa, what the grandfather has done for me! I shall never forget it all my life. And I keep wondering, what could I give him or do for him, that would give him half the pleasure he has given me!"

"That is my dearest wish, too, my child," replied her father.

Herr Sesemann now went to the Alm-Uncle and seizing his hand, said, "My dear friend, let us have a word together. Believe me when I say that for years I have not known such happiness. Money and possessions have meant nothing to me since they have not helped to make my poor child well and happy. You have restored her health and given new life to her and me. Now, tell me, how can I show my gratitude? I can never repay what you have done, but whatever is in my power is at your disposal. Tell me, my friend, what can I do?"

The Alm-Uncle had listened in silence. Now he looked at Herr Sesemann and smiled. "Believe me, Herr Sesemann, I too am over-joyed at the girl's recovery on our Alm and my trouble has been well repaid by that. For your kind offer I thank you, but there is nothing I need; as long as I live I have enough for Heidi and myself. But if one wish only could be fulfilled I should have no more worries in this life."

"Speak, my dear friend," urged Herr Sesemann.

"I am old," continued the uncle, "and cannot expect to be here much longer. When I have passed away there will be nothing for the child and she has no relatives of any account. If you will promise that Heidi will never have to go out and earn her living among strangers then you will have amply repaid what I have done for your child."

"But there could never be any question about it!" exclaimed Herr Sesemann. "The child is one of us. Ask my mother and my daughter. They will never allow Heidi to go to strangers. This I promise you, both during my life and after, the child will never have to go among strangers. But she has made good friends, one of whom is our friend, the doctor. He is winding up his affairs and intends to come and settle here this autumn, in the Swiss mountains, for he has never felt so well and happy as in the company of you and the child. You see, Heidi will now have two protectors. May they both live long!"

"God grant that will be so!" added the grandmamma and shook hands warmly with the Alm-Uncle. Then she embraced Heidi, who stood beside her.

"And you, my dear Heidi, come, tell me, don't you have a particular wish?"

"Yes, certainly," replied Heidi, looking cheerfully up at the grandmamma.

"What is it child?" she encouraged.

"I would like my bed from Frankfurt with the three high pillows and the thick cover, so that Grandmother needn't lie with her head downhill and won't need to put her shawl on in bed any more because she is cold."

"My dear child, it is good you remind me to think of others in our happiness, those who are not so well off as we are. I will wire at once to Frankfurt. The bed will be here in two days and, with God's help, the grandmother will soon be sleeping comfortably in it."

Heidi skipped delightedly round the grandmamma. She wanted to go down at once and give the grandmother this happy message for she felt she had been away from her far too long, especially since the grandmother was in such discomfort the last time Heidi had seen her, but the grandfather said reprovingly, "No, no, Heidi! When you have guests you can't run away like that!"

But the grandmamma supported Heidi. "My dear Uncle, we shall go together. We can then go on to Dörfli and send the wire off to Frankfurt. What do you think, my son?"

Until now Herr Sesemann had not given much thought to his holiday plans. Originally, he had thought of taking a trip through Switzerland with his mother and had wondered if Clara would be fit to accompany them for part of the journey. But now he would be able to enjoy the company of his daughter more fully. He did not want to miss any of these beautiful days of late summer and decided to stay the night at Dörfli and the next morning to fetch Clara when all three would go to Ragatz and start their journey from there.

Clara was a little upset at the thought of leaving the Alm but there was so much to look forward to and so little time to think that she was soon quite cheerful again. Heidi bounced for joy as they all went down the mountain. She told grandmamma all about the grandmother, and how cold she was, and what she lacked in the way of food.

Brigitta was standing outside the cottage when the little company approached and she rushed inside quickly crying, "They are coming, Mother."

"Alas, it is true, then," sighed the grandmother. "Do you think they are taking the child with them? Did you see her?"

Presently the door flew open and Heidi rushed into the room, going at once to the Grandmother's corner and embracing her affectionately.

"Grandmother, Grandmother! My bed is coming from Frankfurt, and the three pillows and also the thick cover. It will be here in two days. Grandmamma has promised."

The grandmother smiled a little sadly, "What a kind lady! I wish I could be happy that she is taking you with her, Heidi."

"What is all this? Who has been telling my good, old grandmother such tales?" said a kind voice. Grandmamma had overheard the conversation.

"No, no, that is out of the question! Heidi will stay with the grandmother, but we will come back to the Alm every year for we have good reason to thank God for this spot, and especially for the miracle He has wrought on our girl."

The grandmother's face lit up. Unable to speak, she pressed Frau Sesemann's hand again and again, and two large tears ran down her wrinkled cheeks.

Heidi clung affectionately to her and said, "Hasn't it all happened as in the hymn I read to you? When the bed comes from Frankfurt you will be much better too, Grandmother."

"Ah, yes, Heidi. God has sent me so many good things. Is it possible that there are such kind people who trouble themselves about a poor old woman?"

"My good Grandmother," interrupted Frau Sesemann, "in the eyes of God we are all equally poor and need His help; and He does not forget us. We must say good-bye now, but only until we meet again next year, and we certainly never will forget the dear grandmother."

Frau Sesemann took the grandmother's hand again, and with the old woman's blessing, Herr Sesemann and his mother continued their journey down into the valley.

Next morning, Clara was very sad about leaving the Alm where she had been so happy; but Heidi did her best to comfort her. "Summer will soon come again, and then it will be better still, for you are well now and we can go every day with the goats up to the pastures."

Clara dried her tears, "Don't forget to remember me to Peter and the goats," she said. Heidi suggested that Clara send Little Swan some salt, for she loved to lick some from out of the grandfather's hand in the evening. Clara promised to send a hundred pounds of salt so that Little Swan would never forget her.

Herr Sesemann had arrived and was beckoning to the children for it was time to go. Heidi stood at the very edge of the slope and waved to Clara until she disappeared from sight.

Frau Sesemann did not forget how cold it could be in winter

on the mountain. She sent a big parcel to Goat Peter's hut; it contained warm clothing of every description so that the grandmother would never again have to sit trembling with cold.

The doctor arrived in Dörfli, and, on the Alm-Uncle's advice, he bought the house where the old man and Heidi stayed during the winter. The doctor decided to have it rebuilt, part of it for himself and the other part for the uncle and Heidi for their winter lodgings.

As the days went by, the doctor and the Alm-Uncle became very good friends and often their conversation would turn to Heidi because, for both of them, it was the greatest joy to have the child with them in their new house.

One day, when the doctor and the uncle were standing together, seeing how the new building was getting on, the doctor said to the old man; "I share your happiness in the child and I feel I am the nearest to her after you; I want to share also the responsibilities and to provide for her as best I can, so that I may hope that in my old age she will stay with me. That is my greatest wish, that Heidi should have the same claims on me as though she were my own child. Then we will be able to leave her free of worries when you and I have departed."

The grandfather pressed the doctor's hand and the doctor could read in the eyes of his friend how greatly touched he was by these words.

At this moment Heidi and Peter were sitting with the grandmother. Heidi had such a story to tell them that she hardly took time to breathe. They had seen very little of each other during the summer, and how much had happened!

It was difficult to tell which of the three radiant faces shone most happily.

Brigitta, with Heidi's help, at last understood the story of Peter's miraculous weekly penny and her face beamed, perhaps most radiantly of all.

At last, the grandmother said to Heidi, "Read one of the hymns to me, child! I want to thank our Heavenly Father for all the mercy He has bestowed on us!"